TALES OF ATLANTIS

THE DAWNING OF A NEW AGE

D. M. WHITE

D WHITE PUBLISHING

First published in Great Britain 2022

Copyright © D. M. White, 2022

Set in Garamond

ISBN: 9798777734952; 9798794346817

Tales of Atlantis

The Dawning of a New Age

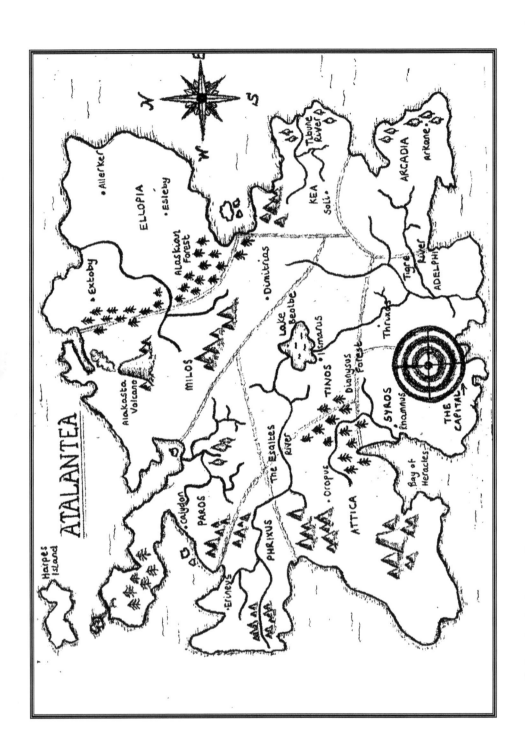

CHAIN OF COMMAND

Order of Poseidon
|
High lord (Critias Atlas)
|
High-lord-in-waiting (Attalus Atlas)
|
Lady of the House (Hestia Atlas)

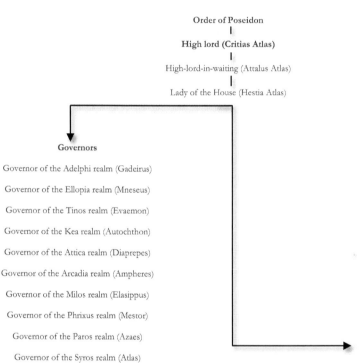

Governors

Governor of the Adelphi realm (Gadeirus)

Governor of the Ellopia realm (Mneseus)

Governor of the Tinos realm (Evaemon)

Governor of the Kea realm (Autochthon)

Governor of the Attica realm (Diaprepes)

Governor of the Arcadia realm (Ampheres)

Governor of the Milos realm (Elasippus)

Governor of the Phrixus realm (Mestor)

Governor of the Paros realm (Azaes)

Governor of the Syros realm (Atlas)

The High Table

Viracocha

High physician

High priest

Captain of the high guard

High lawgiver

High whisperer

Coinmaster

Genealogy Master

THE BARD'S PROPHECY

When the cup bearer's time is nigh,

And the Eagle falls from the sky,

Await a stranger from distant shores,

As a line lost returns once more,

With the only chance to end the curse,

But follow His words, not the weight of a purse,

For He will not forget or forgive,

Those who ignore the reason they live.

PROLOGUE

End of the Second Age

The Citadel

Ten men were seated around a golden table. Some had travelled for days to reach the Citadel, and the meeting had been long and arduous. The morning's good humour had evaporated in the afternoon as the men argued and spoke over one another. As evening descended, all that remained was a residue of resentment and frustration.

'We must offer him as a sacrifice.'

'Don't be a fool, Klemides.'

'The Order requires it.'

'The Order says nothing of the sort. In fact, the Order requires a majority for any State killing, and I will never agree to such folly.'

'You would risk the wrath of the Saviour? For the middling?'

'It is a sign from the Saviour, and you would slaughter him. How many people have survived the mouth of the storm?'

'Nestor has a valid point. There are no records of any survivors.'

'No records, but we've all heard the stories. Whether there's any truth in them is another matter.'

'They're just stories to entertain the children. I agree with Klemides. We must sacrifice the middling. We cannot risk him returning and disclosing his discovery. It would destroy us.'

'Then we must keep him here. He couldn't escape if he wanted to, anyway. He is bound here like the rest of us.'

'If he survived his journey here, who knows whether he could leave?'

'He can barely walk. He won't escape, and even if he did, who would believe him?'

'Let us not forget the prophecy.'

'What of the prophecy?'

'The prophecy speaks of a stranger returning to us, and that stranger—'

'Will mark the beginning of a new age. Yes, yes, I know of the prophecy. We all do. But this is not the stranger of whom the prophecy speaks.'

'How can you be so sure?'

'The middling the prophecy speaks of is not due to arrive for hundreds of years.'

'Hippocrates is right. The Viracocha confirmed it.'

'And do you think the middling descends from one of us? Look at him.'

The middling was sat chained to a wall, his pale, malnourished body shivering despite the intense heat. Two men had found him washed up in the realm of Syros two moons ago. At first, they had presumed him dead, but somehow he had survived his journey from the other world, and now his fate hung in the balance.

'What else did the Viracocha say?'

'The middling spoke only of a great plague that had ravaged his country and of his god.'

'Which god?'

'Just the one. The middling believes in a false god.'

The men fell silent, processing the information. Then the oldest one said, 'There is another option.'

'Go on.'

'If we are wrong and that man chained to the wall is the stranger referred to in the prophecy, then we would make a grave mistake by offering him as a sacrifice. One which might cause our destruction, but we cannot allow the middling to roam freely. To do so would set a dangerous precedent. It would appear to me that the only option is to send him Below.'

'That would be as good as a death penalty.'

'Not necessarily. If he truly is our descendent, the Saviour would ensure his safety, and we would know for sure.'

'An interesting proposition.'

'Yes, I agree...'

'My loyal governors,' said the man with golden bands covering his arms, a hint of sarcasm in his voice. It was the first time he had spoken, and the other men fell silent. 'Thank you for your comments. They have been useful. The Order requires a majority for any State killing, but the Order only applies to kinsmen. Do you agree?'

The men murmured their agreement.

'And the middling may be many things, but he is not our kinsman.'

'No, but—'

'Do you agree?' the man with the golden bands interrupted an edge to his tone.

The men nodded their heads.

'Good, then the Order does not apply. The decision on the middling is mine alone, and I have made it.' The man with the golden bands turned to his guard. 'Ready the prisoner. We will not require the bull today.'

'Show mercy, my lord!'

'You've grown soft, Nestor. Aemon said it himself. The middling has angered the gods. He has forsaken them for an imposter. They have taken their vengeance by bringing a plague down on his kind. He may have escaped their wrath, but we must finish their work. Make ready the prisoner.'

A guard, the size of a boulder with three vertical lines branded on his forehead, grabbed the middling and dragged him off by the scruff of his neck. Such was the guard's strength that he barely noticed the middling's attempts to free himself.

'Now, let us move on to the pledge and have done with it,' said the man with the golden bands.

The men walked in silence through a silver temple dedicated to Poseidon until they reached a red column that stood prominently in the centre. Delicately inscribed upon the column was the Order, and in front of it sat a smooth golden altar that reflected the temple's ivory roof.

After a few minutes, the guard returned with the high priest and the middling. He was dressed in a white linen robe, and a glowing pendant hung loosely from his stooped neck. He gazed at the ground, defeated.

One by one, the men approached the altar and recited the pledge, their voices barely audible. Then the guard forced the middling to kneel on the altar, facing the column. The men could hear his sobs and whimpers, but they couldn't see the fear in his eyes or the tears flooding down his cheeks as the guard held him.

The priest began his prayer. The men had heard it many times before, but they had never borne witness to this ritual. As he spoke, the priest produced an obsidian blade no bigger than a leaf. The sobs from the middling grew louder, but he was powerless in the vice-like grip of the guard. Some men held their breath, some closed their eyes, and some fixed their gaze on the statues surrounding them. Only the man with the golden bands watched the middling, the corner of his lips betraying a veiled smile.

As the priest finished his prayer, he approached the middling. It was time. The guard forced the middling's forehead back with his hand, and the priest stuttered. If that was a pang of conscience, it didn't last. Delicately, he opened the middling from ear to ear, the deadly blade cutting easily through flesh and tissue.
The middling coughed and gargled as his body thrashed, his lifeblood spurting onto the column and altar. For those watching, it seemed to last an eternity.

And then he was still.

Human or animal, it didn't matter. They all reacted the same. The guard let go of the middling's limp body and stepped away, his arms and face painted red. Silence swallowed the room, save for a gentle dripping sound.

The man with the golden bands said, 'This must remain within these walls. No one can know about the middling or what has happened here. The gods will reward us for what we have done today.' He turned to the guard. 'Dispose the body away from here, and make sure no one can find it.'

The men dispersed with haste, the day's events forever etched on their minds. It wasn't the first time the high lord had taken matters into his own hands, and it wouldn't be the last.

*

The guard heaved the middling's corpse through the forest. Disguising the body and removing it from the Citadel without raising suspicion had been a tough task. Sweat drenched him as he negotiated the dense flora, but he had followed the Viracocha's instructions to the letter. It had taken him to a clearing where a vast stone protruded from the ground. He pushed it with all his strength. There was a creak, and it moved, revealing a black abyss. The guard smiled. So that's the entrance to the Below!

He looked around to make sure he wasn't being watched, then kicked the body into the void. It fell silently to the bottom, where it would remain untouched for hundreds of years.

CHAPTER I

November 2007

London

It was the worst day of Alfred Lyon's miserable life. He had worked twelve hours a day for a year and had nothing to show for it. There had been no bonus, no promotion, nothing, and all because of a stupid misunderstanding.

He needed tequilas, lots of tequilas. For the first time in months, he had no plans to log on to his laptop over the weekend to work. He'd be nursing a hangover instead. The first one tasted vile. He gurned and squeezed a lime into his mouth before downing a second. The third tasted better. The fourth was almost enjoyable, and his spirits lifted marginally. That was the curse of tequila. It made him happy.

He moved on to beers and then other magical stimulating potions. He didn't know what, and he didn't care. Not about work, or London, or the green, slimy concoction he was sliding down his throat.

As *Mr Brightside* came on the jukebox, he felt his phone buzz rudely in his pocket, demanding attention. It was an email from his friend Shep. He ignored it. They hadn't spoken in months, and it was probably nothing, but then a mixture of boredom and curiosity got the better of him. After another beer, he opened it to find that Shep had forwarded a message promoting a rowing race across the Atlantic.

Alfred had travelled across Europe with Shep whilst at university, and they had always talked about taking on another challenge. They had touted various ideas and dismissed them all as too hard, too expensive, or too suicidal. Then Shep moved across the pond to work in New York, and the ideas dried up. Until now.

As Alfred read the email, a yearning ignited in his soul. Fate was calling to him. Alfred typed an email back and then decided that a text would be more appropriate, more familiar.

Alfred: *Let's do it!*

Alfred clicked send, hoping Shep still had the same number, and waited impatiently. He re-read the email and got excited at the prospect of a fresh challenge. After what seemed like an eternity, his phone buzzed.

Shep: *Who is this?*

It had been a while since they last messaged each other.

Alfred: *It's Al. I'm responding to your email. I think we should do it.*

Shep's response was quick.

Shep: *Are you drunk? How are you? It's been a long time!*

They exchanged text messages for over an hour. Shep had returned to England a few months ago and was in-between jobs, whatever that meant. It was a strange move. Shep had been well paid in the Big Apple and had his dream job, but Alfred didn't consider it in his drunken state. They agreed to do some research and meet up in a week.

Alfred thought about how they could make it work to distract himself from his more pressing predicament. Their major issue, other than complete lack of experience, but they could remedy that, was funding. Alfred had plenty of savings, but he would need that to live on until he started earning again. He'd decided on his fourth tequila that he'd had his last day with his firm, regardless of whether they fired him.

Then an idea struck him. Jeremy could fund it. Why not? He owed it to his only blood son, and he had more than enough cash. Alfred set to work writing an email to his father expressing his long-burning desire to row the Atlantic. His inability to process thoughts due to his inebriated state meant that the act of typing a simple email on the pixie keys of his Blackberry took him over an hour to complete, but he got there eventually.

Firmly wedded to competing in the race, Alfred then emailed his head of department, expressing, in somewhat colourful terms, his decision to move on to pastures new with immediate effect. It might have taken him a while, but Alfred felt pleased with what he had achieved whilst slumped in the corner of a bar, nursing a whisky or two. The wonders of modern-day technology. He continued drinking into the early hours before collapsing at home with grand plans to spend the following day at the gym.

*

Alfred didn't remember his actions when he woke up. Instead, an ominous feeling followed him around like a bad smell as he tried to shake off his hangover. It felt like his brain was waiting for the right moment to tell him some unwelcome news. A shower and a long stint under the hairdryer delayed the inevitable vomiting episode and piercing headache for a while, but both soon caught up to him. It wasn't until a few hours later after the paracetamol had kicked in and he had turned on his phone to find two emails waiting for him, that the previous night's events flooded back.

The first email was brief and to the point. It was a message setting up a meeting on Monday morning to discuss his resignation. His head of department had emailed at 7:43 in the morning. The thought of being up and working at 7:43 on a Saturday morning made Alfred feel nauseous, and he had to lie down in a foetal position with a fan blowing on his face just to avoid throwing up again.

The email didn't give much away, and Alfred was certain they would quietly shuffle him out the back door to avoid any further embarrassment. Not that he'd done anything wrong. She was the one who'd made the move, but no one would believe him. With plenty of young blood rising through the ranks, keen to impress and more than happy to sacrifice themselves for the status of a big city lawyer, Alfred knew that he was dispensable. He didn't regret his decision. In fact, he felt content for the first time in a long time.

The second email was from his father.

Alfie,

Good to hear from you, son.

How's the job going? Things are nonstop here at present! We've had a few issues with one of our developments. I won't bore you with the details. Let's just say that a few people are standing in the way of innovation and modernisation, but they'll back down. They always do. Could do with knowing a good lawyer… do you know any?

What's this about a transatlantic race? I know you've had a bit of flooding in the UK this summer, but this is excessive, isn't it? It sounds like a challenge! I know a few guys here who row. They're incredibly fit, and they only do a few miles, nowhere near 3000! You up to that?

I'll support you as best I can and see if we can assist with funding. Take it as a marketing exercise, maybe. We usually sponsor a few events.

I'll speak to a few people, see if I can pull a few strings. Any idea what sort of money you'll need? I'll need an idea of what it involves and what timescales we're talking about.

How would you fit it all in with work? What does Josie think about it?

Have a think about it, a long think. For the record, I think you're crazy!

Take care.

Dad

Josie. It had been six months since they'd broken up. She'd grown fed up with playing second fiddle to Alfred's work. One day, after he'd cancelled yet another one of their date nights, it had become too much. She'd walked out without saying goodbye, taking all of her possessions with her. Four years and that was it. She was gone. It was just another part of his life he'd made a monumental mess of. Alfred had returned to an empty apartment, and at first, he thought someone had burgled him. Reality had punched him in the face when he saw that all of his possessions remained in situ. He felt like she'd ripped his heart out, but he couldn't blame her. He toyed with messaging her, telling her he had quit and seeing if she might want to get back together, but then quickly dismissed it. That ship had sailed.

Alfred was clueless about what he'd agreed to with Shep, and so for the rest of the day, after hauling his guts out again and replenishing himself with a full English breakfast and vitamin water, he put his honed researching skills to the test. The more he read, the more daunting it sounded. The amount of work and effort he would have to put in just to prepare for and be able to survive an ocean rowing race was overwhelming. It wasn't just the training. It was learning how to use all the equipment and what to do if something went wrong. The one positive was that he had a while to prepare. They were looking for entrants for the following year, something he'd overlooked in his drunken state. He'd always wanted to take a gap year, though, and at least he'd get a story out of it.

CHAPTER II

Shep was sitting in his underwear on the sofa, playing on his console. He was on a killing streak of twenty, a new personal record. Last night's takeaway sat half-eaten in the kitchen along with a dozen empty beer cans. He'd boldly gone for a vindaloo and regretted it. When he woke up with his bowels in agony, he regretted it again, but he would still eat it for his breakfast as he'd run out of cereal. A sniper ended his run, and he was midway through swearing at his killer, probably a thirteen-year-old nerd, through his headset when his phone buzzed.

Al: *Still meeting at 2? Have spoken to Jeremy.*

He never thought Alfred would take his suggestion seriously. He'd emailed him on a whim, but now things were leaping forwards. Only a week had passed, and already Alfred seemed to have everything mapped out.

Shep responded to confirm their meet-up and then realised he'd have to get a move on. It was midday, and it would take at least an hour to negotiate the London traffic and reach the café.

Shep hadn't seen Alfred for over two years. He'd heard through the grapevine that Josie had split up with him, not surprising given that Alfred had been punching. Other than that, he didn't know what his old friend had been up to or what to expect. He felt on edge, perhaps even self-conscious. They'd met at university and had quickly become friends during the opening week of carnage. The common threads that had bonded them in their youth had largely disappeared, and any attempt to create new ones could make things awkward between them.

Alfred was also the only person who knew he was back in England, and he had a habit of asking probing questions. That was the last thing Shep needed right now.

Shep searched in vain to find some clean clothes and then gave up. Yesterday's would have to suffice. They smelled of sweat, curry, and beer, so he sprayed some deodorant to mask the lingering scent. He left the vindaloo, thinking he might have it for tea, and then almost knocked his neighbour over as he darted out the door. He took the stairs two steps at a time and had to stop at the bottom to catch his breath. If they were serious about this, and Alfred seemed resolute, he would have to work on his fitness.

Alfred was already sitting at a table in the café when Shep arrived. He was always a stickler for punctuality. He'd picked a chair facing the entrance and was sipping a fancy coffee. Alfred spotted Shep and made an exaggerated gesture to his watch. Shep let the reproof pass over him. He was only twenty minutes late.

'Jaffaknacks!' Shep shouted as he made his way over to the table. He knew Alfred hated the nickname. Someone at university had shouted it to him on a night out, mocking his ginger hair, and Shep had found it hilarious.

'Tosser!' Alfred replied and grinned. 'What happened? They run out of food in New York?' Alfred pointed to Shep's stomach, and Shep breathed in, conscious of his weight, which had spiralled since he'd returned to England.

'I'll have you know I'm an Ironman,' Shep commented, recalling past achievements.

'I thought that was Tony Stark,' Alfred quipped.

It might have been a while since they had seen each other, but Alfred looked like not a day had passed. He still had a baby face and a broad, goofy grin that made him look like he'd just passed through puberty. Unlike Shep, his thick red hair showed no sign of receding, and his skin was its usual shade of wallpaper paste. He was even wearing the same plain blue jeans and tight white top that had become his trademark look throughout their time at university.

They caught up over a coffee, with Alfred explaining how his law firm had marched him out of the office earlier in the week following his resignation. Something about a partner's wife and an office event that had resulted in several red faces. Shep only caught half of the story because he was distracted by a waitress. She had the perfect combination of an ample bosom and a low-cut top. Every time she leaned forward to serve a customer, Shep got an eyeful, and he didn't want to miss out. Whatever had happened to Alfred, he seemed uncharacteristically relaxed about his situation.

Whilst Alfred chatted freely, Shep kept his cards close to his chest. No one needed to know about his predicament.

'What happened with Josie then?' Shep asked once they had exhausted their go-to topics. He was straying into unfamiliar territory, but he was keen to keep the topic off himself. He also wanted to know, should he happen to bump into Alfred's ex at some point, whether she was fair game.

'Just drifted apart, I guess,' Alfred replied vaguely, avoiding Shep's gaze. 'How do you know about that?'

'Her relationship status is single on Facebook. You should join. You're possibly the only person I know who hasn't.'

'I thought I had?'

'Not unless you've signed up recently which, knowing you, you won't have done.' Shep laughed. Alfred had never been tech-savvy.

'Not sure I have the energy for it.' Alfred sighed. 'It'll probably disappear in a few months like the other ones, and I don't like people prying into my private life. Anyway, let's talk about this race. Are we doing it?'

'Hell yeah!' Shep sounded far more confident than he felt. 'You've signed us up already, haven't you?'

'Not quite, but I have been looking into it.'

Alfred produced a folder, and Shep smiled inwardly at his friend's efficiency. He'd been the same when they went travelling. Every hostel had been booked in advance, every day pre-planned. Had Alfred left Shep in charge, he'd have just winged it, although that was probably dangerous with an ocean race.

Alfred went through his research with Shep. He'd thought about everything: the equipment they'd need, the courses they'd have to complete, their training regime and diet, how much it was all going to cost, and how they'd finance it. Every deadline had been noted and highlighted. He'd even written to previous competitors for guidance. All Shep had achieved since he'd emailed Alfred a week ago was to binge-watch some dramas on television. From the sound of it, all he'd have to do going forwards was turn up on the day.

'... and I spoke to Jeremy yesterday. He said his company will sponsor the boat. Which is good because that's our biggest expense, and I don't have a spare £35,000 lying around. There are a few conditions but nothing to worry about.'

Shep nodded. He hadn't a clue what Alfred's father did for a living and didn't care, but he was happy to take advantage of his wealth. They finished their coffees and left the café, having agreed that Alfred would submit the paperwork to reserve them a place in the race. Alfred's parting gift to Shep was a week-by-week training rota. It looked intensive. Shep wasn't lying when he said he'd completed an Ironman, but that was a few years ago, and rowing was a different discipline. He felt completely out of his comfort zone, but he couldn't let Alfred down. The whole thing had been his idea.

Sort of.

CHAPTER III

Alfred had grave doubts about what he'd signed up to. The problem was, he found the act of rowing incredibly dull, and so spending hours on end doing it in the gym was tedious.

A professional coach, apparently a former Olympian, had once taught him the correct rowing technique, and so he at least had a foundation to build upon. Most people set the resistance on the rowing machine to its highest setting, which was like rowing through treacle. Good if you wanted to build up resistance, but not if you wanted to row 3000 miles. He knew he needed to lean forward to extend his reach, and the power in his stroke should initially come from his legs. Most people ignored their legs and focused on using their arms, which was a one-way ticket to a back or shoulder injury. Only after the legs had fully extended should the torso and arms be engaged to finish the action before returning to the starting position.

At university, Alfred could row six-minute miles comfortably, and he foolishly set out at that pace on his first training exercise. But whilst he still looked trim, his body had become soft through lack of exercise. There had been a gym on-site at his former workplace, but the equipment was ancient and didn't take too kindly to being subjected to a rigorous workout. So it had been rare to see anyone there.

On his first day of training, the power drained from his legs like an old battery, and he was gasping for air after two minutes. He could see others in the gym looking over in his direction, horrified at the noise his body was making. It was embarrassing.

The second day was worse. He was only just managing eight-minute miles, and it felt like he was running on gas already. It was clear his fast-food diet required a rethink. He would rely on takeaways no longer. And no more beer. Alfred went shopping on his way home and purchased 20 chicken breasts, a boot load of pasta and broccoli, and a big tub of protein. It was the start of a new era, a new Alfred.

Day after day, mile after mile, he pushed himself to the limit. Regularly, he would collapse in a heap on the floor after his workout and find himself so exhausted it was all he could do to stop himself from vomiting. To relieve himself from the monotony of the rowing machine, he interspersed his exercise with running, swimming, and weight training. He even started climbing again, rekindling his love affair with the sport.

After a month, the routine had become familiar, and his fitness quickly improved. Alfred liked what he saw in the mirror again. He slept better and, despite draining his body each day, he felt more alert and observant.

Whilst he was doing everything he could to prepare, always hovering at the back of his mind, was Shep. He didn't know what to make of his wayward friend. When they met up, he'd seemed on-edge and lukewarm to the race, despite his efforts to look enthusiastic. But since then, Shep had found himself a job to keep the money ticking over and was training, although quite what his training involved was a mystery. Alfred knew that he'd signed up to a gym because he regularly sent updates, usually complaining about the beefcakes who hogged the gym equipment. He seemed more bothered about how much he could lift than how far he could row. Shep was a big boy, though. He knew what the race required of him.

The mystery around why Shep had returned to England also bugged Alfred. Every time it came up in conversation, Shep either brushed it off or changed the topic. It was infuriating, as were some of Shep's other ticks, which Alfred mistakenly thought might have disappeared with age. He still displayed a lack of attention to detail, a careless attitude, and an inability to take anything seriously, to name just a few. Even thinking about it put Alfred on edge.

Then there was Jeremy, who wasn't helping things either. He'd taken an almost debilitating interest in every step of their preparations. Alfred suspected it was because his money was in the pot, and he wanted to ensure maximum exposure for his company rather than out of fatherly affection. It had been easy getting his financial backing. Alfred knew which button to press. It was the big one labelled GUILT.

Alfred's mother had died when he was eight, and Jeremy had suffered a meltdown. It had been way beyond his capabilities to look after a grieving child. Soon after his mum's death,

Alfred's school expelled him for fighting. That was the final straw for his father, who wasted no time in shipping Alfred off to a boarding school, out of sight and out of mind.

Then, when Alfred was sixteen, Jeremy moved to Texas with work and found himself a new family. Alfred had visited them a few times, and they seemed pleasant enough, but he was a square peg in a circular hole in Jeremy's eyes. Alfred was a painful footnote to a previous life, which Jeremy could keep pacified by writing the occasional cheque, and he would need a big fat cheque this time.

Alfred had no job, no girlfriend, and no family. The prospect of the race was the only thing keeping him going. He ignored the alarm bells ringing in his head, all the reasons it was foolish to continue, and carried on regardless.

CHAPTER IV
April 2008

Shep was getting cold feet, both literally and metaphorically. After their second ocean training exercise with Tommy-the-Twat, Shep doubted whether he could operate a pedalo with Alfred, let alone attempt an ocean crossing with him.

He thought it would be simple. It was just rowing from A to B, but there was so much to remember and coordinate, and he kept making silly mistakes. Ocean rowing was much more difficult than rowing in the gym. Not that he'd spent much time on the rowing machine. He preferred to spend his time watching his muscles bulge on the weights. It didn't help that Alfred seemed to be a natural. Bloody golden boy and he took Tommy's side every time he made a little slip-up. At university, Alfred had been the clever one, acing exam after exam when Shep struggled to even understand the questions. However, sports had been Shep's domain, and it annoyed him how easily Alfred was picking everything up.

A friend from the gym had introduced Tommy to Shep, and he'd agreed to provide some training in return for a modest sum, paid for by Jeremy. Shep had been proud finally to contribute something to their trip, although Alfred said not to call it a trip because it made it sound like a holiday, and he might have slightly exaggerated the amount of work he'd put in to secure the lessons. It was a futile attempt to stop the endless questions from Alfred about his new job and leaving New York. Alfred didn't need to know he was delivering packages for some old acquaintances, no questions asked, for cash. As to why he'd come back to England, Shep had no intention of explaining his reasons.

The first time Shep got out onto the ocean with Tommy, the size of the task confronting him had become clear. It was far more difficult than he had ever imagined putting what he knew in theory and isolation into practice. He was way behind Alfred in knowing how to operate a boat and still hadn't grasped the terminology and commands. He would have to learn a lot, and learn it fast, if they were to stand any chance of finishing.

It was ludicrous that they were even considering attempting it. Tommy thought they were bonkers. He told them every time he saw them, and he was a skilled veteran. What chance did they have?

It would help if they could train on the boat they'd be competing in. Apparently, there had been some issues. The boat was being custom-built, and the deadline had slipped. Alfred hadn't gone into any detail, he'd just muttered something about his father's empire crumbling, and Shep had decided not to poke the bear. Alfred would find a solution, or he wouldn't, and the less Shep knew, the less he could help, which suited him perfectly.

According to Alfred, Tommy's boat was similar to the one they were having built. Alfred seemed to think that was a good thing, but Shep wasn't so sure. On Tommy's boat, he'd developed unbearable blisters on his hands within a few hours of their first training exercise, kept smashing his shins against the oar, and the waves left him constantly drenched and miserable. He wasn't expecting a hammock on board, but at least something to keep his spirits lifted.

Shep also wasn't sure if he could put up with Alfred for such a prolonged period. Small doses were fine, but days on end? He had enjoyed his travels with Alfred when they were younger. They'd survived many scrapes together without an angry word being muttered, but that was years ago, and a lot had changed since then. Plus, they hadn't been in each other's faces the whole time. They would be sleeping in the same room, sharing the same food, and breathing the same air. Alfred had changed, too. He'd become far more serious and short-tempered. If the training exercises were just the tip of the iceberg, he might go insane. He might end up throwing Alfred overboard or, even worse, himself.

He was in too deep to pull out now, though. With only a few months left to go, they had put in a lot of money. Well, Jeremy and Alfred had, but Shep had still invested a lot in time and effort. They'd raised thousands of pounds in donations for their chosen charity, well, Alfred's chosen charity. The local paper had even run a piece on them, painting them as heroes. He couldn't back out. Alfred wouldn't allow it.

Or could he? If he became injured, or if a family member developed a crippling disease, Alfred could hardly complain…

Shep passively listened as Tommy provided his constructive criticism, which was largely a rant about how he had nearly destroyed the boat, again. He'd been nowhere near the other rowers, and they could have moved out of the way had they needed to. There was no need to be such a drama queen. Alfred stood next to him, silently nodding away and occasionally chirping in. He was trying to be kind and reassure Shep that he was doing a fantastic job, being the good cop to Tommy's bad cop, but it wasn't helping.

'… and you've got to stay clipped in. I don't know what you were thinking unclipping.'

'Yeah, we can't be having you fall out on me, can we eh, Shep?' Alfred smiled.

Shep sucked through his teeth and counted to ten.

The debrief finished, Shep skulked off as quickly as he could to have a long shower and lick his wounds. His confidence had taken a battering. He needed to regroup, de-stress, and think about poor Uncle Roy and his debilitating illness…

Back home, Shep undressed and stepped into the shower, deliberating whether to have a hot or cold one. He'd read somewhere that ice baths were important for athletes after a workout, but he needed the comfort of a steamy shower. He turned up the heat, sat down, and let the water wash away his problems. After a few minutes, he decided he needed a more powerful shower to handle his issues, perhaps a jet wash.

Satisfied that he'd saturated the benefit of the shower, he got out and looked at his ailments in the mirror before checking himself out from various angles and poses. His chest had grown broad and strong from the training. His legs were powerful, the muscles defined and strong. Eventually, he'd gone teetotal, a task which had almost killed him, but he'd lost the tyre around his stomach. For the first time in his life, he'd developed the vague outline of a six-pack. Shep had been receiving a lot of attention lately regarding his body, and he liked it. He smiled, remembering the previous night's conquest. He'd forgotten her name already, not that it mattered because he had no plans to message her.

The loud buzz of an incoming message interrupted his thoughts. He searched for his phone, finding it tucked away in his sports bag, and opened it up, expecting to see another motivational text from Alfred. They usually followed a training session or a meeting, but it was a number his phone didn't recognise.

Unknown: *They switched it off today, and they know where you are.*

Baffled, Shep assumed that someone had sent the message to the wrong number. But then it clicked, and the meaning and purpose of the text became clear. It felt like he'd taken the pin out of a hand grenade. He threw his phone across the room and heard it thump against the sofa.

Was it her? How did she get his number? It could be the wrong number, but that would be too much of a coincidence. Naked, Shep paced up and down, the thought of getting dressed occupying a distant part of his brain. How could they know where he was?

The race!

Alfred's insistence on getting as much publicity as possible meant it wouldn't have been difficult to find him. A quick Google search of his name would narrow it down to London, and the press release had almost named the street he lived on. He debated for a moment if he should respond but decided not. He didn't want to know any more, and if he pretended he hadn't seen the text, he could continue in ignorance.

The ramifications of the message formed an orderly queue at the back of Shep's mind. They were problems for future Shep. Suddenly, the thought of being on a boat in the middle of nowhere seemed far more appealing. Perhaps Uncle Roy's illness wasn't too bad after all.

CHAPTER V

November 2008

Ismarus, Tinos

Aliz sat in a tavern called the Old Oak with a watered-down sweet beer and some questionable meat. She would normally avoid cesspits like the Old Oak, but she was in unfamiliar territory and desperate for replenishments. With its maze of corridors and hideaway rooms, it was the ideal place to stay inconspicuous. The room was dimly lit with a small table and a candle. It only had one entrance and exit, which wasn't ideal, but it was the only empty room in the tavern.

Aliz hacked at her meal with a blunt knife, attempting to remove the fat and sinew from whatever poor animal sat in front of her. It was hard work, and she was quickly losing her appetite. The room darkened, and Aliz looked up to see a towering figure in the doorway. She initially thought it might be the waiter bringing out more food or someone else trying to find a quiet spot. Then the figure moved into the room and sat down on the stool opposite her. He was somewhere in his fifties with warts littering his face. A deep scar ran from his right temple to his left cheek like someone had slashed him in a bar fight at some point in his murky past. He was the most revolting man Aliz had ever had the misfortune of setting her eyes on.

A second man followed. Although *man* was being kind, he was barely out of childhood. He was attractive, compared to his colleague, with straight white teeth, a chiselled jaw bone, smooth, olive skin, and curly black hair slicked through with oil. He looked nervous but sat next to Aliz, boxing her in against the wall and the table.

'What's a pretty girl like you doing in a place like this then?' the ugly man asked. He had a hoarse voice that matched his face.

'Eating my food, minding my business,' Aliz replied. 'You know,' she added, 'it's nice to ask permission before you sit down at someone else's table.'

The ugly man grinned at her, displaying yellow teeth. 'Don't worry, EN62, we won't be staying long. Any of us.'

Aliz cursed silently. She had hoped the men were trying to take advantage of a young female. She could easily deal with that. But someone must have sent them to track her down, and she was irritated at the calibre of her adversaries. Had she not shown them what she could do?

'My name is Aliz,' she said, sticking to the story she had given herself, but the lie was obvious.

'I don't care what you called yourself after you abandoned your post,' spat the ugly man. 'You're EN62, and you refused the Paymaster. No one refuses the Paymaster. You knew that when you accepted the job. I'm not surprised, though. What happened? Was it too much for you to handle? Never send a girl to do a man's job. Always said that, haven't I, Xee?'

The man called Xee nodded but kept quiet.

Aliz kept her mouth shut. She was small and used to being underestimated, but she had other skills more valuable and subtle than pure brawn and power. She tried to think and stay calm, but the ugly man was doing an excellent job of making her skin crawl. It would be difficult to make him uglier, but she could try.

'The job was suicidal,' she said after a pause. It was pointless keeping up the pretence. 'I didn't sign up for that. Get someone else to do it.'

'No, refusing the Paymaster was suicidal,' said the ugly man.

Xee produced a knife and hovered it next to Aliz's neck. She watched the blade shake in his hand and knew he'd never used it, not to cut a human, anyway. He'd be better pointing it at her gut. He'd have more control, a bigger area to aim for, and be less likely to miss. To go straight for the jugular without hesitation would require more confidence than he possessed.

'How did you find me?' Aliz asked, playing for time but also curious. She had moved fast, keeping off the major roads, and had covered her tracks.

The ugly man curled his mouth into what Aliz assumed was a smile. 'We have a snarler with us, and it's not that difficult. We just have to ask if anyone's seen the pretty girl with the white streak through her hair.'

Aliz kicked herself. She had been born with a white line dissecting her chestnut-coloured hair. She'd hated it at first, but now she quite liked the way it fell across her face. It gave her character, but it also made her stand out. It had been a foolish mistake not to hide it.

Were they telling the truth about the snarler? The big-teethed tigers were on the verge of extinction, and hunters could only hope to find them in the depths of the Alaskian Forest. Whilst they were renowned for their sense of smell, Aliz had never seen one, let alone heard of one being trained to track humans.

'So what? You just tied it up outside?' she asked, her face screwed into a picture of disbelief.

'As you know, our Paymaster is extremely well connected,' said the ugly man.

The knife by her neck shone in Aliz's peripheral vision, but Xee's grip was loose. 'What happens now?' Aliz asked.

'You come with us. We take you to the Paymaster and, if he's feeling generous, he might let you live.'

'And if I refuse?'

'The Paymaster left it to us to decide whether to take you in alive, and it'll be lighter if I'm only taking your head. It would be a shame, though, to remove such a pretty head from such a fine body. They work so well together. We could even have some fun on the way back.'

Aliz had heard enough. She pretended to enjoy the compliment and gave the ugly man her warmest smile. Slowly, she placed her right hand on Xee's crotch and gently grabbed her blunt knife with her left hand. Xee didn't know how to respond to the sudden development, and the ugly man was oblivious to what was going on under the table.

'Well,' she said in her most delicate voice.

The ugly man instinctively leaned in to hear.

'When you put it that way…'

Aliz squeezed Xee with her hand, and he looked down. His face was a mixture of delight and confusion. Aliz threw her right elbow back and up into Xee's face. She connected with the sweet spot and felt his nose splatter. Xee's head hit the back of the bench, and he slumped down.

Aliz didn't stop to think. She lunged forward with the knife in her left hand and struck the ugly man in his eye with all her force. There was a pop followed by a scream. The knife that Xee had threatened her with was loose on the bench. She picked it up and thrust it into the ugly man's throat. A waterfall of blood splashed Aliz in the face and created a horrendous mess on the walls and table. The ugly man squirmed, his hands clutching his face and neck. He writhed, gargled, and eventually collapsed heavily onto Aliz's plate. It was all over within a minute.

Aliz checked Xee and found him still breathing. She considered finishing him but decided he'd suffered enough. He was harmless, and she wasn't a murderer.

She cleaned the knife on Xee's shirt and tucked it away in her belt; she might still need it. If they had spoken the truth about the snarler, there were probably more of them waiting for her outside. Carefully, she peered out of the room, worried that the ugly man's cry might have alerted someone, but no one was there. A fiddler was playing music in the bar, and his high energy strumming must have swallowed any noise they had made.

Aliz kept to the shadows, working her way quickly through the warren. She was on high alert, but no one seemed to be in the slightest bit interested in her. She reached an exit and enjoyed the feeling of fresh air against her face. It wouldn't take long for someone to discover the mess she'd made, so she needed to act with haste. Aliz looked around and spotted a movement to her right. Behind a tree in the distance, she could make out the faint outline of a leg and a head. Whoever it was made a run for it, dragging something rather large behind them.

Aliz disappeared in the opposite direction. There was only one place she would find safety.

CHAPTER VI

Attica

Xee's head hurt like Tartarus. There was no escaping the pain. It was a constant dull thud across his eyes. Since his meeting with EN62, Aliz, or whatever she called herself, he hadn't been able to breathe through his nose. He hadn't realised how much he relied on his nose for breathing until he'd lost the ability.

EN62 had made a mockery of them when they'd met. Jared had told him it would be easy, that she wouldn't try anything. Jared had underestimated her, and he'd paid for it with his life. When Xee came to, the first thing that had confronted him was Jared's lifeless body splayed across the table in an inky pool of blood. He'd never seen a corpse before and hadn't expected to see his colleague so brutally ended. The image and smell had made him nauseous.

Xee didn't know how long he'd been out, but no one had discovered him. A party was still in full swing in the main room, so he'd been able to disappear quietly, leaving Jared's body for someone else to deal with. The further he could get away from the scene, the better.

Denby was the third man on their assignment. He handled the snarler. Xee didn't know how he'd managed to train the beast. That alone should have told Xee he was out of his depth, but he hadn't thought too much of it. Jared had told him it was easy money, more money than he'd ever seen in his life. That was the hook that had dragged him out of his easy backwater life.

After leaving the Old Oak, Xee found Denby at their meeting point and relayed what had happened. Xee had hoped Denby would know what to do, but to his dismay, rather than find a solution, Denby had turned a ghostly white and seemed to lose his tongue. He, too, was inexperienced in such matters. In the vain hope the snarler would do their dirty work, they attempted to track EN62, but the trail had gone cold. At least that's what Denby had planned to tell the Paymaster, until things turned ugly.

It turned out that Denby had never hunted with a snarler before, stammering out that he only reared and protected them. He'd kept it hungry during their assignment, believing it would chase EN62 down should she make a run for it. After losing her trail, they'd made camp to get some shut-eye, but the pain had prevented Xee from sleeping. He desperately needed some drugs and a physician to straighten his nose. He'd gone for a walk, hoping a stretch of his legs would help him, and discovered the snarler's gnawed ropes up against a tree. A few seconds later, he'd heard a panicked scream followed by the sound of a brief scuffle, and an almighty crunch, like a giant nut being cracked. It was a sound he'd never forget.

Through the trees, he spotted the snarler standing victorious. The moonlight reflected off its smooth coat, usually white and orange, but now red and dripping. It looked him in the eyes, its long canine teeth menacing in the moonlight, and then returned to its feast. Xee backed off slowly and then fled.

Now Xee had a meeting with the Paymaster, and he couldn't stop shaking. Jared had coordinated everything for the assignment, and he'd only recruited Xee because his other companion had let him down. Xee had been working in his father's tavern collecting glasses and cleaning pots when Jared had walked in boasting that he was about to become rich. He was a regular in the tavern, and his exploits were legendary across their small town anyway. Despite his father's warnings to stay away, Xee had found himself drawn into one of Jared's tales about fighting off three tridents in his youth. They had left him with the scar on his face, but Jared had taken their lives. The story had enthralled Xee, and when Jared asked for someone to help him with his current job, he'd put himself forward willingly. At fifteen, he was old enough to make his own decisions and his own mistakes.

Exactly what he'd agreed to wasn't clear, but it sounded more exciting than cleaning glasses, and he was desperate for adventure. He'd left the following morning whilst his parents were tucked up in bed, with plans to return with enough money to open his own tavern. Everyone would see that he could stand on his own two feet.

Now he longed to see his parents and clean glasses. However, his plan to return home and forget the entire episode changed drastically when a black armored rider appeared the night after the snarler incident. He forcefully collected Xee from his bed with barely a word being spoken. How the rider had found him was a mystery he didn't want to unravel.

The rider followed the Esaltes River to a remote location in the mountains on the border between the Attica and Phrixus realms. Xee bounced along uncomfortably in front of the rider on the back of the horse. They reached a cave on the edge of the mountainside, and Xee was told to wait outside. The rider had told him only that the Paymaster wanted to see him. Xee hadn't asked any more questions. He hadn't dared.

Xee's body was sore from the lengthy ride. His lips felt dry, and he kept licking them, which made them worse. An itch on the side of his head wouldn't go away, and he needed to empty his bowels. He awkwardly hopped as he waited, wondering how long it was going to take.

Finally, a deep voice said, 'Enter.'

Heart racing, Xee obeyed and walked into the cave. It was dark and difficult to see where he needed to go, so he used his hands to guide him, trying not to bang his head on the low ceiling. Then a light appeared ahead of him, and he followed it into a cavern.

A tall man stood in the corner. The three vertical lines branded on his forehead and his distinctive silver armour identified him as a trident. He looked as strong as an ox, and he was probably about as intelligent as one. The warrior stood straight to attention with his arms locked behind his back. He looked briefly in Xee's direction but did not acknowledge him.

A beam of light entered from a slight gap in the cavern roof. The cavern was empty other than the warrior, and Xee wondered if the warrior was the Paymaster.

'Report on the status of your assignment.' The voice filled the room. It was deep and booming with no particular accent. It was unclear who had spoken, and Xee looked around in confusion.

'Report on the status of your assignment,' the voice repeated with more aggression.

'Me?' asked Xee. He pointed to himself and looked at the warrior for help, but the man remained stationary. Xee decided it was best he answered, just in case. 'She got away... master,' he stuttered.

'Where is your leader?'

'Lord... um, sir? Dead, sir, she killed him. At least, I think she did... I suppose it could have been someone else. I wasn't awake. She... Aliz... EN62 knocked me out. Caught me by surprise, and then when I woke, he was dead and—'

'Did you remove all traces of the body?'

33

Jared's lifeless body and the bloodstains on the tavern wall flashed before Xee's eyes. The corpse had been about as conspicuous as it could be.

'It wasn't possible to move the body without the assignment being compromised. So I... left it to pursue the target.' That sounded like an acceptable response, although it came out as a question when it left his lips. What else could he have done?

'Where did you leave the body?'

'The Old Oak tavern in Ismarus.'

There was a lengthy pause. Xee looked around, trying to work out what trick the Paymaster was using to get his voice into the room.

'Did you track down the target?' the Paymaster asked.

'We tried, but the scent was cold. She was good, sir. Lethal.' If he said it with enough confidence, then at least it sounded like he knew what he was talking about.

'Where is the snarler now?'

'It... ahem, escaped. Denby, the handler, was... careless.'

'No names,' barked the Paymaster. 'Has the handler contained it?'

Xee considered his response. 'Not exactly,' he said.

'Explain yourself.'

'Den... the handler's dead.'

There was another painful pause.

'How?'

'The um... snarler ate him... your honour.' Xee saw the warrior raise his eyebrows. It was the first reaction he had seen from him. Xee cursed Jared and his simple assignment. Right now, he was glad he was dead.

Xee waited. Every second felt like an hour, and he startled when the Paymaster spoke again. 'EX6, go with the boy. Bring in the snarler and trace EN62. We cannot allow her to escape. Take as many men as you need, but make sure you deal with her. Then tie up any loose ends.'

What did he mean by loose ends? The warrior called EX6 thumped his chest with his right fist to acknowledge the order, clicked his heels, and marched out. 'With me,' he barked at Xee, who followed, now desperate for the toilet.

CHAPTER VII

Dionysus Forest, Tinos

How dare he keep her waiting! The Botanist tapped her long, thin fingers on the table and checked the sun-aligner again. Ten minutes now. It was plain rude. There was a knock on the door, and her assistant's acne-scarred face peered in tentatively. He was a pleasant boy and bright enough, but he was skittish, which didn't bode well.

'There's someone here for you,' he said in his high-pitched voice that had never graduated from puberty.

'Did you ask who they were and what they wanted?' The Botanist already knew, but she wanted to see her assistant squirm before he left.

'No, sorry. They, um, just said they had an appointment, so, um, I didn't think... I thought you'd know. Sorry. I'll go ask...' he turned away and then looked back. 'Should I ask?' he asked, torn.

'No. Just bring him here, then disappear.'

'Yes. Thanks. I mean, yes, I will.'

The assistant dithered in the doorway, then disappeared to bring her guest.

That was hard work, the Botanist thought. She had contemplated letting him go, but she needed an assistant, and they were hard to find and keep. Plus, she couldn't risk it. He knew too much.

A minute later, the assistant returned and showed a man into the room. He was about forty years old, experienced, but still holding onto the thin shadow of his youth. A thick moustache covered his lips and looked peculiar on his face like someone had stuck it there for a joke. A mop of blonde hair fell carelessly over his forehead, and he wiped it to the side as he entered. He had a broad frame, and his eyes were striking and serious, with a sadness behind them.

'He wouldn't tell me his name,' the assistant whispered loudly and then left.

'You're late!' the Botanist said to her guest.

'You're hard to find,' replied the guest, unapologetic. His accent told her he was well educated, perhaps in Ismarus or even the Capital if he had contacts.

'So you're the famous Botanist. I was expecting a man. And someone older.' The guest looked around the room and inspected a rare cactus with a striking orange flower that sat on a table. Its spikes were poisonous and could cause a rash, but the Botanist didn't warn him.

'What should I call you?' he asked, looking up.

'Madam will be fine.'

'No, that won't do.'

'Then call me what you want. It matters little.'

'Demeter would seem apt if what they say about you is true.'

The Botanist masked a smile. Her reputation was growing. 'If it pleases you,' she replied.

'I'm Axil,' said the guest, 'but you already knew that.' He gave her a hint of a smile, which brought a different, far more pleasant dimension to his face. 'I believe you have something for me,' he said.

The Botanist looked her guest up and down. Axil probably wasn't his real name, but he fit the description given, and he'd found her, so she was confident she was dealing with the right person.

'Very well, Axil, follow me.' She led him through a passage and into a conservatory filled with hundreds of black orichalcum plants.

Axil stopped. 'I'm assuming you don't have a licence for these,' he said, pointing to the plants. It was illegal to grow orichalcum outside designated areas unless the State had granted permission. They harnessed an incredible amount of energy, which the State claimed ownership of. The Botanist had discovered how to triple the potential yield of the orichalcum bead, but she had no desire to share her little secret at the moment. She looked at Axil dismissively and then walked on.

'I could have you thrown in jail for a long time for growing orichalcum, you know,' Axil continued playfully.

'And you're here on legitimate State business, are you?' asked the Botanist sternly. 'Because I was of the understanding that we were working for the same person. Or am I mistaken?'

'Just a comment,' he said and then stopped to stroke one of the orichalcum's furry, black leaves. The orichalcum bead glowed fiercely from inside its black rose-like flower.

'You're not here to study my collection of orichalcum, I assume?' the Botanist said coldly.

'No, just interested,' said Axil, blinking as he tore his eyes away from the bead. 'I'm hoping you might have something else for me.'

The Botanist led Axil through her garden into a second building, which the surrounding woodland had consumed, making it invisible to the naked eye. 'I suggest you spray yourself with this,' she said, handing Axil a container full of liquid.

Axil looked at the container, confused.

'You'd better listen and follow what I say,' the Botanist added. Memories of her previous assistant were still fresh. She tried to remember his name. Theo? Theseus? He had been utterly useless with plants, but he was handy in other ways. The Botanist smiled to herself. It was a shame he had been so careless.

She pushed her memories aside. 'Are you ready?' she asked.

'Ready for what exactly?' Axil replied as he sprayed himself.

The Botanist led him into a huge room flooded by sunlight from a deceptively high glass roof. Plants of a thousand colours and varieties filled the space. They climbed the walls and covered the floor. They interlinked, making it difficult to tell where one plant started and another ended. Some grew straight up from the uncovered floor, towering over the Botanist and Axil, whilst pots and containers constrained the smaller species.

The Botanist looked at her guest. A bead of sweat rolled down his forehead onto his pronounced cheekbone as the heat took its toll. He looked unimpressed. 'I thought you might find some of these to be of interest,' she said, referring to the plants surrounding them.

He looked at her and pursed his lips. 'It's not what I was expecting,' he said politely, 'but carry on.'

The Botanist knew what Axil wanted, but his tardiness had annoyed her, so she would now waste some of his time. She walked up to a plant that stood five feet high. Seven green leaves protruded from a long tubular stem, and each leaf looked like a mouth with crimson lips and long, thin teeth.

'This is a flytrap,' said the Botanist, looking at it fondly. 'The hairs,' she continued, pointing at the teeth, 'can detect the faintest of touches from an insect. When that happens, the trap is engaged, and the leaf closes around its prey, trapping it inside. Remarkable, really.'

As if scripted, a butterfly gently landed on a leaf. There was a nervous pause as the Botanist and Axil waited for a response. Then the plant sprang into action and closed its mouth around the butterfly before it had the chance to fly away.

'It will stay closed now for a few days whilst it breaks down its meal by releasing acids.'

The Botanist smiled, but Axil remained unmoved. She continued her way around the sunroom, pointing out plants and explaining what they did and how. There was a large cactus plant with toxic needles here and a rose with deadly foot-long thorns there. She could sense that Axil's patience was wearing thin.

Finally, they reached the end of the room, where the Botanist pointed at an unusual plant that looked like a large maroon jug with a narrow bottom and broad top. 'This,' she said, 'is my favourite. It's a giant pitcher plant, and it's the most deadly of the plants in this room. It lives off mice and other small rodents, attracting them with its smell. When they fall in, they're trapped and eventually drown. We get plenty in here, so it stays well-fed—'

'Enough!' Axil snapped. 'You know what I'm here for, so please let's move on quickly. There are a lot of places I need to be.'

The Botanist smiled inwardly at her guest's frustration. Sweat was racing down his forehead now, and he looked flustered. He wasn't so cocksure anymore. 'Very well,' she said, producing a phial from a pouch by her side.

Axil laughed a frustrated laugh. 'You had it on you all that time,' he said. 'You could have just given it to me without the tour.'

'Yes,' said the Botanist, 'but you're not just here for the gorgon blood, are you?'

Axil grunted as the Botanist passed him the phial.

'I assume you know how to administer it?' she asked.

Gorgon blood was suicidal to obtain because the snake had to be alive at the point of extracting it. Then the user had to store and administer it correctly for it to work as intended, which was no mean feat. It was the only poison without an antidote, and there was a demand for it on the black market. With no competition, the Botanist could charge what she liked.

'No, but I will not be the one administering it,' Axil commented.

'Who's it for?'

'I don't ask questions. And I suggest you don't either.'

The Botanist shrugged. She'd already received her payment.

'Fine, I understand you have something else to show me,' he said, wiping his brow with the back of his hand.

The Botanist grinned and then led Axil to the corner of the room. Hidden amongst the vines stood a small door. When the Botanist opened it, a vile smell assaulted them. She was expecting it and held her breath, but Axil turned his face away in disgust.

'After you,' she said.

Axil covered his nose and mouth with his arm. He crouched down and walked through the door into a second room. Like the first room, light shone fiercely through a glass roof, but there were no plants. Instead, something far more bestial waited for them.

The Botanist entered and smiled at her creation.

It had the body of the jug-like pitcher plant she had pointed out in the previous room, except it was gigantic and required a ladder to reach the top. A separate thick trunk was attached to the body at ground level and extended as high as the roof. At various heights along the trunk, long, green tubular arms had grown, and at the end of each arm was the terrifying red mouth of the flytrap, each one bigger than a human head. The arms hung limp and covered most of the floor like monstrous coiled snakes.

Axil didn't know where to look or stand.

'It's called Gyges,' said the Botanist. She had named it after the many-handed monster banished to the depths of the dungeon of torment, reserved for the world's most evil creatures and humans called Tartarus. Only a select few people had seen her creation, and whilst she knew most would view it as a monstrosity, she thought it was spectacular.

'What is it?' Axil whispered as though Gyges could hear him.

'It's my child,' the Botanist replied and then watched Axil's face as he tried to process what he was looking at. 'You look confused,' she said. 'A demonstration might help?'

Axil raised his eyebrows. 'Sounds sensible. Then I can be sure what it is I'm looking at before I report back to the Paymaster.'

The Botanist left Axil alone in the room to find her assistant. When she returned, he had scurried into the corner with his back to the wall. He looked like he was holding his breath, and she couldn't blame him. The smell of rotting flesh was overwhelming.

'Quickly,' the Botanist said to the assistant as he bundled a cart into the room and rolled over one of Gyges' arms.

'Sorry... um, excuse me,' the assistant muttered and then stopped. He looked at the Botanist, worried.

'Go on!' she urged.

The assistant removed a cloth on the cart to reveal a man, battered and beaten so badly that the Botanist thought he might be dead. Then the man let out a rasping wheeze, and the Botanist relaxed. The man didn't move, either not having the energy or the means. The Botanist wasn't sure of the extent of his injuries.

'Who is he?' asked Axil.

'Someone who displeased someone,' replied the Botanist with indifference. She wasn't getting paid to have a conscience.

'Madam, should I, um... maybe...?'

The Botanist nodded, and her assistant tipped the cart and dumped its contents in a heap on the floor. The man let out a groan but didn't move.

Nothing happened at first, and the Botanist was worried that Gyges was full. Then its arms slithered inexorably towards the man.

'The arms,' she said, 'have long thin hairs that can detect movement. She isn't interested in us because the spray we used outside is poisonous to her and acts as a deterrent.

But if you haven't taken precautions, then…' The Botanist pointed towards the man on the floor.

A thick, green arm reached the man's ankle and wrapped itself around him whilst the mouth of the arm closed around his leg. From the depths of despair, the man found some energy and tried to unleash himself, but another arm wound around his wrist as he raised his hand. Within a few seconds, Gyges had entangled him. The man let out a muffled scream as he tried to fight his way clear, but he had no means of defending himself.

'Look how the elements work together,' the Botanist continued, mesmerised.

Axil's face was a mixture of disgust and intrigue.

Gyges's arms lifted the man's body off the floor amidst muffled screams and brought him towards the opening of the plant, which pulsated grotesquely in eager anticipation.

'She's hungry!' said the Botanist, pleased that the demonstration was going well.

The arms disappeared into the opening of the body and then re-emerged, having deposited the man inside. They flopped haphazardly on the floor.

Axil watched open-mouthed as Gyges bulged from its dinner punching and kicking it from inside.

'There's no hope of escape,' commented the Botanist. 'He'll be swimming in acidic quicksand right now. He will probably die from drowning once he's exhausted himself. It'll keep Gyges full for perhaps three days. Her last feed was four days ago, and she's growing all the time, so it's difficult to know.'

Axil turned pale and gulped. 'Hmm,' he managed, 'I will report back to the Paymaster. I think he will be… pleased.'

'He should be,' said the Botanist and watched as Axil quickly left the room. She knew he wouldn't be late again.

CHAPTER VIII
San Sebastian, La Gomera

It was another beautiful day in La Gomera. A day for relaxing on a sun lounger with a beer and a book, but Alfred didn't have time for that. He had too much to do. Time had passed far too quickly. They were only a few days away from the start of the race, and his list was like the Hydra's head. He'd slay one job only to have two more appear.

Despite all the potential issues that could arise during their crossing, Alfred was confident. He'd completed dozens of courses and training events and was in peak condition. Shep had joined him for the compulsory ones, at least. Even Tommy, their coach, had seemed mildly impressed by the end, although the challenges they faced tootling about with him were minor compared to what awaited them.

Shep was another matter. An almost tangible nervousness resonated from him, and it had been building over the last few months. It could be the race. He'd hardly been a model student, but Alfred had a feeling that it was something else. Whenever he broached the subject, Shep shrugged off Alfred's concern and refused to engage with him. So Alfred had let sleeping dogs lie. He wouldn't risk upsetting Shep. He might throw his toys out of the pram, and that wasn't a risk he was willing to take, not after all the hard work that he'd put in.

Plus, they had a lot to enjoy. Jeremy had arranged for them to stay in a five-star luxury hotel for the week before the race. A little taste of luxury before they had to spend months confined to a small cabin together. Most of the competitors were staying there, and it created a real buzz of excitement about the place. Overall, thirty-four teams were competing in four races. Alfred had spoken to nearly all the competitors and discovered several other first-time amateurs like himself. Had Shep taken the time to engage with the others, he might not be so uptight, but he had shown little interest in making friends other than two drinking companions.

In the lead up to the race, Alfred's biggest headache besides Shep had been their boat. The global financial crisis had hit Jeremy's company hard, and it had taken far longer than expected to get their vessel ready and kitted out. At one point, it had been touch and go whether they would be able to compete at all, but at the eleventh hour, Jeremy had stepped in with his personal savings, much to Alfred's relief.

When Lyon Heart—the dreadful name Jeremy had christened their boat—arrived at La Gomera's harbour, Alfred had nearly collapsed with relief. Since then, he'd spent most of his free time with his paramour, stroking her, talking to her, searching her every inch. She was twenty-four feet of high-tech, custom-built, carbon perfection oozing sex appeal. Streamlined and pristine, she had been well worth the migraines and sleepless nights. Alfred felt a pang of guilt that he hadn't invited Jeremy to the pre-start party. He'd really come up trumps when it mattered.

Alfred walked the familiar route to the harbour, and his jaw nearly hit the ground when he saw Shep had beaten him there. He'd hoped that Shep would be as enthusiastic as him when Lyon Heart arrived, but he hadn't even bothered to visit her. He'd told Alfred that he would soon have to spend all of his time on her and that he wanted to make the most of his time on dry land. Alfred could understand, but Shep's plans also seemed to involve spending a large amount of time at the bar. It was a concern, but there was nothing he could do about it.

'How do?' Alfred asked as he approached Shep, noticing black rings around his eyes.

Shep stood up sluggishly. 'I thought I should have a closer look before we go. See what all the fuss is about.'

He sounded less than enthused, but that wouldn't deter Alfred. 'Pleased you found the time to join me. There's a lot to sort.'

Shep grunted tiredly and adjusted his baseball cap. They climbed aboard. Despite spending so much time on Lyon Heart, every time he stepped on her, Alfred felt like he was trespassing. It didn't feel real. So much time and effort had gone into getting to this stage. It had felt so impalpable at one point that the reality of the situation was overwhelming.

There was a lot to check, sort, and pack, but seeing as Shep had made an effort to join him, all that could wait. Alfred showed Shep around, pointing out various areas and equipment.

The set-up was like the boat they'd been training in with Tommy, and so nothing would be new to Shep, but everything had its distinct quirks.

'This is our sleeping area,' Alfred said, showing Shep the rear cabin.

'Looks like a coffin with a porthole,' Shep mumbled, and Alfred felt the hairs on the back of his neck prickle and his shoulders tense.

'Well, I think you'll be too tired to care,' Alfred replied flatly. 'All the electrical equipment and our computers are in there, so we need to make sure that the door stays closed. You know what happened on Tommy's boat when—'

'Yes, I remember it well. Wouldn't let me forget it, would he?' Shep said curtly.

'You ruined his GPS.'

'So he said. Repeatedly. It was on its way out, anyway.' Shep peered through the cabin door. 'It looks like the command centre of the Starship Enterprise in there,' he commented.

'I've already packed most of our supplies,' Alfred said as he led Shep to the front cabin. 'The anchors, chains, parachute sea anchor, and drogues are all in there ready if we need them.'

'Okay. What about food?'

'Mostly in the lockers on deck. Each one holds a week's worth of freeze-dried rations, so it's nice and easy for us to control our food intake.'

Shep scratched his head and looked around, bored. 'Seems like you've got it all sorted.'

A thank you would have been nice. 'Getting there. I could do with you picking up a few bits that I've missed.' Alfred waited, hoping that Shep might volunteer his services, but he just stared at his flip-flops. 'Could you get some batteries for the compass? I forgot to bring spares.'

'Yeah, sure, I'll pick some up,' Shep replied as he stared at a bird in the distance.

Would he bother to check what size and type they needed? Alfred shook off his concerns. He needed to trust him with something.

'Remember what these are for?' Alfred pointed to the safety lines that ran the length of the boat. They could use them to get back on board if they fell overboard, assuming they had clipped themselves in. Shep had been notoriously bad at remembering to clip himself in and had felt Tommy's wrath for it. It had become a running joke. Although Shep never found it particularly amusing.

'Hilarious,' he said dryly. 'I'm pleased I don't have him breathing down my neck anymore. "Clip in. Why aren't you clipped in? You've got to clip in,"' Shep mimicked.

'He wasn't that bad.'

'Not to you he wasn't. Had it in for me though, didn't he?'

Alfred kept his thoughts to himself and changed the topic. 'This is our electric water maker. Have a look at that now because it's different from Tommy's, and you need to know how it works. Otherwise, we'll be hand pumping seawater into drinking water.'

Shep crouched down to look and then decided better of it. 'I'll look before we go.' He produced two cans of beer from his bag and said, 'I think we should have a celebratory tipple first.'

'Cheers,' Alfred said. It had been a long time since he'd touched alcohol, but it seemed appropriate to mark the occasion with a drink.

'Cheers!' Shep opened a can and drained it. 'Not bad.'

Alfred wasn't sure whether he was talking about the boat or the beer. They sat down in the seats. There was space for them to row together, but they would take it in turns during the race, so the second seat would be redundant for most of the journey.

'So, we're stuck with the name Lyon Heart, then?' Shep asked as he opened a second can.

The name had been the only thing that Shep had taken a particular interest in. They had considered everything from mythological boat names such as Argo to comedy names such as Stroking to the Finish. However, their deliberations turned out to be pointless, as Alfred's father had put his foot down on Lyon Heart. Given that he was paying for it, Alfred had not voiced his disappointment, but he wished he had gone for something more inspirational.

'What name would you prefer?' Alfred asked.

'I keep saying Bertha!'

'She's not a Bertha. How about Aphrodite, after the Goddess of Beauty?'

'I think you're obsessed.'

Alfred laughed. Perhaps he was obsessed. It was all that he'd been able to think about for the last year, and he'd pushed himself to the breaking point. It felt good to relax. The sun was shining, and the weather was warm without being uncomfortable. Alfred stretched out and took another drink from his can, already feeling the impact. A tsk told Alfred that Shep had moved onto his third.

The tour was over.

CHAPTER IX

It was the night before the race, and Shep felt sick. He had arrived at the pre-race party arranged by the organiser a few hours ago. Most of the competitors were making the most of the free drinks and canapés, but Shep didn't need any more alcohol. He needed Alfred. He had a confession…

On arrival, Alfred had disappeared to speak to one of his friends. The thought of listening to more tips and advice about the race made Shep feel exhausted. Instead, he'd made a beeline for Hendrik and Isaac, two Dutch competitors who had become his drinking companions. They were young and full of confidence and, as they had never competed before, he had a lot in common with them. Plus, they liked a drink, and they didn't reprimand him for getting smashed every so often. Of course, his nasty habits frustrated Alfred, but he needed to make the most of it whilst he still could.

Throughout their entire stay in La Gomera, Alfred had been nothing but a bore, constantly wittering about jobs they had to do and overthinking everything. Shep had taken what opportunities he could to escape. If he hadn't, he would have gone insane. Yes, they needed to get everything sorted, but what was the point of taking part if they pulled the fun out of the experience? On one occasion, Alfred had even turned up with a clipboard. No one has fun when a clipboard's involved.

Hendrik had bought a round of beers and shots, which they'd consumed within a few minutes. Shep then felt compelled to follow suit, and before long, they were being unsociably loud. Inevitably, the conversation had moved on to their route and tactics for the morning, and Hendrik believed that Shep and Alfred were making a colossal mistake. Everyone had their own approach to the race, and everyone thought theirs was the best. It infuriated Shep. What did it matter so long as they all crossed the finishing line in one piece?

To reduce the distance they had to row, Alfred had decided that they would travel in a straight line to the finishing point in Antigua. It sounded sensible, and Shep had gone along with it without question. They had based all their preparations on that route. Apparently, the more experienced competitors were following the longer trade route with the favourable winds. To make his point, Hendrik had brought others into the conversation, just so they could tell Shep what an enormous error they were making. He felt like an idiot. Surely Alfred knew what he was doing. He'd done plenty of research. The weather might not be as good, but they'd just have to tough it out for a bit. How bad could it be?

Unable to stomach any more goading, Shep had stormed off to find some food to soak up the drink. A waiter hovered nearby with a tray of battered prawns, so he grabbed a handful and shoved them into his mouth as he watched Natalia, a competitor from Surrey, order a cocktail from the bar. She wasn't his usual type, but he still couldn't take his eyes off of her toned body and playful smile. It was at that point that Shep spotted someone familiar standing next to Natalia at the bar. A tall, heavily tanned man with a dark mop of hair. Shep didn't know who he was, except he must do because sirens were screaming in his head.

Why couldn't he place him? Excessive alcohol had turned his brain into mush. The man turned around and looked in Hendrik's and Isaac's direction. They were being loud and drawing attention to themselves. The long nose and small, deep-set eyes were familiar. Then Shep's heart rate jumped into overdrive, and he felt sick.

He ducked out of the light and hid behind a group of three women who were talking excitedly at a pace Shep couldn't comprehend. The man at the bar was just standing, looking around. He didn't appear to know anyone. Was it him, or just someone who looked vaguely similar?

At the other side of the room, Alfred was talking to the crew of another boat. Shep didn't recognise any of them. The man at the bar strode off and approached Alfred's table. There was a brief conversation, and Alfred pointed to the bar. As the man walked off, Shep edged his way along the side of the room to Alfred's table, keeping out of sight.

Alfred was mid-conversation and didn't notice Shep as he crouched down beside him.

'We need to get out of here,' Shep whispered.

Alfred nearly jumped out of his chair. 'What are you doing down there?' he laughed.

48

'Doesn't matter. We need to get out of here. I think we need to... discuss tomorrow.'

Alfred looked bemused. 'Bit late, isn't it?' Then he saw the look on Shep's face. 'I've just got a drink in, so let me finish, and then we can go. Why don't you get another one? Actually, it looks like you've had a few already, so maybe water or something soft. I need you fit for tomorrow.'

'I'm fine,' Shep stressed. 'But I'd like to get out of here. Who was that you were speaking to earlier? What did he want?'

'Who?'

'The bloke who you were just speaking to. The tall guy.'

'I don't know who you're talking about.'

'He literally just walked over here and spoke to you and then walked off.' Shep was getting frustrated with Alfred. He was being deliberately obtuse.

'Oh him! I can't remember if he said his name. He was just asking where the toilets are.'

'Did he ask about me?'

'Why would he ask about you? Do you know him?'

Had he said too much? 'No, I... I thought I knew him, but I'm not sure.'

'Oh right. Where from? I've not seen him before.'

That wasn't good. Alfred knew everyone competing. He had to come clean. If something happened, he'd need at least one person to know.

'Listen,' Shep said, keeping his voice low, 'I need to tell you something, but it can't be here.'

Alfred stared at him and then nodded. 'Okay, let's head outside for a bit.'

'It needs to be away from here,' Shep insisted.

Alfred leaned back in his chair and raised his eyebrows. 'Fine, well, let's head off, then. Probably best we get an early night, anyway.'

Shep scurried outside as Alfred politely excused himself from the table. It didn't look like anyone was following them, but he had to be sure, so he led Alfred up the road in silence until they were out of sight of the party.

'You going to tell me what this is all about, then?' Alfred asked as Shep stopped behind a bus shelter.

It was a moment Shep had been dreading, but he needed to unburden himself. 'Something happened in New York,' he said.

'I figured something happened by how edgy you've been on the subject. Does it involve that bloke you scarpered from in there?'

'I don't know. Maybe. My memory is hazy. It happened so fast.'

Alfred took a deep breath. 'I don't think I'm going to like this,' he muttered.

'Hmm.' Shep wondered whether he should say anything. It wasn't too late. He could just make something up…

'So, something happened in New York?' Alfred prodded. 'Something which forced you back to England, and which you've been silent about ever since? I knew there was something you weren't telling me.'

'Hmm,' Shep said again, still deliberating. Alfred would know if he was lying, he would never let it drop. 'It was on a night out,' he said after a pause. 'We'd had a few drinks, me and a few guys from the office, and this girl walked over to me. She was hot. Like, smoking. Like…'

'Yeah, I get it. Keep going.'

'She came over, and we got chatting. She said she liked my British accent and asked where I was from. One thing led to another, and I ended up going back to hers, and—'

'That bloke's her boyfriend or husband?' Alfred tried to speed things up.

'No, but she had a boyfriend, and I found that out after I'd been seeing her for about a month. He'd found out about everything.'

'Okay,' Alfred said. Shep looked like he was waiting for a slap to the face.

'And the boyfriend finds out where I work, and where I hang out, and where I live, and one evening, he follows me on my way back home from a bar.'

'Aha,' Alfred said as he stroked his jaw with his thumb and forefinger.

'I don't know the guy, but he's there with this other guy, and he says all this stuff and starts pushing me around. And then I realise who he is. I'd seen his picture on the internet after Anna told me about everything. I'd looked him up.' Shep was talking fast now, the alcohol acting as a lubricant.

50

'Anna's the girl?' Alfred said, trying to follow.

'Yeah, she's the girl. He was a big guy, like a quarterback, so, you know, I'm fearing for my life when he shoves me down this dark alley.'

'Mm. And you're still seeing Anna at this stage?'

'No, she'd stopped things a while ago, so I was not expecting anyone to come after me. Why would I? She was old news. And then… then he punched me, and my nose exploded. Blood everywhere.'

Alfred screwed his eyes as he looked at Shep's nose. 'It does look wonky! I've never noticed it before, but now you say I can see it. So what happened then?' He'd relaxed his shoulders a little and had a wry smile on his face. He hadn't heard the worst of it yet.

Shep carefully considered his next words. 'Well, I was in a lot of pain. More pain than that time I snapped my ligament playing football. So I threw a punch because I thought he was coming for me again, and I connected with him.' Shep mimicked the action. 'And then he hit the deck.'

'Just like that?' Alfred said in disbelief. 'I thought you said he was big.'

Shep shrugged his shoulders. 'Then his mate, who was playing lookout, runs to him because he was on the ground bleeding and not getting up. And I was not hanging around, so I made a run for it and got out of there.'

Alfred stared ahead as he tried to make sense of Shep's rambling. 'I'm confused. Who's the guy you're paranoid about?'

'The mate, or brother, or whoever it was being the lookout whilst his mate tried to kill me,' Shep said as though it was obvious.

'That's a bit strong. He punched you, and you deserved it by the sound of it. But I don't know why he is here. You're not making any sense.'

'Because,' Shep took a deep breath. 'Because the guy I hit is dead.' Saying it aloud made it sound real.

Alfred barely reacted. 'But not from you punching him? Surely?'

'There was blood. A lot of blood, but some of it was mine. I think most of it was mine. His mate was hovering over him and, I don't know, I got out of there, but then I got a message from Anna saying that he was in hospital in a coma.'

'Not from you punching him, though? Couldn't have been that. Did he hit his head on something?'

Shep wondered whether he should leave it there and pretend that was it. No, he couldn't. Alfred would be onto him. 'Maybe. I...' Shep paused, 'I had a rock in my hand...'

Shep looked away as Alfred burned a hole in his forehead with his eyes.

'So, what you're telling me is you smashed a man over the head with a rock, and he's dead, and now his mate is after you!' Alfred paced up and down, his hands on his head, trying to process Shep's bombshell. 'So what happened next? You found out he was in the hospital? What's Anna doing? Why aren't you in prison? What are you doing here?'

A vein throbbed in Alfred's head, and Shep tried not to stare at it. 'I just... I didn't.' He struggled to think of what to say. 'I felt bad. Obviously. Especially when I found out he was in a coma. But nothing linked me to it, and there was no one coming after me. I mean, I was expecting the cops at any moment, or Anna or his mate, but nothing happened. Then my placement finished, and I had no reason to stay in the US, so I came home. There was nothing to keep me in New York, so I booked a flight to London, messaged you, and here we are. I was half expecting someone to stop me at the airport. Then I tried to forget about it, and I genuinely thought he'd just recover, but then I got a message a few months ago.'

Alfred was staring at the pavement, breathing slowly. 'Why didn't you tell me at that point?'

'Well, I didn't think it was for me at first because I didn't recognise the number and no-one in New York knew my UK number, but then I remembered I had given it to Anna one time and so she must have kept it. The message said that they'd turned it off and were coming for me, or something like that.'

'Turned what off?'

'I don't know. His life-support-machine, I guess.'

'You assume? What do you mean? And didn't you think of mentioning this to me at the time? What the hell have you gotten me involved in?'

Shep had never seen Alfred this angry before. He was often grumpy, moody, and demanding but not angry. It was strange, almost funny.

'Why, why are you telling me this now?!' continued Alfred. 'What do you expect me to do exactly? Are you even sure he's dead?'

'Yeah, he's dead,' muttered Shep. He'd checked out his social media profile and discovered a wall full of condolences. 'But if that guy we saw today is who I think it is, then he must be here for me. For revenge or... I don't know, but he's not here to pat me on the back, is he? So I needed to tell someone in case, you know, I suddenly die or something.'

Alfred shook his head dismissively. 'Why the hell aren't the cops after you if you've killed someone?'

'It was self-defence, and from what I've seen, my name hasn't been mentioned. Remember, they came after me. They attacked me. It's them who should be worried. I should have pressed charges. Why would I attack two massive blokes? Look what they did to my face. It was an absolute mess.'

Shep had rehearsed his defence in his head many times, but it didn't impress Alfred. 'Yeah, well, one of them is dead, so...' Alfred said and pursed his lips.

It was such a condescending look and one Shep was all too familiar with. It was typical of Alfred to take someone else's side over his.

After a few seconds, Alfred relaxed a little. 'So you think that bloke is here for revenge?'

'Possibly,' Shep mumbled. It had been dark, and everything happened so quickly.

'Possibly? How sure are you?'

On reflection, it sounded ridiculous. Why would someone follow him to La Gomera? 'I don't know,' he admitted.

Alfred threw his arms into the air. 'Right, so it could be anyone! Well, we can't pull out now. Not on the eve of the race.'

'I'm not suggesting we do!' Shep sighed. He'd just confessed to having killed someone, and all Alfred could think about was the race.

'Head back. Go into your room. Lock your door. Put a chair up against it or something. If anything happens, bang on the wall, and I'll hear you. I'll call for you in the morning, and we'll get ready and head down together.'

Shep nodded. 'Cheers,' he said.

'Don't thank me. If anything happens, I'll be standing aside. I'm not getting involved. As far as I'm concerned, we haven't had this conversation. Agreed?'

'Yes.' Shep breathed.

'Agreed?' Alfred forced.

Shep felt like a little child being told off by his parent. 'Yes,' he said, louder.

'Good. Let's head back then and get some rest.'

They walked back to the hotel in silence. It seemed inappropriate to talk about anything else, and neither wanted to bring up the incident again. Shep got into his room, locked his door, and put a chair up against it, just in case. Whilst he hadn't wanted to tell Alfred, or anyone, about what had happened, the revelation had unburdened him from the guilt he had carried. And Alfred didn't need to know any more about what had happened. He wouldn't mention it again. They could forget all about it.

Shep helped himself to a drink from the mini-bar. The walk back had almost sobered him up, and that wouldn't do. Not on his last night of freedom.

CHAPTER X

Alfred sat poised, ready to set off. He'd been waiting for this moment for over a year, but instead of feeling excited, he felt utterly deflated. Shep's confession had poleaxed him, and he'd spent most of the night searching the internet for any reports he could find about the incident. The only thing he'd found was an article about someone who had been left in a critical condition after an altercation following a night out. The police were appealing for witnesses. The timing and location matched, but the article stated that someone had stabbed the injured man, so Alfred had given up. It was probably better if he didn't know any more.

After exhausting his internet searches, Alfred had tried to sleep, but it was hopeless. Every time he drifted off, he thought he heard someone in Shep's room and immediately braced himself for action, expecting the worst.

Then, in the morning, it had taken fifteen minutes of shouting and kicking the door before Shep had finally answered. He was alive and untouched, but he'd emptied the contents of the mini-bar and smelled like death warmed up. That explained the rustling and clinking Alfred had heard with his ear pressed against the wall. Alfred dragged Shep onto the boat, but he was in no state for rowing. He was passed out in the cabin sleeping off his hangover.

Alfred had checked everything on board a hundred times, clocked up thousands of hours of training and preparation time, and considered and carefully planned for every eventuality. Everything apart from spending over two months trapped on a boat with a murderer, but there wasn't much he could do about that. Despite his vigilance, he still felt ill-prepared for the challenge, especially with Shep a dead weight in the back. As he waited for the horn to tell them to go, he tried to bury his doubts, but they kept resurfacing, and his mind was awash with elaborate excuses he could reel off to pull out of the race. His conscience was telling him to report Shep. Then the courts could deal with the matter in the proper way. But the humiliation he would face if he accepted defeat before he'd even started, after all the effort he'd put in, forced him to ignore his principles and bury his head in the sand.

After what seemed like an eternity, a foghorn broke the silence, and the 14 boats in Alfred's race set off amidst a loud cheer. Euphoria pushed away his worries. There was no turning back now. He could decide what to do with Shep during their voyage. He'd have plenty of time to think about it and make the right decision.

Alfred smiled. Next stop, Antigua.

The plan had been for Alfred and Shep to take it in turns to row, each rowing for two hours before switching for a two-hour break. That way, they could keep moving for twenty-four hours a day. After three hours of rowing, Alfred was tired. He'd shouted repeatedly for Shep to take over but to no avail. Just as Alfred was about to explode, he heard a movement, and Shep appeared from his cesspit and hurled over the side of the boat.

'That's better!' Shep said. His skin was pale and creased. 'We made it out then?'

Alfred gave him a scathing look, but Shep wasn't paying attention.

'Sorry,' Shep muttered. 'I think everything just caught up with me.'

'I had to pay the mini-bar charge,' Alfred barked. He could barely look at Shep. 'It was a lot. Anyway, get sat down. It's your turn. And get yourself clipped in, for god's sake.' Shep had failed on the number one health and safety rule already. 'And make sure that door's locked. Come on Shep, get it together!' Shep had left the door to the cabin open as he'd run to be sick. Rule number two was already broken.

'Sorry!' Shep said sheepishly. 'Is it my turn already? And where are all the other boats?'

'I've been rowing for three hours, over three hours, so, yes, it is your turn. And where every other bugger is.' Alfred looked around. 'They are somewhere on the horizon or somewhere behind us. I don't think we'll have much company from now on.' Alfred had expected to stay within a pack for at least a day, but the teams had separated quickly after the start.

'Okay, okay, sorry, didn't realise how long I'd been in there. I heard the foghorn, but that only seemed like a few minutes ago. I must have drifted off again. It felt like someone was driving a needle into my brain. Man, it's hot out here.'

Shep looked in no state to row, but Alfred didn't care. He was too tired to be mad, so he made his way to the cabin for a nap, but Shep's lingering smell, a mixture of vomit and cheese and onion crisps, put an end to that. Instead, he watched as Shep struggled to settle into a rowing pattern. The oars smashed into his shins, and a rogue wave left him drenched. Shep cried out miserably, and Alfred felt a little happier.

After their initial mishap, Alfred and Shep settled into their two-hour rowing shifts, and Alfred soon realised the enormity of their challenge. Neither could sleep during the first night, and both suffered from seasickness. They couldn't see the waves to counter them in the darkness, and they struggled to steer the boat whilst suffering from extreme sleep deprivation.

By day two, Shep looked like a broken man, and Alfred didn't want to admit that the race was already far more challenging than he'd expected. He knew he needed to be the strong one, so he rowed in quiet contemplation. The low point was a three-hour silence broken only when a flying fish collided with his face and caused his sunglasses to fall off. It was a literal slap in the face.

Alfred had taken some medicine to counter his seasickness, and it had worked a treat, but it also dulled his appetite. He'd hardly eaten since setting off. Shep was having a similar experience. With a lack of calories fuelling their engines, rowing became a struggle, and their lack of progress was tedious.

On the sixth day, a pod of dolphins lifted Alfred's spirits. They appeared from nowhere as if sent by some divine spirit to provide a lift. Such beautiful and majestic creatures, they made gliding across the ocean look so easy. Alfred fell into a trance as he watched them. How much easier it would be if they could just throw a harness over them and let them do the hard work. Then the splash from a wave brought him back to his senses, and he realised he was rowing off course.

Whilst they were travelling far slower than Alfred had hoped, and were behind schedule, the first week went by without any major mishaps. Everything was in working order, and the routine and life at sea were starting to feel familiar. Alfred had drawn a line under everything that had happened on land. They were in another world now, a world where they could write off all previous worries as a host of fresh ones emerged. With each mile that passed,

Alfred felt increasingly positive, even optimistic, about their chances of completing the race. It wouldn't last.

*

During the third week, they received news that Hendrik and Isaac had been forced to pull out. The organisers hadn't specified why, and whilst it gave Alfred confidence that they weren't the worst out there, it also highlighted how vulnerable they were.

Shortly after, the light on the compass stopped working.

It seemed fairly innocuous at first. It wasn't the end of the world, it just made navigating in the dark a little more complex.

But the incident played on Alfred's mind.

All it needed was new batteries, and Shep had forgotten to buy spare ones. Alfred had only given him a handful of jobs, and he couldn't even do them. What else had he forgotten to do? What else hadn't he told him? To make it worse, Shep was the one being critical.

Shep had been tracking the progress of the other teams and had become increasingly vocal about their choice of route. Yes, the other competitors had made better headway taking the longer trade route, but they also had a longer distance to travel, so what did it matter? Alfred knew he'd taken a gamble, but it could work to their benefit. He was only gambling because he feared Shep would struggle with the longer distance. Having to defend his choices when Shep was equally responsible for them was driving him mad.

Things came to a head on day thirty-five of the journey. It was Boxing Day, a day when Alfred usually ate his body weight in food in front of the television. Instead, he was on a boat crawling along in horrendous conditions. Both he and Shep were desperate for a sense of normality.

'Good nap?' Shep asked.

It was a loaded question since Alfred had overslept. 'Not too bad,' Alfred yawned, 'but I'm in agony now. I've woken up with claw hands.' Alfred showed his claw-like hands to Shep and winced as agonising pains shot up his arms when he tried to straighten his fingers. He'd read it was normal for rowers covering long distances, but that didn't make it any better.

'Well, I'll swap with you, give my balls a break. I don't think they'll ever be the same again.' Shep had complained about salt sores on his nether regions for a few days. He always had to turn everything into a competition, even ailments.

Alfred checked their progress. 'We're going off course,' he muttered to himself.

'It's difficult to keep on course when we're constantly drifting,' Shep replied with venom. It was another dig at Alfred's choice of route because the weather had been battering them for days.

'No,' Alfred said through gritted teeth, 'it's difficult to stay on course when we can't see the compass to know we're rowing in the right direction. And we can't see the compass because someone forgot to bring spare batteries.' Alfred was beyond caring if he annoyed Shep.

'I keep saying we need to switch routes.' Shep's muscles tensed as he regurgitated his argument.

'Switch routes?' Alfred said, his voice high. 'Are you serious? Now?' Alfred tried to get himself settled in the seat, but in his distracted state, a wave caused the oars to crash into his shins, and he cried out.

'Yes, I am serious,' continued Shep, ignoring Alfred's screams. 'We need to switch before it's too late. It will only get more difficult.'

'It's already too late! What is it you don't understand? We can't switch now. We might as well give in. Is that it? Do you want to give up? Go join Hendrik and Isaac for a few beers?'

Shep shook his head and looked away. 'I swear, sometimes—'

'What? You want to hit me over the head with a rock? Add to your kill count?'

Shep looked like Alfred had punched him in the stomach. Perhaps he'd gone too far. It was the first time he'd mentioned the incident since the eve of the race. They had an unwritten rule that they'd leave it be, and Alfred suddenly felt guilty.

Shep cursed under his breath and shoved Alfred aside as he disappeared into the cabin.

Alfred watched him go. Part of him wanted to apologise, but he needed to let the atmosphere simmer down first. Otherwise, it could explode like icy water on hot oil. Alfred used his anger to fuel his rowing instead. Another week and they'd be at the halfway point. They needed to hold on. They just needed something to hold on to.

Alfred was so busy arguing with Shep in his mind that he didn't notice that he was heading straight into a storm. The first he was aware of it was a lick of sharp, chilly wind and rain across his face. The sudden change of atmosphere was noticeable, if not dramatic, and it knocked thoughts of speculative arguments with Shep out of his head. He needed to focus.

The wind whistled in the distance, and after a few seconds, its fingers reached out and tickled the boat. They were within its grip now. Rolling waves arrived head on to the boat and became increasingly intense and volatile as Alfred kept rowing. He felt loathe to leave his station to spoon Shep in the cabin and preferred to take his chances with nature instead. The wind growled at his temerity and sent watery gusts his way. Alfred struggled to keep his eyes open as an immense wave lifted the boat, then crashed it back down with malice. The impact juddered Alfred, and it reminded him of the time he'd tried to ride a bucking bronco on a night out. He spat out seawater as another wave lifted the boat even higher.

Time and time again, the boat rose out of the water and dropped back down. Lyon Heart was being thrown about like a dog toy, and Alfred had no choice but to go with it. Fog and darkness descended and made it difficult for Alfred to see where he was going. The waves became so violent and sporadic that it was impossible to predict when they would arrive. All Alfred could do was brace himself and try to hold on.

A few minutes passed, but it felt like hours. Alfred shivered uncontrollably as conditions continued to deteriorate. The waves started rolling across the boat, which told Alfred they were moving in the wrong direction. To avoid being dragged further off course, Alfred released the parachute sea anchor, but it required a level of skill that Alfred didn't possess, especially in such terrible conditions. Rather than keep the boat stationary, the anchor dragged them further off course, and Alfred's inability to stay sure-footed for longer than a few seconds prevented him from bringing it back on board.

Alfred's chest thumped as panic overcame him. He was sodden, shivering, and out of his depth. He wanted to give in. Maybe Shep was right…

Another wave broke over the boat and covered everything with gallons of ice-cold seawater. There was no way he could continue in the conditions. He needed to call for help. No sooner had he made that decision when Alfred looked up and saw the end of the world riding inexorably towards them. Alfred thought his eyes were tricking him as he watched the wave of Herculean proportions grow to at least forty feet high.

How was their tiny boat supposed to deal with that? It was too late to move about. He checked he was secure and braced himself for the impact. Then Alfred spotted something from the corner of his eye. Had the cabin door moved? It looked closed. Perhaps he'd imagined it. Then it swung open, and Shep's forlorn figure appeared in the darkness. Alfred tried to shout, but it was too late.

CHAPTER XI

The Capital

The high lord was dead. According to the official report, he died of a heart attack, but Hestia knew her father didn't have a weak heart. He was fifty-four and still young and fitter than most people half his age. Determined to judge for herself, Hestia went to look at his body after they'd finished cleansing him for burial. It was forbidden, and she was violating a strict, ancient code. But a small bribe to the watcher bought her entrance to the high physician's chamber after the funeral rituals had ceased for the day.

Hestia nearly turned and fled when she saw her father's corpse on the table. They had dressed him in the flamboyant ceremonial clothes for the burial festivities. What had they done to him? He was not a man who sought attention, and he would have hated the fuss made on his behalf. She had half expected him to open his eyes and say, 'Hello darling', as he always did when he saw her. When he didn't, the fact that she would never hear his voice again struck her like a lightning bolt.

She sniffed and forced herself to look at the body. She tried to pretend it was a training exercise and focused on what she'd been taught studying medicine. There was nothing obvious on initial inspection, but it was difficult to tell because the high physician had tampered extensively with the body to prepare it for burial. When she looked closer, she could see a strange discolouration around his neck, like a water stain on wood. She hated what she would have to do, but she needed to know.

Hestia found one of the high physician's scalpels and, apologising profusely to her father, made a small incision in the middle of the discolouration. It drew no blood at first, and then a small black glob appeared. Hestia knew the cause of death immediately. A heart attack, whilst not wrong, was only half the story.

She heard a noise in the distance and, not wanting to get caught, she hurried out of the chamber. The watcher diverted his gaze as she slipped past him and let out a deep breath, relieved that they hadn't been caught.

Quite what Hestia would do with the information, she didn't know. She could hardly shout about her findings. That would be an admission to tampering with the holy ritual. She didn't even know who might do such a thing. Her father had no enemies. He had been fair and just, treating everyone as equals. Perhaps that was his mistake. Hestia had nothing to go on without a suspect or a motive, but she knew that something was wrong, and the only lead she had was the high physician. If he'd taken a bribe, then he had to know something.

Hestia's opportunity came the following day. The high physician had completed the cleansing and gathered Hestia and her brother, Attalus, to see the body one last time before the burial ceremony. Hestia was pleased she had snuck in the night before. It meant she could easily mask her disgust at what they had done to her father. They confirmed that the high physician had suitably prepared the body for the afterlife and then completed the arrangements for the burial. As Attalus departed, Hestia hung back, feigning a need to be alone with her father's spirit. Attalus snorted his derision and left without another word.

The high physician made his way back to his chamber, and Hestia followed. When they were alone, she caught up with him. He seemed on edge.

'Lady of the House?!' Her sudden appearance startled him.

'I know my father didn't die from natural causes.' She got straight to the point, and he hesitated a second too long.

'What are you suggesting?' he asked, composed once more.

'I'm suggesting someone murdered my father, and you're protecting them.'

The high physician forced a laugh. 'That's preposterous and bold, I might add. If you're making claims like that, I hope you have some proof.'

'I have a witness,' Hestia lied. She'd gone down the rabbit hole, so she might as well see where it led.

The statement stumped the high physician. 'Witness to what exactly?'

Hestia had to think on her feet. She needed to find out what she could, but if she slipped up, she'd be on the back foot and would lose any ground she had gained. She sighed. 'I had hoped you'd be helpful and that we could resolve this without bringing the matter before the lawgivers.'

It was the key moment. If he were innocent, he'd know she was lying about the witness. If he were hiding something, he'd either have to gamble or hope she was lying, and it would be a big gamble. Any matter brought before the lawgivers could mean his removal from the high table, whether or not he was innocent.

He scanned the area and scratched his forehead, then looked back at Hestia. 'Not here,' he said. 'Meet me at my chambers tonight. Now go. You can't be here.'

The high physician's tone ruffled Hestia's feathers, but she had what she was after and didn't want to push too hard. She was already on shaky ground.

Hestia's mind raced. Who would want to kill her father, and why? His abolishment of the Trident Programme had caused controversy, but that was a few years ago. Who would hold a grudge about that? The only other controversy during his reign, his Equality-For-All Motion, was being brought in over fifty years to allow everyone to adapt to the change. It had caused no violence, so why would it suddenly flare up now?

Had he become mixed up with something? If he had, he hadn't let on. His demeanour had remained calm and jovial, like always. The thoughts plagued her. Had he known it was coming? Was he scared? Did he die in pain? Who else knew? The minutes crawled by, and the questions multiplied.

Hestia arrived at the high physician's chamber on time. She had taken the scenic route to make sure no one followed her, figuring it was better to err on the side of caution. Her father's body had been moved for the funeral, so there was no watcher. She knocked on the door, but there was no response. A shiver went down her spine. It was too quiet, and the air was deathly still.

She knocked again. She didn't want to shout out in case anyone heard her voice and recognised it. Still, there was no answer.

Hestia pushed the door. It was unlocked and opened an inch. She peered in, but it was too dark to see anything. Had he fled? Where would he go? She opened the door further to allow some light in. The high physician's implements hung on the wall, but there was no sign of life. Hestia searched each room but found nothing amiss. Maybe he'd forgotten their meeting? No, you don't forget an appointment with the Lady of the House!

She waited half an hour, but there was no sign of him, so she made her way back to the palace, where Attalus was waiting for her.

'Where have you been?' he demanded.

Attalus stood up from the marble seating area in the palace courtyard and walked towards her. He was the same height as Hestia, but where Hestia was lean and dainty, Attalus was stocky and clumsy, like an overfed terrier. Although he was the younger sibling by four years, Attalus had the misguided impression that he was the one in charge.

'For a walk,' she said, which wasn't a complete lie. Hestia tried to walk straight past him, but he hadn't finished.

'You didn't tell anyone.'

'Since when did I have to tell anyone about going for a walk? And since when do I answer to you?'

'You'll answer to me soon.' Attalus smirked.

Hestia's blood curdled. She had never been fond of her little brother. He was cruel and vindictive, and at twenty-two, he still behaved like a spoilt brat. According to the Order, the position of high lord would pass to him, even though he lacked all the skills required to make a competent leader. It should have passed to Dyon, who was two years older than Attalus, but he had gone missing a few years ago. Time hadn't diluted how much Hestia missed Dyon. They had been inseparable as children. Everyone said that he was dead, but she'd never given up on him. Dyon had been the only one who'd been able to keep Attalus in check. Even their father, normally so authoritative, had held little control over him.

'You're a *taur*,' she said, cursing him.

'And you're hiding something.'

'What is it you want, little brother?'

'You missed the commotion.'

'What commotion?'

'They found the high physician.'

Hestia's heart jumped. She tried to hide her reaction, but she was sure she'd given something away. 'Why's that important? We saw him earlier.'

'He's dead!'

'He's dead? What? How?' she spluttered.

'He hung himself, apparently. I didn't see it myself, but a boy found him in the woods behind his chambers.'

Hestia couldn't think straight. Dead. Why? Who would kill him? It made no sense. She looked at her brother, who was wearing a smirk she wanted to slap off.

'Suicide, or so they say. Now, why would he do such a silly thing?' he added accusingly.

'How would I know?'

'I don't know, but I know you've been sniffing around and acting strange, and you were the last person seen with him before it happened. You were alone with him earlier, were you not?'

Hestia didn't answer. She didn't know what her brother was playing at, but she didn't like it. 'What are you suggesting, Attalus? That I killed the high physician? Do you know how ridiculous that sounds? What have I got to gain?'

'I'm just stating facts. It's for the officials to determine what happened and why. You should be careful, though. Wouldn't want you on the wrong side of an investigation, would we? It would embarrass the high lord if his sister left such a stain on the family cloth.'

'I'm going inside.' Hestia was too tired to entertain Attalus's accusations, so she turned and walked towards the palace.

'See you at the reading,' Attalus called after her, but Hestia wasn't listening. Her cat, Toszka, was rolling playfully in the sun and needed a stroke.

*

With all the excitement, Hestia had forgotten about the reading of her father's will. She arrived late and spotted her brother sat on the edge of his seat at the front of the room. He beamed as she entered. She avoided him.

Borus, the high lawgiver, looked authoritative in his official scarlet robes as he presided over the reading. He had asked the ten governors to attend, which was unusual. It was typically only family members.

'Thank you for gathering with us today on this very sad occasion,' Borus said solemnly.

Hestia sank back in her seat, realising it wouldn't be the short reading she had hoped for. Borus had known and advised her father for many years. He had probably written the will and so would make the most of his opportunity in the limelight.

Borus continued with a twenty-minute eulogy, which only finished after a governor let out an audible sigh.

'… and so we come to the reading of the high lord's will, which I prepared on the high lord's instructions. My apprentices, Cato and Tray, both of whom are sitting here with me today, witnessed the will and are here to verify its contents.'

Borus read through several pages of legalese whilst everyone sat uncomfortably in their seats, oblivious to what was being read out or why it bore any significance. And then he got to the important part.

'I, Critias Cresta Atlas, High Lord of the State, hereby order that in the event that my death occurs before the ratification of the final movement of the Equality-For-All Motion instigated during my tenure as high lord, the governors shall, at the first annual governors meeting following my death, discuss said motion with a view to ratifying it with immediate effect. Once the governors have determined the outcome and, if applicable, amended the Order accordingly, the position of high lord will be inherited under the then applicable law. In the event of a deadlock at the annual governors' meeting regarding the aforementioned motion and, in my capacity as high lord before the event, I hereby vote in favour of the motion.'

Hestia wanted to laugh. She smiled at Attalus, who looked like he was chewing a wasp.

'What are you saying? Do I need to wait until after the next annual governors' meeting before you appoint me high lord?' Attalus asked.

'If you are to be high lord, then yes, it will follow the outcome of the next meeting of the governors at the next full moon,' replied Governor Gadeirus of the Adelphi realm.

'What do you mean if? It's my birthright. It's written in the Order. You can't refuse me. How dare you!' Attalus raised his voice at Gadeirus, who shrugged sympathetically.

'As you know,' Gadeirus slowly explained, 'each governor rules over and has autonomy regarding his realm. However, various matters affect all realms, and we all have to abide by the Order, and so once a year, we have a meeting to discuss and determine those points by majority rule, and the agreed outcome is binding on us all. As Head of the State, the high lord acts as chair at the meetings and, if there is a deadlock, he determines the outcome. As Head of the State, it is also within his power to propose motions, such as the Equality-For-All Motion, and unilaterally impose sanctions on any governor, and their realm, if they fall out of line. Your father, acting as Head of State before his untimely death, has brought forward the last part of the Equality-For-All Motion by fifty years.'

Hestia couldn't sit still. 'That means that if it's agreed at the governors' meeting, the birthright of all governors and high lords will go to the firstborn, not the firstborn son,' Hestia interjected. She couldn't resist winding up Attalus. 'That's right, isn't it?'

'Yes, that's right,' confirmed Borus.

Attalus had turned crimson as every sinew in his face strained. 'He can't do that!' he shouted. 'He's dead. How can he do that?!' He was about to explode.

'It was within his power when he was alive,' Borus said calmly, ignoring Attalus's outburst. 'And the high lord's instructions bind the governors, regardless of how hot or cold they may be.' Borus looked at the governors sternly as though expecting a challenge.

'Ridiculous,' sighed Governor Mneseus, who presided over the Ellopia realm. 'We should never have passed the motion. We anger Him with our actions. The State cannot be governed by a girl. What does she know of State matters?' He gave Hestia a scathing look.

Hestia was about to argue back, but Gadeirus beat her to it. 'Now is not the time nor the place to discuss this matter. We have already passed the law. We just need to determine whether to bring it forward. You can voice your arguments at the meeting.'

'You cannot—'

'At the meeting, Lucan!'

Borus interrupted the spat. 'If you are finished,' he said, 'I will complete the will reading so we can all go home.'

The governors sat back, some more reluctantly than others, and Borus continued with the reading, which contained nothing else controversial. Hestia looked around as he spoke. In two weeks, she could become the first-ever high lady, and the thought made her excited and nervous at the same time. Would the governors vote for it? She didn't know them well, and so she couldn't gauge what their response would be. Governor Lucan Mneseus clearly didn't approve. There were no surprises there. But no one else had spoken against it. She was certain she'd make a better high lady than Attalus would a high lord, but would they know that? She would make it her job to make sure they did.

The reading finished, and everyone was quick to leave. Attalus, who was still a beetroot colour, made a point of storming off and slamming the door in the face of Governor Gadeirus. Hestia smiled to herself. Maybe Attalus would convince them for her.

CHAPTER XII

Rhamnus, Syros

Axil waited for his audience with the Paymaster. He'd had six meetings with the Paymaster so far, and all six had been in the same remote location. A cave in the mountainside between Attica and Phrixus. This time it was different, and Axil had been told to enter a penitence booth in Demeter's Temple on the outskirts of Rhamnus. The location was far more public than Axil was used to, and he didn't like it. It meant something urgent must have happened.

Axil waited in the booth and then heard the familiar sound of the Paymaster clearing his throat on the other side. A wooden wall separated them, and Axil wondered what his employer looked like. He imagined him to be old, perhaps bald or going bald, and with a gap between his front teeth which caused him to occasionally whistle when he spoke. To have the funds he was throwing around, he had to be well-connected, but there were lots of rich old men on the island who could hold a grudge. It was better not to overthink it. To overthink was to open Pandora's Jar, and all Axil wanted was to get paid.

'We have a problem,' a voice hissed. There was anger there, although not aimed at Axil. 'The girl may inherit the high lord's seat.'

Axil knew better than to ask why that was a problem. 'How? It's against the Order,' he asked, instead.

'I know it's against the Order,' snarled the Paymaster, 'but the high lord recorded the demand in his will, and so the governors will vote on it. We are at a crucial moment in our history, and she could put the future of our great nation in jeopardy. The governors are blind to it.'

Hestia, the girl, would make a far better leader than her oaf of a brother, but Axil knew to keep his views to himself. He wasn't being paid to have an opinion. 'What would you have me do?' he asked and braced himself for the response.

'We need to know who intends to vote in favour of the motion. There was a deadlock for the Equality-For-All Motion. Five governors were for it, five against. It only got through because the high lord voted in favour of it. Those who voted against the motion are likely to vote against this ludicrous proposal. Use your connections to find out what you can. We might need to,' the Paymaster took a deep breath, 'sway a couple into our line of thinking.'

Axil grimaced and wondered again how he'd managed to get embroiled in such a mess. It was his ego's fault, always driving him towards more money and power. He'd been working as an apprentice to the Whisperer for the Tinos realm when he'd uncovered information about a plot to assassinate Governor Evaemon of the Tinos realm. The action he'd taken had saved Evaemon's life and brought him to the attention of some powerful people. For a healthy sum, he had agreed to become the Whisperer for the Paymaster, but his role had since expanded beyond recognition. Axil didn't know who or what he was now. His latest job was well outside of his comfort zone, but he knew what happened to those who displeased the Paymaster. The vile creature the Botanist had shown him sprung to mind, and he shivered.

'Very well,' he said. 'It will be difficult. The governors are almost impossible to communicate with.'

'I will pay you handsomely.'

'Even so, I will,' Axil paused to weigh his response, 'do what I can.'

'Work quickly. The governors will make their decision in less than two weeks. They are staying in the Citadel for the funeral and will stay there until after their annual meeting. You will need to be discrete.'

That much was obvious. 'What if I cannot sway them?'

'That would be unfortunate. Take whatever action you need to, but make sure, whatever you do, there's no trace. The mess with the high physician raised a lot of questions, and we cannot face such exposure again. Do I make myself clear?'

Axil had been told that the high physician was a liability who needed dealing with. He didn't know why, but he had his suspicions.

71

'Yes.' Axil noted the Paymaster's threatening tone. 'The incident with the high physician was against my orders. It will not happen again. I have dealt with those involved. The report on death will say suicide.'

'Good. I have another task for you. Behind your chair, you will find a scroll.'

Axil felt around with his hands and found it under his seat. His instructions had always been verbal, and the sudden formality made him uneasy.

'It's a list of names,' explained the Paymaster.

Axil opened it up and found a list of names. They meant nothing to him. He took a deep breath and closed the scroll.

'I'm sure you don't need me to tell you what I require of you. I suggest using the Botanist. From what you said last time, she's likely to come in handy. Now go, I will be in touch.'

Axil left the booth in a stupor. He had men he could pass the list of names on to, but the other task was impossible. It came with grave consequences, whether he succeeded or failed. One small slip up, and everything would come crashing down.

CHAPTER XIII
Atlantic Ocean

A feeling of revulsion was expanding in Shep's chest like a balloon. Alfred, and everything about him, was infuriating. Shep hated his posh voice, his plastic facial expressions, the way he breathed through his nose, and the way Alfred spoke to him, like an unwelcome pet. Alfred had become obsessed with the race, and Shep hated that too. He should never have sent that email. It was the biggest mistake of his life... other than the time he killed someone.

He'd nearly died during the storm. If he hadn't strapped himself in, he would have fallen overboard, and there was no surviving that. Why Alfred hadn't sought to take cover from the storm was beyond him. The only reason he'd peered out was to check Alfred was alive, and that was more than he deserved. Not that Alfred cared. He only cared about his stupid boat and finishing the crossing. The storm had battered Lyon Heart and, whilst both of them had somehow come through unscathed save for a few bruises, she was another matter altogether.

All the electrical equipment had been drenched after Shep opened the door to the cabin. Seawater had contaminated everything, and it was mostly useless. That included their GPS beacon, which kept track of their location and progress. To their families, the race organisers, and anyone else who was following them, they had all but vanished. They had contacted the support boat briefly to inform them about what had happened, but the satellite phone had cut out before they'd received instructions, and it hadn't worked since.

The water maker relied on solar panels to function and appeared to have survived the event, but the day after the storm, it, too, gave up. It died with a gurgle, a wheeze, and a clunk. Now they had to hand pump all the water they required, adding further calories to the 7000-odd they were already burning off and eating into important sleeping time.

The light igniters for the gas stove were the next casualty, which meant they couldn't boil what water they had to cook the freeze-dried rations. They were up the creek without a paddle and desperate for the organisers to send a rescue party. For that to happen, though, the search party would need to know where to look, and they had been dragged helplessly off course.

Shep looked hopefully at the sky for signs of a helicopter. More than once, his imagination had overpowered reality and cruelly convinced him he could hear the familiar sound of blades rotating, but he only saw blue sky and one faint, wispy cloud.

Whilst Alfred tried to resuscitate the water maker, Shep worked on the satellite phone, but neither had any luck. If anything, Shep was making things worse. The one positive was that the weather was warm and still. They could work on things without bouncing around and attempt to dry off.

Shep knew Alfred blamed him for all the issues they were having. He hadn't said anything, but that was the problem. Alfred had barely spoken a word, and it riled Shep up. It was pointless starting an argument, though. They had nowhere to go, and nothing either said would help resolve things. They needed to work together as best they could to get out of the mess they were in. If they achieved that, they could have a fun round of the blame game.

'How's the water maker looking?' Shep asked, breaking a five-hour silence. He couldn't take it anymore.

'Not good,' Alfred grunted back. 'I've read all the instructions, and I don't know what's gone wrong. We must have broken it the last time we used it.'

Shep had been the last one to use the water maker, and Alfred knew that. Shep was about to respond that they'd have had plenty of time to figure out how everything worked had the boat arrived on time but stopped himself.

'Well, at least we still have the ballast water,' Shep said, referring to their emergency drinking water, which was being used as a ballast to give the boat extra stability. Under the rules of the race, any water they drank from their emergency supply would result in a time penalty being added to their finishing time, but their finishing time was the last thing on Shep's mind. Alfred grunted his response. He still thought they could finish. He was deluded.

'I've been trying to dry out the electrics,' Shep said. 'They might come on again once they're not swimming in saltwater.'

'Mm.'

Shep gave up on the conversation and went back to playing with the satellite phone. Then Alfred cried out loudly as though something had stung him.

'What is it?' Shep asked.

'Look!'

'Look at what?'

'Can't you see it?'

'See what?' Shep was in no mood to play games.

'Shh,' Alfred put his fingers to his lips.

He was acting peculiar. Even more so than normal.

'Don't startle it,' Alfred whispered.

'Don't startle what?' Shep asked, keeping his voice low. Perhaps Alfred had spotted something in the sea or an unusual bird.

Alfred pointed at the top of the water maker. 'I found out what's wrong with it,' he said.

'What?'

'Can't you see it?'

'No, what are you pointing at?'

'That.'

'What is that?'

'The tiny leprechaun.'

'The tiny lepre... sorry, what? Tiny leprechaun? Is that a part of the water maker?'

'No, it's a... well, you know. You must know what a leprechaun is? It's a bearded fairy feller, I guess.'

Shep laughed out loud. It was the first time he'd laughed in a long time, and it felt like a release.

'Shh,' Alfred urged, 'you'll scare it away.'

'I'll scare away the leprechaun? You're joking, right?'

'Just look!' Alfred said, pointing at thin air.

Shep remembered that both he and Alfred had taken medication to help them sleep. One of the side effects was vivid dreams and hallucinations. More than once, Shep had suffered from sleep paralysis. His mind would wake up whilst his body remained paralysed, making his dreams of dark alleys seem a reality. Alfred had hardly slept since the storm and, combined with the lack of food and water, heat, and exhaustion, he was delirious. Shep wasn't feeling great himself. Every inch of him ached like hell, but he looked in good health compared to Alfred. Black rings hung loosely under Alfred's eyes. He was malnourished and even paler than usual, despite spending so much time in the sun. Much as he despised him right now, Shep didn't want another dead body on his conscience.

'Have some water, Al. I think you need to take a break,' Shep urged.

'Where's it gone?' Alfred cried and then glared at Shep. 'I think you scared it away,' he said viciously.

'Al, here,' Shep said, handing Alfred a bottle, 'have some water and then go have a rest. I'll keep trying with the phone. You go get some sleep in the cabin.'

Alfred followed his suggestion without a fight. He looked like a lost soul as he crawled away to get some sleep.

Shep played with the satellite phone a little longer, but it was no use. He had no idea what to do with it. He threw it on the floor in frustration and sighed.

Then a drop of rain fell on Shep's nose, and he looked up, unsure of where it had come from. The sky had been clear a second ago. A couple more drops fell, and a sudden chill replaced the warm breeze. Heavy, black clouds emerged from every angle and raced towards the boat, which rocked unsteadily as the sea reacted to the change.

Then a flash of lightning struck a few feet away from Lyon Heart. Shep looked around, trying to make sense of what had happened, and then winced as the sky roared at him.

'What's going on?' he muttered to himself.

Another explosion struck nearby, and more followed, each one getting teasingly closer to the boat. Driving wind and rain stifled Shep's vision as he tried to navigate his way through the deluge that had arrived without warning. None of his training had prepared him for this. 'How is this happening!' he screamed, but he couldn't hear himself.

Two converging waves collided over the boat and Shep felt water wash over him. He cursed out loud as the boat flew into the air on the crest of another wave. As it crashed down, Shep was sure the boat would tip over. He held his breath, waiting for the inevitable, but then it corrected itself just as another wave lifted him again.

Adrenaline pumped through Shep's body. His situation was dire, but he tried not to panic. He was sure he would get through it. But then the boat corkscrewed, and he saw a giant wall of water moving towards him, and all rationality faded away.

It couldn't be real. It wasn't possible. The wall was getting closer, rising so high that Shep had to crane his neck to see it. Maybe the drugs he'd taken earlier had caused him to hallucinate as well. He watched it for a few seconds and then resigned himself to his fate. If it was real, there wasn't much he could do. It was an unstoppable force, rising high into the clouds. It would pulverise him and the boat. So Shep watched and waited.

Fear rose in him, and he shouted, challenging the sea. He challenged the wave. Challenged anyone who could hear him. It was the only thing he could do. The wave was seconds away from consuming them when Shep spotted a face appearing from the wall of water. It was small at first, but then it grew, unmistakable and terrifying.

Then Alfred appeared from nowhere. He was shouting, trying to tell him something, but there was no way Shep could hear him over the storm. Alfred waved his hands frantically towards the face. He wanted Shep to row towards it. The wall of water was almost upon them, thirty feet away at most. For once, Shep followed Alfred's instructions without question. He didn't know why, but it was better than doing nothing.

The features of the face became clear with angry, hollow eyes, a small straight nose, and a thin, cruel mouth that opened as if screaming. Shep flinched but composed himself and strained every muscle to turn the boat towards it. Even his cheeks ached.

Water closed in from every direction, flooding Lyon Heart, but she was still going. It felt like she could break into pieces at any moment.

The mouth opened wider, and Shep let out a yell as he used up the last of his energy reserves. The wall of water smashed into the front of the boat, lifting the bow. They were moments away from being flipped and were powerless to do anything. Shep stared into the mouth. They'd almost reached it. Or had it reached them? The boat tipped further, the bow pointing at the stars. Shep clung on as gravity became his enemy. His body was at breaking point. Just… another…

Then there was darkness, a brief reprieve amidst the chaos, like a rollercoaster suspended at its highest point. Shep looked around and allowed himself to relax for a second. Where was Alfred? He didn't have time to think of anything else before Lyon Heart plummeted forwards, and he screamed.

CHAPTER XIV

Kea

Kaspa sat at the back of the temple to avoid being seen. He was half-listening to the sermon, which had been going on for far too long, and half-considering what to eat later. The latter was more interesting.

'And unto us, a stranger shall appear,' the priest said, 'and that stranger will mark the beginning of the third age, and that third age will be the beginning of the end. The beginning of the end, my friends. The prophecy is clear on that.'

A few gasps rang from the congregation. Kaspa didn't know why; the priest had been hammering that point home throughout the entire sermon. He wasn't right. The prophecy wasn't clear about anything. It wasn't even a genuine prophecy. Who knew what the oracle really told the bard all those hundreds, if not thousands, of years ago? It was foolish to think it meant anything, but you would have to be brave to say that out loud.

'The time is nearly upon us, friends,' the priest boomed, his voice bouncing around the temple. 'Soon, the Saviour will test us. He will test us. And what should we do?'

The priest spoke hypothetically, but a few responded.

'Should we welcome this stranger, this middling, with open arms as our brother? The one who would destroy us?'

There were cries of, 'No!' and, 'Never!'

'There are many that will tell you we should. The State has already challenged the Saviour, and He is angry.' The priest was referring to the State's decisions to pass the Equality-For-All Motion and to disband the Trident Programme that many had contested. He believed them to be against the Order, but he was being vague to avoid alienating any members of his congregation who had supported them. Members such as Kaspa, who were growing tired of the priest's propaganda.

'Should we anger Him further?' the priest asked amidst cries of dismay. 'There are some that will tell you that the middling's arrival is a wonderful thing and that his arrival will lead to our return. They believed the Saviour has trapped us here. Do you feel trapped? Do you want us to return? What is out there, beyond the fog? Do you know? I do! There is nothing but destruction and desolation. Is that what you want?'

The congregation was growing animated now, with many standing up and displaying their anger at what was being put forward by the priest. Kaspa sat back and watched, keeping his head low. Even if a middling appeared, would it be so terrible? Was there a need for such a fuss?

The priest signalled for everyone to sit down and listen.

'No! The Saviour has not trapped us here. He has kept us safe for thousands of years. He has guarded us, protected us, and looked over us. We are all his children. Now we challenge Him, and there are some that wish to castrate Him like Uranus.'

Kaspa crossed his legs. In his sermons, the priest liked to refer to the story of Kronos overthrowing his father, Uranus, by removing his manhood. He always managed to shoehorn it in. The priest had a strong penchant for violence given his occupation.

'The Saviour wants to test us. He thinks we will turn our backs on Him at the first opportunity. And can you blame Him? We ignore His rules. We pray to others over Him and spit in His face. So He will send the middling to test us. It is a test we must pass, or our world will end. Hear me now! Believe me now!'

The priest was shouting, his passion infecting most of the congregation. He walked his ample frame around the temple, and Kaspa sunk lower into his seat.

'If we accept the middling, we accept degradation and the poisoning of our line! In doing so, we reject the Saviour, and He will take his vengeance on us. He will remove His protection and let in the impure and the unholy. He will let everything we hold dear crumble before us, and we will only have ourselves to blame. Would you allow that?'

There it was, the killer blow. For most Atlanteans, the thought of sullying their family's line back to the Saviour was sacrilege. Most would happily switch off their brains and pick up an axe if they thought their holy lineage was at risk, no matter the consequences. Despite all that had happened over the millennia, religion still resonated through their bones. Kaspa had never understood it. He didn't believe he was related to the Saviour, and he didn't care if he was. What had He ever done for him?

'Would you allow that!?' the priest shouted, unhappy with the previous level of response. This time, a wave of noise responded.

'We cannot allow it. We must not allow it. The middling must not live. They will tell you it is written in the Order that we may kill no man without the approval of the State. If we breach the Order, we will anger the Saviour. But since when did the Order apply to middlings?'

The priest laughed, and others joined him. He had them on his hook. People who Kaspa considered quiet and reflective, who would barely utter a word as they went about their daily business, had found a voice for their inner angst. It terrified him.

The priest calmed everyone down. 'My friends, the time is almost upon us. I have news that the eagle has fallen from the sky. The prophecy is coming true. Now we must do what is necessary for the good of the State and everyone and everything you hold dear. When the middling arrives, and that time will be soon, we must offer him back to the Saviour. Only He can decide the middling's fate. It is in the Order.'

Kaspa had heard a rumour that a metal contraption had fallen from the sky somewhere in the neighbouring Milos realm and that a picture of an eagle adorned the side of it. Rumours often passed from realm to realm, but there was rarely any truth in them, and it was all rather convenient for the priest. He was also certain that there was nothing in the Order about sacrificing middlings, but no one else in the congregation seemed to care. They would lap up whatever the priest told them.

'When the time comes, I know that you will do the right thing. May the Saviour give you strength. Now let us pray.'

The priest raised his head and hands towards the sky, and many in the congregation did the same. Kaspa remained seated. He felt uncomfortable at the thought of joining in. No one would see him tucked away at the back, anyway.

'Saviour,' the priest said. 'Protect us this day and save us from sin. May your strength and courage guide us. Let us stand beside you as your loyal army. We are your kingdom, your subjects. May we never flounder with trident in hand. For you are within us and upon us. You are everything and everywhere. We will honour you and obey you. Love you and fear you. Today and forever. Our Lord, Poseidon.'

Only the priest said the last line, for only priests, the high lord, and governors were worthy of whispering the gods' names. Everyone else had to refer to them by alternative names to avoid suffering their wrath for insolence. Kaspa thought Poseidon would have bigger things to worry about and so often flouted the rule in private. He was still alive.

Kaspa quietly let himself out of the temple as soon as the priest finished. It was a legal requirement for him to attend at least once a week, and he had satisfied that archaic obligation, but he wasn't obliged to hang around.

The sermons were usually intense, but this was the first time the priest had encouraged violence. Kaspa had heard talk of similar sermons taking place in neighbouring realms from people who had visited his bakery, and it worried him. If a middling appeared, then it meant only one thing: trouble.

CHAPTER XV
Atlantic Ocean

Alfred's body somersaulted through the water. He didn't know what had happened or where he was. Lyon Heart had disappeared. He'd been standing on her one second, and then she'd vanished.

His lungs demanded oxygen. He took a breath and inhaled water. He felt a burning sensation and started coughing. Then his body stopped turning, and he kicked his legs with all his might. He needed to get to the surface, but he couldn't tell if he was pushing in the right direction. A voice begged him to breathe, but he couldn't. Everything was on fire. He couldn't take it any longer.

He kicked and flapped his arms with everything he had left. Then he breathed out and fell into darkness.

When Alfred came to, he was a dolphin cutting effortlessly through the water. He glided through a stunning underwater world and passed over exotic, colourful fish and a bumbling metropolis of coral reef.

As his eyes darted from side to side to absorb his surroundings, something unusual flashed past him. It was just a glimpse, and then it disappeared. At first, he thought it was someone snorkelling, but he was certain he'd seen a tail. He tried to slow down to look back, but something, or someone, was pulling him along, and he had no control over where he was going. They were heading up and away from the magical, vibrant world he had only just discovered.

They kept going, higher and higher. And then, as the sun's image broke through the water, a beautiful sound hit Alfred's ears. It was enchanting, and every sinew of his body strained to move towards it, to bask in its beauty, but whatever had hold of him wasn't letting go. The sound faded, and Alfred felt exhausted. He closed his eyes, and sleep welcomed him.

Alfred felt snug in his bed at home with the duvet pulled up over his head. It was the weekend, and he had no school, so he could enjoy a long lie-in. The smell of bacon and pancakes wafted up to him, and his taste buds pricked up in anticipation. His mum liked to make pancakes as a treat for him at weekends, but Alfred decided that breakfast could wait a few more minutes. He scrunched up his eyes and relaxed into the mattress.

From downstairs, his mum shouted for him. It was nice to hear her voice. Alfred felt like he hadn't heard it in such a long time, and it filled him with warmth. She shouted again, and Alfred tried to respond, but he was so relaxed he could barely muster a word. Perhaps he should get up. He wanted to see his mum. For some reason, he was struggling to picture her face. He tried to piece it together like a jigsaw, but a few pieces were missing. Why couldn't he picture her? His mind seemed to want to block her out.

Then his brain hit fast forward…

He was sitting in a hospital waiting room with a bottle of fizzy drink. His dad wheeled his mum around in a wheelchair to see him. She looked frail and could barely lift her chin. Her skin was hanging off her like an oversized coat, and tufts of hair were all that remained on her head. She used to take such pride in looking after her hair. She gave Alfred a weak smile that he tried to return, and then he broke down, an avalanche of tears running down his cheeks…

Then he was sitting on his bed with his dad, wearing a swollen eye and a cut on his nose. 'I can do better, Dad,' he kept saying. 'I can do better.'

He hadn't started the fight. The others had been mocking him for not having a mum, and he'd charged at them. There had been three of them, but they said that he'd started it. He didn't know what had happened. He hadn't meant to hurt them.

'It just won't do,' Jeremy said, unable to look at him.

'Don't send me there,' Alfred pleaded. 'Please, Dad, I can do better. Don't send me there.'

'It's too late. You'll start after the holidays.' Jeremy stood up and walked out, stopping at the door briefly before closing it…

The door opened to a group of boys dressed in sportswear. They ran into the dormitory, throwing a rugby ball between them. Alfred was sitting in the corner of his room with his books, trying to complete some homework. It was physics, one of his favourite subjects, and he'd just finished. It had taken him most of the afternoon. One boy threw the ball, and it landed in amongst his papers, causing them to fly up into the air. The boys didn't apologise. Instead, they formed a scrum to retrieve the ball with Alfred wedged in the middle, desperately trying to collect his books and pens before they got trampled.

Then a wayward knee smashed into his face, and one of his teeth came loose. Alfred was livid, and hatred coursed through his veins. He let out a cry, and the next thing he knew, everyone was on the floor. He was the only one conscious, blood swilling around his mouth and confusion etched on his face...

He was standing in a queue, a file of papers in his backpack. The person in front of him looked around hesitantly, a few papers crumpled up in his hand. He was good-looking with soft brown eyes, a small nose, and an easy smile. His white V-necked t-shirt showed off the hours he spent in the gym, and he was sporting a goatee, which Alfred could only dream of growing.

The stranger turned to Alfred and said, 'Is this the right queue for enrolling in the law course?' He had a Scottish accent which suggested that he might be from Edinburgh or somewhere nearby.

Alfred nodded, and they carried on waiting in the queue for another minute before the stranger turned around again. 'I'm Sheppard, by the way. Sheppard Mills, but people call me Shep. I'm guessing we're on the same course?' He let out a laugh and held up his crumpled papers. It looked like he had completed them in a rush.

Alfred smiled. He didn't know what to make of Shep, but he was the first person he'd met on his course, and so he had to give him a chance. 'Looks like it,' he agreed. 'I'm Alfred, but you can call me Al. It'll be a long time before we reach the front of this queue. I knew I should have arrived earlier.' It looked like he would have to make small talk with Shep...

'You're always working!' shouted Josie. Alfred was standing in his flat. He had a bunch of flowers in his hand, which looked half-dead. Josie's hands were glued to her hips, and her eyes were wide and red with mascara smudged in the corners of them. She'd been crying, but it looked like she'd run out of tears. 'I don't know why I bother.' She had her apron on, and Alfred could smell the remnants of a beef wellington in the kitchen.

'I had to help with a deal,' Alfred mumbled, disgusted with himself. He'd let her down again, and on their anniversary. 'We can still have it now, though, make the most of the rest of the night?' he tried weakly.

'You have it!' spat Josie. 'Fish it out of the bin. I'm going out.' She took off her apron and threw it on the floor, downed her glass of red wine, and stormed into the bathroom to freshen herself up.

'It's ten o'clock,' Alfred said through the door, desperate to redeem the night. 'Where are you going?'

'Leave. Me. Alone,' came her measured response. Then Josie emerged, wearing the red dress she had picked out for Alfred. She looked a million dollars, and Alfred kicked himself as she stormed past him. She put on her heels, picked up her bag, and slammed the front door behind her. Alfred went into his room to lie down on his bed…

'Alfred, you need to get up,' said Jeremy, banging on his door. He was back at home in bed. 'Get up, son. You need to get up!'

Alfred ignored Jeremy's shouts, but then they got louder. It sounded like his father was standing in the room right next to him. Except it didn't sound like him anymore? It didn't sound like anyone Alfred knew. It didn't even sound like a language he knew.

He needed to get his duvet off, but he couldn't find the end. It had trapped him in his bed in a cocoon, and he was running out of air. He scrabbled around, desperately searching for a way out, but every movement exhausted him. His body wanted to give in, but his head was telling him to keep going and fighting. With an almighty effort, Alfred reached the edge of the duvet with his fingers and pulled. He could see light, but his strength was fading. He pulled down faster, but the cover seemed never-ending.

The light grew. He was so close. He pulled with his last bit of strength, and finally, the duvet came off as reality flooded in.

CHAPTER XVI

Kea

Kaspa strolled along the beach, enjoying the heat of the sun's rays on his back. It was a secluded spot, difficult to access through the dense forest terrain. But Kaspa knew the route well, and he didn't mind navigating his way past low-hanging trees and thick shrubbery to enjoy some peace.

Sad news of the high lord's death had reached his town shortly after the priest's sermon, and rumours were spreading like wildfire. Many believed the prophecy was coming true and were spoiling for a fight. He had heard talk of marching on the Capital, although with what aim or purpose, he didn't know. People were panicking, and mob mentality was taking over.

Warm sand sunk into Kaspa's sandals and tickled his toes. He could happily stay there all day if he didn't have other jobs to do. He reached the sea and followed the coastline, letting the waves lap over his feet.

The stretch of beach funnelled an array of treasures from a faraway land. They fascinated Kaspa, and he kept a collection of them at home. There were mostly bottles, cans, and general tat, but each had its own mysterious story. He longed to know where they came from and what they did.

This time was no exception, and as he walked, Kaspa noticed a small black item on the beach. He quickened his pace to look at it, excited at the prospect of adding to his growing collection. The item was the size of his hand, and it had a cracked screen with strange writing on it. Most items that washed up had spent a long time at sea and were dirty and broken, but this one was different. It looked as though it had washed up recently. When Kaspa picked it up, it came alive, vibrating in his hand and displaying more unusual text. It was like a magic trick, and Kaspa threw it on the ground, scared of what it might do next. When it went quiet again,

Kaspa popped the item into his satchel and decided that he would inspect it once he got back home.

Further along the coastline, Kaspa spotted something else. An animal had washed up, but it was too far away to make out what it was or whether it was alive. The odd fish and jellyfish had washed ashore before, but this was much bigger.

As he approached it, Kaspa realised it was a person, and he felt a pang of anger that someone else had discovered his special spot. It looked like they were sunbathing, and Kaspa kept a distance, not wanting to disturb them. However, something about the positioning of the body was strange, and their clothes looked peculiar. Kaspa moved closer to get a better look.

When he was a few feet away, Kaspa shouted to the intruder. There was no response, and he realised something was wrong. He approached and knelt next to him. It was a man with a pale complexion and ginger hair. He didn't look Atlantean, but Kaspa hadn't seen many people from the southern or western realms, so perhaps it was a fisherman who had been caught out in a storm. Kaspa nudged the intruder again, but he was unresponsive and didn't appear to be breathing.

Kaspa panicked. He was a long way from help, and it would be impossible to drag a dead weight through the forest. It was hard enough for just one person to get through by themselves. He had to do something, though. Kaspa beat on the man's chest, recalling that someone had taught him that at some point in his life.

There was no response, and Kaspa applied more force, increasing the intensity. Still, the man didn't wake. Kaspa put all his body weight into it and shouted at the man in frustration. Why did he have to wash up on this stretch of beach?

He was about to give in when the stranger coughed seawater violently into Kaspa's face. Pleased with himself, Kaspa moved the stranger onto his side to help him control his breathing. He looked around to see if anyone had witnessed his triumph, but he was alone.

The stranger continued to cough and gasp, so Kaspa patted his back. 'Are you okay?' he asked, but the stranger was in no state to reply. 'Are you okay?' Kaspa tried again a few seconds later.

The stranger didn't answer. He was still gulping at the air but was sat up now, hugging his knees and looking at his feet.

'What happened to you? Where have you come from? Can you talk?' Kaspa was getting frustrated. He'd just saved the man's life. The least he could do was acknowledge his existence and say thank you.

The stranger gingerly rolled onto his knees and put his head between his hands on the ground, vomiting seawater onto the sand. He was coming around, but he still didn't register Kaspa. The stranger looked at his hands and arms, studying the bruises and cuts on them. Then he carefully felt around his face and head, grimacing as he touched a sore spot.

'Are you hurt?' Kaspa asked.

This time, the stranger looked at him. His eyes were red, and he squinted with his mouth agape as though he hadn't realised that he had company. He spoke, but it was an incoherent garble. Kaspa wondered whether he might have suffered brain damage during his traumatic experience.

The stranger looked young, perhaps in his late twenties. He had prominent front teeth and ears that stuck out a little too much. His lips were cracked, and he looked weak, but he had managed to stand up, which was something. He was talking quietly and slowly, taking deep breaths between sentences and gesticulating. Kaspa still couldn't understand a word he was saying.

Then a thought crossed his mind. What if this was the middling that the priest had pontificated about? Surely not. He could barely open his eyes, let alone cause a revolution.

Whoever he was, and wherever he had come from, he didn't speak the common tongue. Some isolated islands with small tribes spoke an unfamiliar language; perhaps he had come from one of them. Suddenly, Kaspa wished there was someone else in his secluded spot to pass the problem on to.

Kaspa patted his chest with his index finger and said, 'Kaspa.' He repeated it several times, hoping the stranger might understand him.

'Yaspa,' the man repeated and nodded. 'Yaspa,' he said again and then pointed at Kaspa, who smiled hesitantly. Now was not the time to correct him.

The stranger pointed to himself and said, 'Eimalfred.'

Kaspa repeated it, and Eimalfred smiled before strangely putting the thumb up on his right hand. He then pointed towards his mouth. Kaspa realised he must be thirsty and so offered him some water from his skin. Eimalfred drank greedily, leaving Kaspa with nothing for the journey back.

Kaspa pointed towards the forest and tried to tell Eimalfred that he should wait whilst he went to get help. It proved to be a waste of time because Eimalfred followed, anyway. The two of them walked in awkward silence, with Kaspa repeatedly stopping so that Eimalfred could keep up.

By the time they reached the edge of the forest, Eimalfred was already wheezing, and they'd just started. They would have to navigate their way through a host of challenges to get back, and Kaspa was already losing his patience. What was he supposed to do with him? At first, he'd considered leaving him on the beach to find a way back on his own, but his conscience had stopped him. He could hand him in, but to who? And what would he say? If he said he thought Eimalfred was a middling, they would either laugh at him or kill Eimalfred. Neither sounded good. He could take him to the Capital, but that was a long way away, and there was a rumour that the position of the high lord was passing to the Lady of the House, which meant trouble. It was too much to process.

They entered the forest, and Kaspa grabbed hold of Eimalfred's shirt as he tripped and almost fell into a manchineel shrub with poisonous spikes capable of causing severe blistering. A spider, startled by the commotion, scuttled its way past. It was the size of a foot and harmless. Eimalfred whimpered in fright when he saw it and squeezed Kaspa's arm, making him wince.

They pressed on, and as they walked, Kaspa played arguments back and forth in his head about what to do with his strange find. He couldn't decide, but Erik, his brother, would know what to do. He always knew what to do.

A branch snapped nearby, and Kaspa froze. Something heavy was on the move. Kaspa put his hand over his mouth to tell Eimalfred to be silent. He seemed to understand and nodded his head.

They crouched down and waited. Snarlers had been spotted in the forest recently, and they were becoming increasingly aggressive as powerful men destroyed more and more of their habitat. It seemed there was a sudden demand for Kea forest yew trees, and it was having a devastating impact on wildlife. Boar and deer were far more common in the forest, but it was better to err on the side of caution. They waited, and the sound of two men talking confirmed the source of the noise. Kaspa relaxed a little, but it was still better to avoid them and any awkward questions they might have.

Eimalfred was shaking, his energy almost spent. Kaspa put his hand on his back to provide some support, but Eimalfred didn't respond. He was staring straight ahead, his eyes wide and his jaw clamped. Kaspa followed his gaze to spot a gorgon slithering towards them. Its distinctive brown skin and green rings were almost impossible to see on the forest floor, but the movement of the leaves gave it away. This time, he was right to be frightened. If the gorgon struck one of them, they would die in agonising pain within a minute. It was mesmerising and terrifying in equal measure. Kaspa had never seen one. Even Erik, who was far more adventurous, had never seen one.

The gorgon slithered brazenly towards them. Kaspa found a stick and beat it on the ground to deter it, but it just made it angry. Kaspa pounded the ground, and the stick snapped. Eimalfred let out a strange, almost comical, shriek. The serpent raised its head, looked around, and then darted away in another direction. Kaspa breathed out, but his relief didn't last. The scream had given away their position.

'Who's there?' came a shout. Kaspa didn't recognise the voice. Eimalfred looked at him questioningly, and Kaspa put his fingers to his lips, hoping he understood the command.

'Who's there?' said a second voice.

This one Kaspa recognised. It was Breon, a bully and fool of a man. Not someone Kaspa would want to meet in a crowded marketplace, let alone deep in a forest. A crescendo of hurried footsteps and crunching leaves forced Kaspa to reveal himself, having first signalled Eimalfred to stay put.

'It's Kaspa,' he declared. 'Kaspa Kolinska from town. Sorry, I didn't mean to startle you.'

Kaspa recognised the second man as Timolt, Breon's long-time accomplice. Breon had a dent in his forehead, apparently from where his father had dropped him as a child. Timolt had a birthmark in the shape of a crescent moon on his neck. Their shaved heads and squashed noses made them look related, and they probably were. Kaspa disliked them both and tried to avoid them. They were nothing but thugs and were often before the Kea lawgivers for their various misdemeanours. By their weapons, Kaspa guessed they were hunting illegal wildlife for ivory and fur.

'I know you,' Breon said coldly. 'You're the one who hides in the back at sermons and doesn't join in. The one that thinks he's above us all.' Breon paused, waiting to see if Kaspa tried to defend himself.

Kaspa stayed silent.

'Why didn't you answer when we shouted?' Breon asked.

Kaspa cleared his throat. 'I did,' he said.

'That you making that scream?'

'I almost stepped on a gorgon,' Kaspa explained.

Breon looked at Timolt, and the two exchanged a wicked smile. 'It can be dangerous in this forest if you're not careful,' Breon remarked. 'One false move and you could step on something unpleasant or, even worse, slip down an entrance to the Below. I hear a few have opened up if you know where to look.'

Was that what they were up to? Were they searching for an entrance to the Below? The State used to send people Below as punishment for heinous crimes, but that practice had stopped over a hundred years ago. Now people believed there was treasure down there.

'I've been for a walk to the cove. I need to get back, and I'm sure you have things to be getting on with—'

'You're in a hurry,' Timolt commented suspiciously, cutting Kaspa off.

'I've got jobs to run, and I'm late,' Kaspa responded, his voice shaking. He scraped his long, dark hair behind his ears and looked at Timolt, who didn't move.

'What are you hiding?' Breon asked.

'Nothing,' Kaspa muttered, but his eyes betrayed him. It was the briefest of glances in Eimalfred's direction, but it was enough for Timolt and Breon to spot his outline quivering behind a tree.

'Well, well,' said Breon smirking, 'you're lying to us, Ka spa. What have you brought us?'

As Kaspa dithered, Eimalfred emerged from the trees, his hands in the air, shouting nonsense in his peculiar language. Kaspa wanted to warn him, but it was too late.

'Who on Mount Olympus is that?' Breon laughed.

'What is that he's wearing?' Timolt asked. 'And why is he so pale? Have you been hiding him in a cave?'

'He's a fisherman from Paros,' Kaspa said, thinking on his feet. 'A storm caught him off-guard, and he washed up on the beach. I'm trying to get him back, but he's hurt.'

'A fisherman from Paros,' Breon repeated. 'Do you expect us to believe that? Who is he? I won't ask again.'

Kaspa looked at the thugs. They were both powerful-looking men with big biceps and strong backs. They wouldn't be able to overpower them, but they could try to outrun them. But if he ran, Eimalfred might not follow. The only option was to try to talk their way out.

'He's not from Paros,' confessed Kaspa. 'I don't know where he's from, but he washed up on the beach, and he's got some injuries, so I'm trying to get him back to town to get some help. He's called Eimalfred. That's all I know.'

Kaspa gave Eimalfred his fiercest look as he started talking again. He wasn't helping things.

'Breon, the prophecy,' said Timolt.

Breon was staring at Eimalfred. 'I know,' he said.

'It's not the prophecy,' Kaspa pleaded. 'He's just an Atlantean who's—'

'Shut up!' Breon spat as he stroked his chin. He drew his machete, and Timolt copied.

The time for talking was over. It was time for Plan B. 'Run!' Kaspa screamed at Eimalfred. 'Run, run, run!'

CHAPTER XVII

Kea

Alfred's body ached, and his head felt like it was in a vice. His dreams had been so vivid, and he couldn't work out whether he was awake. A boyish man, called Yaspa, with olive skin and long, dark hair, was standing in front of him. Although his unusual white tunic and leather sandals made him look like he belonged in ancient Greece, he seemed genuine enough. His language was a concoction of strange primordial noises, unlike anything he'd ever heard. Alfred half wondered whether he'd stepped back in time.

He was on a pristine beach, the sort you would find proudly displayed in a holiday magazine, but he didn't know how or why. The last thing he could remember was being angry with Shep about something, and then his mind turned into a foggy mush. Thoughts about where he was and Shep could wait, though. The two muscular men with looks of hatred on their faces were his more pressing concern.

Yaspa turned towards him and started yelling one word at the top of his lungs. It was the first thing he'd said that Alfred could understand: run.

Every inch of him groaned. He could barely stand, let alone run, but adrenaline became his fuel as the men closed in. Yaspa was already on the move, and he grabbed hold of Alfred's arm, pulling him towards a path through the forest. Alfred struggled to keep up. Yaspa was slim, quick, and a few years younger. Plus, Yaspa wasn't recovering from a near-death experience. The path narrowed, and Yaspa went ahead, swinging his machete wildly to chop down anything in their way.

Why are we running? Alfred thought to himself but knew it wasn't the time to ask.

The men were close behind. Alfred didn't dare look to see how close, but the sound of footsteps rhythmically pounding the floor was evidence enough. Each branch he had to duck, and each root he had to jump required a huge effort. He was running on fumes. Still, he forced himself to keep going, telling himself that he was faster than his pursuers. But he knew one slip or one misplaced footstep, and they'd have him.

Sweat dripped into his eyes. He tried to blink it away, but the salty liquid spread painfully across his eyeballs, blinding him. Yaspa's footsteps and his occasional shouts were Alfred's only guide now. As he tried to clear the sweat with his hand, he smeared grime over his face, and then the inevitable happened. His left foot caught itself on a vine, and his body fell forwards. He landed heavily, his shoulder taking the full impact of the fall. Desperate, Alfred shouted out, but Yaspa's footsteps, along with his hope, faded into the distance.

He had nothing left. The hairs on his arms tingled, and his throat felt like he'd swallowed an apple whole as he watched his pursuers approach him in slow-motion. Half of his brain was freaking out whilst the other half tried to think rationally. Why would they want to hurt him?

As he edged backwards his voice returned, and he tried to explain what had happened, but the men just looked at him with blank faces. He tried pidgin German, Spanish, French, but nothing. Months and months of studying the route, yet he had no idea where he could have washed up.

He watched, wide-eyed, as the men talked to each other, listening for a word he might understand, but they spoke so quickly it was impossible. They seemed to be arguing about what to do with him.

Taking advantage of their distracted state, Alfred edged backwards on his bottom. They didn't notice. They were too busy yelling at each other.

The gap extended by two feet.

Was it enough? He didn't think about it. He was too tired, but his legs had a mind of their own. In a smooth motion, he'd sprung off the floor and turned to flee. He'd caught his pursuers off-guard. If he could just lose himself in the forest, they'd have no chance of finding him. There was a cry from behind as the men reacted, but they'd been slow. Too relaxed and sure of themselves.

Alfred was away, but no sooner was he congratulating himself than his feet disappeared from underneath him. He tried to correct himself, but it was too late. His weight was pulling him down into a hole. He scrabbled with his hands to grab hold of something, but there was only dirt and dust. Then the ground disappeared, and he fell into darkness, the sound of the men's voices following him as he clawed at the air. Minutes later, at least that's what it felt like. His body splashed into a pool of water. The impact sent waves of pain up Alfred's body. When he hit the bottom, he collided with jagged rocks that lacerated his feet and arms. The fresh injuries made him feel alive and jump-started his body into survival mode. He ignored the pain and pushed himself up, breaking the surface.

The only visible light came from the hole through which he had fallen, no more than a tiny dot in the ceiling. It took a few seconds for his eyes to adjust to the darkness. The faint voices of his pursuers drifted into his ears and then disappeared.

He swam to the edge of the pool, and on the fourth attempt, pulled himself out. To escape via the same route, he had fallen in was impossible. The exit was far too high, and the walls arched inwards, making any attempt suicidal. The ledge he had crawled onto was small, perhaps eight feet square. Water surrounded him, and it was the only solid floor he could see. Alfred cursed and sat back, resting his exhausted body. He was trapped.

CHAPTER XVIII

New Year 2009

The Capital

Vast crowds had gathered for the high lord's funeral, and they lined the streets of Outer Atalantea in an array of colourful garments. Funerals were a celebration of an individual's achievements in life rather than a time of mourning, but Hestia didn't feel like celebrating. She wasn't even sad. She was angry, and she wanted answers.

A band played the upbeat 'Fond Farewell', and choirs sang songs of love and praise, but all Hestia wanted to do was get the day over with so that the governors could have their stupid meeting and make her the first high lady. Then she would have the power to investigate what had happened and bring justice to those involved.

Dancing groups and acrobats led the funeral procession, followed by a dozen drummers who kept a steady beat to match their pace. Behind them came the members of the high table, who served as the high lord's most trusted advisers, minus the high physician, as that position was still vacant.

The high priest's entourage of disciples followed the members of the high table. The high priest's role was to oversee the funeral and ward off any evil spirits that might try to steal the deceased's soul, thus ensuring safe passage to the afterlife. Various ointments and candles were lit and sprayed to achieve this, and their sweet smell lingered for days afterward. As he walked, the high priest recited incantations in an ancient language no one other than he and the Viracocha understood. Some believed it to be the language of the gods. Hestia thought they made it up to appear divine.

The wailers came next, all dressed in black cloaks and wearing masks of sorrow. They acted out the grief of the people for the loss, thus enabling everyone else to celebrate. The sight of the wailers sobbing and screaming uncontrollably whilst walking at a steady pace was something to behold, and most people in the crowd tried to avoid looking at them.

Next came the ten governors, each one proudly waving the flag of his realm.

Hestia stood with Attalus behind the governors and in front of the carriage carrying their father. They were the only immediate family members remaining, and so they alone occupied the principal spot in the procession. Attalus wore bronze armour, beautifully adorned with intricate carvings of interweaving flowers. If one believed their history, Zeus's son, Hephaestus, the blacksmith, had forged it for Poseidon. Then it had been passed down to his son, Atlas, the first High Lord of Atalantea. Since then, the armour had passed to each successive high lord as a symbol of their position.

The holder wasn't supposed to wear the relic, but Attalus wasn't one to follow rules. He had seized the armour before their father's body was cold, and now it clinked and clanged as they walked, the breastplate loose on his shoulders. He waved happily at the crowd, enjoying the moment, oblivious to how ridiculous he looked. Her brother made her sick.

Hestia wore a black funeral cloak that covered her from head to toe, save for a slight gap for her eyes. Other than the wailers, she was the only one permitted to wear black and mourn at the funeral. However, tradition dictated that she hide her emotions from view so as not to darken the day for everyone else. The funeral cloak was another relic handed down from time immemorial. Apparently, Arachne had woven it before Athena transformed her into a spider for her insolence in claiming to have superior weaving skills to the goddess.

The sun was fiercely hot, and the funeral cloak was heavy and uncomfortable, but Hestia didn't mind because it meant that she didn't have to speak to her brother. They hadn't spoken since the reading of the will, and she had no desire to end that period of silence.

Attalus, however, had other ideas. He leaned in close as they walked. 'I know you can hear me under all that garb,' he hissed into her ear, a fake smile painted on his face.

Hestia tried to glare at him through the cloak.

'I know you're keeping something from me,' he continued. 'And I don't like it. I know you went to see the high physician before he died, and I know you were poking around asking questions about things you shouldn't have been. Our father is dead, and the quicker you learn to accept that, the better. It's just me and you left now.'

Hestia thought she'd been careful. How did Attalus know that she'd been to see the high physician? Had he been watching her?

'Don't fool yourself into thinking you'll be high lady,' he continued, his jaw clenched, 'because there is no way the governors will vote for you. After their meeting, everything Father had will be mine. And you... well, it would be wise to do as I say.'

The fabric of Hestia's cloak prevented her from sending a verbal tirade back at her brother, and all that came out was an angry mumble. Attalus waved cheerfully at the crowd, and they cheered back. They weren't cheering for Attalus. They were cheering for the armour and what it represented, but he wouldn't see it like that.

'Once we've finished today, you will make a public announcement. You will support me as high lord, and you will confirm your decision to become a Lady of the Fountain. Otherwise, everyone will know about your involvement in our father's death, and they will blame you. I will make it so they hate you. Is that clear? Nod if it is.'

Subtlety had never been one of Attalus's strengths, but his suggestion was beyond the pale, even for him. The Fountain was a female-only temple on an island to the north of Phrixus. It required those who devoted themselves to it to excommunicate themselves from society for the rest of their lives. Historically, the second daughter of each noble household joined a temple, but that tradition had faded a long time ago and wouldn't have applied to Hestia, anyway. If Attalus thought she would disappear meekly to a faraway temple to devote her life to a god she didn't believe in, he was grossly mistaken. She was so shocked by his demand that she didn't know how to react, and so she said nothing.

Attalus grabbed the inside of her arm forcefully. 'I'll take your silence as acceptance of my terms,' he said.

She shrugged him off, and they carried on walking in silence.

The distance between the Pagaros Pyramid, where the procession started, to the Golden Pillars of Heracles overlooking the sea was less than a mile, but it took them over two hours to walk it. The pillars had stood for thousands of years and reached at least two hundred feet into the sky. Heracles had built the pillars himself, in-between completing his twelve labours.

Hestia recalled it was purportedly after he had captured the Cretan Bull. Or was it after he had captured the Ceryneian Hind? She could never remember. Not that it mattered. The pillars marked the only entrance into the Capital via the sea, and sailors could see them standing proud from miles away.

The pillars stood on either side of a man-made canal that ran from the sea and uphill to the Citadel in the centre of the Capital. The water flowed thanks to powerful pumps created by the famous architect, engineer, and scientist, Daedalus. A high stone wall surrounded the Capital, separating it from the neighbouring Syros and Adelphi realms. As they walked the last 100 yards along the canal towards the pillars, the wailers stopped, and there was silence. Then a bell rang out, slow and methodical. The procession parted, allowing Hestia, Attalus, the high priest, and the carriage through. Members of the public had packed themselves along the stone wall to watch. As Hestia looked up, she grimaced as someone grappling for a position fell backwards to the stone ground below.

A boat, built especially for the occasion and filled with her father's prized possessions, sat moored on the canal. Pallbearers placed the open casket on top of a pyre on the boat. For the first time, grief truly hit her. She tried to control her breathing, not wanting to appear weak in front of Attalus. But it kept hitting her in waves, and she gulped at the air uncontrollably as her funeral cloak wrapped itself around her like a python, suffocating its prey. She pulled at the hood to let some air in and sucked at it slowly, counting the seconds of each breath until she gained some composure.

The high priest walked onboard and sprayed the body and pyre with various ointments. Traditionally he lit the pyre, but Attalus had insisted that he should have that honour, no doubt believing it was symbolic of him taking control. Attalus pushed past Hestia and marched towards the boat. Part of Hestia hoped he would slip and fall into the canal, but he was disappointingly sure-footed and avoided such ignominy.

After lighting the bottom of the pyre, Attalus returned to his place next to Hestia and placed his arm around her. He was playing the caring brother in front of the crowds. She bristled and looked away, numb to his mind tricks.

The high priest untied the boat, and it drifted into the centre of the canal before slowly passing through the pillars of Heracles into the sea. It was burning quickly, and it wouldn't be long before her father was feasting with Poseidon. Hestia didn't believe in the gods, but she allowed herself this one exception and smiled at the thought of it.

As she watched her father disappear, another boat came into view in the distance. It was creeping towards them, although it was difficult to see because of the stone wall. She had cancelled all patrols for the duration of the funeral and ordered that no other boats enter the vicinity as a sign of respect for her father. Hestia felt her grief turn to anger. She would punish whoever it was for their impertinence.

Those watching from the wall had noticed the second boat as well, and they were pointing in its direction. Solemn silence had turned into excited murmuring. Hestia wanted to shout at everyone, to tell them to be quiet and ignore the second boat, but she was powerless.

'What is that?' muttered Attalus to himself. He had only just noticed the intruder.

The boat was close enough now to see strange writing on its side, and it was heading straight towards the pillars. It didn't look like any boat Hestia had seen before.

Then a cry from the wall echoed over the crowd. 'It's the middling!'

Hestia tutted. She was growing fed up with hearing about the middling predicted by the bard's prophecy. It was unhealthy for such nonsense to be piped into the public's conscience by people who should know better. There had to be another explanation. She looked to her right just in time to see the back of Attalus as he raced off.

What was he up to now?

CHAPTER XIX

The Capital

Shep scratched his head and rubbed his eyes. He had no memory of what had happened during the storm, but his stomach was doing cartwheels, and he felt like he'd spent an hour spinning around in circles, which told him he'd had quite a ride.

He was alone on the boat. He had a vague recollection of Alfred being stood next to him during the storm, but every time he tried to think about it, the memory floated away. A voice deep inside was telling him that Alfred must be dead, that he must have fallen overboard, but he refused to acknowledge it. Not yet. He needed time to think.

In the distance, an unusual structure blotted the horizon. He rubbed his eyes again and squinted to see if they were playing tricks on him. The structure still stood, so he rowed towards it. As he got closer, he could see two pillars reaching high into the sky. They appeared to mark the entrance to a walled city, and Shep felt his spirits lift at the thought of getting off the godforsaken boat. He quickened his strokes, excitement and relief washing over him.

He smelled it before he saw it. There was a heavy, pungent odour hanging in the air, and then the source became apparent. A flaming boat was drifting inexplicably towards him. Shep's immediate thought was that he'd stumbled on a festival or celebration, but something about the boat, and the horrible smell emanating from it, made him feel queasy.

Beyond the flaming boat, he could see the pillars more clearly now. He strained his neck to look at them. They were magnificent constructions, glistening a fantastic golden colour in the sun. Geography had never been his strength, but he felt like he should know what they marked the entrance to.

He could hear the faint sound of a bell ringing in the distance, fast and frenzied, like a call to arms. The stone wall adjoining the pillars stretched out, hugging the coastline as far as he could see. The wall was far higher than he'd originally thought, and there was no place for him to moor the boat. He would have to head between the pillars.

The pillars were close now, close enough to see people high on the stone wall peering down at him. Shep had an ominous feeling that he had interrupted something sacrosanct. He debated turning away to head for somewhere less imposing to land, but tiredness hounded him, and God only knew how long he'd be rowing before he found somewhere else. A bed and some food were what he needed. Then he would figure out what had happened to Alfred.

There was a loud cheer as a grand wooden boat emerged. It had a serpent figurehead and one giant sail. It looked fit for a king. Shep watched in awe as it glided effortlessly through the water, past the pillars, and out into the open sea towards him.

As the boat approached Lyon Heart, he noticed hundreds of oars moving with perfect timing, each one disappearing and emerging from the water at the same time. For reasons he couldn't understand, he felt nervous. Was it a coincidence, or had someone sent the boat for him? A sixth sense was telling him it was the latter, and he hadn't had time to prepare. How would he explain what had happened or how Alfred had disappeared? What if they sent him away, or even worse, threw him in prison?

The boat closed in, and he could see five people standing onboard. One man was wearing golden armour and appeared godlike. He was waving his arms and yelling at the other men, clearly in charge of whatever was going on. When he was close enough to Lyon Heart, he shouted something in a peculiar language to Shep.

'Hello?' Shep replied and noticed how weak his voice sounded. 'Do you speak English? Is there something going on? I can get out of your way. I'm a bit lost.' Shep heard a clang as the crew threw grappling hooks onto Lyon Heart, securing the two boats. 'Hang on,' he yelped, his voice shaking, 'there's no need for that. I'm lost. Or are you helping? Does anyone speak English? American?'

No one responded.

Then the man in the golden armour shouted something at his crew, his tone threatening, and he pointed at Shep and the boat.

Shep put his hands up in the air defensively. 'Pardon? I'm sorry, I don't understand. Do you speak English? I need help. I'm lost.' Shep wondered where he could have landed to receive such an unusual reception. 'I've been taking part in a rowing competition, and I got caught in a storm and… and…'

Lyon Heart rocked unsteadily as a man carrying a spear boarded her. What on earth was he doing carrying such a weapon? It had to be some sort of show, and the people on the wall must be spectators.

'Sorry, I've disrupted your show. If you could just tell me where I am…' Shep trailed off as the spearman gave him a seething look. Should he play along?

Wild cheering erupted all along the walls. Shep turned to look, wondering what had caused the sudden commotion, and then his legs collapsed from under him. He was on his knees, stunned, still conscious but no longer able to see. And then he felt something against the side of his head, and he crumpled into a heap on the floor. As he drifted in and out of consciousness, he heard a horn blowing behind him, and then the cheering turned to euphoria.

CHAPTER XX
Adelphi

The White Horse was a tavern on the outskirts of the Capital in the Adelphi realm. It was notorious, but not for its food or ale. Axil sat at the bar and ordered a fruit beer, waiting.

The funeral had been an eventful occasion. He'd watched the drama unfold from a distance, keeping a close eye on the governors at all times. He kept track of who spoke to who and how they responded and reacted to each other. It was his only opportunity to get close to them, but then all Tartarus broke loose following the middling's arrival, and his carefully crafted plans had fallen by the wayside.

The upstart, Attalus, had made a bold move by capturing the middling in front of the crowd. They had whooped with delight at the sight of their so-called persecutor being taken down so easily. People were calling him a hero and comparing him to the likes of Theseus and Achilles, but they hadn't seen what Axil had seen. Far from being the champion of Atalantea, Attalus had hidden onboard his vessel out of harm's way whilst his protectors did the dirty work.

Attalus had taken the middling straight back to the Citadel in the centre of the Capital on the high lord's trireme. It had been intended for use as part of the ceremony until Attalus commandeered it. Most of the crowd had followed, eager for a closer look at the middling. The funeral was long since forgotten. They had found their way blocked by tridents at the bridge leading from Outer Atalantea into the Limbal Ring. Some had tried to storm the bridge and regretted it. Axil had heard that tridents had gutted three men as the protests turned violent, and that had taken the sting out of the crowd's enthusiasm.

The governors had ignored the furore and remained at the funeral for a brief period out of respect before saying their farewells to the Lady of the House and dispersing. Axil had almost given up at that point. His task was already impossible.

The Order required the line of all governors and the high lord to remain pure. That meant governors married their sons to the daughters of other governors to ensure that rule of their realm passed down with no claims of illegitimacy. It was archaic and draconian and, despite some spurious unions, no one had ever challenged the legitimacy of a governor's position- not in recent times, anyway. The result was complex alliances, often forged before anyone had been born. Add to that the historic oaths which bound many realms to one another and which the governors refused to break for fear of facing the gods' wrath, and the result was a tangled web of organised chaos.

By Axil's reckoning, the Ellopia and Milos realms in the northeast would vote against the motion. The governors had been vocal about their opinions. The southern realms always voted with the high lord, which was unlikely to change. That left Kea in the east, the western realms of Paros and Phrixus, and the landlocked Tinos. Axil knew little about how the governors in those realms intended to vote. He would need to find out and ensure they shared his point of view, or his neck would be on the line.

Governor Castor Azaes of Paros was the youngest of all the governors at the age of thirty-one. He had inherited the position a few months prior, and he was still finding his feet. His father had been a popular leader before his untimely death. Castor was still trying to emerge from his shadow and make a name for himself. He had no wife and no heir. Axil had heard whispers that he spent most of his time cooped up in his mansion, allowing his father's advisers to rule in his absence. Axil had noticed how Castor had hovered awkwardly around the other governors during the funeral, unable to strike up a conversation. He didn't look like much of a leader, nor did he appear to have much interest in leading.

Castor had been the first to leave the funeral, and Axil had followed him out of instinct. Curiously, he had headed out of the Capital rather than towards the Citadel where the governors were staying. At first, Axil thought he might take a longer route to avoid any trouble, but then Castor had removed and hidden his silver band and blue robe, denoting his position. He jumped on board a passenger boat, heading to Adelphi with the common folk. He blended in well. No one knew who he was, and he didn't have the natural air of someone in a position of power.

Axil followed him for over an hour and watched him walk into The White Horse, a watering hole he had heard about in some of his more sordid escapades. Few knew its location, and Axil could see why. The tavern was positioned at the foot of a cliff in the middle of nowhere, surrounded by farmland and trees. It was a wonder how people came to know about the place. Axil didn't know what to expect as he walked in and was disappointed when he discovered a fairly common-looking bar and a few tired and dishevelled punters who eyed him warily. Castor wasn't there.

'What's in the backroom?' Axil asked the bartender who handed him his drink. The tavern had to have a hidden room somewhere. Castor hadn't just disappeared.

The bartender looked at him blankly. 'What backroom?' he said, unhelpfully, and Axil handed him a copper for the fruit beer along with a couple extra to see if that would move things along.

'I don't know what you're talking about,' the bartender whispered but took the coins on offer. He was young and unskilled in the art of lying. His eyes were too pure.

'I believe you do, and I would like to know more. I have plenty of coin.'

'Coin doesn't work here,' the bartender said carelessly whilst rubbing the coins in his hand.

'Then what does?'

The bartender ignored Axil's question and looked over to the corner of the room to where an obese, bald man was sat, nursing a beer. He spotted the bartender's plea and stood up. It was evident that he had spent many years perfecting his colossal midriff, and as he marched over, the timber floorboards creaked from the weight. He stood so close to Axil he was almost on his toes.

'There a problem here?' the bald man asked, puffing after his short exertion. His two front teeth were missing, and his breath smelled rancid. The bartender looked at Axil, who shook his head and stepped back out of the obese man's shadow. Not out of fear but revulsion.

'No problem,' Axil said and smiled.

The obese man looked at the bartender, who shrugged his shoulders. He grunted and slowly plodded back to his chair.

'Point taken,' Axil muttered to himself. He had no desire to start a fight. He preferred more subtle forms of attack. The fruit beer was pleasant, and so he sipped it slowly as he decided on an alternative approach.

Axil left and walked around outside, keeping to the shadows. The tavern looked like it extended into the cliff face. There had to be another entrance. Axil climbed on top of the building with the help of an apple tree to get a bird's-eye view.

After a few minutes, a man appeared from nowhere below him. Axil watched the spot for a little longer and saw a steady thread of people coming and going from the same place. Concealed within the cliff face was a secret entrance, invisible to the eye until someone revealed it. That must be where Castor had disappeared to.

Axil waited. Eventually, a man in his sixties with a stooped back, a weather-worn face, and a nervous disposition appeared. Axil followed him as he made his way slowly along a winding path up the cliff. There was no cover, and it was impossible to stay hidden. So Axil covered his face with a black mask he carried for such occasions and when he was sure they were alone, ran up behind the man. He pushed him so that his face was up against the red rocks of the cliff. The man let out a whimper.

'Where have you just come from?' Axil growled in the man's ear, switching his accent seamlessly to that of a subject from the Ellopia realm.

'The White Horse,' the man whimpered pathetically.

'Where exactly?' Axil pushed the man's face harder into the rocks and heard something click. Perhaps it was his nose.

'The Diphetroa area. Please. I have a wife and children. Take what you want.'

'The Diphetroa area? What's that? What's the Diphetroa area?'

The man fell silent.

'Answer me,' Axil barked as loud as he dared.

'Please, I can't say it. There are girls, women… boys, whatever you want. Please. I was just there with a friend. I've never been there before. I didn't know what it was… please. Take what you want, but please have mercy.' The man begged pathetically, and Axil almost felt sorry for him.

'How do I get in?'

'What?'

'How do I get in?'

'Please, if I tell you, will you let me go?'

'How do I get in?' Axil said again, this time showing a knife to the man. He had no plan to use it, but it did the trick.

'The code. You need the code. You knock three times, then four, and then another three. Then they ask you for the code. You tell them, then they let you in.'

'What's the code?'

'Will you let me go?'

'If you don't tell me the code, this knife is going in your gut. So I suggest cooperating.'

'Anchises. The code is Anchises.'

Anchises was one of Aphrodite's mortal lovers, and Diphetroa was an anagram for Aphrodite. It wasn't the most complex of codes, but it made sense. Axil loosened his grip on the man.

'Thank you,' the man said as he breathed a sigh of relief.

Axil smashed the man's head on the rock, knocking him unconscious. He didn't like to use force, especially on a frail old man with a humpback, but he needed to be certain there was no risk of being caught.

Axil removed his mask and walked back to the secret entrance. He followed the old man's instructions and waited. There was no response, and he wondered if the old man had lied to him. Then a voice said, 'Speak your purpose.'

'Anchises,' Axil said to the wall. He sensed he was being watched and looked around, but there was no one there.

After a brief pause, a gap in the cliff appeared. Axil walked in, carefully studying the entrance to fathom how it worked. It was like a magic trick, and he could find no clues. The entrance closed, and the aromatic smell of bocardium smoke greeted him. It was a plant local to the area, and it hung thick in the air and stung his eyes. The smell alone made him feel intoxicated.

He walked into a gloomy room, which was empty save for one candle hanging from the wall. It flickered, carelessly casting monstrous shapes onto the wall. The faint sound of groans and moans echoed around him. 'Where are you, Castor?' Axil muttered and took a deep breath.

No one was there to greet him, so Axil followed a corridor with rooms on either side, each doorway lit up by candlelight. Thin curtains did little to hide the silhouetted actions of the people behind them. Axil averted his gaze and tried to think. Castor could be in any room, but he could hardly search them without raising suspicion. Why would Castor visit such a place? It was an enormous risk. If anyone caught him, it would humiliate his house.

Axil reached the end of the corridor, and it opened out into a larger room that appeared to be a meeting point for the workers and their customers. It was almost impossible to see anyone through the smoke coating his senses, creating a warped reality. His thoughts drifted, and his eyes caught creatures lurking in the shadows, waiting for him to drop his guard. Axil slapped his face and scratched his neck, using the pain to focus himself.

'You look lost,' a voice said in a soft whisper, floating on the fumes.

Axil looked around, confused. A scantily clad girl stood in front of him. Axil blinked, and her face shifted into a serpent for a moment before returning to normal. 'I'm looking for someone,' he said, ignoring the demons.

'Maybe I can help you find her. And if you can't, maybe I could help instead?'

Axil felt uncomfortable. She was young enough to be his daughter, and he had no intention of staying around for any extracurricular activities.

'I'm looking for a customer. He's in his thirties, around my height, skinny, and good-looking with long blonde hair. He came in around an hour ago. He might have left by now.' Axil tried to remember any other distinguishing features, but his brain refused to help.

The girl looked despondent. 'I've not seen anyone here with that description,' she said.

'He might be in a private room.'

'If anyone good-looking came in, I would know. I've been here all afternoon, and you're the first.'

Axil ignored the compliment. 'Is there anywhere else he could be?'

The girl dropped her shoulders and turned away to look for another customer, having realised he was a lost cause.

'I can pay you,' Axil said.

'How much?' the girl asked, casting Axil a sideways glance. Her tone had moved from flirtatious to businesslike.

'Two orichalcum beads. That's worth more than you could earn here in a month.'

'Where am I going to sell orichalcum beads without being caught?'

She had a valid point. Perhaps she was cleverer than Axil gave her credit.

'All right, three gold coins. That should be more than enough.'

'Show me.'

Axil produced the coins from his purse and slapped the girl's hands away as she tried to snatch them.

'Your turn to show me.'

The girl smiled and undid her top button, pretending to misunderstand.

'You know what I mean,' he groaned. He didn't have time for games. The smoke was making him delirious.

'Why not hang around for a bit first? You've got plenty enough coin in there to pay for anything you want. An-y-thing!'

Axil knew what she wanted. She would take him to a quiet room and then try to rob him at the first opportunity. 'No games,' he said. 'Show me to the other rooms.'

'You need to relax,' she moaned and wrinkled her nose. She led Axil to the far side of the room and down another corridor, passing two guards who raised their eyebrows as he passed. The smoke disappeared, and Axil's head cleared slightly. A small blessing.

'We reserve these two rooms for our special guests, and it looks like one is free. Maybe we could carry on the conversation in there?'

She was persistent.

'Which room is taken?' Axil asked.

The girl shook her head and pointed to the room on the right. 'But I don't know who is in there,' she added quickly.

'That will be all. Here are your coins. You can leave now.' The girl raised her eyebrows at his bluntness. He hadn't meant to be rude, but he had no time for conversation, and the quicker he could leave, the better.

'You can't go in there!' she said as he walked towards the room she'd pointed to. 'Our customers pay a lot of money for our discretion. If you go in there—'

'Trust me, this guest won't be complaining. Now leave me. Please.'

The girl stomped off without looking back. Axil made sure he was alone and then put his ear against the door. He could hear talking and laughing, but it could be anyone.

He put his mask on and carefully opened the door. He held his breath, expecting a noise, but he was in luck. The bed in front of him was big enough for an entire family to sleep in with drapes surrounding it. Two people were on the bed laughing and rolling around, but he couldn't see them. Whoever they were, they were too busy in their own company to notice him as he crept closer. Axil reached the foot of the bed and composed himself. If it wasn't Castor, he would be in trouble, but it was too late to turn back now.

He took a deep breath and tore open the drapes. There was a scream as two naked bodies searched for the sheets to cover their dignity.

'Governor Azaes,' Axil said, smiling out of relief. 'Lady Nefali, does Governor Mneseus know you are here? I saw him earlier at the funeral. Didn't see you, though…'

'Who are you?' demanded Castor, finding his voice. 'And how dare you barge into our room like this! There will be repercussions from this, you hear me?'

'I'm sure there will be repercussions,' said Axil calmly, 'but for who will depend on how cooperative you are.'

Nefali sat rigid with the blanket drawn up to her shoulders, her face drawn. Her wide green eyes darted between Axil and Castor, trying to make sense of the situation. Dark, curly hair flowed over her gentle features, and Axil felt sorry for her. Her father, Governor Autochthon of the Kea realm, arranged her marriage to Governor Mneseus to keep their families tied, but there was no love in the union. Mneseus was old and repulsive. Axil recalled that when the union was announced, it had caused some consternation, although he couldn't remember the details as it had been over a decade ago.

Nefali had barely been seen since her marriage, but there she was with Governor Azaes, naked save for a thin cotton sheet. Axil could see why Castor would risk his life for her.

'What is it you want? Money?' Castor asked, flustered.

Axil snapped out of his daydream. 'To talk,' he said.

'All I have to do is shout, and guards will storm in here. I can have you left for dead in some ditch somewhere.'

'I don't think you're in a position to be making threats, Castor. We both know you don't want anyone to know you're here. If you shout out, your secret will be whispered in the darkest alleyways, and it won't take long for the wind to spread them to more influential ears. Why take that risk when all I want to do is talk?'

'Talk then and begone.'

Axil sat on the end of the bed. 'Perhaps put on some clothes,' he said. 'It's somewhat distracting talking to you when you keep winking at me.'

Castor looked down and saw that he was revealing himself. He stood up and put on his silk gown. He was skinny but toned, like a long-distance runner, with a hooked nose, intense blue eyes, and thick flowing hair which was scraped back behind his ears. Axil could see why Nefali was drawn to him. Where Governor Mneseus was old, fat, and visibly decaying, Castor was young and athletic. They made a pretty couple.

'You will be aware,' said Axil once Castor had dressed, 'that there is about to be a rather important vote.'

'Of course, I am aware. Everyone in the ten realms is aware. What of it?'

'You will vote against the motion.'

'I will vote how I choose,' Castor said defiantly.

'Let me phrase this differently. You will vote against the motion, or I will spread your dirty little secret throughout Atalantea. The gods only know what sort of punishment Mneseus would have in store for you and Lady Nefali if he found out. You've clearly gone to great lengths to conceal your affair. Who would ever expect to see you here?'

Nefali squeezed Castor's shoulder and looked at him, desperation in her eyes. Axil suspected she had suffered by Mneseus's hand before.

'I could just kill you here,' Castor said, his eyes burning a hole in Axil.

'You could try, but I didn't get to where I am without getting my hands dirty.'

Axil suspected Castor wasn't much of a fighter. Most governors liked to show off their skills at the Games, but Castor had never taken part or shown any interest in them, suggesting he had never trained. However, his skills with a lyre were renowned.

'If I vote against the motion, you will leave us alone?'

'You and Governor Autochthon.'

Nefali gasped. 'I have no influence over my father,' she begged. 'Why would he listen to me? We've barely spoken in years. Not since he sold me to that monster.' She blinked her long eyelashes to stem the tears.

'Then I suggest it's about time you made amends with him, don't you?' Axil said, keeping his eyes on Castor. He couldn't deal with tears.

'He will always pick my brother over me, and my brother is in love with Hestia. He always has been. My father wouldn't vote against her if it meant upsetting my brother. What you are asking is impossible.'

Nefali's brother was the beautiful Ganymede. He could have his pick of any woman on the island, and so he'd gone for the only one that was unattainable.

'If the governors pass the motion,' Axil said, an idea forming as he spoke, 'the Lady of the House will become the first high lady, and your brother's chances of a union will all but disappear. However, if Attalus becomes the high lord, then he could marry her off to someone who has been loyal to him. Ganymede and Hestia are both of an age where they need to form a union. It would seem to me that your father would be doing Ganymede a favour by voting against the motion.'

'Even if Tomos, Governor Autochthon, and I voted against the motion, you still wouldn't have the numbers,' Castor interjected. 'Hestia has made pledges to all the governors, and they like her far more than her brother. Attalus is a fool, everyone knows it, and his little stunt at the funeral didn't help. The governors think he is out of control. What is it to you, anyway? Why do you care?'

'That is my business. Who has said they'll vote for the motion?'

Castor hesitated. 'Everyone, other than Governor Mneseus and his lapdog, Governor Elasippus, but I don't know. People say things and change their minds all the time. If Tomos and I voted against the motion, then that would make four votes against. You need six.'

Castor was right. He'd been lucky in finding Castor and Nefali together, but the task now looked even harder. He needed two more votes, and time was running out. 'I'll worry about that,' he said. 'If you and Governor Autochthon vote against the Motion, I will keep your secret.'

Castor nodded, and Nefali stroked his hand.

'Now, if you've said all you have to say, go,' Castor added crossly.

Axil backed out of the doorway and disappeared into the shadows. He had work to do.

CHAPTER XXI
The Below

Alfred's stomach rumbled angrily. It felt like days had passed since he'd found himself stuck in the cave, although in reality, it was probably only hours, but he had no way of telling. At some point, his body had succumbed to sleep. Then the dawn chorus had blasted out a raucous tune and snapped him back into consciousness. That he was no longer sleepy suggested he'd been out for a while, but he was still feeling like an empty, broken shell. The last time he had eaten a proper meal was a distant memory, and his body was feverish. He drank a gulp of water from the pool, beyond caring whether it was safe to drink. He'd watched enough survival programmes to know if he didn't drink, he would die.

No one was coming for him. The two men who had chased him had stayed around for a while and then lost interest. He'd been relieved at first, but now all he wanted to do was escape by whatever means he could. The case of the Speluncean Explorers came to mind. A hypothetical case he had debated at university about a group of cave explorers who, trapped and facing starvation, had eaten one of their comrades to survive. They had then faced trial for murder on their escape. He'd argued that the jury should absolve the men of any wrongdoing and won the debate, joking afterwards about what he would have done. Never did he think he would face the same dire situation. How many days had the explorers faced starvation before they thought of doing the unthinkable?

His mind was a swamp of angst, and he needed to do something, anything. He was in no state to move. Deep cuts covered his arms and legs. His body was more plum than peach, but his situation would only get worse, and before long, he wouldn't be able to move at all. Gingerly, he stood up and grimaced as a host of injuries shouted at him. He ignored them and listened to a voice from deep within, urging him to keep going.

If there was a way out, it had to be via the pool. Alfred dipped his toe into the water and recoiled. He cursed loudly and took a deep breath before gently stepping in. The iciness spread to his extremities, and his shivers made gentle waves. The only noise was the sound of his teeth chattering. They felt loose in his gums.

Gently, he edged his way around the outer rim of the cave. The water reached his waist, and then he gulped as it climbed to his chest. He went to his tiptoes as the water crept up to his mouth. He kept moving around, feeling the wall with his hands and feet, not entirely sure what it was he was looking for but pleased to be doing something. Alfred was about to give up when his foot disappeared through the wall. He kicked forward but only kicked water. There was a gap.

Alfred took a deep breath and dunked his head to inspect. It was too dark to see anything, but as he felt his way down, he discovered a crevice with his hands. He returned to the surface and allowed himself a minute to catch his breath. His body was feeling slightly better for moving, and he was loosening up. He was glad because he knew he needed to see if the crevice led anywhere.

Alfred took a deep breath and dived back down. The gap was sufficient for him to squeeze through, but just. It appeared to be an underwater tunnel. Alfred pulled himself along, using the wall to help, relying on his sense of touch alone in the pitch black. The tunnel narrowed, and he forced his shoulders through, the effort almost draining him of his reserves. If it narrowed any further, he'd have to turn back. He needed air badly, his comfort zone abandoned.

Alfred tried to control his heart rate as he crawled forwards. In a few seconds, he would pass out. His body screamed at him to turn back, but it was too late. He had committed himself. This is it, he thought to himself. This is how I die.

Then sweet relief as his head reached into an air pocket. It was a lifeline, possibly his only one, and Alfred devoured the oxygen in great gulps. It was too small for him to stay for more than a few seconds, so he carried on, his body still writhing in agony.

The tunnel ended abruptly. There was no way through. Alfred felt around desperately and discovered a dog-leg. He followed it and batted away a wave of panic as the passage narrowed further. He scrabbled his way through, scraping his body against the wall, not caring that the skin on his back was shredding against rocks like cheese against a grater. All he needed was to just keep going, but it felt impossible. He was about to give in and let the tunnel have him, but then it widened, and he could see a light.

Alfred pushed himself along. He could use both his arms and his legs now, so he pulled and kicked with everything he had left. It felt like a frog was jumping around in his chest. His lungs screamed. His head was about to burst. And then he broke the surface. Relief swept over him at the realisation that he'd made it out.

Using what energy he had left, he doggy paddled until his feet could touch the ground, his loud gasps echoing all around him. He'd swam through to another, larger pool. This one was lit from within, and as his senses and breathing returned to normal, Alfred saw the light was emanating from something perched at the edge of the pool. At first, Alfred thought it was sticks or stones, but when he got closer, he discovered a pile of bones. He recognized them as human bones, and he suddenly wished he was back in the other chamber.

He swam towards the nearest ledge and pulled himself out with a struggle. 'Hello?' he mumbled in case anyone was around, but there was no response. The skeleton looked intact, and it was lying nonchalantly just out of the water. The light was coming from a pendant hanging from the skeleton's chest.

Who are you? Alfred wondered. Had he, or she, swam through the same tunnel as Alfred, or had they come from a different direction?

Across the skull was a clear break, like an egg that had been carefully cracked. The body was positioned in a way that made it look like it was taking a quick nap. Alfred removed the pendant, careful not to disturb the rest of the remains, and placed it around his neck. The light would come in handy. Then he examined his surroundings.

Like the previous room, there was no way of climbing out. The roof looked solid, but there were several tunnels to explore, which could lead somewhere. Alfred wanted nothing more than to sit down and have a rest, but he knew he needed to press on. If he didn't, he would wind up spending eternity with the skeleton.

The first tunnel led to a dead-end.

The second appeared promising, but as Alfred followed it, the tunnel looped back to the cavern.

The third tunnel led to another cavern with a sudden, deep drop.

The fourth tunnel narrowed so much that it became impassable.

Alfred returned to the skeleton, despondent. 'Any advice?' he asked, and its hollow eyes seemed apologetic. The presence of the skeleton was strangely comforting.

His eyelids felt as though they had two hooks in them, pulling them down, but he knew he couldn't stop. So he went back to the third tunnel to take another look. The drop was deep, and he couldn't see to the bottom. If he climbed down, he might get stuck, but he could try to climb around the outside. There were enough hand and footholds to make it achievable, and the gap was only about twenty feet. Fully fit, the climb would be easy, but in his current state… If he fell, he would die, but he would die if he did nothing, so it didn't look like he had much of a choice.

Mind made up, Alfred climbed about a yard off the ground and made his way across. The wall had plenty of nooks and crannies, but they were difficult to see. He had to feel his way around for them. His fingertips were sweaty and, combined with the moisture on the wall, it was difficult to grip anything, so his progress was excruciatingly slow.

Alfred hit his first problem at the midway point. His toes kept slipping against the wall as he searched for purchase with his right foot. He took his shoes and socks off to make it easier to feel and grip, but it wasn't helping. He brought his foot back to its original resting place and took a few deep breaths. The muscles in his arms and legs were aching. He searched for something with his right hand instead and reached into a crack with his fingertips. It wasn't as secure as he would have liked, but it would suffice. He moved his left foot next to his right foothold and his left hand to where his right hand had been previously. Now he had a better reach with his right foot, and he searched, desperate for something to secure himself. All he could find was a crevice at an awkward angle. It would have to do.

Sweat covered Alfred's hands, and he tried to wipe it off on his shirt, but his adventures in the pool had left him drenched. Usually, he would have chalk while climbing to keep his hands dry. Trying to climb without it was insufferable, and his fingers were working overtime.

With all of his weight on his right leg and his foot precariously in place, Alfred reached out with his right hand. He could feel a gap, and his fingers reached into it. Then a cramp shot up his right calf, all the way from his ankle to the back of his knee. Alfred gritted his teeth and flapped at the gap with his right hand, but he couldn't get a clean hold. His heart was in his mouth. He needed to find a point of contact to take the weight off his leg. Then his right foot slipped, and he couldn't hold on anymore. Alfred let out a scream as he fell backwards... straight into a pool of water.

Confused, Alfred looked around. It had been an illusion. The deep abyss he had been climbing around had been a pool of water reflecting the high ceiling of the cavern like a mirror. He thumped the water in frustration and laughed. For a split second, and not for the first time that day, he'd been convinced he was about to die. 'Water!' Alfred shouted hysterically. 'Water!'

The sound echoed through the cave. 'WATER, WATer, WAter, Water, water...' And deep within the dark, something stirred.

CHAPTER XXII

The Capital

Shep opened his eyes to see his reflection staring back at him a thousand times. Mirrors covered every inch of the walls, ceiling, and floor. They were positioned at awkward angles to make his figure contorted and repulsive. He was naked save for his briefs and socks. The floor was cold, hard, and impossible to sit on comfortably. Shep curled himself into a ball and groaned. He touched the side of his head and felt a tender bruise. He couldn't remember what had caused it. When he closed his eyes, they ached, but he couldn't open them without feeling sick. He squeezed his head to take away the pain, but it only made it worse. Shep found a compromise and peeled open the corner of one eye, looking around for a door. He needed to get out of there, but it was impossible to find an exit.

Shep couldn't tell which of his memories were real and which he had created in his battered and delirious state. He had been in a rowing race, and there had been a storm that had nearly killed him, and then he'd landed somewhere. That much was true, but all the events in-between were hazy. Was he even awake? The bruise on the side of his head told him he had to be.

A vivid memory of a high stone wall and two gigantic pillars flashed in his mind, but it was so extraordinary that it didn't seem possible. None of it seemed possible. Even the strange mirror room he'd woken up in.

Alfred! He'd been travelling with Alfred. Where was he? How had he escaped this punishment? His mind hurt thinking about it.

Shep's body ached from his toes to his forehead. That he could move everything and was in one piece was a miracle.

There was a sharp, angry growl as Shep's stomach woke up. He tried to remember the last time he'd eaten a proper meal. It felt like weeks ago.

'Hello!' Shep tried to shout, but his mouth was so parched he could barely raise his voice above a whisper. 'Is anyone there? Hello? Help me, please. I need water.'

It was useless. No one could hear him. Instead, he tried to bang on the walls with his hands, but his efforts were feeble, and he'd tired himself out within seconds. Exhausted, Shep closed his eyes and tried to sleep, but his brain was on overdrive and refuted his request.

He waited, growing insane at the sight of his image grimacing back at him like a pitiless gyroscope. Minutes turned to hours, Shep drifting in and out of a cruel consciousness. Each time he came to, the same question confronted him. Why am I here? He couldn't help but think it was divine retribution for what he'd done. The blood on his hands…

At one point, he tried to feel his way around the room to find an exit. He quickly concluded there was no escape from his torment.

Just as reality squeezed the last remnants of hope from his soul, Shep heard a slight movement and saw a door open. An old man with a cane appeared, his image reflected hundreds of times. He had long, straggly, white hair flowing around a tired, sagging face, and his nose was long with juts of hair growing from it. His cane was supporting most of his weight, and he looked like he might collapse at any moment. He was wearing a white tunic that reached his knobbly knees and sandals that showcased his bulging bunions. Exhaustion rendered Shep too feeble to react, but if he could, he would have laughed. Was this his saviour?

The old man didn't speak. Instead, he beckoned Shep to follow him. Shep tried to stand up, but he had lost all sense of balance. As soon as he put any weight on his feet, the room spun, and he collapsed in a heap on the floor. After several attempts, the old man hobbled into the room. Shep noticed that his cane looked like a cobra coiled and ready to pounce. It was so intricately carved that it looked lifelike, and Shep almost fell into a trance looking at it. The old man held the cane out for Shep, and he reached out to grab it. Hundreds of snakes sprang at him, and he wailed, drawing his hand back. Was that a smile on the old man's face? Was the old man playing with him, tormenting him?

The old man left the room and was replaced by a younger man who Shep took for a wrestler. Shep's vision faded, and the last thing he could remember as the wrestler hauled him over his shoulders was a strange fork tattoo on the wrestler's forehead, like some sort of satanic symbol.

*

Shep woke up on a bed as soft as clouds. He looked around, his eyes slowly adjusting to his new setting. The room was large, with high ceilings and stone walls. It had no furniture other than the bed, a cabinet, and two wooden chairs. A painting of a bull hung from the wall. The room looked old like he was in one of the stately homes his parents had forced him to visit as a child. The curtains over the bay window had been left open, and the room was filled with sunlight. Shep couldn't see much from his bed, which he had no intention of leaving, but the blue sky told him it was a beautiful day.

His head no longer hurt, and whilst he still carried cuts and bruises from his ordeal, the pain had subsided. On the cabinet, a large jug of water and some bread and fruit greeted him. Shep's stomach let out a thankful growl as he shoveled it into his mouth. The fuel awoke memories of the mirror room, and his heart rate quickened. Had that been a nightmare? He felt so safe now.

He was too tired to think, so he snuggled into the mattress to sleep. Just as he was drifting off, he heard the creaking of a door opening. Curiosity overcame his urge to rest, and he sat up to welcome the intruder. An old man with a cane stood in the frame of the doorway. Shep recognised the creased face immediately. It was the man from his nightmare, his tormentor. The hairs on Shep's back stood up, and his muscles tensed.

The old man said nothing and crept into the room without an invitation. His eyes penetrated Shep, reading his inner thoughts. Grey, soiled clothes hung loosely off his boney body, but despite his appearance, Shep had the sense he was formidable. Neither spoke, and a feeling of unease hung in the air.

'Hello!' Shep said after an endless pause. 'Thank you for the food and drink.'

The old man narrowed his eyes and turned his left ear to Shep. It was filled with thick, white hairs.

'Where am I?' Shep asked, sitting up.

123

The old man studied him as though deconstructing the question. 'Hel-lo,' he said in a strange accent. Shep wasn't sure whether it was a greeting or a question. The old man forced a smile, showing his yellow teeth hanging precariously from his receding gums. 'You have woken from your sleep.' He spoke slowly, as though considering each word before it left his mouth. 'You will have questions, but first, welcome to Atalantea. I am the Viracocha. What is your name?'

Shep screwed up his face. Had he heard him correctly, or was the old man playing tricks? 'I'm Shep,' was all he could manage.

'Hello, Shep. Where have you come from?'

Thoughts were at war in Shep's head, and he barely heard the question. 'England,' he responded absently.

'And how did you get here?'

'On a boat. I have a friend. He was with me. Alfred. He's called Alfred. Is he here as well?' Shep had a terrible feeling that something bad had happened to him.

'Your friend, Alfred, was on the boat?' the Viracocha repeated, puzzled.

Was he? 'Yes… no. He was. I can't remember. We sailed into a storm, and he was there. And then… there was a mouth.' The dam had burst, and his memories were flooding back, but they were sporadic and in no particular order. 'There was a mouth in the wave. I can't remember what happened. Alfred wasn't there when I woke up.'

Where had he gone?

'You were alone when you arrived. Perhaps your friend didn't complete the journey, but we will look for him.'

Shep remembered how Alfred had been hallucinating before the storm. There was every possibility he could have jumped out or fallen overboard. What other explanation could there be?

'Where am I?' Shep asked. Perhaps he'd misunderstood his host.

'Atalantea,' the Viracocha said plainly.

Clearly, the old man was doolally. 'Am I close to Antigua?' Shep pressed. 'We were heading for Antigua.'

The Viracocha smiled in response as though he hadn't understood the question.

124

'Do you have a phone? Or a computer with internet? I need to make some calls and find out what's happened. They'll be people looking for me. For us.'

The Viracocha squinted. 'No,' he said after a pause.

Shep didn't know what to say to that and so gawped at his host, his tongue flopping around loosely in his mouth.

'You will have many more questions, but rest now. You have eaten your food and water, I see. We will get you more, and we will have a physician look at your pains.' The Viracocha pointed to the bruises and cuts on Shep's arm. 'We will bring fresh clothes for you. We will talk again soon.'

Questions. He had so many questions, yet his mouth wouldn't function. The silly old man hobbled his way out of the room, and Shep closed his eyes, a traffic jam of thoughts beeping loudly in his head.

Sleep came and went in a blur. Maids brought a stream of fresh food and drink. There was a salad with pomegranates and figs; peppers filled with sour cheese; earthy fruit juices; mince and mint potatoes. Shep ate it all, shoveling heaped spoonfuls into his eager mouth. In an adjoining room, he bathed in a white, milky liquid. It penetrated his injuries and absorbed his pain. Then another maid applied an aniseed smelling lotion onto his cuts, which had an instantaneous healing effect. A tunic and a cloak had replaced his normal clothes, and a maid with soft hands and an inquisitive face helped him dress. The clothes were loose and comfortable, and they carried a strange odour he couldn't place. Not unpleasant, but distinctive, like burning incense.

Still lurking at the back of Shep's mind was the thought of the mirror room he'd initially woken up in. It contradicted everything about his current treatment, but the memory was too tangible and vivid to be false.

Shep still didn't know where he was. The old fool had said Atalantea, which sounded a lot like Atlantis, but he didn't even know what a phone was, so he was probably deluded. The bay window in his room looked out onto a courtyard garden. It was beautiful and regal, but it didn't reveal much about his whereabouts, other than that he seemed to be on the second floor of a very grand building.

The only person who had attended to him that could speak English was the old fool, and he hadn't been back since his visit earlier in the day. The maids didn't speak. They barely looked at him, and when they did, he saw fear in their eyes, as though he could turn them to stone like that monster in Greek mythology. What was she called? Medusa? Alfred would know. What had happened to Alfred?

On a few occasions, he'd made to leave the room, but every time he did, someone would come in with more food or drink and signal that he needed to rest. It was as though he was being kept there, forced into staying against his will. More than once, he thought he spotted a guard outside as the door swung open, and he wondered whether he was a prisoner or a guest.

After a day, Shep felt fully replenished and rested. With no television to watch or games to play, he was bored with lying on his bed waiting for some instructions. As he debated whether to march out and demand some answers, the old fool who called himself the Viracocha returned. He looked slightly less dishevelled this time. It was clear he had attempted to wash the muck out of his hair, and he'd put on some clean clothes.

'You feel better?' the Viracocha asked as he walked in.

'Yes, thank you. Much!' Shep said and wondered if there were any customs he should follow when addressing and speaking to his host.

'We are looking for your friend, but maybe he is not here. We will go now for a walk if you are able?'

It was more a statement than a question, but Shep was happy to agree. He was desperate to escape his room and stretch his legs, even though they still ached. 'Yes, please,' he said, swinging his legs off his bed.

They walked out of the room. There was no guard on the door. Perhaps he'd imagined it. The hallway outside his room was grand, with huge paintings of landscapes and battles hung majestically from the walls. Busts of important-looking people stood guard in the corners, watching as they passed. They walked in silence down a wide and decadent staircase towards the entrance. Shep noted that the Viracocha was alarmingly agile for someone who had exceeded his best before date by at least fifty years.

'I will show you the palace,' the Viracocha commented as Shep gazed up at a vast mural that covered the ceiling. A fierce battle was taking place above them, and Shep was caught in the midst of it, with gods and monsters fighting on either side.

'Thanks,' Shep muttered as his eyes tried to process what he was looking at.

The Viracocha followed Shep's gaze. 'Ah, yes. Spectacular, isn't it? Worthy of the muses themselves. It depicts the end of the First Age, which resulted in our isolation,' he said. 'The Athenians in red are being overrun by the superior Atalantean army. But you can see that other forces are about to become involved and, well, here we are. Ultimately, for the greater good. Not that everyone sees it that way. But they will. In time.'

'Hmm,' Shep mumbled. The Viracocha wasn't making much sense. Perhaps it was a biblical reference. He'd never been good with religion.

'Shall we?' the Viracocha asked and gently nudged Shep on.

A guard with a smooth black spear stood at the entrance to the building and let them out. They walked through an archway into a courtyard that had a pathway lined with olive trees and a marble seating area surrounded by potted plants. A colourful mosaic on the floor provided the focal point, and above them, large wooden beams created a pergola with wild, vibrant flowers hanging from it, releasing a herby fragrance into the air.

A ginger cat strolled up to them, and Shep, forgetting himself, bent down to stroke it. He couldn't resist petting cats, and this one looked friendly and well cared for. The Viracocha shook his cane, and the cat hissed before walking off towards the palace. The guard let it in as though it owned the place.

The evening sun was still warm, and Shep was thankful for the loose clothing as they followed the line of olive trees out of the courtyard into another garden.

'What is this place?' Shep asked, pointing to the building behind them. Shep hadn't appreciated how magnificent the building was from his room, but now that he could see its huge white stone pillars, archways, and central tower, he was almost speechless. How could such a place exist without tourists swarming all over it? It was as jaw-dropping as the Taj Mahal but without the clutter and fuss.

'This is the palace and gardens of the high lord and his family, which are located within the citadel,' the Viracocha said. 'You are lucky. Very few are permitted access to the citadel, let alone the palace.' The Viracocha raised his eyebrows and looked accusingly at Shep, as though he had somehow forced his way there.

The palace was perched on top of a hill and looked like it belonged in a fairytale. The gardens flowed downwards via a series of stone steps that levelled out at various points to showcase an exotic garden display or an inspiring water feature, each one more elaborate and impressive than the last. They followed the steps down, and as they walked, the Viracocha commented on the architecture and the history of the gardens. Most of it went over Shep's head, and nothing he said explained why or how Shep was there. The constant flow of information buffeted Shep like a boxer unable to break free of his opponent's embrace, suppressing the questions he was desperate to ask.

They reached the bottom of the last set of steps and arrived at a tall wall that enclosed the palace. Towers intersected the wall, and the only visible way out was through the closed iron gateway.

'This is the only way in and out of the palace,' confirmed the Viracocha. 'The high guard, our very best, man the gates, so you are safe here. The high lord would like you to enjoy his hospitality for a while. You may explore the gardens whilst you recover. You will find them therapeutic.'

It didn't sound like he had much of a choice, but Shep didn't argue. He could be in a worse setting.

The Viracocha carried on the tour, following the wall around the outside of the gardens. The sun was setting behind the palace, casting a perfect ruby semi-circle over it. The sound of cascading water preceded the pièce de résistance. Shep stared in wonder at the tropical waterfall flowing down like a dream into a pool at the bottom. White spray fanned out around it, bringing to life an array of flora. On either side of the waterfall, two streams flowed inexplicably upwards, defying the laws of nature. Steam rose from the one on the left, and little grew near it. Both disappeared into the ground near the top. Questions formed and then crumbled in Shep's head as the conversation turned to his life and his journey. He wondered if it was conversation or interrogation.

The natural light faded as they walked and talked. Shep couldn't tear his eyes away as bioluminescent plants came alive, casting the gardens in a miraculous glaze. Disappointment filled him when the Viracocha led him back to his room, where some food and nightclothes awaited him. Shep felt shattered and mentally exhausted by the tour, but the Viracocha looked like he could still manage a trek up Ben Nevis.

'We will talk again tomorrow,' the Viracocha promised and disappeared. Shep was sure he heard the click of the door being locked from the outside, but he was too tired to check. It would take a nuclear disaster to move him from his bed. The old man had proved himself to be not quite as foolish as Shep had first thought.

Was Atalantea the fabled Atlantis? If he believed his eyes, then, perhaps…

CHAPTER XXIII
The Below

Alfred pushed, squeezed, and climbed his way through the cave network, following the path of glowworms that lit the way like icy blue stars in the night sky. Had he not been suffering from severe hunger pains, he would have marveled at the beauty of nature's phenomenon. Right now, he couldn't care less. Desperation was spreading like a cancer through his resolve, but he wouldn't give in. He'd made it so far.

Every so often, he found unusual markings on the walls, crude carvings made by hand. Someone had been there before and left markers, but try as he might, Alfred couldn't decipher them. So he kept going, relying on instinct and willpower.

Without the sun to guide him, there was no way of knowing how long he'd been awake. Hours? Days? Weeks? Did it matter? He was beyond tired, whatever the time frame.

Unusual sounds occasionally floated through to his ears. Perhaps it was the wind chiseling its way through the rock, perhaps someone shouting for help, or perhaps just his imagination. There had to be a way out. There just had to be.

Alfred squeezed through another tunnel and emerged into a giant chamber. It looked lived-in and homey, in a Neanderthal way. Huge stalagmites rose from the ground, and someone had sawn off the tops for reasons which Alfred wouldn't understand until later that day. Crude tools made from bone and tied with bits of fabric lay discarded in a corner. They could have been there for millennia, although when Alfred inspected one, it looked coated in fresh blood.

He walked to the wall and gently rested up against it. Alfred almost jumped out of his skin when what looked like a centipede the size of his forearm scuttled past on long delicate legs. He felt disgusted at himself that he wanted to bite into it to release some precious calories, but it had long gone by the time he'd decided to catch it. A few of those would keep him going for a few more hours. That was assuming he could bypass his gag reflex. He wasn't sure he could ignore the crunch as he bit into it or the taste and feel of its squelching innards swirling around his mouth.

Alfred heard a scuttling sound from the other side of the cavern. Tiny legs skittering across the hard floor. He went to investigate and discovered red roaches feasting on the remains of a bat. The roaches looked pumped up on steroids, and when they sensed Alfred's approach, they quickly dispersed, leaving the bat's hollowed-out carcass for him. He looked at its tattered, ripped wings and decided he could manage a little while longer without food.

Tunnels led off in various directions from the cavern. As Alfred decided which one to take, he heard a grunting sound, like a bear clearing its throat. He wondered if he'd imagined it, but then he heard it again, this time clearer and closer. The hairs on the back of his neck stood on end. He ducked behind a rock and covered his pendant to hide its light.

Two figures emerged from a tunnel on Alfred's right. He could sense them and hear their footsteps, but he could only see their distorted shadows on the wall. They could be cavers, but the way they crept on their toes and felt their way around the cavern seemed odd. Their grunts and sniffs were animalistic. They came closer to where Alfred was hiding, and he could smell them now, sewage mixed with rotting flesh and vomit. He held his breath, his eyes stinging.

Suddenly, he had a great desire to cough. A tiny feather was brushing up and down the inside of his throat, and it was unbearable. The two figures became animated and communicated in grunt-like noises, confirming to Alfred that whatever had entered the cavern was not human.

They moved around into Alfred's field of vision, and he froze, his eyes unblinking as he watched the creatures in disbelief. They looked like humans who had escaped from a lifetime of torture. Their bodies were naked save for scraps of scraggly hair that saved some of their dignity. They were sinewy and deformed, with tumours growing grotesquely from their limbs and necks. Their drawn, pale faces were a vision of torment. Their broad noses and big ears would have looked comical had it not been for the sockets where their eyes used to sit.

Alfred held his breath and watched as they switched to moving on all fours. The tickle was getting worse. He needed to clear his throat. One cocked its head in Alfred's direction, and its empty sockets stared straight at him, seeing everything and nothing. The creature sniffed the air and made a deep gurgling noise. Its companion added its voice, and the noise intensified until it was deafening. Alfred coughed gently into his hand, hoping it would go unnoticed.

It didn't.

They moved with lightning speed. Before Alfred even had the chance to look up, they were on him, knocking him onto his back on the floor. Alfred swung his arms and kicked his legs. He smashed something with his foot and then felt sharp teeth bite into his hand. He screamed, convinced the creature had ripped it clean off. Another set of teeth clamped down on his thigh. The grip was vice-like, his pain unbearable.

He kicked out with his other leg, but it was weak, and his shin collided with a stalagmite. He felt like an antelope, caught by two lions. A sharp fingernail scraped across his chin, over his mouth and nose, and then eased inexorably towards his eye. Something inside of Alfred snapped. He tensed and then, with all the strength he could muster, pushed his hand deep into the first creature's mouth and down its throat, forcing it to gag and release him.

Alfred grabbed the finger that had been teasing his face and bit down hard. The first creature let out a high-pitched scream and withdrew as Alfred spat its bony digit onto the floor. Alfred switched his attention to the second creature, which was pinning down his leg. He kicked at its face with the bottom of his foot and felt a deep satisfaction as he connected with its nose, and it fell away.

Alfred scrambled to his feet. His left hand was in tatters, and he couldn't straighten his middle three fingers. His trousers had largely saved his thigh, but he could still feel blood running down his leg and couldn't put much weight on it. The two creatures regrouped and circled him, their mouths deep pits of anger.

What the hell are you? Alfred thought to himself. He had fought them off the first time, but he wouldn't be so lucky again. The creatures were conditioned perfectly for moving and climbing around the caves, and he'd used up all of his energy.

Alfred stood still, hoping that if he didn't make a sound, they wouldn't be able to detect him. But even without eyes, they knew where he was. They could smell him.

The second creature climbed effortlessly around the wall into Alfred's blind spot. The first creature, the one whose finger he had bitten off, moved in front of him. Alfred braced himself for an attack, hoping they would make it quick.

He sensed a movement from behind and turned as the second creature jumped towards him. Something whistled past Alfred's ear, and the creature's lifeless body landed on him. The first creature had disappeared out of sight, but Alfred could hear it screaming. Then the screaming stopped and was replaced by the sound of footsteps moving unhurriedly towards him.

Someone, or something, dragged the second creature's body off of him. Alfred sat up and watched as a man put his foot on the creature's back and wrestled his spear out of its head. He stared at the pendant that had come loose from around Alfred's neck with a puzzled expression on his face and then looked away.

His rescuer didn't look like a typical hero. He was skinny and dressed in rags, which hung loosely off his skeletal frame. His hair and beard were long, and a large scar ran across his milky right eye. He was impossible to age. He could have been as old as the caves or just out of childhood.

Alfred began to thank him and then trailed off when he saw his rescuer's death stare. Instead, he followed him to the first creature that sat crumpled in a pool of blood, multiple stab wounds evidence of its violent death.

The man wrapped Alfred's hand and thigh with some of his rags to stem the bleeding without saying a word. The bites had penetrated deep and would need stitches, but he had broken no bones or suffered any irreparable damage, which was a miracle. The man bent down and pretended to rub the creature's blood on his body. Alfred watched bemused before realising that he was being asked to copy in order to mask his smell. He reluctantly obeyed, unable to look at what he was doing.

The rescuer nodded and then walked away. Unwanted but desperate, Alfred followed. The man was quick and agile, and Alfred fell behind, his injuries hindering him. Then the man disappeared down a tunnel and was out of sight by the time Alfred crawled his way through.

'Slow down,' Alfred pleaded.

The sound of scurrying echoed around him, and he realised his mistake. A cold, firm hand grabbed him and dragged him forcefully into a small crevice. A minute later, a dozen creatures scuttled their way past, sniffing the air through their pronounced noses.

Alfred's entire body was shivering. His hand and thigh were pulsating. He felt sick, and he was certain the creatures could smell his blood-drenched rags, but then their footsteps faded, and the man led him deeper into the caves. This time, more slowly.

The tunnels grew darker and tighter, and Alfred once again found himself submerged in an underground lake. This time, the passage through was less claustrophobic. When he came out, he discovered that the man had led him to his home, or what passed for a home in a cave. Markings covered the wall, and a makeshift bed was in the corner, made from what looked like skin, although Alfred didn't want to investigate. Tools and weapons covered the floor, along with the remnants of a half-eaten animal. It was impossible to tell what it was.

The man offered Alfred some water in a bowl, and he took it gratefully. It was only as he took a deep gulp that he realised the bowl was the top half of a human skull. He dropped it on the floor in shock. It clattered and rolled, making a horrendous din that seemed never ending. The man looked at him, horrified. His mouth looked for the words but couldn't find them. Instead, he said something which Alfred assumed was a curse, picked up his makeshift weapons, and ran.

Alfred, sensing he was about to lose his only hope of survival, followed.

CHAPTER XXIV

Rhamnus, Syros

Axil scratched his chin and cleared his throat in the penitence booth. The seat was wooden and uncomfortable, with curves and spikes on the armrests and back. It made it impossible to rest for any longer than a few seconds in the same position without picking up an injury. He'd been waiting for over an hour.

He'd returned to his room the previous night to find a sealed note waiting for him. Axil had told no one where he was staying, but the Paymaster had eyes and ears everywhere, so his silence made no difference. It was always the same whenever the Paymaster wanted anything. A cryptic sealed note was delivered anonymously to whatever room he was staying in, demanding an urgent meeting.

Axil heard a movement in the booth next to him and took a deep breath, pleased the Paymaster couldn't see his expression.

'I hope you have good news for me,' a familiar voice said, with no apology or explanation for the tardiness.

Axil had practised his response the night before. 'I've made some interesting discoveries,' he said. 'Some good, some not so.' Alfred paused, waiting for a response, but the Paymaster remained silent. Axil cleared his throat. 'Mneseus and Elasippus will vote against the decision.'

'That much was obvious. Everyone knows they hated the high lord. I hope you have more than that.'

'Yes,' said Axil, a little too sharply. The Paymaster seemed in a particularly foul mood this morning. 'Castor, Governor Azaes that is, will vote against the move.'

'Governor Azaes?' The Paymaster sounded surprised. 'On what basis? His father was a great ally to the high lord.'

'I found him in a compromising position, and he was quick to see my point of view after that.' Axil held some information back.

Silence met his comment.

'And Governor Autochthon will also vote against the motion,' Axil said after a pause.

'His son, the irrepressible Ganymede, will not be happy if his father votes against his beloved.' The Paymaster didn't sound convinced.

Axil felt irritation creep over his skin and prickle him. 'No, but if Hestia becomes high lady, any chance of a union between her and Ganymede will disappear.'

'True,' the Paymaster conceded. 'Good. Who else?'

Was that a compliment? Axil took a deep breath. It was the moment he had been dreading. 'All the other governors intend to vote in favour of the motion,' he blurted.

The Paymaster grunted. Axil screwed up his face, waiting for a reprimand or a snide comment, but the Paymaster remained silent. Axil waited nervously.

'Hestia has been making promises to the governors, buying their votes,' Axil said to break the silence.

'What sort of promises?'

Hestia had been clever and used her time wisely. She had approached each governor and set out a detailed plan on how she could help each one invest and develop their realm. Her actions had impressed Axil. She had the drive and tenacity needed to become a very popular high lady, but Axil kept his opinion to himself.

'She's promised to commit funds to improve the canal network throughout the Adelphi realm to ensure Governor Gadeirus stays faithful to the Capital. Not that he would go against his closest friend's wishes, but opening up additional trade routes will improve efficiency and bring in more money for the Capital through taxes, so it's a smart move. For Syros, she's told Governor Ampheres that she will help complete the extension and restoration work on Demeter's Temple, which is… needed.'

Falling masonry had almost killed him as he'd walked into the temple, and Axil mused that the work would need completing sooner rather than later. Otherwise, there would be no temple to restore.

He continued. 'To Governor Diaprepes, she's offered to revisit the payments for the dissolution of the tridents to ensure that Attica has sufficient time and resources to replace its primary source of income with an alternative.'

Attica had been solely responsible for training the tridents, Atalantea's elite soldiers. The other realms had supported it for this service, but there had been no wars for millennia and so no requirement for elite soldiers. When the high lord dissolved the Trident Programme, Attica's income went with it, and so the high lord had agreed to provide funding to Attica to offset the harm suffered. The period of funding was about to end, and Attica's towns were still falling to rack and ruin. Axil had heard that Hestia had placed conditions on the additional funding, which would give her greater control over Diaprepes's spending. Technically, it was contrary to the Order, which required governors to have autonomy over their realms, but Diaprepes had no option but to accept it. His subjects were on the verge of an uprising.

'What else?' the Paymaster said impatiently.

'She's promised the next Games to the Tinos realm to keep Governor Evaemon happy. For Governor Mestor, she's promised to supply him with ten boats to help him shift his supplies to the other realms. His fleet needs replacing, and he has limited funds, so he was planning on taxing his subjects, which wouldn't have gone down well. I don't know about the rest, but she seems to have a plan for everyone, and she's very convincing.'

'Her brother hasn't helped things. His petty act at the funeral hasn't gone down well with the governors, and now he's holding the middling hostage at the palace and refusing to let anyone other than the Viracocha see him. I heard he planned on letting the middling rot or go insane in the reflection room, but the Viracocha talked him round. He convinced Attalus we need to learn what we can from him. It doesn't help that the Viracocha is the only one who can understand a word the middling says. Apparently.' Axil wasn't convinced the Viracocha understood anything the middling was saying. It seemed inconceivable that he could learn the language so quickly.

'How did you come by this information?' The Paymaster sounded mildly impressed.

'Mostly housekeepers and maids. They hear and see things. Lots of things, as it happens, and they're cheap.' Or free if you treat them well enough, Axil thought to himself. Castor had been wise to take his affair outside of the Capital.

'Unless Attalus relaxes his approach and lets the governors decide the middling's fate, the others are unlikely to vote for him, and I can't see that happening. He's set his guards on the gate to the palace, and there's no way in or out. If Attalus used the middling to bargain with the governors, then there's a chance, but he's a fool and won't listen to reason. He sees himself as the hero who single-handedly saved Atalantea. He doesn't realise that the middling divides the people. Half want to kill him, half want to welcome him. His actions have already caused riots.'

'His actions were… unfortunate, but necessary. We must offer the middling to appease the Saviour. The girl would no doubt try to save him. It is a weakness in the fairer sex and another reason we cannot allow her to succeed. What is your plan to convince the other governors?' asked the Paymaster.

Axil thought he'd made the position clear, but he should have known better. The Paymaster didn't accept failure. 'There is one thing,' Axil said. It was his last resort, and it was perilous, but he was desperate.

'I cannot gain access to the palace or influence Attalus, but…' he reflected on his next words, 'there is a possibility of getting one more vote. But it still wouldn't be enough,' he added hastily.

'One more vote would be enough,' said the Paymaster.

Axil was about to argue that they needed six votes for the motion to pass but thought better of it. The Paymaster was not an idiot and would not take kindly to any inference that he was. Axil took a deep breath. 'Governor Evaemon would never vote in favour of Attalus. I know him. I worked for him, and he's clean. But his son, Alec, has spoken out against the motion, and I've heard that he's held rallies in Tinos whilst his father has been in the Capital.'

'Yes, I have heard about those. It has all been very embarrassing for Governor Evaemon. How does that help?'

'When there was the attempt on Evaemon's life a few years ago, the one I prevented, the incident left him too shaken to travel to the Capital for the governors' annual meeting. He sent his son instead.'

'Yes,' the Paymaster said impatiently.

'The power Evaemon signed, which entitled Alec to vote on his behalf, has never been revoked. It's still valid. I've seen it, and I have a copy.' Axil let the sentence hang.

'Yes, I see,' the Paymaster muttered to himself. 'If the father is absent, then the son can take his seat, and we have another vote. What of the daughter? What happened to her? Would she not be a problem?'

'Kallista. She ran away when her father tried to force her into a union with Governor Mneseus's son, Leonidas. No one's seen her for years. I don't even know if she lives. Probably not if Mneseus had his way.'

Axil had been young when it happened, around thirteen. Kallista was only slightly older. Leonidas was double her age and had a fiery temper. It was said that he had macabre inclinations, and he never sought to quell the rumours. His first wife had died under suspicious circumstances, and Axil couldn't blame Kallista for running away.

'Yes, I remember now. So, remove your old master, and we will have Alec's vote. Will you be able to remove him?'

Axil's eyes grew wide. He hadn't meant to suggest that he would carry out the act. He was merely pointing out some information.

'It would have to be clean,' continued the Paymaster, oblivious to Axil's stuttering. 'Nothing that would arouse suspicion. They will use trackers to find him if they think there's been foul play. Use the Botanist. Her methods have been very successful recently.'

Axil shivered at the thought of the men on the Paymaster's list who had no doubt been sent to her. On his orders.

What have you got yourself involved in?

He couldn't think straight. He felt like he was drowning.

'It would have to be outside of the Capital,' he mumbled when he realised the Paymaster was waiting for him to speak. 'There's no way I could remove him whilst he's in the Capital. There are too many people.'

I'll die before I get close!

'Evaemon will receive a letter,' the Paymaster said. 'It will require him to attend a meeting at the old temple ruins on the outskirts of Dionysus Forest in two days. Do you know the place?'

Axil's head was spinning, and he didn't register the question.

'Do you know the place?' the Paymaster asked again.

'Yes,' muttered Axil.

'The meeting will take place when the sun is at its highest point. He will be alone. Take him to the Botanist and let her take care of him with her... methods.'

'Yes,' Axil responded as he stared fixedly ahead, pinching his forehead.

'Do not fail me in this,' the Paymaster said threateningly. 'The hope and future of Atalantea rest on the motion failing. We have pushed the Saviour too far already. We must right the wrongs made by the former high lord before it's too late.'

'Yes,' Axil said again, unconvinced by the Paymaster's theology but too afraid to dissent.

'If the governors pass the motion, it will take more extreme measures to right the wrongs. That will be on you. Think on that. Now leave.'

Axil left quietly, wondering what the Paymaster meant by his last comment.

CHAPTER XXV

Kea

Kaspa felt ill. It was just nerves, but that didn't help.

'You got the supplies and ropes?' his brother, Erik, asked. He didn't look worried at all, but that was typical Erik, calm and collected no matter the situation. He never seemed to break into a sweat, and Kaspa wished he could take after him. Instead, he was more like his mother, a worrier, always overthinking things.

He'd lost Eimalfred in the forest as he'd run away. When he'd gone back to find him, he'd spied Breon and Timolt hovering over a large opening and assumed the worst. He'd quickly left the scene, afraid of what the pair would do to him if they discovered him. Kaspa made his way home, only for the incident to gatecrash his mind at every opportunity. He hadn't been able to sleep, and his mind kept shooting down rabbit holes where he would imagine different outcomes, all of them grave and sickening.

It had been Erik who had forced him to open up about the incident. When he did, the words had exploded out in a muddle, and he'd overlapped and confused events. By the end, Kaspa wasn't even sure what had happened. Erik told him to forget about it. There wasn't anything else Kaspa could have done, and he'd tried his best. If Eimalfred had fallen Below, then only the gods could save him.

Erik's reassurance had put him at ease, but then he heard news that a middling had washed up in the Capital during the high lord's funeral, which made no sense at all. If Eimalfred was the middling, there was no way he could have travelled to the Capital so quickly after running away. There was no plausible explanation. Who had fallen down the hole? He needed to know.

The stress had reached boiling point, and Erik found him one day shaking uncontrollably in his bakery. Erik had listened to Kaspa's hysterics silently and patiently, and then told him what they needed to do. They had to find the entrance to the Below and look. If Eimalfred was down there, then the likelihood was he'd be dead, but they could recover the body and hand it to the authorities. Erik was insistent that Kaspa wasn't to blame for what had happened, but if recovering the body was necessary to clear his conscience, then so be it.

Erik always had the answer, whatever the situation, and he always knew how to make Kaspa feel better.

'Take this, just in case,' Erik said, handing Kaspa a machete. It was far larger than the one he usually carried, but it looked small in Erik's hand. He didn't think he'd need such a weapon, but he knew better than to challenge his brother.

They walked to the spot where Kaspa had initially found Eimalfred on the beach and retraced Kaspa's steps through the forest until they reached the path where Breon and Timolt had confronted them.

'I shouted at Eimalfred from here,' Kaspa said, crouching down in the spot, 'and we ran in that direction.' He pointed towards the dense forest terrain, and the incident played out in his mind. He could almost hear Breon and Timolt's voices and was pleased Erik was there to act as his safety blanket.

'I can see tracks,' Erik said as he squatted down. 'And there's a footprint here.'

Erik spent days, sometimes weeks, tracking down wild animals in the forests of Atalantea just to say he'd caught a glance of a pigmy elephant or a snarler. Kaspa would listen, fascinated, when Erik returned from his latest adventure, hanging on to his every word, wishing he was brave enough to go with him. Most of the more unusual species were on the brink of extinction, but Erik had tracked down most of what remained of the island's fauna. He'd even claimed to have spotted the woodland nymphs once, although Kaspa was fairly certain he must have been mistaken.

'There are some obvious tracks here!' Erik shouted.

He was almost out of sight, so Kaspa caught up with him.

'You must have been running fast because the footprints are far apart. And you can see here that Breon and Timolt must have been right behind because their prints are mixed. I wonder what they were doing here.'

After a few minutes, they reached the clearing. It wasn't as deep into the forest as Kaspa remembered.

'This is it,' Kaspa commented. 'The drop is over there.' He pointed to a hole in the ground on their right.

'There?' Erik said, confused. Long grass obscured the opening, and from a distance, it looked no bigger than a rabbit burrow.

'I kept on running. I didn't even see the gap,' Kaspa said. 'I guess I'm lucky because I could have easily fallen down there.'

'Thank the gods,' Erik muttered as he peered down into the void. 'Oh, wow, it really opens up!'

'Can you see anything?' Kaspa asked and leaned over to look into the hole. He felt faint. He hated heights.

'No, there's quite a drop there, and I can't see the bottom. Hello?!' he shouted hopefully, but there was no response. 'We'll go look,' he said.

Kaspa felt bile rising and couldn't respond.

'I'll go look,' Erik said upon seeing Kaspa's green face.

Kaspa hovered, kicking grass, as Erik tied the ropes around a sturdy-looking rubber tree and created a harness.

'I'll need you to take my weight and help me back up,' Erik told Kaspa.

Kaspa nodded as Erik climbed down the rope that hung loosely into the abyss. Kaspa kept hold of the rope attached to Erik and let it gently slide through his fingers as his brother made his way down. Then the rope became slack as Erik reached the bottom.

'Water!' Kaspa heard his brother cry. 'I'm in a pool of water.'

'Do you see him?' Kaspa shouted back.

'Give me a chance!'

Kaspa waited impatiently, wondering what his brother was doing down there. Then there was light as Erik lit a torch.

'I can't see him, but there's blood on the walls,' Erik shouted up. 'It looks fresh! I think he was here!'

'Has he gone?'

'He's not here, but there's nowhere for him to go, so I will check the water!'

Kaspa paced as he waited. The thought of Breon and Timolt stumbling into the scene made him nervous. Why was Erik taking so long?

A shout interrupted his thoughts. 'Nothing! There's nothing down here, but there's a small gap that seems to head somewhere. I can't fit through, but someone smaller could. I'm coming up now!'

Kaspa breathed out, relieved.

'Pull me up, then!' Erik shouted.

Kaspa pulled on the rope.

'Not so much!' Erik yelled, and Kaspa muttered his apologies.

Erik's drenched body eventually appeared, and he scrambled out of the gap onto the grass. 'That was an effort,' he said after he'd gotten his breath back.

'What do you think happened?' Kaspa asked.

'I think he was there, or someone definitely was. There was blood splattered in various places. I had a good look and couldn't see or feel anything, so I think he must have tried to escape through the tunnel. I couldn't see any other way out. It's funny, though. I was sure I could hear something down there, like a rumbling.'

'I wonder if Breon and Timolt pulled him out?' Kaspa thought aloud.

'No,' Erik replied with conviction. 'We would have seen another set of tracks if they'd returned here, and we would have heard about it. Those two wouldn't be able to keep something like that secret.'

A thought struck Kaspa. 'I think there might be another entrance to the Below. I spotted it a while ago when I took a different route through the forest. It's a bit of a walk, but I'm sure I can find it. The tunnel could connect through to it. If we shouted for him there, then maybe he could follow our voices.'

'It's a long shot, Kaspa. He could be anywhere. Maybe he got trapped in that tunnel and drowned. He could even be the person they're talking about in the Capital.'

'We've got to give it a go,' Kaspa pleaded. 'At least then we've done everything we can.'

Erik looked at him for a moment and then smiled. 'Right then, lead the way. We'll give it a quick check, then head home. Then, please, you'll just have to let it go.'

Kaspa led Erik back to the beach and then along a path through the northern edge of the forest. Although it wasn't much of a path at all, it looked vaguely familiar but had become overgrown and was difficult to follow.

'What in the underworld were you doing here?' Erik asked as a branch flew back and hit him across the top of his head.

'Just walking. Exploring, I guess.'

'Well, make sure you take care when you go off on these little expeditions. If you ever went missing, we'd never know what had happened to you. There's no way we'd find you.'

Kaspa smiled. At eighteen, he was a man, but he'd always be a little brother. And Erik was hardly one to talk, given the sort of dangerous adventures he went on. 'I don't stray too far, don't worry. We're nearly there, I think.'

'Good, I was beginning to think you had no idea where we were.'

The vegetation grew thicker until it became impassable. 'This is where I followed it around to the left to find a way past. We're not far away.'

Kaspa felt a surge of energy and picked up the pace. The ground rose steeply on their right, and they followed it for about ten minutes until they reached an entrance obscured by leaves and branches. 'This is it.' Kaspa grinned as he led Erik into a small cave hidden in the hillside.

On the ground in front of them was a circular opening, just big enough for one person to squeeze through.

'Well, it must go somewhere,' Erik muttered as he leaned in with a fresh torch to look. 'There's a platform a short distance down and then another drop. Let's get roped up. I can't see properly from here.'

Kaspa waited as Erik found somewhere to tie the ropes, and then they both squeezed through the opening down to the first platform.

Erik lit a torch and threw it. They watched as it fell through the air, lighting up the cavern. It took a few seconds for the torch to hit the ground, and Kaspa felt his stomach jump into his throat when he realised how steep the drop was. The ledge suddenly seemed minuscule.

'Good job, the ropes are long.' Erik smiled as Kaspa sat down and hugged his knees, his world spinning.

Erik climbed down using the rope and wall whilst Kaspa closed his eyes and took some deep breaths.

'I'll have a look around!' Erik shouted as his feet hit the ground. Kaspa barely heard him, using meditation to control himself. It was a trick his sister, Ariadne, had taught him to use whenever he was feeling overwhelmed, and it seemed to work well.

After a few minutes, Kaspa's breathing returned to normal, and the world stopped spinning. He could even look down into the cavern without feeling sick, but something didn't feel right. He didn't know what it was, but it was something. The air was electric. With each minute that passed, the feeling grew. Time seemed to slow. Every few seconds, he crawled closer to the edge of the platform. When he looked down, the torch was fading, and it was difficult to see anything.

What was Erik doing? He was just supposed to take a quick look.

'Erik!' Kaspa shouted angrily.

There was no response.

'Erik!' he shouted again, but still nothing.

Kaspa knew something wasn't right. They weren't supposed to be there. The cave seemed to be... howling. He couldn't just sit when Erik could be in danger. He had to go down. Before he changed his mind, Kaspa gripped the rope tightly and descended.

In through your nose. Out through your mouth. In through your nose. Out through your mouth.

It seemed to take forever, but then his feet hit the floor, and he relaxed a little. He shook his arms and legs to release the tension, but they still tingled. The torch Erik had thrown down earlier had burned out, and it took a few minutes for Kaspa's eyes to adjust to the darkness. He shouted for Erik again, but there was no sign of him. There were four potential routes he could have taken. Kaspa took a quick look down each one and shouted, but nothing. Why wasn't he responding?

A quick look, he'd said. He should have been back by now.

146

A high-pitched screech came from a tunnel. He couldn't tell which one, but it made him jump. What in Hades made that noise?

Kaspa could hear his heartbeat thumping wildly. He should have trusted his instincts. He shouldn't be down there. Where had he taken Erik? They should have gone home.

'Erik!' Kaspa screamed desperately. He needed to control his breathing.

In through your nose. Out through your mouth…

Then footsteps echoed through the cave. Someone, or something, was running. The sounds grew louder, and Kaspa shouted for Erik again, edging back towards the rope. The walls seemed to be closing in. The footsteps were getting closer. They were fast and panicked. He could hear other noises now, heavy breathing and panting.

In through your nose. Out through your mouth…

Kaspa shouted again, and three figures emerged from a tunnel. The first had long hair and a thick beard that emphasised his gaunt face. His eyes were wide, and there was a look of fear in them. The second was Eimalfred, and Kaspa's heart lifted when he saw him. The third looked badly injured and was at the back, his swollen face staring at the ground. All three carried weapons and had the same wild and desperate expression on their faces.

'What hap—'

'Climb,' urged the one at the back, and Kaspa gasped. It was Erik. What had happened to him? Had he fallen?

'Erik, what's going on?'

'Climb!' he begged.

Kaspa heard the panic in his brother's voice and started the long climb to the first platform, survival instinct overriding his fear of heights. He'd been so distracted that he hadn't heard the noises coming from the other tunnels, but they were clear now. Snarls and growls so haunting, Kaspa wondered whether Hades had let loose the Furies. Adrenaline pushed Kaspa up the rope quicker than he thought possible. The bearded man followed, and then Eimalfred. All three of them dangling precariously.

The noises grew louder and then exploded into the cavern. Erik shouted desperately at the bottom.

Was he climbing?

Kaspa tried to look down, but all he could see was the bearded man's bulging eyes urging him up. His arms and legs were exhausted from the effort. Going down had been a lot easier. Then his hand hit the first platform, and he hauled himself up. The bearded man followed a few seconds later, but Eimalfred was slow. It looked like he was struggling to grip the rope with his hand and was having to use his legs more. Erik was nowhere to be seen. Kaspa could only hear the snarls and screeches of whatever monsters lurked in the darkness below.

Was he climbing the rope? Please let him be on the rope.

Kaspa found another torch in Erik's supplies. He lit it and dropped it into the cavern. He let out a moan, seeing Erik was still at the bottom of the rope. Every time Erik tried to climb, a creature jumped at him, and he had to fight it off. More creatures were entering the cavern every second.

'Climb!' Kaspa shouted desperately. He was in tears, searching desperately through Erik's bag for something that might help, but there was nothing.

Eimalfred's bandaged hand reached the platform, and the bearded man dragged him up. The climb had taken everything out of him, and he could barely move.

'Cut the rope!' Erik shouted as he slashed his machete at two creatures.

'No!' screamed Kaspa. 'Climb! You have to climb!' He could barely get the words out. Tears were streaming down his face as he watched his brother slash at another monster.

'Cut the rope! There are too many of them, and they will reach you!' Erik shouted back between breaths. Kaspa gasped when he realized a creature had almost reached the ledge. The bearded man plunged his makeshift spear into the top of the creature's head, and it fell to the ground.

'We have to cut the rope,' the bearded man said softly.

'We're not cutting the rope! We can't leave him. That's my brother,' Kaspa sobbed.

Climb! Just climb!

His head was telling him it was impossible, but his heart wouldn't give up. It was his brother, and he'd forced him to go down there.

Then Kaspa saw a creature jump on Erik. He slashed at it but couldn't fight it off, and the creature dragged him to the floor. Kaspa watched helplessly as three more joined in, scratching and biting.

Erik punched and kicked, but to no avail. He couldn't get his arms and legs free enough to gain any leverage.

Kaspa screamed at them to leave Erik alone, but his words caught in his throat. He couldn't comprehend what he was seeing, refusing to believe it.

Still, more creatures entered the cavern. There had to be over one hundred of them now, and without Erik protecting the rope, more were climbing up. Kaspa couldn't breathe. It couldn't be real.

'Climb,' Kaspa whispered. He was on his knees, sobbing. Unable to function.

'I'm sorry,' said the bearded man. Kaspa didn't hear him, his conscience having left his body.

The bearded man cut the rope to stop the beasts from reaching them, and someone forced Kaspa up the second rope to the safety of the forest. Minutes passed, but it could have been hours or even days. He felt numb and had no words for what he'd just seen.

It was a quick look!

Why had he taken him there? Even now, he refused to believe what had happened. It had to be a joke. Erik would appear in a minute, and they would laugh. So, Kaspa sat on the ground, his head in his hands, waiting. But Erik didn't appear.

Eventually, the bearded man approached him. 'We need to leave,' he said.

Kaspa knew it was true, but he didn't want to, so he didn't respond. He didn't have the energy. Then the tears came, and he didn't attempt to stop them.

'What were they?' Kaspa asked when he could speak again.

'Androphagi,' the bearded man said.

Kaspa vomited on the ground.

CHAPTER XXVI

Dionysus Forest, Tinos

The orichalcum plants had caught black rot. It attacked the roots, and by the time any symptoms were showing, it was usually too late to do anything. The Botanist had discovered it before it had destroyed the whole nursery, but it had wiped out at least a quarter of the plants. Still, she should have spotted it earlier.

No. Her assistant should have spotted it. The stupid boy had a lot to learn.

There was a knock on the door. 'What?' said the Botanist sharply.

Her assistant's face appeared, and he nervously cleared his throat. She had been hard on him earlier, and she'd scared him. Good.

'What?' the Botanist said again.

'There's um... he... the man. Axil? I think he said that was his name last time. He's here.'

The Botanist smiled absently, then pursed her lips when she remembered her assistant was looking at her. 'Very well. Bring him through to the front room.' She didn't want him to see the state of her orichalcum nursery.

'There's... um, something else.'

'Yes?'

'He's got someone here with him.'

The Botanist felt anger surge inside of her. How dare he disclose her whereabouts to others! 'Who?' she said, her voice calm amidst the yelling in her head.

'I don't... I don't know. Should I ask? He's... well... I don't... I don't know if he's conscious. He's like the others.' Her assistant whispered the last sentence.

The Botanist breathed out and relaxed. The Paymaster had paid her well to deal with a steady influx of unconscious, or barely conscious, bodies since her last meeting with Axil. She didn't know who any of them were, and she didn't know what they had done. It was safer that way, for her conscience, anyway. Axil didn't seem the sort to get involved in that side of the business, though. Something must have happened.

'Bring the body to the front. I'll deal with it,' the Botanist said and waved her assistant away.

The Botanist looked at her reflection in the window and tried to sort out her hair. It was a tangled mess. Mud caked her fingernails, and it had smeared all over her face. She was in no state for seeing anyone, but duty called. She tidied herself up as best she could, annoyed that she even cared what she looked like, and then went to see her guest.

'Axil,' she said as she walked into the front room. The man looked different. He had lost the confidence and surety he carried with him when they first met. He looked as though he hadn't slept in weeks. 'What do I owe the pleasure?'

'I need to make use of your services,' Axil muttered, unable to make eye contact.

He didn't make a joke or introductions, just a demand. She felt disappointed. 'I didn't think you were here on a social visit. What is it you require?'

'I need someone to disappear.'

'Not possible. Not right away, anyway. Usually, I get notice when my services are required?' She was being short with him, but she was disappointed with how formal he was being.

'Why?'

'It's too soon since the last feed. Why can't you get rid of him? I assume it's a him? The rest of them have been. Throw him in a hole. Bury him deep. Why do you need me?'

Axil's brow furrowed as though she'd offended him.

'I have explicit instructions that there can be no trace of this individual. Trackers can dig up a hole and detect human traces.'

'Trackers? Who on Mount Olympus have you brought me? You could lead them straight here,' the Botanist said, fear creeping in. Trackers were only used when it was someone important or someone with money.

'Yes, but they wouldn't find him, would they?' Axil said dismissively.

'No,' said the Botanist crossly. He was missing the point. 'They would find a lot of other incriminating evidence, though, wouldn't they?'

'We have been careful to ensure that his absence can be accounted for so that there is no suspicion of foul play, and we have covered our tracks. If you have concerns, you should take appropriate steps or take it up with the Paymaster.'

What did he mean by "appropriate steps"?

'You need to make sure that monstrosity of yours does its job,' Axil said.

The Botanist pushed down her fury. It would be unseemly for her to let her emotions control her. This was business.

'Who is it? Why is he so important?' The Botanist knew she shouldn't ask, but the stakes had been pushed up, and she wanted to know what she was getting herself into.

'It's better you don't know. The less you know, the better,' Axil said forcefully.

No. Not anymore. This was too much. 'He's alive, I assume?' she asked.

'Obviously! You told me that monstrosity only senses live food.'

Gyges is not a monster.

The Botanist fixed Axil with a stare, and he weakened.

'If you must know,' he said, 'the Paymaster called him to a meeting at the old ruins, and I ambushed him there. He didn't even see me. He's unconscious but unhurt. I used seed of valerian to subdue him.'

The Botanist grunted. She had probably provided it. 'Where is he?' she asked.

'Outside.'

'Show me.'

Axil led the Botanist outside to where he'd tied his horse. A cart with several large sacks in the back sat nearby. Most of the sacks appeared to contain vegetables, but one looked different from the rest, and she knew it must contain the body. She could tell, just from looking, that whoever was in there was around 6 feet tall and slightly overweight. 'I won't be able to do anything for at least a day,' she said. 'How long will he be out?'

Axil let out a deep sigh and scratched the top of his head. 'I don't know. Twelve hours at most, and he's already been out for two hours. Just do whatever you need to do. You can keep the cart.'

'I will do as you ask, but only if you tell me what's going on.'

'You know I can't. That's not the deal.'

'The deal's changed. I never agreed to this. And it seems you need me more than I need you.'

'It's better you don't know.'

'I'll decide what is or isn't good for me. No man has ever told me what to do.'

Axil weighed her up, but the Botanist wasn't playing around. If trackers could get involved, she needed to know what she was up against. How else could she properly prepare for the potential repercussions?

'Or do you want to dispose of him yourself?' she asked, and Axil bridled at the suggestion.

'Before his death, the high lord brought forward the Equality-For-All Motion—'

'I know that much. I may be cut off here, but I have my ears.'

Axil ignored the interruption. 'There's a vote on whether to bring the motion forward. If it passes, then the girl will be the first high lady.'

'Hestia?' The Botanist liked the sound of that. She didn't know a lot about Hestia, but it was about time a female took charge of the pompous governors. A female leader might get something done.

'The Paymaster needs it to fail. The boy, Attalus, must succeed his father.'

'Why?'

'What more do you need to know? The Paymaster wants the boy to succeed, and we're paid to make sure it happens. I didn't ask him to explain himself to me.' Axil sounded frustrated.

'So you don't know. You just blindly walk into whatever he tells you to do, and you expect me to do the same?'

'Yes, I do. And if you don't, you know what will happen.'

'Who's in the sack?' the Botanist asked again, this time with more authority.

Axil looked at his feet. His shoulders were slumped, and he looked exhausted. 'I tried to convince the governors to see the benefits of voting for Attalus,' he muttered, almost to himself. 'But he is such a fool, and Hestia has been clever. The numbers are against us, so I had to think of something else—'

'You've brought a governor here!' The Botanist interrupted him. She didn't like it. She didn't like it one bit. 'You fool,' she chided. 'Have you any idea what this could mean for me?'

'I have been careful. Do not underestimate me,' he said impatiently.

The Botanist scratched her chin and took a few deep breaths. She needed to think. Axil stood with his hands on his hips, waiting for a response.

'What has Attalus done?' she asked. 'You said he has been foolish.'

'You don't know?'

'Would I ask if I knew?'

'I thought you had ears,' Axil said and gave a weak smile to the Botanist, taking the sting out of the comment. 'He's taken the middling and put him under house arrest without seeking the approval of the governors. He's already acting like he's in charge, and the governors don't like it. They think they should decide what to do with the middling, not some boy playing at high lord.'

The Botanist had heard rumours about the middling, but everything she'd heard had been contradictory, so she didn't know what to believe. Some had said that he had arrived on the crest of a wave, carried by Poseidon and that on his arrival, a group of Atlanteans led by Attalus had wrestled him into submission. Others said that Attalus had staged it as part of the high lord's funeral. She'd even heard a rumour that two petty criminals had discovered the middling in Kea, and that he'd fallen Below.

'He's also organised Funeral Games in honour of his father and demanded money from every realm to fund it. The governors have not responded well to the demand,' Axil continued.

'Where is the middling now?'

'At the palace with the Viracocha, who's finding out what he can about him as far as I know.'

154

'Could be a fake. Seems a bit of a coincidence that he turns up on the day of the funeral.'

'Could be,' Axil admitted. 'But I don't think so. The middling's arrival makes no difference. I need five votes. This will give me five votes. That answer your questions?'

The Botanist had plenty more, but she decided not to push it further. 'We need to move him,' she said. 'But don't worry, I'll get my assistant to do it. You've made your thoughts on Gyges perfectly clear.' It was the Botanist's time to tease.

Axil gave a wry smile. 'Good. I have other jobs to see to. I'll leave him in your capable hands.' With that, Axil turned and strode off towards his horse. He looked back briefly, then cantered into the forest, leaving the Botanist alone with the body.

She looked at the shape of the sack and felt the hairs on the back of her neck bristle. Carefully and slowly, she untied the knot of the sack. She could hear the man inside breathing small, shallow breaths. She pulled the sack down just enough so she could see his face and gasped.

Not you. Why did it have to be you?

A hand touched her shoulder, and the Botanist nearly jumped out of her skin.

'Sorry, I... um, didn't mean to frighten you. Not that you were, you know, um, but I didn't know if you needed some help.'

'Don't creep up on me,' the Botanist said to her assistant. She stood up and tried to regain her composure before facing him.

'Do you, um, do you know him?' the assistant asked hesitantly.

'No,' replied the Botanist before tying the sack closed again.

CHAPTER XXVII
The Citadel

Hestia tapped her fingers as she waited for the governors to sit down. It was the first time that a female had entered the decision room at the Temple of Poseidon, but the historical moment felt lost with everything else that was going on. Usually, only the governors would attend the annual meeting, but because any decision would directly involve Hestia and Attalus, they had permission to view the discussion, along with the high lawgiver, Borus, who would document the decision reached.

Paintings of past governors hung from the walls, and a large stain-glass window depicting the Titanomachy, the war between the Titans and the Olympians, allowed a vivid array of colours to wash over them. A large golden table sat in the centre of the room, with a candelabra hanging over it. The candelabra hung from a chain attached to the ceiling, at least 100 feet high, and Hestia wondered how they got it up there hundreds of years ago.

The governors were slowly seating themselves in the heavy golden chairs that sat around the table. Each governor had his allotted seat, and the governors sitting closer to the high lord were considered to have greater influence. Governor Gadeirus of the Adelphi realm and Governor Diaprepes of the Attica realm occupied the seats to the high lord's right and left, respectively. Hestia knew that her father regularly sought their counsel on matters involving the state.

The high lawgiver was sitting in the high lord's chair at the head of the table. That seat would be Hestia's if the governors passed the Equality-For-All Motion, and she felt aggrieved that Borus had assumed that position, although he had little choice as there was nowhere else for him to sit.

Hestia sat in the corner of the room, and Attalus was a few seats along, sucking on a lemon. He hadn't acknowledged her. They hadn't spoken since the reading of the will, and she had no intention of speaking to him now. He looked up as Mneseus and Elasippus entered together. They nodded at him in unison. They were talking quietly under their breaths and took up seats at the opposite end of the table to the high lord's seat.

They were just waiting on Governor Evaemon of the Tinos realm to make up the quorum. Hestia had spent a lot of time negotiating with Evaemon since the reading of the will, and she was relying on his vote. She had agreed that Tinos would host the next Games if he supported her, and she was quietly confident that she had his backing.

Usually, he was punctual. He'd even lectured Hestia on the importance of time-keeping when she'd arrived a few moments late for their meeting. Something didn't feel right. She'd had the same feeling with the high physician.

Borus cleared his throat loudly. 'Fellow governors,' he said.

The room fell silent.

'I received a letter from Governor Evaemon two days ago. He has, unfortunately, been taken ill and has returned to Tinos with haste to recover at his residence. He has asked for his son, the governor-in-waiting, Alec, to vote as his proxy. I have here the required authority signed by Governor Evaemon, and the request, whilst unusual, is perfectly lawful. However, before I invite the governor-in-waiting, Alec, into the Decision Room, does anyone have any quarrels with the proposal?'

The governors shuffled uncomfortably in their seats, and some muttered under their breaths, but no one objected.

'Good,' continued Borus. 'You may enter,' he shouted.

Alec, who must have been listening at the side door, walked in. He wore a white robe rather than the traditional blue robe worn by the governors, and he sat in his father's empty chair.

Hestia had not seen Alec since they were children, but he had always held strong traditional views. No doubt his mother's influence and, from what she had heard, he hadn't mellowed. The development smelled foul.

Borus waited a moment for Alec to settle himself. 'It appears, gentlemen, that we have a quorum, so let's begin, shall we?'

Hestia watched nervously. The days had dragged since her father's funeral, but she had done everything she could to ensure that the vote went her way. Attalus, in contrast, had occupied himself with the so-called middling. He hadn't allowed her, or anyone other than the Viracocha, near him. Quite what he was up to was a mystery, and his actions had angered most of the governors. They thought he should have handed the middling over to them. The situation was unprecedented, and no one had intervened, presumably because they were waiting for the meeting so they could reach a consensus. No one had even verified if the man was a middling or just a stray Atlantean with an unusual boat.

'First order of business is to vote on the Equality-For-All Motion, which will determine the next high lord,' Borus said and looked briefly in Hestia's direction. 'You are all aware of the motion put forward by the high lord before his death. You previously passed the Equality-For-All-Motion. We are now voting on whether to bring forward the implementation date of the last elements of the motion to today's date. For the sake of clarity, I am aware there are people here today who weren't at the reading of the will. The effect of bringing forward the last elements of the motion is that the heir to all seats will, from today, be the firstborn child, not the firstborn son.'

'We will shortly vote on the matter. However, a governor has queried whether the vote can be made anonymously. I have considered the proposal under the laws. There is nothing for or against such a proposal. We must demonstrate transparency and fairness, but ultimately it is a decision for you, the governors.'

'Then I vote against it. I will not hide under a veil of anonymity when I vote, and I call anyone who does a coward,' said Governor Gadeirus, and there was a general murmuring of agreement.

'In that case,' said Borus, 'we will decide on matters in the usual way.' Borus paused for a moment in case any of the governors challenged him, but they remained silent, unwilling to be called out as a coward.

Suddenly, the air felt heavy, and Hestia's stomach turned itself inside out.

Governor Diaprepes shuffled in his chair and scratched his face. He seemed fidgety. Hestia wondered if the deal she had reached with him was weighing heavily on his mind. He had agreed to relinquish a lot of control over Attica to Hestia. In return, she had offered a loan that he desperately needed to keep Attica from falling into ruin. The deal could cause controversy if it became public.

'Very well,' said Borus. 'Let us vote on the motion. Those in favour of the motion, please raise your hand.'

Governor Gadeirus raised his hand.

Governor Ampheres and Governor Atlas raised their hands.

Governor Mestor raised his hand.

Hestia's heart leaped. She had four votes and needed just one more. Then there was a pause.

She looked around at the governors. She thought she could count on Autochthon and Diaprepes. What had happened that they'd turned against her? And surely Governor Evaemon had instructed his son to vote for her?

'Any others?' asked Borus.

Attalus leaned forward and looked at Hestia, a smirk on his face. Her eyes were wet, and she was struggling to breathe.

Governor Autochthon cleared his throat. He looked in Hestia's direction, a strained look on his face. She could see the cogs working. Had they not agreed to a deal?

'Anyone else?' Borus pressed.

Autochthon cleared his throat loudly. 'Before I cast my vote, may I first propose a union between my son, Ganymede, and the Lady of the House?' he asked.

Hestia felt herself blush. Autochthon wanted her to marry his son, the beautiful and gallant Ganymede, who comfortably won every tournament he entered. Everyone in the kingdom either wanted to sleep with him or wanted to be him, everyone except Hestia.

Ganymede had made it clear on a multitude of occasions he wanted a union with her and she, or her father, had always politely refused him. There was just no spark there, but he didn't take rejection lightly. It was alien to him. Hestia was of an age where a union was well overdue, but there was no one Hestia was interested in. There had never been, and her father had told her she could pick her suitor when the time came. It was such an archaic and foolish rule. If she were high lady, she would change it. She would change a lot, but she wasn't high lady, and the rule stood.

Had it been Autochthon's plan all along to back her into a corner? He must have known that she would have rejected his suggestion had he proposed it during their discussions. He hadn't even raised it. If she agreed, she would have his vote, and she would be high lady, but it would tie her into a marriage she wanted to avoid. A union that went against everything she believed in. Marriage should be for love, not politics.

If she rejected his offer, though, Attalus would become high lord, and he could pick someone for her. That thought made her skin crawl.

Hestia looked around hopefully at the other governors. Governor Diaprepes studied his hands and tapped his foot. Governor Azaes couldn't even look at her. Were they in cahoots with Autochthon?

The rest of the governors were watching her as they waited. She had no choice and nodded her head slowly, agreeing to the deal. Hestia gulped and glanced away, wiping her eyes with the back of her hand. She looked back as Autochthon raised his hand, and Governor Diaprepes followed suit. They must have agreed to a deal. She felt betrayed.

Hestia thought she'd been clever, but she was new to this game and had a lot to learn. Then she realised that was it. There were six votes in her favour, a clear majority. She pushed her feelings for Ganymede aside. She wanted to yell and jump but knew that would be unseemly, so she smiled and remained seated as the governors clapped, some of them begrudgingly.

'Motion carried,' said Borus matter-of-factly. 'May I invite the new and first high lady to the table so we can proceed with further business.'

All eyes were on her, and she felt overwhelmed. She hadn't even thought about the meeting itself. What was she supposed to do? No one had trained her in this. The governors' meetings were shrouded in mystery.

Her limbs felt like jelly as she stumbled to her seat at the table, replacing Borus, who stood for her. How did she normally walk? Did she swing her arms or hold them still? Why was the chair so large and heavy? Would people think her weak if she struggled to move it?

'High lady,' Gadeirus said and smiled warmly at her. Hestia returned the smile.

'Welcome, high lady,' said Diaprepes. He smiled with his mouth, but his eyes cursed her. What had she done to make him so angry?

'As I have overseen the selection, I have fulfilled my role here,' said Borus. 'I will leave you to your deliberations.'

Borus walked out. Attalus must have skulked away as well because he was no longer in his seat.

'First order of business,' said Gadeirus, 'is the middling.'

As the eldest governor, Gadeirus had the unfortunate title of Uranus after the Primordial deity, and his role included progressing the governors' meetings. Hestia knew that much, but little else.

'We are all aware,' continued Gadeirus, looking at Hestia, 'of the unfortunate events that unfolded at the high lord's funeral. And I think we all know that whilst Attalus might have believed he was acting in the interests of the state, it is now up to us, as the guardians of the state, to determine the fate of the middling. I would ask the high lady, as the only one with access to the palace, if she knows anything about the current state and whereabouts of the middling.'

Hestia sat upright. 'My bro… Attalus has placed the middling under house arrest, and the palace is under guard. The guards would not listen to me before, but they will now.'

'Will they?' Mneseus muttered under his breath.

'Yes, and Attalus battered the middling over the head and threw him into the reflection room,' said Atlas, ignoring Mneseus. 'What sort of impression is that creating?'

Hestia had heard of the reflection room. It was located underground somewhere within the Citadel, but she had never seen it nor thought to look for it. Previous governors and high lords had used the room as a punishment to drive prisoners insane. Her father had never used it, preferring more humane ways to deal with any trouble.

'He did the right thing,' said Elasippus. 'No one else was stopping the middling. We had no patrols to intercept him. He showed leadership when we needed it the most.' Elasippus looked scathingly in Hestia's direction, and she ignored him.

'He acted without authority,' said Gadeirus sternly. 'But we are not here to debate his actions, rather what we should do now. The middling is under house arrest at the palace, but I have not heard or seen anything during my stay. What else do we know?'

'The Viracocha has been questioning him,' said Diaprepes. 'I understand that he has been with him for most of his stay, learning everything he can.'

'How do you know this?' questioned Gadeirus, perhaps too fiercely.

'Because I spoke with the Viracocha. I am allowed to, I believe.'

Gadeirus grunted in response. 'And what has he learned?'

'We know he arrived here from a place called England. He said he was in a boat race, and they passed through the Mouth of the Storm.'

'They?' said Elasippus.

'He was travelling with one other,' explained Diaprepes. 'It would appear that his friend died as they entered the Mouth of the Storm, but somehow he survived. He can't remember much else.'

'Are we sure the other one is dead?' asked Autochthon.

'Patrols have been looking for him, but no one could survive the Mouth of the Storm. And the bard's prophecy does not speak of two middlings,' commented Diaprepes.

'No one knows for sure what the true prophecy was,' snapped Mneseus. 'All we have is a bard's account of it.'

'Even so,' said Gadeirus, 'people believe in it, and that is the key. If we are not careful, we could find that the public turns against us. There has already been fighting in several realms. His sudden arrival has confused the people. We need to stand united on this.'

Hestia sat back and wondered if the governors always spoke so harshly to each other.

'What do you propose then?' asked Mneseus. 'We welcome him, and the public turns against us because they think it will lead to our destruction. Or we rid ourselves of him, and people think we are smiting the Saviour and ruining any chance we have of removing the fog that binds us here. What do you suggest, high lady?'

Mneseus spoke with venom, but Hestia wasn't afraid of airing her opinion. 'We wait,' she said. 'We should not rush into a decision until we know what we are dealing with and can gauge public opinion. I will not be the high lady who started her term by provoking a civil war. We need to know more about our guest. We need to learn about the outside world. Attalus kept the middling contained on the pretence that he was acting as temporary high lord until the governors reached a decision. Well, you have reached a decision, and Attalus has no authority.

I will take control of the middling and, once the Viracocha has gathered all the information we require, we will meet again to discuss how we act.'

'She talks sense. We don't know what we are dealing with,' said Mestor.

'Would you keep a snarler tethered to investigate how strong its bite is?' asked Alec, leaning forward in his seat and staring at each governor in turn. He knew how to hold the room. 'The longer we wait, the more he learns, and the more dangerous he is. How can you all sit idle? Each day that passes, he brings us closer to ruin. What we need now is decisive action. A leader who leads, not one who sits on their hands.'

Alec's comments felt like a punch to the stomach. Hestia hadn't expected such a personal attack, but she tried to brush it off. She would need to become hardened to such criticism.

'Is this your father speaking, or you?' asked Gadeirus.

'My father would say the same if he had any sense.'

'What would you do then?' Mneseus asked Alec. Hestia could tell he was playing him off against her.

'We don't need to know what he would do as he has no say on the matter,' snapped Gadeirus.

Hestia smiled at Gadeirus. 'Let him answer,' she said, trying to settle things down. She didn't intend to follow Alec's suggestion, but she knew that his voice was loud and that he had influence around the taverns. She had heard about priests inciting the public to take action against the state, and she suspected Alec was behind it. The more she knew about her adversaries, the better.

'Offer him Below, let Poseidon deal with him as He intends. If the middling proves himself worthy, then we accept him. If he is of the blood, then he will be saved.'

'He speaks sense,' said Elasippus. 'All heroes have to overcome challenges. If he will lead us into a new world, if he is here to rescue us as some believe, then let him prove himself.'

'You would send him to his death,' said Gadeirus through gritted teeth. 'An innocent man. We do not do that.'

'His life could save thousands by preventing a civil war. We have to act for the good of the State, Minos, the good of the state,' Mneseus responded.

'Even if we were to send him Below, surely you want to know as much as you can about him first,' said Hestia, remaining calm despite the tempers flaring around her.

Mneseus grunted a response.

'So let's delay the decision for now,' Hestia urged.

'I agree with our high lady,' said Gadeirus.

Alec sank back in his chair and breathed out loudly as he shook his head and rolled his eyes.

'I agree, delay the decision,' said Mestor.

'Very well, but for how long?' asked Mneseus.

'Three months should suffice,' said Hestia with confidence. She'd plucked the timeline from the air, but she felt like she needed to exert her authority. Nods met her suggestion, and they voted in favour of it, with only Alec dissenting.

Each governor then provided an update on any concerns and issues within their realm that required input from the other governors. Most were fairly trivial matters. As Hestia had spoken to most of the governors separately, they had already voiced their concerns to her in private, and she had agreed to help where possible. However, there were a few matters which troubled her.

A metal contraption bearing the picture of an eagle had fallen from the sky in Milos near the Alakasta Volcano. Elasippus had sent men to investigate, and they had found dead men inside. Elasippus was calling the contraption the Icarus Device. The name was a nod to the legendary boy. Icarus had escaped imprisonment in Crete using wings created by his father, Daedalus, but fell to the earth, having flown too close to the sun against his father's instructions. The grieving Daedalus had continued his flight and had eventually landed in Atalantea. His ingenious inventions were fundamental in developing the infrastructure of the Citadel, and a statue of him stood at the palace.

Elasippus had a team investigating the Icarus Device, but he refused to share any information. Whilst it wasn't unusual for things to wash up from the other world, this was on an entirely different scale. What they could learn from the highly sophisticated contraption could prove crucial. However, it was clear that Elasippus didn't like the decision reached on the issue of the high lord and would do everything he could to undermine Hestia's authority. For the time being, she would let it slide, but she wouldn't forget it.

Autochthon also had disturbing news. People were going missing in the Kea realm. And not just one or two isolated cases. Entire families had purportedly disappeared without a trace. The villagers had sent out search parties, but they had found nothing. Autochthon wanted a unified response to find out what was happening, but no one had the resources to commit to it, and the governors deemed it an internal problem. Hestia didn't like the decision, but there was a clear majority, and she had no say on the matter.

The meeting continued for most of the afternoon, and by the time they finished, the sun had nearly set. Hestia concluded by confirming that the Funeral Games in her father's honour, proposed by Attalus, would still take place but that the Capital would fund it. For the first time, the governors unanimously agreed to something. It was a chance for them to show off their athletes and warriors. They were eager to gain bragging points without having to spend coin. She would let Attalus organise it. Perhaps it would pacify him for a bit.

Hestia left the meeting feeling uplifted. It had gone well. Autochthon might have forced her into a union with Ganymede, and she would have to come to terms with that, but it was a huge step forward. It was a day that would go down in history. She would go down in history as the first high lady. It sounded good.

She could make a difference. A real difference, and any governor who voted against her would soon realise that they were wrong to undermine her.

It was late, but Hestia needed a walk to reflect on the day's events. The evening breeze felt comfortable against her skin, and the palace gardens were deserted, save for Toszka, who came to join her. He arched his back and ran playfully between her legs as she walked. He was getting old now and seldom ventured much further than the gardens.

The night was clear, and the stars shone fiercely in the sky, lighting up the paths. It was quiet. Too quiet, but Hestia didn't notice. Nor did she notice that the night lights hadn't come on. She was too busy deconstructing each conversation and each point discussed.

Toszka became spooked by something and ran back towards the palace. Hestia watched him go, and only then did she see the two men walking down the steps towards her. She carried on, assuming they were palace guards, but why would they be patrolling the palace gardens? Had Attalus changed their instructions? Hestia turned to confront them, but they had disappeared.

She continued with her walk and turned into the rose garden. The gardeners were clearing a section to plant new roses, but a number were still in full bloom, and their perfume hovered in the air. Hestia forgot about the men and turned her attention back to the day's events. She had performed well, but there were a lot of areas where she could make improvements. At times, she had allowed herself to be swayed on matters. On reflection, as counter-arguments made themselves visible, she could see that she had perhaps been a bit too hasty in some of her comments.

Up ahead, through the archway to the herb garden, she saw a movement, someone else taking a stroll, perhaps the middling. Attalus had given him the freedom to explore the palace gardens, although she had never seen him. What would she say to him? The thought of bumping into the middling made her panic. She didn't have the energy to deal with him now.

The sound of slow footsteps behind her caused her to turn, and she spotted the two men from earlier walking down the path towards her. They were around fifty feet away, and they had covered their faces. They wore light leather armour and carried swords, but they didn't look like palace guards. Had Attalus brought in more men to protect the middling?

Hestia considered speaking to them but decided that she would resolve any issues with the guards in the morning when her head was clear.

She turned to walk on, but two more men appeared in front of her. They stood shoulder to shoulder on the path, blocking her way. Intimidation poured off of them. They wore the same armour as the other two men and also carried swords. They walked towards her, and only then did Hestia recognise the danger. She was a target now. Lots of people stood to gain from her demise, especially Attalus, and she had no protection. Hestia looked around. Her only escape was through a flowerbed thick with rosemary, thyme, and sage.

'What are you doing here?' she shouted.

They ignored her.

'I asked you a question. Who are you with, and what are you doing here?' Her body was rigid, and she was short of breath.

They continued to ignore her.

'What do you want?'

A clash of steel cut through the air, and two yellow warblers took flight. Hestia turned around. The two men behind her were on the ground, blood slowly pooling around them. A man in a black cloak stood over them. A hood covered his face, and he looked like a servant of Hades. He cleaned his blade on the inside of his left arm and then walked towards her.

Hestia backed away. She wanted to scream, but no sound passed her lips. She had never felt so… helpless or terrified.

The two other men drew their swords. Hestia stumbled back into a hedge as the man in the cloak walked straight past her. Hestia gasped when she saw his face under the hood. 'Father?' she whispered. He looked just the same, but with a slightly longer, wonkier nose and a few scars on his cheeks.

The fight was over in a few seconds. Despite being outnumbered, the man in the cloak was lightning fast, and his two opponents weren't used to fighting together. The first one went down to a heavy blow to the head. He was dead before he hit the ground, his brains leaking onto the gravel. The second one fell to a thrust through the stomach. He attempted to run away but stumbled after a few steps and expired, clutching his injury.

Hestia looked on in astonishment at the scene. She had rediscovered her voice, and the man in the cloak no longer appeared a threat to her. 'What is the meaning of this?' she shrieked. 'Who are you?'

She didn't know whether to run or hug the cloaked man.

'We need to go. There's more,' the cloaked man said, ignoring her questions and taking off his hood.

'Uncle?' Hestia gasped.

She hadn't seen her Uncle Klemides in years. He'd joined the Trident Programme when he reached adulthood, giving up all of his rights and privileges. Hestia had heard stories about him, but she'd only seen him on the odd occasion when he had business with her father, and even then, it was only fleeting.

'Move, now. We'll go this way,' he said.

'I'm not going anywhere until you tell me what's going on.'

'You can't trust the high guard, and the palace is swarming with mercenaries. Stay here, and they'll kill you,' he said quickly.

'What? Why?'

'I don't know, but you need to come with me so I can get you somewhere safe. I can't take them all on.'

'What about Attalus?' Hestia asked. She didn't like her brother, but she didn't want him to come to any harm.

'As far as I know, they don't care about him. You need to move now. You're lucky I found you in time.'

Hestia froze. She didn't know what to do. She was being asked to put all of her trust in a man who was a stranger to her, a man who had just killed four men without breaking stride. 'But… but I'm the high lady,' she pleaded.

'You'll be a dead lady if you don't come now.'

The sound of running and clinking of armour helped Hestia reach a decision.

'Now, please, if you don't mind,' said Klemides.

She followed her uncle into the shadows of the gardens and to an exit which only those who had grown up in the palace would know about. It was a concealed entrance in a small woodland area to the east of the palace that led to an underground tunnel. The passage wound its way under the Citadel to an exit on the side of the canal. Hestia had used it as a child to escape the palace, but she'd never used it as an adult, until now.

Klemides led her through the passage to a small fishing boat tied up on the canal.

'Get in and hide under those sheets,' Klemides said.

Hestia was about to protest but then saw her uncle's face and knew better than to challenge him. Instead, she hid away and silently sobbed as Klemides rowed them out of the Capital.

CHAPTER XXVIII

Rhamnus, Syros

This time, the Paymaster was waiting for Axil when he entered the penitence booth. 'She escaped,' he flapped before Axil had even had the chance to sit down.

Axil took a deep breath, knowing it wouldn't be a pleasant conversation. 'Who escaped?' he asked, playing dumb.

'The girl,' snapped the Paymaster.

Axil knew the governors had appointed Hestia as the first high lady, and the knowledge had given him insomnia. That the Paymaster had already taken steps to remove her showed how desperate he was.

'Escaped from who?' Axil asked, trying to piece together the chain of events.

'I had men ready to intercept the girl should the governors appoint her as high lady. We paid the guards to let them into the palace, but she escaped, and four of my men are now dead.'

Axil swallowed to suppress a smile. 'How?'

'She had help. There's no way she could have taken out four of my finest fighters.'

Who could have known the Paymaster's plans? Axil didn't even know, but then, the Paymaster kept him in the dark until he needed him.

'You must have someone with liquid lips on your pay.'

'Do not think to tell me about my men,' the Paymaster chided. 'We would not have been in this position had you carried out your job properly.'

Axil opened his mouth to protest and then closed it again. He didn't want to agitate the Paymaster any further.

'It wasn't all your fault,' the Paymaster conceded. 'Governor Autochthon sold his vote to the girl in return for her union to Ganymede. I am a reasonable man. No-one could have predicted he'd be so bold to proposition her so.'

Axil wondered how the Paymaster knew about the discussions at the governors' annual meeting. Only the governors, the high lawgiver, Hestia, and Attalus had been in attendance. Had he spoken to Attalus? Was the high lawgiver, Borus, on his books?

'How did they die?' Axil asked. He had so many questions buzzing around his head.

'Sword wounds.'

'The high bodyguard?' That was the most obvious person who could take on four mercenaries and live to tell the tale.

'No, he'd retired for the evening, and he's on my pay. Whoever helped came from outside the palace.'

The Paymaster's reach was far greater than Axil had feared.

'We have cleared away the mercenaries,' the Paymaster continued, 'and now I need you to find Hestia and bring her back.'

Axil's bowels loosened.

'What's your plan?' the Paymaster barked, challenging Axil to defy him.

Axil stared at the wooden door in front of him, his mouth agape. He had no plan. He'd only just learned about the previous plan. He stuttered, but nothing intelligible passed his lips.

'It's what I pay you for, isn't it? Whisperer!' the Paymaster hissed, obviously desperate.

No, it's not! Axil thought to himself. 'I will need to do some digging first,' he said after a long pause. *Might as well dig my grave whilst I'm at it.*

'That's two young girls who have evaded me,' the Paymaster muttered to himself.

'Two?'

'Do your digging, but be quick,' the Paymaster said, ignoring his question. 'She couldn't have travelled far since last night, and people will recognise her. We need to find her and deal with her before she regroups. Have your men look for her. All of them.'

'Yes,' said Axil and thought about where he would go if he were in her shoes. 'Won't everyone notice her absence?'

'Yes, there will be an official ceremony to announce the new high lady. Until then, she is still, technically, just the Lady of the House. People will expect the ceremony to take place in the next few days, and rumours will start spreading if there isn't one.'

Axil had forgotten about the swearing-in ceremony. It was a simple formality, but without it, the high lady couldn't give her pledge to the Saviour, and allow Him to sanction the appointment. 'Understood,' Axil said and squeezed his forehead. He could already feel a migraine coming on.

'Do not fail me again. Now leave.'

Axil nodded and stumbled out without saying another word.

*

Axil sat in a tavern in Outer Atalantea, reflecting on his meeting with the Paymaster. He had thought long and hard about Hestia, but he didn't know where she could be or how she had escaped. The only conclusion he could come to was that someone had betrayed the Paymaster, but that much seemed obvious.

His first step had been to set all his men looking for the high lady in the Capital, but he held little hope in them finding her. The fact she'd escaped the palace meant she was getting help, and they wouldn't be sticking to the obvious routes. She was probably out of the Capital by now, anyway. If he was in her shoes, he'd go to stay with a governor he could trust. But all the governors were still in the Capital, and there was no one she could trust.

What had the Paymaster meant by a second girl getting away?

A drunk man stumbled into the seat next to Axil. 'Beg your forgiveness,' he said, and Axil grunted at him. 'We're celebrating,' he continued, oblivious to Axil's mood. Axil looked at him but didn't respond. 'My best friend, the ugly one over there, is getting married, so he is.'

Axil's patience was wearing thin. He just wanted to drink in peace. 'Very good,' he said, hoping that a brief response would pacify him.

'Marrying the love of his life, so he is.'

'I'm very pleased for him. Would you mind? It's just that I'm—'

171

'See, I said,' the drunk man continued leaning into Axil, 'that she was too pretty for him. Too pretty for any man.'

'I'm sure she is.'

'I said that she was destined for the Love Temple.' The drunk man burped and stole a few nuts from Axil's jar on the table.

'Yes... wait. What did you say?' Axil asked, thinking aloud.

'Love Temple. You know, where they put all the goddesses to keep them away from people like you and me.'

The drunk man winked and carried on talking, but Axil wasn't listening. The Love Temple was what many people called Aphrodite's Temple, and it was in Paros on a parcel of land isolated from the main island. The only way to and from the temple was via a long rope bridge suspended high above the sea. Aphrodite had forbidden men from crossing the bridge to the temple. It was the ideal location for women to escape to. It was a long way from the Capital to the temple, and it would take at least a week to get there using the main trading routes. Undercover, it could take two or three.

That's where she would be heading. It had to be.

'... and I said, the gods must be on his side because he's too ugly to—'

'Thank you,' said Axil. 'That's been most helpful.' He downed his drink in one gulp and left the tavern with the drunk man still talking behind him. If he was quick, he might get ahead of them.

CHAPTER XXIX

The Capital

Attalus left the governor's meeting reeling. The fools! He had been so close to the decision going his way, and then Governor Autochthon had stepped in with his stupid proposal.

However, his frustration had been short-lived because Hestia had disappeared. It was the first day of her tenure as high lady, and no one could find her. The Viracocha had informed him that there had been a commotion in the palace gardens during the evening. The palace guards thought she had left with someone, but they were still investigating. It was highly negligent of his guards to have let intruders enter the palace, but Attalus didn't care. Until the high priest completed the swearing-in ceremony, he was still in control. And the high priest couldn't do his duties if Hestia was missing.

He'd set trackers to look for her. It would be remiss of him not to, but he had been slow to react and even slower to pay their fees.

In a rare moment of wisdom, Hestia had placed Attalus in charge of the Funeral Games. It was the one piece of good news to have come out of the meeting, and Attalus had decided that they would be the focus of his attention for the rest of the day. The sooner the Funeral Games could take place, the better. The people needed a hero and a champion right now. They needed him. He would let others worry about his sister's whereabouts and what had happened to her.

A knock on the door interrupted his thoughts of the format for the sword fighting competition. 'Yes,' he said sharply.

'High lord.' The Viracocha smiled as he opened the door.

Attalus smiled. He liked that the Viracocha used that title for him, even if he was a slippery eel with a quick tongue. The Viracocha had talents Attalus could barely comprehend.

He could pick up languages with ease and had encyclopedic knowledge on every subject. He was also as old as the mountains and could barely walk without his snake-like cane. The walking stick had scared Attalus as a child. He had a vivid memory of fire coming out of the snake's mouth. His father had told him he must have dreamed it, but he wasn't so sure. Every time Attalus saw the Viracocha, he thought it would be the last, but somehow the old man plodded on. He had already outlived at least two generations of high lords, and he would probably outlive Attalus.

Over twenty viracochas had existed at one time, and they had been active in each realm, guiding the governors and the high lord. Attalus knew very little about them. Only that their training was intense, shrouded in mystery, and very few had the abilities to succeed. It was something to do with the way the mind works. Ancient practices which few could understand, let alone master. Now only the Viracocha remained. He was the last of his kind. At least, that's what he told anyone who would listen.

'A word if I may,' said the Viracocha.

Attalus sighed. It was never just a word. 'Come in, take a seat.' But don't get too comfortable.

'Is there any news of your sister?'

'No, nothing.'

'I'm sorry to hear that, especially after your brother disappeared in such similar circumstances.'

Why was he bringing up Dyon? What did he have to do with anything? His disappearance had been years ago, under entirely different circumstances. Attalus grunted a response, keen for the Viracocha to make his point and then leave.

'And how are the preparations for the Funeral Games going? I know everyone is keen for a lift right now.'

'Yes, fine. They will take place in ten days, so plenty to sort.'

'Good, good.' The Viracocha exhaled loudly and slumped forward. For a moment, Attalus wondered whether he'd expired right in front of him, but then the Viracocha sat upright and clicked his knuckles. 'There are certain State matters which require urgent attention, and I'm afraid they won't wait.'

'What sort of State matters?'

'We'll get on to them, but as the high lady is absent without reason, and we have not made her position official, you are legally still acting high lord.'

It seemed extreme for anything to require such urgent action, but Attalus was happy to play along. 'What sort of decisions?' he asked.

'First, I feel I should make you aware of some… discontent.'

'Discontent? What do you mean?'

'There are those who oppose you and your actions with the middling.'

'Who?'

'It's just whispers, but whispers are like clouds. They collect, and before long, you have rain.'

Why did the Viracocha insist on talking in riddles?

'What do you suggest?'

'I suggest that, if rain is to fall, you decide where and upon whom it pours.'

Attalus sighed. He'd lost him. 'Speak plainly.'

The Viracocha coughed into his hand. He shuffled in his seat, trying to find a comfortable position. 'The middling divides public opinion. Unite the people, and they will favour you.'

Attalus had also heard rumours of discontent. 'Am I not the one who saved them? Do I not protect them, even now? Even after the governors rejected me? How can they not see that?'

'There are some who have a different opinion. Some who think the governors should determine the middling's fate. They are being quite… vocal. It could cause a disturbance in the Capital, perhaps even further afield, if it continues unchecked.'

Attalus let out a laugh. 'We cannot trust the governors with anything. They've already shown that.'

'I have spent many hours with the middling now. I have garnered what I can. He is simple and not of Atlantean stock, but where he comes from and what he represents poses a catastrophic risk to the future of Atalantea. If we allow him to divide us, it could cause a war, but you could use him to unite the realms. Do that, and your subjects will love you. Even if Hestia returns, it is you who they will consider their true leader.'

'At the risk of repeating myself, how?' Everything the Viracocha had said sounded like an impossible dream. There was no way he could satisfy everyone.

'First, look after him, show him around, and let him enjoy himself. He is simple. He's likely to want simple things, carnal things. Entertain him and let the people see him at the Funeral Games. If you are open about what you are doing with him and show the people that you are not hiding him away, they are more likely to trust you. Then, when you have their trust, you can make clouds and decide where it rains.'

Attalus nodded slowly, still not clear on what the Viracocha was saying. 'Very well, we'll relax his house arrest, satisfy his… carnal desires, and we'll show him around. But what of those who are still speaking out against me?'

'What do you suggest?'

'I don't know. That's why I asked you.'

'What would your father have done?'

'Probably nothing, but he's not around anymore, is he?'

'Are you saying he was weak?'

Attalus wasn't saying that, but perhaps the Viracocha had a point. 'Maybe.'

'One thing I have learned during my tenure with many high lords is that the public requires a powerful leader they can stand behind. A weak leader is worse than no leader at all. A powerful leader is someone who can make tough decisions and stand by them. The outcome is usually irrelevant, so long as your subjects have a direction of travel and believe in it.'

Attalus looked at the Viracocha, his brain in knots. 'Fine,' he said. 'Find anyone spreading your clouds about and deal with them.'

'Deal with them?'

'Yes, deal with them, in the same manner we would deal with anyone inciting violence against the high lord. Did you have something else you wanted to speak to me about?' Attalus barked when the Viracocha remained stubbornly seated. He'd just realised he could enter young Theagenes into the bare-knuckle boxing, and he wanted to write to him.

'Yes,' said the Viracocha solemnly. 'It is to do with succession and forward planning. Unfortunately, there is an issue involving Governor Atlas.'

'What sort of issue?' Attalus sighed. He'd had a fantastic idea for the chariot racing, and he wanted to make a note of it before he forgot.

'He is dying.'

The Viracocha said it plainly, and the revelation shocked Attalus. 'Dying? How? I only saw him at the governors' meeting, and he seemed perfectly fine then. He's young and healthy!'

'Yes, but looks are deceiving, and what he's suffering from is a hidden monster, which doesn't show its teeth until the very end.'

'How long?'

'From what I have heard, a few weeks if he is lucky. Days, if he is not.'

Attalus was shocked that Governor Atlas had voted against him, but he still didn't mind him. Of all the governors, he was the only one who had been pleasant to Attalus as a child. They were also distantly related, third cousins or something like that. 'Well, thank you for letting me know. Obviously, when the time comes—'

'I think you miss the point,' said the Viracocha.

Attalus sensed a note of frustration in his voice. 'Enlighten me then,' he snapped.

'Atlas has no heir.'

'Asterion has Cassandra,' Attalus retorted, using Governor Atlas's first name. 'And seeing as the law has changed, she is next in line, is she not?' The old man was frustrating him now.

'Cassandra is eight. She is not of an age to become a governor.'

'No, then what are you saying?'

'If… when Governor Atlas passes, the high lord must appoint someone to take over the role of governor of Syros until Cassandra is old enough.'

'Yes, I suppose they will.'

'I have consulted the governors' family trees in the library.'

'I'm sure you have.'

The Viracocha ignored the jibe. 'The governor with the strongest line, and therefore the strongest claim, is Diaprepes. His line is nearly unbroken. He has three sons, all of an appropriate age. Aenas will take over from his father in time and will become the governor of Attica, but Damaris, the second eldest, is the strongest candidate for shadow governor of Syros. Until Cassandra is old enough, of course.'

'Doesn't it need to go to the governors to decide?'

'The governors all have a vested interest, and so they are conflicted. The decision is for the high lord or high lady alone. I am afraid time is short on this. If I could wait for the high lady's return, I would.'

Attalus scratched his head. 'Very well, what do I need to do?'

'I have drawn up the papers. If you are happy to, you just need to sign and stamp them. If we do not resolve this matter quickly, the governors may fight amongst themselves when the time comes, and that would not be good for the State. This will ensure that there can be no disorder.'

The Viracocha produced some papers from his robe, and Attalus rolled his eyes. He couldn't help but think he was being played somehow, yet everything the Viracocha had said made sense, and was he not supposed to guide him? 'Where do I sign then?' he asked, and the Viracocha showed him.

Attalus's hand hovered over the papers, reluctant to commit but unsure why. He ignored his gut and slammed the stamp down. He didn't have time for this.

'Is that everything?' Attalus asked as the Viracocha rolled the piece of parchment back up.

'I will leave you in peace,' he nodded. His rickety frame groaned as he stood up from his chair and hobbled towards the door. 'I suggest you find your sister quickly,' he said as he left. 'If she remains absent, there might be an argument that the governors' decision was a gross error that should be reversed.'

Attalus didn't see or hear the Viracocha close the door. He was too deep in thought.

CHAPTER XXX

The Capital

A hand caressed Shep's shoulder, and he felt a soft, warm breath on his neck. Katalina. Was that her name? Or was Katalina the girl from the previous night?

He was enjoying his time on Atalantea, and his thoughts of leaving had evaporated. Other than a few faint bruises, he had recovered from his injuries. The food was plentiful and delicious, the bed comfortable. The gardens were as beautiful as anything he had ever seen, and the nighttime entertainment was exquisite. Far better than anything he had experienced in Amsterdam or the Reeperbahn, and as far as he was aware, he didn't have to pay!

He'd barely even thought about Alfred or contacting the outside world. Why would he want to leave and return to a painful reality when he was being treated like a king? A few more days wouldn't hurt.

The Viracocha's daily visits had dried up around a week ago, and with them, Shep's sense of anxiety eased. His endless stream of questions and riddles left Shep drained and frustrated but none the wiser about where he was or what was going on. In his absence came a young, bullish-looking man who a translator introduced as the high lord, whatever that meant. He looked familiar, but Shep couldn't think why. The high lord had told him, or more correctly, the translator had told him, that he was free to explore the palace by himself. Until that point, the Viracocha had babysat him. They'd locked his door whenever he was alone, which made him feel like a prisoner, despite the Viracocha telling him it was for his own protection.

He'd been nervous about leaving his room, like a rabbit that had just had its cage opened. He was sure that as soon as someone saw him, they would rugby tackle him to the ground, but when he eventually ventured out, the guards hadn't even acknowledged him. They stood statue-still at various points in the palace, each dressed in the same linen shirt, bronze breastplate, knee-high leather boots, and a helmet that revealed only the wearer's eyes and mouth. They each carried a short sword and a shield with a strange circular crest engraved on it. Shep assumed the costumes were for show, like the Beefeater guards at the Tower of London, but there was still something unnerving about them.

He hadn't ventured far on his first foray into the palace. He'd kept to the paths he'd walked with the Viracocha. When he'd returned to his room, he'd discovered a girl waiting for him. She was pretty and petite, with jet black hair and large curves he wanted to get lost in. She couldn't speak English, but when she removed the clasp on her shoulder and allowed her dress to fall to the floor, Shep realised she wasn't there to talk. He was happy to follow her lead.

With his confidence growing, Shep had explored further afield the following day. The Viracocha had shown him the majority of the grounds and the palace during their daily walk-and-talks, but there was still a lot to explore. The gardens were enchanting, and he quickly lost himself in exploring the different sections. Each one was so unique and spellbinding in its design that Shep could have easily spent an entire day just revelling in one area, but his curiosity kept him moving.

The plants were so full of life that it wouldn't have surprised Shep had they started talking to him. The birds, whose songs filled the air, were all the colours of the rainbow. They were a far cry from the dull blackbirds and sparrows Shep was used to seeing back home. Shep had never understood how gardens could improve health. But as he breathed in the intoxicating perfume of the plants and listened to the sound of nature, he felt uplifted. His worries melted away, along with any thoughts of escaping.

On his return to his room, another girl was waiting for him. This one had dimples you could store your M&Ms in, along with his supper. The girl could wait. He hadn't eaten all day, and he was starving. Supper was a salad with pomegranate, figs, and what he assumed was chicken. It was delicious. He greedily devoured it as the girl undressed and gave him a massage.

Shep enjoyed her fingers gently kneading his shoulders, ridding them of any tension that had built up from his walk. They worked their way down his back and along his spine. Shep finished his food and then allowed himself to be undressed and pushed onto the bed. The girl straddled him and carried on the massage. He closed his eyes as she worked her magic.

Afterwards, Shep rolled onto his side and fell into a deep and peaceful sleep. He didn't hear the girl leave. Nor did he hear the Viracocha check in on him or see the Viracocha's thin mouth twist into a smile at the scene of debauchery that greeted him.

And so the pattern continued. Each day a different walk. Each night a different girl.

It was a life he could get used to.

CHAPTER XXXI

Kea

Hands gripped at Alfred, rough, leathery skin and long fingernails. They scratched and clawed at him. He could feel them grabbing at him, and he could smell their breath on his face like rotting flesh. He was running, but they were quicker. Hundreds of teeth bit into him, and he couldn't run anymore. His body ached. He slowed down, needing to rest, and then they brought him down.

Alfred cried out, and his shout jolted him awake. He was upright, panting loudly, his heart thumping. It had been two weeks since he had escaped the caves, and it had been the same every night, the same nightmare at the same time.

A gentle hand rubbed his back, and he looked across to see Kaspa's sister, Ariadne, trying to calm him. Her beautiful hazel eyes looked at him with softness in their depths. They could convey a thousand words her mouth could not. If it hadn't been for her, Alfred would have been lost.

She mopped his sweating brow with a damp cloth and gently hushed him. Alfred felt himself relax. He had bandages covering his body and was still in a lot of pain, but he was getting stronger with each day that passed. Yesterday, he managed a short walk around Ariadne's house and even sat outside in the sun for a while. Ariadne had refused to let him go any further.

The events leaving the cave had unfolded in a series of still frames. He could remember climbing the rope and feeling every inch of his body strain as the dying embers of his resolve blew away. But somehow, he had reached the top, and Kaspa, not Yaspa, Ariadne had corrected him on that, or the man of no-name had hauled him to safety.

A grief-stricken Kaspa had led the no-named man and Alfred to a house on the edge of the forest. They were three broken men, and they had walked in stunned silence. The walk had taken many hours, and more than once, Alfred had collapsed from the effort. Demons whispered in his ear, telling him it should have been him. They told him he should have stayed down there, that he didn't deserve to live. When they finally reached their destination, the relief had nearly brought him to tears.

A girl had appeared in the doorway, and such was her likeness to Kaspa that Alfred assumed they must be twins. She was introduced as Kaspa's older sister, Ariadne. Ariadne had shouted something at Kaspa. Upon hearing her voice, Kaspa dropped to his knees as though shot through the head. Like a pin, she had popped the bubble of his emotions, which he'd kept contained until then.

Ariadne had run to him and, although he couldn't speak the language, Alfred knew that in-between sobs, Kaspa was relaying what had happened. Ariadne listened, shaking her head, barely able to look at her brother. When Kaspa finished, she cried silently, her head in her hands.

Alfred had watched from a distance, guilt stabbing away at his exhausted body. He couldn't take his eyes off Ariadne. He didn't know her, but he had an overwhelming urge to comfort her. Make everything better again. Her pain was his fault, and that cut him more than any of his other injuries.

When they'd both run out of tears, Ariadne had spoken quietly to Kaspa. Alfred knew they were talking about him because they kept looking in his direction. Kaspa left without another word, and Ariadne led Alfred and the man of no-name into her house, where she tended to their wounds, her eyes blank and her demeanor cold.

For the first week, Alfred barely moved from his bed. Every movement was an effort. Even sitting up caused his bones to creak like an old garden fence.

Initially, he shared his room with the man of no-name, who wasn't a talker. Ariadne eventually christened him Theseus, so she had something to call him. From Theseus's appearance and manner, the caves must have been his home for a long time, but how long was anyone's guess.

Kaspa visited Ariadne most days, and Alfred assumed he lived nearby. Not once during those visits did he attempt to see Alfred. It was as though he was trying to block him out. Alfred owed him his life, and the debt weighed heavily on his conscience. He had to repay him for his sacrifice, but he didn't know how.

Theseus recovered swiftly from the ordeal, and after a week, he disappeared with Kaspa, leaving Alfred alone under Ariadne's care. Deep down, Alfred was pleased that Theseus had gone. He still didn't know what to make of his mute friend, and he loved his moments alone with Ariadne, even though they couldn't understand each other.

Every day Ariadne undressed his wounds and gently applied strange smelling ointments and bandages with a care he didn't deserve. Then she disappeared for a few hours, and Alfred counted down the seconds until she returned, like a dog waiting patiently for its master at the door. He spent most of this time thinking about what she was doing and how he could say thank you. When her figure appeared in the distance, an overwhelming current would course through him as though someone had suddenly plugged him into an energy source.

Alfred loved the way her long brunette hair fell over her right shoulder, pushing out her ear. He loved how she scrunched up her nose and how her eyebrows furrowed when she tended to his bandages. He loved her dainty fingers and how gentle they felt on his bruised skin, providing instant pain relief whenever they touched him. If only she could touch him all the time.

At first, Ariadne did not speak to Alfred. She fed him and tended to his injuries as though he was in a ward with a hundred other patients clamouring for attention. It had taken two days for her to even tell him her name.

On day four, she smiled at him. She squeezed his hand on day five. On day eight, just after Theseus left, she sat with him all afternoon as they tried to untangle each other's curious tongue. Alfred listened to her voice melt in his ears, but he couldn't place her accent or pick out any words. Ariadne, though, put Alfred's efforts to shame. She was a natural linguist.

After that, their conversations became a daily occurrence. Ariadne grew tired of trying to teach Alfred. So they spoke in English, with Ariadne only switching to her native tongue to curse, usually after she'd made a mistake or pronounced something wrong. With each day that passed, the conversation grew longer. Alfred grew stronger and happier.

Ten days later, when Alfred looked into Ariadne's eyes, he no longer saw anger. They had softened. Her gaze lingered for longer, and she smiled when she saw him. It was a beautiful smile that lit up her face, and you couldn't help but return.

Shortly after that, Kaspa called by as Ariadne was tending to Alfred. He'd been fooling around, and Ariadne had laughed. Kaspa was furious. He'd had an argument with Ariadne in the room next door. The wall did little to stop the sound, and Alfred knew it was about him. He'd even heard his name mentioned, but he didn't care as long as he could stay there and let Ariadne tend to him.

The house itself was small and basic. Some might have called it cosy. The walls were made from the striking red stone that filled the landscape. Large south-facing windows flooded the house with light for most of the day. There were two bedrooms, a bathroom, and a large living quarter. Strangely, there was no kitchen other than a sink and a small inbuilt oven heated by logs. Ariadne always brought food back with her from somewhere. It was perfect if you wanted a secluded trip away from all modern amenities but terrible if you needed to contact the outside world, which was something Alfred was desperate for.

The language barrier, combined with Alfred's injuries, meant that he had found out very little about his temporary home, and he wasn't sure that he was ready for the answers. He had once asked Ariadne, and she just kept repeating the word Atalantea.

Atalantea… Atlantis? He must have misunderstood, but with everything that had happened and everything he had seen…

The thought kept returning to him, and each time he batted it away. Atlantis was nothing more than a myth. He had watched documentaries on it, and even read Plato's *Timaeus* and *Critias* when he was younger. Thousands had searched for it, spending their lives in the vain hope of finding it. No one had been successful. For it to not only exist but to still have inhabitants? It was impossible!

But…?

Ariadne sat herself down on his mattress and idly stroked his hair. Alfred closed his eyes and enjoyed the touch of her skin. Her weight on the mattress caused it to sink, and he felt himself roll towards her. She put her arm around him, and he reciprocated. It felt natural. They sat in a gentle embrace, each enjoying the feeling of the other's steady breathing. They needed no words this time. Then there was a loud knock at the door, and Ariadne sat up abruptly. The knock became frantic, ruining the moment, and Ariadne left to see who it was.

Kaspa's voice reverberated through the house. He sounded upset, angry even. It sounded like he was reprimanding Ariadne. Alfred felt his heart rate increase and his muscles tense. He wanted to protect her, but he knew it wasn't his place, not now, anyway. They started shouting, and Alfred was sure he heard his and Theseus's name a few times, but his ears were still adjusting to the strange language, and so he couldn't be sure. Then the door slammed shut, and Alfred could hear crying.

A few moments later, Ariadne walked back to Alfred's room. She'd composed herself, but the lines on her face told the real story. She got onto the bed next to Alfred and curled herself into a ball. Alfred put his arm around her. It was his turn to be the rock.

'Kaspa, he fight,' Ariadne said after they'd been lying together for a few minutes.

'Fight?' asked Alfred.

'Yes, against,' she struggled to find the word, 'against monsters who took Erik. He go. Theseus go. They get more… fighters and go.'

Alfred sighed. He'd tried to block out what had happened. It was bad enough when it returned to him in his sleep.

'Kaspa no fighter.' Ariadne started crying again. 'They take him, too.' She was struggling to get her words out now. 'I tell him no but he…' She pointed to her ears. 'If he goes…' She let the sentence hang.

Alfred held Ariadne as she sobbed into his shoulder. She was shaking, and he wished he had some words of comfort, but he had seen what those monsters were capable of.

'Perhaps he'll change his mind,' he said feebly.

Part of Alfred felt like he should go, too. Erik had died saving his life, and he owed it to Kaspa, but he was still recovering. He would be as much a liability as an aid and, he selfishly didn't want to leave Ariadne. His every thought went back to her. Would she think less of him if he didn't offer to go? He watched her body rise and fall as she tried to control her breathing.

'Should I go?' he asked before he could stop himself.

Ariadne looked at him, her eyebrows almost touching her hairline, then shook her head. 'No. You no strong. No fighter,' Ariadne said.

Alfred felt his confidence dive into an abyss.

'You no fight,' she continued. 'We need fighters to kill monsters. You…' She pointed at Alfred's injuries.

'Okay, okay,' Alfred said, feeling hurt. 'No need to destroy me.'

'Stupid, stupid,' Ariadne continued.

Alfred wondered if his character assassination would ever end.

'You no leave me,' she said. Then she grabbed Alfred's face and kissed him.

Her lips felt soft, and Alfred felt his body relax as he fell into her. Josie was the last girl he had kissed, and that had been a long time ago.

Ariadne pulled away and smiled. 'You stay, stupid,' she said teasingly, and Alfred couldn't help but laugh, his smile a crescent moon on his face.

Then Ariadne turned serious. 'I check you,' she said, pointing to Alfred's bandages.

He let her check his body. This time her touch felt different, sensual rather than routine, and Alfred struggled to control himself.

'You much better,' she breathed into his ear, and then she kissed Alfred again more forcefully. He relaxed back on the bed, thoughts of monsters and fighting a distant memory.

CHAPTER XXXII
The Capital

A loud knock on the door woke Shep. He was expecting breakfast, and his stomach groaned in anticipation. Instead, the high lord walked in with his translator. It was the first time the high lord had visited Shep since he had granted him freedom of the palace. The sudden intrusion made him nervous.

The high lord looked at the girl in Shep's bed with a wry smile and then said something to the translator. 'The high lord asks if you are enjoying your stay and the company?'

'Yes,' said Shep, fumbling around with the sheets. In truth, he was getting bored. He had explored every inch of the palace he could gain access to and had run out of things to see and do. A television and a games console would make things far more bearable, but they didn't seem to have anything like that. They didn't seem to have electricity, full stop. Shep had spent an entire day searching in vain for a power socket. 'Thank you,' he added as the girl grabbed her clothes and left, under the watchful eye of the high lord.

'Today, there are Funeral Games. The high lord would like you to attend with him,' the translator said.

'Yes, thank you,' Shep said again, excitement bubbling in his stomach. Finally, something different to break up his day. He might finally get some answers, although they were unlikely to come from the translator, who struggled to understand anything Shep said.

'The high lord would like you to wear these clothes.' The translator passed Shep a white linen shirt, trousers, and a red robe with colourful golden markings on the sleeves and neck. It looked expensive. He'd spent most of his time in the palace dressed in a long white tunic. It fell loosely past his knees and made him feel like a hippy, so the new outfit was a welcome development. He didn't know what had happened to the clothes he'd arrived in.

'Thank you.'

'We will return soon. Be ready.'

'Thank you,' Shep muttered as his guests left.

The translator's tone was curt, and the high lord looked more interested in the paint job on the wall than Shep, but the Funeral Games sounded exciting. He wondered what they would entail and quickly dressed, sensing the high lord would be angry if he wasn't ready on time.

*

'Ouch!' Shep shouted and covered his eyes. He could barely watch.

A beast of a man dressed in a green kit picked up a ball that had a handle like a kettlebell. He swung it violently at his opponent, who was late ducking. The ball smashed into the opponent, and he clattered to the floor, his skull rattling. The beast-man let out a roar and climbed the wall.

Shep was as close to the action as he could get. He was looking down on an H-shaped pitch in seats segregated from the rest of the crowd. Both teams had five balls to defend and five balls to steal. Once a team had wrestled a ball from their opposition, they had to pass it to a climber who would scale a wall in the horizontal section of the pitch and pass or throw it through a hoop similar in size to a basketball hoop. The major difference was it was positioned thirty feet above the ground. Each team had eight players, six who would attack or defend, depending on the team's tactics, and two climbers. The climbers also had the role of stopping their opponent's climbers before they could pass the ball through the hoop by catching them on the wall. It was utter chaos, and it had taken three games before Shep had understood the basic premise.

Both teams had passed three balls through their hoop, and the game was evenly matched. The team dressed in green had lost a climber to injury after his opponent threw him from the wall. The team in blue had lost a defender thanks to the beast-man clattering him over the head. The defender was slowly getting to his feet, but he looked dazed and was staggering around. Shep couldn't believe that they hadn't stopped the game for him to receive some medical attention, but no one seemed to care about safety.

The climber for the green team continued to ascend the wall with the ball. He was quick, and the two blue climbers in pursuit quickly gave up the chase. An enormous cheer erupted as the green team made it 4-3. But now, the blue team had stolen their two remaining balls, and their climbers were ascending the opposite wall with them. The green climber threw himself to the floor and immediately gave chase. One of the blue climbers reached the hoop and sank the ball amidst a wild cheer, but the second blue climber was slower. He was about four feet away from the hoop when the green climber caught him and grabbed his ankle. He needed to give up the ball, but the pull was strong, and he lost his grip. The crowd gasped as the blue climber fell to the floor on his neck and fell silent.

The game continued.

The crowd supporting the green team cheered. Shep peered out from between his fingers at the fallen climber. He looked like a wooden puppet carelessly discarded on the floor. It would be a miracle if he survived. Why hadn't they stopped the game? Not that it was surprising, given the other events he had seen that day.

The crowd let out another cheer. The green team had stolen the fifth ball and thrown it to their climber. He scaled the wall in a matter of seconds to pass the last ball through the hoop and win the game. The green team celebrated, along with most of the crowd. Shep realised he was on his feet, cheering. To Shep's left, the high lord and the translator were slowly clapping their hands. Several other important-looking men dressed in blue robes sat with them. Only one of them, an old frail-looking man with thin white hair and a long, bony nose, appeared happy about the result.

Shep's trip to the Funeral Games had been eventful. He had left the palace in a horse-drawn carriage sandwiched between two guards, facing the high lord and his translator. They had travelled in silence to an arena about thirty minutes away. The arena reminded Shep of the time he visited the Colosseum in Rome as a child, except it was in perfect condition and even more grandiose. It had golden statues of athletes and bulls surrounding it, with large marble arches at the entrance.

He had watched in awe as archers showed off their skills with their longbows. One woman was comfortably the best, hitting the bullseye with ease no matter how far she stood from the target. She left wrapped in a winner's wreath and a pocketful of coins.

Bare-knuckle boxers followed the archers. From his ringside seat, Shep could feel every punch, taste the sweat and blood. The brutality had been devastating and only marginally offset by the free food and wine.

The final had been between a scarred old-timer who looked like he had been fighting his entire life and a muscular young man who looked like he should be on the cover of Vogue. The young man had danced around the older man and landed punch after punch. The old man's face was bloody and mushed, yet he kept going, only once hitting the floor. Shep was sure the young man had the fight. But then, as he danced forwards on his tiptoes to make the killer blow, the older man feigned with his left and landed an uppercut with his right. The young man was knocked out before he hit the ground. The high lord had cried out in frustration and slammed his fists down on his chair. Shortly after, Shep saw him hand a purse full of coins to a young boy who looked apologetic.

After leaving the arena, they travelled to the H-shaped stadium and watched the strange game with the climbing wall. The stadium itself was located close to a white pyramid that glowed on the horizon like a beacon to the gods. Shep had seen nothing like it and wondered whether the pyramids in Egypt looked as magnificent. Whenever Shep had seen pictures of pyramids, they had been falling to pieces, but this one looked as modern as the Gherkin in London. He didn't know whether to watch the game or gape at the magnificent structure.

Despite being treated like royalty, something didn't feel right. And it wasn't just that he was in a strange, ancient, yet weirdly modern city alongside people who looked like they had walked off the set of Troy. It felt like he was being constantly watched. People kept looking at him, whispering behind their hands. When he looked at them, they turned their heads away like they were afraid of him, but perhaps it was just the wine going to his head.

Shep had assumed that as soon as he left the confines of the palace, he would find something familiar that would give him some home comfort. A Starbucks, a McDonald's, or someone walking with a phone, but there was nothing. There were no tourists, no electricity, or modern amenities. The people wore strange clothing with no logos or branding and spoke a peculiar language he couldn't place. The more he saw, or didn't see, the more convinced he became that he had found an advanced ancient civilisation, trapped in time. Perhaps Atalantea was the legendary Atlantis, however inconceivable that might sound. What other explanation could there be? Where else in the world could he be?

'We go to the final event,' the translator said, snapping Shep out of his daydream. The green team was being presented with their trophy in front of the crowd.

'Great, thank you,' Shep replied. He didn't know what else to say. The translator had ignored his questions all day, and it was pointless asking any more.

They left the stadium, but this time they walked through the streets rather than travel by carriage. Guards carrying long, heavy-looking swords surrounded them, and Shep wondered what on earth they were expecting. The crowds had been raucous, but not violent. He had seen worse at almost every football game he had been to.

As they walked, a man pointed at them, his manner aggressive. Then he shouted something and spat on the floor. Shep assumed him a non-conformist, rebelling against authority. They existed in all corners of society. A guard left their ranks to confront him, and the man skulked away into the shadows. The incident made Shep uneasy. Suddenly, he wanted the comfort of his room in the palace. He felt like he was walking through a minefield and that at any moment, there would be an explosion.

About a hundred yards further down, a group of five bare-chested men started shouting. They were drunk and sounded angry. When they saw the high lord, they started throwing stones. Then a second group of men ran into them at full speed, causing a melee. The high lord's guards were quick to react, throwing themselves into the mix to separate the two fighting groups. The high lord watched, an amused grin on his face, like a schoolboy watching a fight after school. It was the first time Shep had seen him smile all day.

A high-pitched scream cut through the fog of the fight and brought it to a stop. A boy, no older than sixteen, stood holding his stomach, desperately trying to prevent a mixture of blood and guts from spilling onto the floor. Blood foamed from his mouth, and his eyes darted from side to side, searching for understanding.

A guard stood next to him, cleaning his sword. The boy fell onto the floor, still clinging to his stomach, now making a gurgling noise. He pulled his knees up to his chest, and his neck stretched backwards as he tried to contain the pain. A woman ran to him and dropped to her knees. Blood soaked into her dress as she tried to help, but it was no use. It would take a miracle to repair the damage.

The guard sheathed his sword and shrugged his shoulders. Three lines were branded on his forehead. Shep had noticed that most of the guards had the same mark, and he wondered if it was a badge of honour.

The boy's movements slowed down and then stopped. Shep was shaking and couldn't tear his eyes away. Bile rose in his throat, and he forced it down. He looked around, wondering what he should do, but no one seemed remotely shocked or in a great hurry to report it. The guard wasn't even reprimanded. Instead, someone patted him on his back. Shep made an O shape with his mouth and took a few deep breaths to quell his desire to vomit.

Then they carried on, walking as if nothing had happened. After a few minutes, and perhaps sensing Shep's shock, the translator said, 'Sometimes emotions can run high at these events. The people are passionate. What you witnessed was... unfortunate.'

A boy's guts were spilling out onto the floor, and it was unfortunate. Shep tried to shut the incident out of his head, but when he closed his eyes, the image was there, clear as day. The last events involved horse and chariot racing. It should have enthralled Shep, but the incident wouldn't leave him alone. The boy's eyes had been desperate and pleading for help. He'd seen that look before.

They arrived back at the palace, and Shep went quietly back to his room. He wanted nothing more than to see a friendly face, to ring his parents, or to catch up with Alfred. What had happened to Alfred? His gut was telling him he was alive, that somehow he'd survived. But how?

There was a knock on his door, and a curvaceous brunette stood in the doorway. She took off her top, but Shep wasn't in the mood. He smiled at her and, as politely as he could, indicated she should leave.

She didn't need to be asked twice.

CHAPTER XXXIII
Aphrodite's Temple, Paros

A phrodite's temple stood on top of a cliff, separated from the rest of the mainland. To the north, east, and west, the sea lashed wildly at the cliff face. To the south, a large wooden footbridge provided the only access to and from the temple, but all Hestia could see was a large swinging bridge disappearing into sea spray. She'd heard about the bridge to Aphrodite's temple, but she never thought she would see it. Until her father's death, she'd barely set foot outside of the Capital.

'I cannot travel any further with you,' said Klemides. He was squatting down, breathing heavily after their long journey. After escaping from the palace, Klemides rowed them out of the Capital to the north of Adelphi via a canal network. From there, they'd continued the journey on foot, avoiding any other humans. They'd barely stopped other than to eat and rest, and they were both exhausted. 'You'll be safe here. No man would dare pass beyond the bridge.'

What about a woman? Hestia thought. There were plenty of female mercenaries and tridents. Still, it was about as safe as she could be.

Hestia didn't want her uncle to leave. He'd saved her life and guided her safely to the temple. He was the only person she could trust. She still couldn't understand what had happened. How had she gone from being high lady to a fugitive in the blink of an eye? She had spent every second thinking about it, but the more she thought, the more questions she had. Someone must have infiltrated the high table and paid the high guard. The same person must have had some involvement in her father's death. But why? What did they have to gain?

At first, Attalus had been at the top of her list, but he wasn't wily enough, and he only had limited access to the high purse. She would have known if he was paying people off. The governors were the only people with the money and influence required to pull off such a stunt, but what could they have to gain from such drastic action?

All her uncle knew was that someone had put a price on her head should the governors appoint her high lady. The rumour had come from someone in his unit, but his source knew nothing else, and Klemides believed him. He had travelled to the Citadel following the revelation and walked straight into the palace. The guards at the gate hadn't bothered questioning him. Presumably, someone had paid them to turn a blind eye to tridents entering the palace. Klemides was adamant that none in his unit had taken the contract. They were warriors, not murderers. Other tridents didn't have the same level of integrity, and there were plenty of mercenaries and assassins who wouldn't think twice about taking on the job.

Hestia had wanted to stand and fight, show everyone that she wouldn't wilt away at the first obstacle she faced. But Klemides had pointed out that she needed an army to do that, and the high guard, her army, had been compromised. She would need to rely on the governors' armies to restore order, but she didn't know which governors she could trust. All she had was an ageing warrior with a bad back and knees that hurt in the cold.

'What should I do?' Hestia asked as they sat by the bridge. They had discussed this before, but she needed to hear it again.

'Cross the bridge, and stick with the story we discussed. Don't reveal your true identity, or word might get out. You'll be safe there. The priestesses will look after you.'

'But what if they make me swear allegiance to Aphrodite? I won't be able to leave.'

'They make you complete an apprenticeship before that happens, and that takes time, at least a year. I need to find out what's happening, but once I have, and it's safe, I'll come back for you. Then you can raise your army and get back to ruling. In the meantime, keep your head low.'

'Where are you going to go?'

Klemides took a deep breath and laced his fingers. 'Strange things are going on at the moment. People are going missing, and there is fighting within realms. I think it's all linked, but I don't know how or why. I have some contacts, degenerates mostly, but they know things. They'll talk to me, but the less you know, the better. Now go, you know all this. The less time we're stood around here, the better.'

Hestia felt like a lost little girl, not the leader of the mother of all civilisations. She looked at the rickety bridge and gulped. The wood looked rotten. If she fell through, she'd impale herself on the jagged rocks below.

'Go!' her uncle urged.

'Thank you,' she said, suddenly bombarded by emotions. 'And good luck. Come back soon.' She turned and marched off before she broke down. She needed to stay strong and pray that a man she barely knew could save her.

The bridge swayed, and Hestia turned her attention to the more pressing danger. Her legs almost buckled beneath her as she stepped onto the bridge. She clung to the ropes on either side, her knuckles white. Mist from the sea spray attacked her face, and she turned away.

She kept going, unable to see in either direction, carefully testing each footstep before committing to it. A gust of wind swung the rope bridge high, and Hestia let out a scream. She was sure it would collapse, but somehow it stayed intact and settled back down. Her muscles tensed, and her jaw ached, but she kept going, telling herself it couldn't go on forever.

Just when she was doubting her own assertion, the mist lifted, and Aphrodite's temple stood in front of her. The figure of a beautiful woman covered in gold emerged from the rock face. Hestia gasped and whispered a prayer to the Goddess of Love. It was the first time she had prayed since she was a little girl, and it felt silly. It was just the work of a talented individual. Nothing more. Yet, she felt, somehow, like she was being watched.

Legend had it that the sculptor was Pygmalion. Thousands of years ago, he carved the stones in the likeness of his true love, Helen, after the sea claimed her. He'd devoted his work to Aphrodite as any attempt to depict Aphrodite herself would only anger the goddess. No mortal could capture her beauty. Pygmalion had fallen in love with his work, and after learning that he could not cross the bridge to see it again, he had thrown himself off the cliff in despair.

As she crossed the bridge, Hestia could see a figure leaving the temple between Aphrodite's legs. The figure approached her. It was a young woman, perhaps in her late teens or early twenties. She was pretty and wore a long red robe tied at the neck with a clasp. She had short chestnut-coloured hair with an unusual white stripe through it, which brought out the sky blue in her eyes. Hestia suddenly became conscious of her appearance. She had been on the run for ten days, during which she had not bathed. She felt mucky. Her face itched, and her limbs ached.

The girl stopped about ten paces away. 'Welcome,' she said in a tone that belied the message. The girl had a stern face, and Hestia thought she would look prettier if she smiled.

Hestia nodded, unsure what to do. The two of them stood in awkward silence for a few seconds. The girl didn't look like a natural fit for the temple, and Hestia wondered how she had found herself there.

'Do you seek solace, or do you wish to join the Love Temple?' the girl asked. She made it sound like a challenge.

'I seek solace,' Hestia said.

'For what reason?'

The question startled Hestia. She hadn't expected an interrogation. 'I come from Arcadia. I have travelled a long way to get here. My partner disappeared, and I seek the guidance and wisdom of Aphrod... the Love Goddess.' Hestia remembered her uncle's instructions and relayed her story to the word, trying to make it sound convincing.

'And what is your name?'

'Agrippina,' Hestia said. It had been her grandmother's name.

'Welcome to Aphrodite's temple, Agrippina. I am Aliz. I am an apprentice here, and so I have no control over whether you stay. The high priestess will decide that, but I suggest you work on your story if you want to stay. Remember, you're in the realm of the Goddess here, and they say she addresses the high priestess, so if you can't fool me, you've got no chance in there.'

The bluntness startled Hestia, and she did not bother proclaiming her innocence. Instead, she looked at the apprentice and wondered once again what her story was. Aliz returned her stare, and Hestia turned away.

'You need a bath,' Aliz said.

Hestia laughed. The girl had no tact. If only she knew that she was talking to the high lady.

'Come with me. I'll show you to your quarters for the night. You must join in prayers at dawn. You'll meet the high priestess tomorrow. Or you won't. She works on her own timetable.'

Aliz led Hestia into the temple through Aphrodite's legs, where a spiral staircase greeted them. It rose into what Hestia reckoned would be Aphrodite's stomach. The top of the staircase opened out into a large stone hall with high ceilings. There were carvings on the walls, and Hestia blushed when she realised what they were.

'Graphic, aren't they?' Aliz said, seeing Hestia's reaction, and then she smiled for the first time. Hestia turned her eyes away as Aliz gently ran her finger along a phallus protruding from the wall. She seemed to find Hestia's awkwardness amusing.

Candles flickered on the wall, and the lick of the flame made the carvings dance. A smell of burning incense brought on waves of intoxication, and Hestia swayed as she walked.

'This is the main hall where we worship,' Aliz explained. 'We pray three times a day, but visitors only have to attend the prayers at dawn. Although, you're welcome to attend all of them, should you wish.'

Hestia watched as Aliz pushed some hair behind her ear, exposing the soft skin of her neck. She realised she was staring at her and quickly averted her gaze. What had come over her? Whatever it was, she needed to snap out of it.

Aliz led Hestia through an impossibly narrow corridor, and Hestia wondered if it was the only route into the temple or if Aliz was being purposefully difficult. The corridor led through to a room with rows of tables. It had a roaring fire, and Hestia could smell more incense burning. Two women dressed in white and gold robes sat at a table. They spoke in hushed voices and halted upon seeing Aliz approach. Aliz either didn't notice or didn't care about the sideways looks the women were giving her.

'This is the food hall,' Aliz said before carrying on with the tour.

They climbed a second stone staircase up into Aphrodite's bosom and a room filled with beds, each one separated from the next by a thin curtain.

'You are our only guest at the moment, so you'll have this room to yourself,' said Aliz.

'Where do you sleep?' Hestia asked. The question left her mouth before she'd thought about it, and Aliz met it with a bemused look.

'The apprentices sleep on the next floor. The priestesses on the floor above that, and the high priestess sleeps in the head. At least, that's what I'm led to believe. Any other questions?'

'No,' Hestia answered, annoyed that she'd allowed a common apprentice to make her feel so insignificant.

'Good. The washroom is through there.' Aliz pointed to a doorway adjoining the bedroom. 'I suspect you'll want to freshen up. There are spare robes in the wardrobe. Get changed into them after your wash. Food will be served in the food hall shortly. You will hear a bell.'

'Robes?'

'Yes. If you want to stay here, then you must wear them. And it looks like you have no spare clothes of your own, so rather fortunate, I would say.'

'Yes, thank you.' Hestia's clothes were filthy after the journey and felt welded onto her.

'If that's everything, I'll see you at dinner.' Aliz turned and walked off before Hestia responded.

It wasn't ideal, but it was safe. If Klemides could find out what was happening, she might only be there for a few days. Hestia walked around the room and looked out of the window. She was high up and had a magnificent view of the surrounding area. She saw mostly trees and farmland, but there was also a small village in the distance, perhaps four or five miles away. The Parosean Forest stretched out into the distance, dissecting Paros. They'd been careful to avoid it on their way to the temple. Everyone knew about the dangers that purportedly lurked in the forest. She suspected most of it was exaggerated fairytales, but neither Hestia nor Klemides had wanted to shorten their journey by cutting through it.

The washroom comprised a pool sunk into the floor. It was large enough to have a short swim. Hestia removed her clothes and walked in. The steaming water eased her aching muscles, tension evaporated from her body, and her mind relaxed, free from the stresses that had shackled her.

Hestia closed her eyes. She needed to plan her next move, just in case her uncle didn't return, but her plan could wait until she had rested. The water was too good not to enjoy, and she was so tired—

'Ahem,' said a voice.

Hestia jumped. She'd only closed her eyes for a second. At least that's what it felt like, but the wrinkles on her hands told a different story. Hestia turned to see Aliz staring at her and tried to cover herself with her hands, her face turning crimson.

'The bell for food went a short while ago,' Aliz said, still staring at Hestia. 'When you didn't show up, I thought you might be lost. I can see I was wrong. I'll see you in the food hall.'

'Yes, um, sorry... I...' Hestia muttered, but Aliz had already walked off.

Hestia quickly dried herself and put on a robe, noting that it looked old and in need of a wash. She walked down to the food hall and spotted Aliz sat at a table with several other girls, all wearing red robes. Hestia went to sit with her, but before she could sit down, Aliz pointed to another table.

'Guests, apprentices, and the priestesses eat separately,' she explained, her mouth full of food.

As the only guest, Hestia ate alone. There were around thirty priestesses, and apprentices sat at the tables, but not one of them acknowledged her existence. It was as though she was invisible. Occasionally she would see someone look in her direction, but they avoided eye contact, as though afraid that they might turn to stone if they looked straight at her.

Hestia's eyes kept drifting to Aliz. There was something about her that was intriguing, but she couldn't think what. She had an urge to talk to her, but she knew it would be inappropriate, and the thought gave her goose pimples. Hestia watched her for a while, careful not to make it obvious. Whilst Aliz was sitting at a table with the other apprentices, she was alone in their company. She was adrift from the conversation, her head down, ignoring the surrounding babbling. A part of Hestia felt sorry for her, but Aliz didn't seem to care. Hestia tore her eyes away. Why did she care? She had bigger problems to deal with than some apprentice who had shown nothing but indifference towards her.

Bells rung from the corner of the room, interrupting Hestia's thoughts. Their clangs made a dreamlike sound, and everyone fell silent as a priestess said a prayer to Aphrodite. There was a low murmuring as everyone joined in. When the prayer finished, Aliz was the first to stand to leave. She walked over to Hestia, and Hestia felt her pulse quicken.

'I'll show you back to your room,' Aliz said plainly.

Hestia nodded, dismayed at the formality of the statement.

200

CHAPTER XXXIV
Erineus, Phrixus

EX6 laughed loudly and slammed his hammer of a fist on the table, causing the drinks to fly into the air.

Xee looked over, wondering what was so funny, and then returned to his meal of gristle and gravy stolen from the left-overs of one of his company, although they weren't his company at all. They were nothing but brigands and mercenaries, former tridents brought together for the sole purpose of hunting down and taking out the elusive EN62.

After leaving his meeting with the Paymaster, Xee had led EX6 to where EN62's trail had gone cold. From there, trackers had tried to resuscitate the trail with no luck. Instead, they had followed leads that had taken them on a merry dance around most of the ten realms until they found themselves in a seedy tavern on the outskirts of the town of Erineus in the Phrixus realm.

The majority of the company were horrendously drunk, having made the most of the cheap ale. Two had started fights with the locals, and three had collapsed on the chairs and wouldn't be moving until the morning. EX6, their leader, was midway through a drinking competition with another of their number. They had been going at it for over an hour, and neither had given any ground. The bartender stood cowering behind the bar. He had been drying a glass with his towel for the last ten minutes, a look of horror sewn onto his face. He knew it wouldn't end well, but he also knew better than to stop it.

Xee watched quietly from his corner, keeping to himself. The last thing he wanted was to make himself the centre of attention. He had some food and a cup of water, which was more than he usually got. He was only there for the amusement of EX6, having long since served his purpose. Xee was just an abused dog, loyally following its owner. If EX6 grew bored with him, he wouldn't think twice about running a sword through him and leaving him for the wolves.

The door swung open, and a group of men walked in. The branding on their foreheads told Xee that they were also tridents, so he tucked himself further into the corner. There were seven of them. With their group, that meant fifteen tridents in the small tavern. It was bad news for the landlord. He would be lucky if he had a tavern in the morning.

'Zeus's beard!' EX6 shouted, and the bartender looked like he expected a lightning bolt to crash down through the ceiling.

The new group looked over in EX6's direction as he clumsily stood up.

A hard-faced woman marched over to him. 'Of all the turds in all the taverns,' she said and smiled. They clasped wrists in greeting. 'What brings you here, EX6?' she asked and took a seat on the bench next to him. 'Ale!' she yelled at the barman.

Xee peered up at her. She was tall and muscular, wearing black leather armour. At a guess, she was in her forties, but she had a shaved head that made her look like a young boy. Her features were harsh like they needed sanding down, and she had small, deep-set eyes, which gave away nothing. Xee took an instant dislike to her. She looked over at him, and he glanced away, but she'd clocked him.

'We're on a job,' EX6 slurred as the bartender scurried over with an ale. EX6 grabbed hold of the bartender's arm, pulling him down forcefully. 'Two more,' he said and then pushed the bartender away.

The newcomer studied EX6. 'What sort of—'

'What are you doing here, EX9? Not that I'm not delighted to see an old comrade, of course.' EX6 burped loudly and finished his drink in one large gulp.

'We're on a job as well—'

'Funny story,' EX6 barked, interrupting his old comrade. 'You hear of a contract a few months ago? Worth a lot of money?'

'I may have done.' EX9 looked around uncomfortably.

EX6 laughed into his fist. 'EN62 won it. She'd not even finished her training. Beat the rest, then refused to take it on. So,' EX6 laughed again, 'our benefactor, calls himself the Paymaster, put a price on her head. He sent one of ours to find her with some mercenary called

Jared, except our guy got himself into a fight and lost half of his face. Then this Jared took on the job himself and...' EX6 was struggling to get the words out through his laughter. He slapped the table and took a deep breath.

Xee was listening, and he knew what he was about to say. He desperately wanted to leave, but he knew that any movement now would only draw more attention to himself.

'... and... and so he got him instead.' EX6 pointed at Xee and roared with laughter. 'That rat to take on a trident.'

Xee looked away, embarrassed. Half of the bar was listening to the story now, and most joined in laughing.

EX9 looked at EX6 and gave him half a smile. 'So what happened?'

EX6 cleared his throat and spat phlegm out onto the floor. 'So she escaped, and we've been looking for her ever since. She's vanished, and we might as well be looking for the Helm of Darkness. Trackers couldn't even find her.' EX6 took a few deep breaths and composed himself. The bartender brought out a couple more drinks. EX6 opened his throat and downed one in a second.

'We're also looking for a stray girl,' EX9 whispered, trying to be discreet, 'and it sounds like we're working for the same person.'

Xee tried to filter out the background noise to hear what she was saying.

EX6 sat back. With each drink, he was sinking further under the table. 'And she's here?' he said in an attempted whisper, which was loud enough for those on the other side of the bar to hear.

'No,' replied EX9. 'We've been told that she's sought refuge at Aphrodite's temple, and so that's where we're headed.'

'Aphrodite's temple!' EX6 proclaimed loudly and sat up straight. EX9 gave him a stern look.

'You've not attempted there?' EX9 looked around at their all-male group.

EX6 was staring straight ahead. 'No, I never even...' He drifted off, the thought lost.

'I have three of my strongest female fighters with me. Perhaps we could help, given your men won't be able to enter the temple. Unless you want to piss off the Goddess of Love, that is.'

EX6 nodded.

'Obviously, we would want half of the price on her head if we found her.'

EX6 continued nodding. He was too drunk to negotiate. They spat on the floor and then grabbed wrists to seal the deal. Then the conversation turned to more trivial matters, and Xee focused on his meal, pleased the focus had moved off him.

After a few minutes, Xee spotted an opportunity to escape unseen, and he left hastily by the backdoor. He ran to the stable next to the tavern that would serve as his bed for the night. He could leave right there and then, disappearing whilst he still had the chance. If ever there was an opportunity, it was now, whilst everyone had alcohol in their blood.

The sound of a door slamming brought him to his senses. Footsteps approached, and then someone relieved themselves up against the stable wall.

They'd come after him. He knew too much, and they couldn't risk it. He didn't dare think about what they would do if he fled and they found him, so he curled up in a ball on some hay and tried to get some sleep.

CHAPTER XXXV
Aphrodite's Temple, Paros

It took three days for the high priestess to grant Hestia an audience, and the only person who spoke to her in that time was Aliz, who was still to reveal even the slightest chink in her armour.

In her spare time, which was plentiful, Hestia had explored the temple. On her first day, she discovered the underground baths. Natural hot springs heated them, and the warmth cleansed her pores and numbed her aches and pains like a miracle elixir. On her second day, she got lost exploring a myriad of hidden passageways and uncovered a secret prayer room that led through to a garden overflowing with flowers. It was tranquil, and the sound of waves and the occasional bird call made it the perfect place for meditation. Hestia had been so lost in her thoughts she had nearly missed the bell for food.

There was a lot more to the temple than the barren rock it appeared from the outside. On her third day, Hestia had been about to explore further when Aliz knocked unexpectedly on her door and told her to prepare for a meeting with the high priestess. The strange corridor she had discovered on her previous expedition would have to wait.

Aliz waited whilst Hestia dressed, and then she led her up a set of stairs. All routes leading into the head of the temple were locked, and Hestia wondered what strange delights she was going to witness. Not much other than a staircase, it transpired. They climbed until Hestia's legs felt heavy. When they reached a large, ornate wooden door, Aliz knocked and then disappeared as Hestia looked on, confused. She didn't want Aliz to leave and stood at the door waiting, trying to control her breathing. Suddenly, she was aware of an itch spreading over her arms and face. She reminded herself that she was the high lady and that the high priestess was one of her subjects, but her inner voice was weak.

The door opened to a pretty lady dressed in a simple white robe. Hestia recognised her as the priestess who led the prayers at mealtimes. She beckoned Hestia into the room and then left, closing the door behind her.

'Welcome to Aphrodite's temple,' said a lady, her voice filling the room. She was sitting on a large stone throne carved into the wall. On either side of her, the wall disappeared, providing huge open windows. Hestia assumed that from the outside, the gaps must be the eyes of Aphrodite. The wind whistled into the room, and Hestia felt a chill. She squinted and tried to block out the sun with her hand. The high priestess was sat in a shadow and was barely visible.

'What brings Hestia Atlas, the first High Lady of Atalantea, to Aphrodite's temple? To worship? To pay your respects? Or to cower behind its walls?'

Hestia took a step back and then steadied herself. All that time planning her cover story had been pointless. She opened her mouth to answer and then closed it again.

'Did you think the story you fed to our apprentice would fool the high priestess? That you could hide here? Do you think the Goddess would accept your duplicity?'

A faint murmur was all Hestia could manage in response.

'And what have you brought as an offering?'

The high priestess fell silent. Hestia opened and closed her mouth again, like a fish grasping for food. She didn't have an answer, not a satisfactory one, anyway.

'I... I... need help,' Hestia said, having recomposed herself. She realised she sounded pathetic. 'Are you able to provide it, or are you throwing the high lady out of your temple?'

'That is not within my power,' the high priestess responded curtly. 'All guests are welcome to sanctuary for ten days. It is the rule. But after ten days, you must either become an apprentice, in which case we will bind you here for five years to complete your training, or you must leave. You have seven days left, so what is your plan after that high lady?'

Hestia didn't know about the ten-day rule. Klemides had told her to stay at the temple until he brought news, but it was unlikely he would know anything before that deadline.

'I will have left before your deadline.'

'Even if your path is blocked?'

'I will have left before the end of the tenth day,' Hestia said firmly and wondered what the high priestess meant about her path being blocked.

A plan was already forming about how she could uncover who was behind what was happening. She would put her trust in the governors her father had relied on. Gadeirus and Ampheres had voted for her and, although their armies were weak, their counsel would be invaluable. Diaprepes had the strongest army, and he had been one of her father's closest friends. He would not turn his back on her either, but the journey to Attica would be more perilous.

'I can see you have tough decisions to face. Perhaps if you submit yourself to Her Holiness whilst you are here, She will provide you with some answers.'

Hestia grunted. It couldn't hurt.

'Step forward, high lady.'

Hestia stepped forward. As she did, the sun faded behind a cloud and removed the shadow from the high priestess's face. Hestia couldn't help but stare. She had an ageless complexion, with soft features and skin like caramel. Her charcoal hair was braided in a plait that flowed loosely over her right shoulder, and her eyes shone like diamonds.

The high priestess leaned forward and rested her hand on Hestia's forehead. Her touch was soft, and Hestia felt calmed, like a baby being handed back to its mother. She closed her eyes and listened as the high priestess spoke in an ancient language.

Nothing happened at first, but then images burst into Hestia's mind. Dyon. Her father. The governors. The Viracocha. Attalus. Her uncle. Tridents. A strange man with red hair she had not seen before. They came and left so quickly, Hestia could make no sense of it, and then there was darkness.

Cold, frightening darkness consumed Hestia. It sounded as though she'd found the entrance to Tartarus and was listening to tortured souls trapped there. Something was coming for her. She wanted to run, but her feet had grown roots, holding them to the ground. She tried to shout, but she couldn't open her mouth. It was sewn shut, but she screamed through the corners of her mouth until her body was exhausted. Then she collapsed.

When Hestia came to, someone had returned her to her bed. She didn't know what her vision meant, but she knew that something was coming and that she wouldn't need to worry about the ten-day rule.

CHAPTER XXXVI

Aphrodite's Temple, Paros

Aliz knocked on Agrippina's door. She was warming to her curious guest, even if she didn't believe a word of her story.

'Come in.'

Aliz walked in. Agrippina was lying on her bed, staring at the ceiling. Aliz didn't know what had happened during her meeting with the high priestess, but whatever it was had left her scarred.

'Fresh clothes,' Aliz said and laid them out.

She hated the menial tasks she had to do. The life of cooking, cleaning, and tending to the priestesses and guests wasn't for her. She was a fighter, and she felt like an amputee without her sword by her side. Nevertheless, Aliz kept telling herself it was her only option. She had a price on her head, and until things calmed down, mercenaries would hunt her, but it didn't make the reality any easier.

'Thank you,' said Agrippina without looking up.

Aliz walked off, then hesitated at the door. She wasn't a people person. A life spent talking with her fists meant she lacked the personable skills most people learned as they grew up. In the tridents, it didn't matter whether you could get on with someone, just whether you could take them down. Aliz liked that. She found human interaction dull, but Agrippina intrigued her. She felt like she should try.

'You should come with me,' Aliz said, trying to sound friendly. It came out awkward and forced.

Agrippina looked at her, and her eyes flashed. 'Why?'

'I want to show you something.'

Agrippina weighed up the offer and nodded, some colour returning to her cheeks.

Aliz led her along the hidden corridors and secret tunnels until they reached a door at the back of the temple. They walked outside, and there sat hidden amongst the rock face, a short climb down, was a rock pool. Despite searching the temple from top to toe many times, Aliz had only discovered the pool recently and by pure luck. She suspected few knew about it because to enjoy the pool, the timing had to be perfect. If you got it wrong, either the waves would bombard you every few seconds, or the water would have drained away, leaving an empty cauldron.

Aliz stripped off, forgetting Agrippina was there. She climbed the short distance to the pool and jumped in. The seawater felt good against her skin and washed off the layer of sweat the sun had applied.

'Come on then,' Aliz shouted, suddenly remembering she had company.

'Should we be here?' Agrippina replied, her arms folded tightly across her chest.

'Why not?'

'I don't know. Is it allowed?' She crossed her legs and looked away as she spoke.

'No one knows about this place or that we're here. Be quick, though. We don't have long before it'll disappear. Come on! It's relaxing.'

Agrippina looked like she wanted to say something, but if she did, she decided better of it. Instead, she undressed behind a rock and joined Aliz in the pool, looking around all the time as though someone might disturb them. They sat silently, Aliz enjoying the sound of the waves and the sun's ray against her back, Agrippina hugging her knees.

'You have a lot of scars,' Agrippina said eventually. It was more of a statement than a question.

'So do you,' Aliz replied, pointing to a scar across Agrippina's forearm.

Agrippina covered her arm with her hand and looked aghast.

'You shouldn't do that,' said Aliz. 'Be proud of them. You earned them.'

'Earned them?' Agrippina protested. 'I did nothing to earn this.'

'What I mean,' Aliz backtracked, 'is that they are part of you, whether or not you like them, so you might as well learn to love them.'

'Well, I don't love this scar.'

'I think it gives you character.'

Agrippina was upset, but Aliz couldn't think why. It was only a little scar. She had loads of them all over her body, and they didn't bother her.

'I used to hate my hair,' Aliz said, trying to make amends. 'I did everything I could to make it less noticeable, but now I like it.' She had decided she no longer needed to hide her hair in the temple. 'How did you get your scar?'

Agrippina gave her a venomous look. 'You've never told me anything about you, and now you bring me here for information?'

'Well, before I saw the light,' Aliz said mockingly, 'I trained as a trident.'

'You don't have the—'

'The branding? No, they disbanded the tridents before I completed my training, and then I came here.' Aliz missed out on the bit in-between. No one but the high priestess knew the true reason she had joined the temple.

'This scar,' she continued, pointing to a small scar on her collarbone, 'was from a sword-fighting competition a few years ago. The guy I was fighting was quick, and I let my guard down. He struck me hard and broke my collarbone.'

'What about the scar on your arm?' said Agrippina, moving closer to Aliz and pointing to a long thin scar along Aliz's upper arm.

'That was during a training exercise. We were climbing, and I fell. Broke my arm in three places.' Aliz pointed to a scar near her neck. 'This one nearly killed me.' She was enjoying reminiscing about her time in the tridents. 'It was after I won a melee. There were two of us left, and the man I was up against was older, fitter, and stronger than me. At least that's what he thought. When I beat him, it humiliated him, so he tried to kill me when I was asleep. Such a coward. It's a good thing I'm a light sleeper and always carry a blade.'

'What happened to him?'

'Well, he won't be stabbing anyone else anytime soon or talking.' Aliz smiled, and then she saw Agrippina's face and stopped.

'So why did you join the temple?' Agrippina asked, changing the topic.

'You first.'

'I've not joined.' Agrippina looked away and stared at her hands.

'No, but you're here, and it doesn't look like you're going anywhere soon,' Aliz pressed.

'People attacked me, and I needed to get somewhere safe.'

'Me, too. Not too dissimilar, are we?'

'But you're a warrior. You can defend yourself. You've been defending yourself your whole life, so what suddenly changed?'

'I can defend myself, yes, but not against what was coming for me.'

'And what was that exactly?' Agrippina stared intently at Aliz, and there was a power behind those eyes, a natural tone of authority.

Aliz felt comfortable speaking to Agrippina. It felt safe.

'After they disbanded the tridents,' Aliz said after a pause, 'the warriors were in demand. Lots of people wanted protection, and the tridents were cheaper than anything else on the market because there were so many of them... of us. Some, like me, stuck around to continue protecting the State. There was still funding for a few units, but most were told there was no place for them, and so they went to work for any crook they could find.'

Aliz paused, the water shimmering around her. I nodded, hoping she would continue.

'Then there was a rumour of a contract. It was for a colossal sum, but no one knew who it was with or what it was for. Then a few of us were invited to this secret location, and when we got there, they made us fight. It was brutal. Usually, we train and fight with blunt swords, but these were the real deal,' Aliz said, her tone going cold.

'There were nine of us fighting in a clearing for a contract no one knew anything about for a person we didn't know. It was madness. We could have walked out of there. We should have walked out of there, but some of my comrades were too proud, and so we started competing. It's what we're trained to do, except this time the blades cut. People fell, and others got angry. It was a mess, a horrible mess. I was fighting the only family I'd ever had, but they'd gone berserk. In the end, I got the contract and a load of coin.'

'You won?'

'No one won, but I was the last one standing. Then I watched, helpless, as men came and finished anyone still breathing like they were slaughtering cattle. It was a warning, letting me know what would happen if I stepped out of line. They gave me an assignment and some money.

Then they promised the rest of the contract value on completion, but I couldn't do it. The assignment was suicide, so I ran, and they followed. I ran faster and further. And now I'm here.'

'What was the assignment?' asked Agrippina through gritted teeth, her skin translucent. She was digging her nails into her skin and staring fixedly ahead.

Aliz furrowed her brows and shuffled awkwardly. She thought she might get some sympathy for her plight, not disgust. 'They wanted me to assassinate someone,' she murmured.

'The high lord?' Agrippina said and looked at Aliz's face. She had tears in her eyes.

Aliz licked her lips and looked away. She didn't answer, but she didn't need to.

Agrippina started sobbing.

Then the pieces fell together in Aliz's mind. 'You're Hestia, aren't you? You're the daughter. I'm sorry I—'

'Why didn't you tell someone?' Hestia cried, barely able to get the words out. 'If you'd have told someone, he might still be alive.'

Aliz stood up and walked out of the pool. Hestia's wave of grief was drowning her. 'Tell who? I didn't know who I could trust. I was being hunted. I could barely keep myself alive.'

'There must have been something you could have done. Why would someone want him dead? I don't understand. Why would anyone want him dead?' Agrippina's face had crumpled, and she was gasping between each word.

Aliz looked around, wondering what to do. She could bandage a wound and splint a broken leg, but helping someone with their emotions was way out of her comfort zone. Her natural response was to walk away. This was exactly why she avoided human contact.

A bell rang, loud, crisp, and clear. It wasn't the lunch bell. Aliz's mind snapped into focus.

'Who knows that you are here?' Aliz demanded.

'No one other than my uncle. Why?'

Aliz ignored her and cursed loudly. She needed to find her weapons.

CHAPTER XXXVII
Aphrodite's Temple, Paros

Xee stood at the foot of the bridge to Aphrodite's temple, closed his eyes, and took some deep breaths. They had hunted Aliz for months, slowly tracking her across the country, searching every nook and cranny. With every dead-end, a voice inside Xee's head had whooped with delight, despite it prolonging his miserable journey. Now they had finally found her hideout. He knew this was where she was hiding because it just felt different, inevitable. His conscience was screaming at him, but what was he supposed to do?

They would have to search Aphrodite's temple for her, and that created a problem. Many claimed to no longer worship the gods, but deep down, they were still believers. No man dared cross the bridge for fear of retribution from Aphrodite, and there was no other way to access the temple unless they grew wings.

The party sent to look for the high lady had four female tridents. Tough and brutal warriors, but that still might not be enough. Xee knew how fearsome a warrior Aliz was, and he had no desire to face her again, with or without backup.

Xee watched as the female warriors donned their bronze masks. It was a sign that battle was imminent. He stayed out of their way and made himself as invisible as possible. The masks were chilling. They were all the same haunting face of torment with hollowed-out eyes and mouths. They were supposed to represent the Keres, the spirits of violent death, and there was a proverb that any enemy who looked upon the mask would soon wander the Underworld. One warrior had told him it used to be common practice for tridents to screw their masks into the side of their skull during a battle, but they had discarded the practice after it caused too many injuries. Xee believed him.

'Is everyone clear on the plan?' EX6 shouted amidst a burst of sudden activity. Xee wasn't aware that there was a plan other than to storm the temple. There was a general murmuring of agreement. The four female warriors stepped onto the bridge, and sea mist bombarded them. EX6 walked over to him. 'You too, worm,' he snarled.

Xee nearly jumped out of his skin. 'I can't,' he protested. Suddenly, all eyes were on him. 'Men can't cross the bridge. It's forbidden. It could damage the mission.'

Surely he knew that.

'Men can't cross the bridge, no, so you'll be fine. I can chop that thing off between your legs if it would make you happier. Might feed a fish or two.' The other men laughed, and Xee felt a knot in the pit of his stomach.

'I haven't got a weapon or a mask,' Xee muttered.

'You don't get a mask. You're not a trident. But if you want a weapon, you can take this.' EX6 threw Xee a small knife designed for cutting branches and chopping meat. The men hooted at their leader.

Xee picked the knife up off the ground. It was humiliating but better than nothing. The sound of laughter rang in his ears as he followed the warriors across the bridge. He took a deep breath and wiped his eyes, refusing to look back. He wouldn't give them the satisfaction.

Xee had already lost sight of the warriors ahead of him to the sea spray. Did they know he was behind them? Perhaps he could hide and wait until the trouble was over and then quietly head back home. Maybe they would let him be. The plan comforted him as he crossed the bridge. He didn't care that the wood was rotten and slippery or that the bridge was swaying in the wind.

Then the spray eased, and Aphrodite emerged in front of him. All thoughts disappeared, and Xee dropped to his knees, begging forgiveness for his slight. He tried to explain that it wasn't his fault, that they had forced him to cross the bridge. Then he opened his eyes and realised that he was looking at the entrance to the temple, not the actual goddess. He jumped to his feet and coughed indignantly into his hand.

The four tridents were standing at the end of the bridge, waiting. With their bronze masks and black leather armour, it looked like death had arrived at the temple. He stood a few yards away as they spoke to each other in hushed tones. They glanced at him and then continued with their discussion, and then a bell tolled.

Was it an alarm? Or was it a call to prayers? When the tridents ran towards an entrance between Aphrodite's legs, they brought about a sense of urgency. Xee followed, unsure of what to do, thoughts of hiding away now forgotten.

They climbed up a spiral staircase and entered a large room filled with carvings on the walls. Xee stared at one of them, momentarily distracted by the graphic eroticism which was at odds with their current purpose. Someone pushed him on, and they ventured through a tight corridor into a room filled with tables. There was no sign of life.

They split off with two climbing to the top of the temple and the other two searching the lower floors. Xee joined the search on the lower floors, trying to ignore the striking sculptures and paintings that jumped out at him around every corner.

The warriors didn't need or want him there. Xee had considered hanging back and escaping, but he didn't like the thought of coming face-to-face with EN62, and the temple was such a maze he'd probably be wandering the corridors for the rest of his life. So he stayed with the tridents, and they continued with their search.

They went up and down corridors, through secret tunnels, past the kitchens and washrooms, and just as Xee thought they must have looked everywhere, they found the priestesses huddled together in a small room, praying. Candles flickered brightly on the wall, and a thick fog of incense brought a strange sense of calmness to the scene. The priestesses ignored them and continued with their prayers. They seemed to be in a trance and were slowly rocking backwards and forwards, muttering a strange, rhythmic chant.

EN62 wasn't amongst them. Xee smiled. Perhaps they were mistaken.

'We are looking for a girl that calls herself Aliz and one called Hestia. They will be new here and may go by different names,' said EX9, drawing a small black sword menacingly from her hip. She was in command of their recce. 'We mean no harm to anyone else.'

The priestesses ignored her and carried on with their prayers. Xee suppressed a laugh at their indifference and coughed instead. The tridents held no threat here, not in Aphrodite's house.

'We are looking—' EX9 started again, a little louder.

'There is no one here by those names,' a priestess in white said, interrupting her, and then carried on with the chant.

'We will use force if required,' EX9 said threateningly and took a step forward.

A young girl in a red robe saw the look on EX9's face, the sword in her hand, and broke. 'She's here,' she stuttered. 'Aliz, that is. I don't know about the other one. The only other person here is a guest called Agrippina. She arrived a few days ago.'

'Hold your tongue!' shouted the priestess who had spoken earlier but then said no more as EX9's weapon pierced her chest. The priestess looked down at the strange obstacle stuck in her and slowly pulled it free before dropping to the floor.

The priestesses shrieked.

'That is for lying before the Goddess,' EX9 said angrily before retrieving her weapon. 'No more blood needs to be spilled. Where are they?'

The priestesses looked around, too afraid to speak. Then the girl in the red robe said, 'I don't know. I've not seen her today. She can't be far.'

'Go look for her,' EX9 said to the other warrior. 'And take her with you,' she added, referring to the girl in the red robe. 'She seems eager to please.' Then she turned to Xee. 'You stay here, worm, and watch the door.'

Xee did as he was told. He was quivering, and his legs felt heavy. He held his pathetic knife in his hand, but he knew it was EX9 who the priestesses feared, not him. They looked at him with a mixture of confusion and disgust, but there was no fear.

They waited in silence. Each second dragged, and Xee wondered what was taking so long. Then he saw her approaching. He'd recognise her anywhere with the white stripe in her hair and the confident swagger. EN62, or Aliz, as she liked to call herself now. She was the girl who broke his face. He thought he'd feel anger towards her for what she did to him, but he felt pity. Who was he to pity anyone?

She walked purposely towards him, dragging the tip of her sword along the floor. It made a horrible screeching sound. A second girl tiptoed behind her, looking like a gentle leaf in comparison. The trident sent to look for her and the girl in the red robe, where nowhere to be seen.

216

'She's here,' Xee tried to shout, but the words lost their confidence on the way out. He wasn't going to block her way and moved into the corner of the room.

EX9 drew her sword.

'You need to come with us,' EX9 shouted. 'There has been enough bloodshed because of you already.'

'Too late for that,' Aliz responded and pounced. She flew across the room with the elegance of a ballet dancer and caught EX9 off-guard. There was a clash of steel, and EX9 stepped back defensively.

EX9 was stronger and had the better reach, but Aliz was quicker. The blades danced backwards and forwards as the priestesses darted out of the room. Xee's untrained eyes couldn't pick a winner. They were both highly skilled and showed no obvious weaknesses.

EX9 mounted an attack of heavy swings, which forced Aliz back towards the door, deflecting the thrusts as she went. The attacks intensified, and EX9 grunted angrily as she failed to find a breakthrough. Aliz blocked and moved, blocked and moved, her feet never stopping. Xee couldn't look away.

Then EX9 tired. Her leather armour was heavy, and her mask restricted her vision. She made a wild, desperate lunge, which even Xee could have predicted. Aliz parried it, turned acrobatically, using her momentum to swing at EX9's exposed midriff.

EX9 let out a scream and held her side with her free hand. Xee cheered silently and then wondered why. Aliz would likely come straight for him afterwards.

EX9 carried on fighting, her movements restricted. Now it was Aliz's turn to attack, and she could take her time. She slowly advanced on her wounded opponent, who was bent over, trying to stem the bleeding from her cut. She held her sword up defensively, and Aliz knocked it out of her hand.

'Sit down,' Aliz said just as a high-pitched horn sounded. 'What's that?' she wondered aloud.

It was a distraction, a split second, nothing more. But it was enough for EX9 to retrieve a hidden dagger from her belt and lunge at Aliz. Aliz's guard was down, and the attack would surely have killed her had Xee not been alert to the danger. He had been watching EX9 the entire time, and as soon as the horn sounded, he'd spotted the danger.

Instinctively, he threw his pathetic knife at EX9 from across the room. His aim was true, and the hilt hit her on the side of her head. It was enough to confuse EX9 and delay the lunge. It gave Aliz a chance to raise her sword, which EX9 stumbled onto. She fell limp, and the dagger dropped out of her hand, clattering onto the floor. The horn continued to sound outside.

Aliz looked at Xee, an eyebrow raised and a slight smile on her lips. 'You come with me,' she said and grabbed hold of his elbow.

Xee meekly followed, wondering whether his actions had helped or hindered his cause. The girl who had arrived with Aliz and who had quivered behind her during the ensuing fight joined them as they navigated the maze of corridors out of the temple.

'There are more of them,' Xee said as they walked. 'Three more in the temple. The rest can't cross the bridge.'

'I see you didn't have any problems.'

'I… I didn't have a choice.'

'Hmm, and there are only two more in the temple. I've taken care of the other one. And I suspect the other two have found what they're looking for.'

They reached the bottom of the spiral staircase leading outside and peered towards the bridge. A priestess was standing there, her arms tied behind her back and her head down. Stood behind her were the two tridents who had searched the upper rooms of the temple. One had hold of the priestess, and the other was blowing a horn. Aliz, Xee, and the girl ducked back into the doorway, out of sight.

'The high priestess,' Aliz muttered. 'That was probably their tactic all along. Either take us down or find a hostage.'

Xee looked at the woman who stood next to Aliz and realised that it must be Hestia, or the high lady, or whatever her title was. He never thought he would come so close to royalty, and he wondered if he should bow to her.

'EN62, Hestia!' the trident holding the priestess shouted, and Xee snapped back into reality. 'Hand yourselves over to us, and we will release the high priestess!'

'They'll kill you both,' said Xee unhelpfully.

'Follow me,' Aliz said to Hestia.

218

Xee wondered what he should do, but then Aliz grabbed him by the scruff of his neck and stuck the tip of her blade into his back. Xee cried out and pushed his chest out as the blade pierced his skin. 'What are you doing?' he cried.

'Walk forwards and trust me!'

Xee did as he was told. If she was hoping to use him as a bargaining chip, then she'd be disappointed, although he kept his thoughts to himself.

'The high priestess for your man,' Aliz said.

The tridents laughed at her suggestion, and Xee shook his head.

'Kill him. Save us a job,' said one of them.

Aliz froze, and Xee held his breath. He knew she wouldn't kill him. She wasn't a murderer.

'Fight me then,' said Aliz and pushed Xee to the side. 'Two on one. You win. You kill me and take the high lady, but leave the high priestess. She has nothing to do with this.'

Xee wondered where that left him in the deal and edged out of the eyeline of the tridents. The day was still warm, but he felt a chill in his bones.

The tridents looked at each other. Honour dictated they accept the challenge, but they feared Aliz. Xee could see it in the way they stood. She had already taken out two of their party.

'No,' the trident holding the horn said. 'Drop your weapons and hand yourselves over to us, and then we will let the high priestess go.'

'Me for the high priestess,' said Hestia, stepping forwards. 'Aliz is an apprentice of the temple now. You have nothing to fear from her.'

'No,' Aliz barked and put her hand on Hestia's chest, forcing her to stop.

'Both of you for the high priestess,' the trident holding the horn said. 'That's the deal.'

No one moved.

'We've waited long enough. We'll send her back in pieces until you come over. You have no other option.'

Aliz and Hestia remained frozen, staring at each other as though having a conversation through facial expressions alone.

The high priestess squealed as her captor forced her to kneel and locked her arm above her head so that her hand was flopping down, powerless. Aliz opened her mouth to say something and then closed it again.

'I'll start with the little finger and work my way along,' said the trident and showed them a small, sharp knife.

'Zeus,' mumbled Xee under his breath, putting his head in his hands. Now would be a good time to run.

Hestia bit her lip, and Aliz drew her sword, but neither moved. They didn't know if she was bluffing. An attack on the high priestess was as bad as an attack on Aphrodite.

But Xee knew the tridents didn't bluff.

A scream cut through the air as the trident delivered on her promise.

'Stop!' shouted Hestia. 'Enough. Stop it.' Hestia barged past Aliz and walked towards the bridge.

The trident stopped, a severed finger in her hand. She threw it carelessly to the side and let go of her grip on the high priestess, who fell to the ground, cradling her hand against her midriff, whimpering. The trident stood over her, preventing her from moving. Xee felt a sword dig into his back as Aliz forced him to walk towards the bridge. Not this again, he thought to himself.

'Let her go,' said Aliz through clenched teeth.

'Drop your sword,' replied the trident who had cut the high priestess.

Aliz threw her sword down, allowing Xee to relax his back.

The trident wiped blood onto her armour and then looked at the high priestess. 'You can go,' she said plainly.

The high priestess struggled to her feet and then looked at the two tridents, her strength returning. She recanted something in an ancient language, which made her sound tongue-tied. Xee assumed she was uttering a curse or calling on Aphrodite to avenge her. The thought made him anxious, and he prayed he wasn't part of her retaliation. Then she turned and marched back towards the temple, her head held high, splatters of blood flowing from her finger onto the floor. She didn't stop or look back.

'Collect her sword, worm,' the trident with the horn ordered.

Xee did as he was told and then was forced to bind Aliz and Hestia with ropes. He couldn't bring himself to look at them as he secured the knots. They walked back across the bridge, led by the surviving tridents. Xee dragged his heels as they went, blocking out thoughts about what they might do to him and unable to register what everyone else was doing. He decided he would run as fast as he could at the first opportunity. He was quick, and he might have a chance—

A loud cheer disrupted Xee's thoughts, and he looked up to see that they'd emerged on the other side of the bridge. The cheer became muted as the tridents realised that two of their number hadn't returned.

No chance of running!

'Excellent work!' boomed EX6 to his comrades, beaming. He looked at Aliz and crouched down next to her. 'I liked EX9,' he said. Then he slapped Aliz across her cheek with the back of his hand. The slap was powerful, and Aliz nearly fell over, but she steadied herself. She stood up straight and spat blood in EX6's face. Xee cringed. It was brave but foolish. EX6 would make her pay for that.

EX6 wiped the blood away and laughed. He looked around and encouraged his comrades to join in. Then, as the laughter reached a crescendo, he turned and punched Aliz in the face.

Xee winced. It was a powerful punch, starting from the hips, flowing through his chest and arm in one fluid motion. It caught Aliz off-guard, and she collapsed to the ground. Her nose crunched, and a river of blood cascaded from it. Her eyes looked dazed, and she struggled to stand up. She spat something out which looked like a tooth, and then she slowly got back to her feet, her core still vibrating from the impact. Xee wanted to help her, to do something. Instead, he cowered and looked away.

EX6 smirked and stepped towards Aliz. He unbound her as she tried to steady her legs and passed her a sword. 'Kill him,' he said to her.

Xee looked around. Kill who?

Aliz hesitated and then looked slowly at Xee.

Xee's eyes widened as realisation dawned on him. Everyone was watching them. He edged backwards, but he had nowhere to go.

'You kill him if you have to,' Aliz said, unable to breathe through her nose. She threw the sword back at EX6.

'It's an order, EN62. Kill him, or we kill her.' EX6 pointed at Hestia.

Xee's limbs felt like jelly, and he'd lost the ability to speak.

Aliz stumbled towards him, the blow still affecting her. Dark rings had already formed around her eyes, and blood was flowing in a series of streams down her face. She wiped it away with the back of her arm, but fresh blood quickly appeared.

Xee looked at her. He opened his mouth, but he didn't know what to say. 'Please…' was all he could manage, and he put his hands together.

'On your knees, head down,' Aliz said, her voice barely above a whisper.

'Please,' Xee said again, tears forming in his eyes. This couldn't be happening. Why couldn't they just let him go home? He just wanted to go home.

'It'll be easier with your head down,' Aliz said and looked away.

'You don't have to,' Xee begged.

'Yes,' Aliz replied, 'I do. You need to go down after the first strike.'

Xee kneeled and scrunched his eyes closed. He didn't see the sword fall.

CHAPTER XXXVIII

Attica

Axil entered the cave on the border between Attica and Phrixus for his meeting with the Paymaster. They were back at their normal location. The long ride had left him exhausted, but Axil felt relieved that he didn't have to sit in the penitence booth again. He wasn't sure his conscience could take much more of a hammering.

He'd sent all his tridents north to Aphrodite's temple on the back of a drunk man's ramblings, and that thought made him nervous. What if he was wrong? What if she was hiding somewhere else, and he'd wasted valuable time and resources? The Paymaster was not a man who took failure lightly. He had seen the repercussions. Usually, Axil didn't have issues with his confidence, but recent events had caused him to question himself constantly.

Axil cleared his throat and looked around the empty cave, suddenly feeling a need to relieve himself. An insect scurried along the wall and then disappeared into a crevice. Axil watched it reappear a few seconds later, pleased to have something to distract himself whilst he waited. It was an ugly-looking thing with a red and black striped body and pincer-like legs. Deeper in the cave, Axil spotted a strange blue-green glow lighting up a tunnel. The caves were famous for their glowworms, although Axil had never noticed them before. Perhaps it was to do with the time of day.

'A hawk arrived yesterday,' a voice said from nowhere, breaking the heavy silence.

Axil took a deep breath.

'It seems your suspicion was correct.'

Axil breathed out.

'They found the girl, along with another problem. Well done. You have…redeemed yourself.'

Axil allowed himself half a smile. He nodded at the empty room and looked around again. The relief had made him giddy, but he didn't want it to show.

'I have sent instructions. We will bring her back here. The girl's death cannot be suspicious. It would create too many issues, and we cannot trust the tridents. The incident with the crowds at the Funeral Games is a prime example.'

Rumours were already surfacing about Hestia's absence from the Funeral Games, and the fact that the governors had not set an official date for the swearing-in ceremony where she would be officially appointed as High Lady and Protector of the Ten Realms. Her sudden death would only fuel those rumours.

'We can now move on to stage two.'

'Stage two?' Axil said, aghast. The words just fell out.

'Is that a problem?'

'No, no,' said Axil, shaking his head. He opened his mouth to explain his reaction, but he didn't have an explanation, so he closed it again.

'We need to make the boy's position permanent.'

'Once Hestia is…' Axil swallowed, 'dealt with. Then he is the next in line.'

'Yes, that part is simple, and the swearing-in will be on the eve of Saviour's Day. Attalus will be sworn in instead of Hestia. It's what comes after that I'm interested in. You were a lawgiver in a past life, were you not?'

'Well, I trained...' He'd quickly lost interest in his chosen profession, and his other skills were more valuable, more interesting. He wished now that he'd stuck with the simple life.

'In what circumstances can the high lord overrule the governors?'

Axil racked his brains. It was a long time since he'd studied the rules, and they were ambiguous, to say the least. 'A high lord can propose a motion to overrule a decision, and if the governors pass it, then it will overrule whatever went before it.'

'How else?' said the Paymaster impatiently.

Axil tried to think. 'There's only one other circumstance I can think of, and that's if a motion carried opposes the Order.'

The Paymaster was silent. And then he said, 'And does the Equality-For-All Motion oppose the Order?'

Axil knew the Order well. The State required everyone to study and learn it from an early age. 'I suppose you could argue the Order only refers to the masculine and that by permitting the line of the governors and high lord to pass to a daughter is against a strict interpretation of the Order. I mean, it's long since been ruled—'

The Paymaster cut him off. 'My thoughts exactly.'

Axil wasn't sure what the Paymaster was up to, and he didn't want to know. Putting Attalus on the throne was one thing, but manipulating him to do his bidding? Was that what the Paymaster had intended all along? If so, what was his aim?

'It would be a bold and unpopular move,' continued Axil, backtracking. 'The high lord will no doubt have received counsel from the high lawgiver when he proposed the motion in the first place, so I don't see how such an argument could be successful.'

'A high lawgiver who was no doubt set to benefit from the motion, which weak governors then approved. The high lawgiver needs replacing with counsel that isn't corrupt, don't you think? Who would you suggest?'

'What?' Axil stuttered. He was busy trying to work out what the Paymaster was up to. He wasn't doing this just to appease the Order and save Atalantea from the Saviour's wrath. No, there was something more. Something personal. Something that was staring him in the face, but he couldn't put his finger on it.

'It would be highly unpopular to take such action. I imagine the governors will contest the move. It could even lead to a revolt. And public opinion is already against Attalus. If people think something's wrong, there will be riots. There's already been rioting over the way Attalus dealt with the middling.'

'I am very aware of the position,' snapped the Paymaster. 'Matters will be taken care of. Your job now is to find me a suitable replacement for the high lawgiver. Someone who appreciates the Order and understands the ramifications of bending the Order to your will. Given your recent escapades, I would have thought this would be a simple one for you.'

'I'm sorry,' said Axil, stepping back. 'I spoke out of turn but was merely pointing out...' Axil trailed off, realising it was pointless raising it again.

'Do you have a plan?'

Axil thought about it. 'Attalus can pick his own counsel once he's in place, but I have no way of getting an audience with him to influence him.'

'You don't need to worry about getting an audience. I just need a name. Someone who will provide good counsel to the high lord. Someone who understands the Order as the original governors intended it, and someone who can understand the order of inheritance.'

A name sprang immediately into Axil's mind, a devious snake of a man, and one reason he left the profession. He would be perfect for the Paymaster. Axil would not enjoy approaching him. It would be like cutting a deal with a Titan.

'Do you have a name?'

Axil took a deep breath, stalling. 'Yes,' he said, eventually, 'my old tutor, Solon.'

CHAPTER XXXIX
Aphrodite's Temple, Paros

Xee's first thought was, I'm alive! His second was, Why? His third was, Who is that man standing over me?

Then he saw the mark of the trident on the man's forehead, and a surge of energy pulsated through him, awakening the pains in his body. He tried to stand up, but the effort made him dizzy. He could feel dried blood on the back of his head, and a vague recollection of kneeling to receive his death sentence came back to him.

'Where is she?' the man said aggressively and put his foot on Xee's chest to stop him from getting up. It was the heavy boot of an old warrior who had walked many miles. It was crushing the air out of Xee's lungs with nearly no effort at all.

'Who?' Xee winced as he received a kick to the groin. He recoiled and felt his eyes water from the fresh pain.

'The girl,' grunted the man.

'Which girl?' Xee asked and immediately regretted it as the man kicked him again.

The man looked down, and Xee could see anger in his grey eyes. His face looked incapable of smiling. His unshaven, deep-lined face was filled with nicks and cuts from years of putting himself in front of danger. The beard that lined his jaw had patches of white, and his hawk-like nose had been broken and poorly put back into place. Xee briefly mused that they had something in common.

'The high lady. Where is she?'

Xee initially thought someone had sent the man to finish him off, but perhaps he wasn't with the other tridents. He seemed the same but different in a way that was impossible to pinpoint.

'Your lot took her,' Xee replied as the man removed his foot from Xee's chest.

'My lot?' the man asked. He dragged Xee to his feet.

Xee stood for a second, then collapsed back down. His legs weren't communicating with his brain. 'Warriors like you. They found her here, and they took her away.'

'Where are they taking her?'

'I don't know,' said Xee and put his hands up in defence as the man clenched his fist. 'I wasn't with them.'

'What are you doing here, then?'

'They sent me to bring back the other one.'

'What other one?' the man snarled, losing patience.

'One like you. They sent me to bring her in months ago, but she escaped, and we were tracking her. Whilst we were searching, another group of warriors joined us. They were hunting Hestia, the high lady—'

The man cursed and, when Xee flinched, wafted his hand to tell Xee to keep talking.

'We all ended up here, and the two of them came out together. Why? Who are you with? Are you not with them?'

The man ignored his questions. 'Who were you tracking?'

'EN62. But she calls herself Aliz now,' Xee said, desperate to please.

'An enforcer? Why were you tracking an enforcer? And on whose instructions?'

Xee had always wondered what the EN stood for. He still wasn't sure he knew what it meant. 'I don't know why. She's dangerous. I don't know who the instructions came from. It's just someone they call the Paymaster. Look, I shouldn't be here. I shouldn't. I just want to go home. My parents own a tavern, and I was serving this man called Jared. He needed someone to help with this job—'

The man cut him off, not interested in Xee's tale. 'So, how did this person called the Paymaster get instructions to you if you don't know who he is?' the man asked, shaking his head.

'Like I was saying, a friend, well… not really a friend, someone who came into my parents' tavern, asked for my help with a job because someone had let him down. He said it was a quick and easy job. All we had to do was bring in a girl. He offered me lots of money, so I said yes. It's the worst decision I ever made. That's all I knew, though,' Xee said, rubbing a hand over his face.

'Next, he's dead, and I'm hunted down and forced into a meeting with the Paymaster at some secret location. But he's not even there. And then this voice fills the cave and gives some instructions to this EX6 weapon who's there. The next thing I know, I'm being dragged across the country by a load of your people. We arrive here and go in and get them, EN62 and the high lady, that is. Then they tell EN62, Aliz, or whatever you want to call her, to either kill the high lady or me. She picks me. Anyway, she botched it up, and here I am. So go on, you might as well finish it.'

Xee looked up at the man with defiance. If he was going to kill him, he'd have to look him in the eyes when he did it. Surely the gods would punish him for killing a defenceless and unarmed man. The man handed him one of his spare swords, and Xee cursed silently. He was no longer defenceless and unarmed. His trick had failed.

'She didn't botch it,' said the man who had relaxed his tone.

'What?'

'She didn't botch it. If EN62 wanted you dead, you'd be dead. She's the most talented and natural fighter I've ever seen. She wanted you alive, but I'm not sure why yet. You seem about as useful as a eunuch in a brothel.'

'I saved her life,' muttered Xee. He was fed up with people hurting his feelings.

'I'm sure you did,' replied the man flippantly.

'So you're not with them?' asked Xee.

'No. They are tridents, and no doubt I trained some of them, but they left the service and are now working for the Paymaster. Whoever this Paymaster is. EN62 must have refused an instruction—'

'And that instruction has to die with her,' continued Xee, finishing the man's train of thought.

'Yes. I don't know why they're after the high lady, but it must be linked.' The man fell silent as he continued to think.

'They said something about reversing decisions,' Xee said as the silence became uncomfortable. He'd heard EX6 discussing it drunkenly one evening, but nothing he'd said made any sense.

'Reversing decisions?'

'Yes, I didn't hear much else—'

'The dismantlement of the Trident Programme?' said the man, interrupting him. 'Or the Equality-For-All Motion. It must be one of those. Hestia wouldn't allow anyone to control her, but Attalus? Why? Why would they want to? And how?'

The man was pacing up and down, talking to himself.

'We need to know who the Paymaster is,' the man said, turning to Xee. 'That seems to be the only way we'll find out. He's not only paid off the tridents but he's also paid off the palace and high guards. He probably has control over the high table as well. Whoever he is has a big pot of coin somewhere, and there's no one who can have that amount of wealth and stay hidden. Can you tell me anything about your meeting with him?'

Xee shrugged. It seemed like such a long time ago, and he'd tried to erase his memory of it.

'Where was it?' asked the man when Xee shrugged.

Xee hesitated. He could roughly remember where it was, but he would struggle to find it again. 'You follow the Esaltes River to the mountains between Phrixus and Attica, and then there's a cave. But I don't know if I could—'

'Attica?' The man seemed surprised. 'That's Governor Zetes Diaprepes' realm. How could the Paymaster…'

The man trailed off, leaving Xee in suspense. 'What?' he asked.

The man ignored him. 'Did they give any indication of where they were going or what their plans were?' he asked.

'No, nothing,' said Xee. The man gave him a hard stare, and Xee added, 'Honestly.'

'And you didn't see the Paymaster?'

'No, I just heard his voice in the cave. Must be some sort of trick.' Xee imagined him to be fat and old, with red cheeks and thin hair, but he kept his suspicions to himself.

'I'd say they're a day ahead of us, and they'll be heading to the Paymaster for instructions. They'll be going by land, keeping off the roads and waterways. If they are seen, rumours will start flying. Rumours are already surfacing after Hestia didn't show up for the Funeral Games. Everyone thinks she is ill, which probably serves the Paymaster well if everyone thinks she died of natural causes just like her father.'

Xee watched as the man clenched his fists.

'The governors have announced that the swearing-in ceremony will take place on the eve of Saviour's Day, so the Paymaster will have to make his move before then. I think they'll take her through the Parosean Forest to Paros. That would take them almost into Phrixus, and from there, they could go across the mountains to Attica.'

Xee gulped. He'd heard stories of the Parosean Forest. Every realm had its myths and legends, but Paros was awash with them, and almost all of them involved the Parosean Forest. Stories involving unicorns, nymphs, and many other creatures he couldn't even name. No one ever travelled through it, and most thought it impassable. They had skirted around the huge forest on their way to Aphrodite's temple. In the night, Xee had been sure he'd heard strange noises carried by the wind, whispers and warnings. He had no desire to test them.

'I can't help you. I've told you everything I know,' he pleaded.

The man met his comment with a stony stare. 'I wish that were true,' he said sincerely. 'But I'm going to need your help. If we don't catch them, we're going to have to find the Paymaster, and you're the only one I know who knows where his hiding place is.'

Xee knew it was true, and he didn't have the energy to argue. At least he was safe for now. 'I'll help you as best I can,' he said and tried to stand up. He still felt weak, and his head hurt. 'I need some food and water,' he muttered.

The man threw him a flask of water. It hit him on his arm and fell to the ground. He took a deep drink and felt marginally restored.

'We'll find food as we go,' the man said and made to go.

Then Xee sensed a subtle change in the atmosphere. He turned around and stared into the point of an arrow. He jumped back, letting out a high-pitched wail, and tripped over his feet. Five arrows were pointed at his companion, who sighed as though he were expecting it.

The six archers surrounded them in a semi-circle, blocking their exit. They looked ready to kill them in a heartbeat, but Xee wasn't afraid. Instead, he stared in awe, unable to tear his eyes away. Each wore thin white armour that neatly hugged their bodies. It had extra protection around the neck, elbows, hands, wrists, and midriff. They wore knee-high leather boots and had their hair tied back in a tight plait that enhanced their facial features. A large gold medallion engraved with a bow and arrow hung around each of their necks, showing they belonged to the Temple of Artemis in the neighbouring Milos realm.

The Artemisiai.

Xee almost whooped with delight, despite the imminent danger he was in. He never thought he would set eyes on them. He thought they were just a myth.

'We mean you no harm,' said his companion, slowly raising his hands.

'We received word of a great sacrilege here,' one of the Artemisiai said. Xee couldn't tell which one. He was busy staring love-struck at the one in front of him, who stood perfectly poised with her fingers on the bowstring. Her muscles were tense, and Xee was sure that she hadn't blinked.

'The high priestess was mutilated,' continued one of the Artemisiai, 'and an apprentice was taken. Worst of all, a man crossed the bridge and set foot in the temple. We take crimes against our sisters seriously.'

'I rode here to stop them,' said the trident. 'And now I'm going to find her and bring her back. If she's still alive.'

'I wasn't talking to you.'

Xee jolted. 'I… they forced me. I didn't want to. They made me. Honestly. I would never. I wouldn't…' he stuttered.

'He's with me,' said the trident.

'Yes, I'm with him,' Xee bumbled. 'I'm showing him where to go to get her. He needs me.'

'Where are they, then?' asked the Artemisiai, who appeared to be in charge. She had gold interwoven into her armour and looked slightly older than the others, the few lines on her face not detracting from her beauty.

Xee hesitated. 'They're travelling to Attica, through the Parosean Forest,' he managed, blurting out what the trident told him.

The Artemisiai looked at each other before the one in charge said, 'They have taken the southwest passage. We have been watching them and you. You will travel with us.'

'No,' replied the trident, although he was in no position to argue. 'These are trained warriors. They will kill you if you go after them.'

'You will travel with us,' said the one in charge, her tone forceful. 'You do not know the Parosean Forest as we do. It is not the warriors you need to fear.'

Xee heard his companion breathe out deeply. 'Very well, we travel together. There's no time to argue, but I need him,' he said, referring to Xee.

'And we want the warriors,' said the one in charge. 'Alive. The high priestess at the Temple of Aphrodite has plans for them, and we would assist her.'

'Do what you want with them, but I can't promise they'll be alive. Agrippina comes with me, though.'

The Artemisiai in charge smiled. 'You think you can cast shadows in our temple, Klemides? We know they have the high lady, but know your fight is not alongside your niece. It is your nephew who will have need of you.'

Klemides! Xee didn't know that tridents had names. He thought they all went by a number. Klemides... It sounded familiar.

CHAPTER XL

Ismarus, Tinos

'What in Hades do you want?'

Axil and felt bile rise in his throat as he looked at his old tutor.

'I hoped never to set eyes on you again.'

'The feeling is mutual, I can assure you.' It had been a hard day's ride, and Axil hadn't slept. His bones ached, and it was an effort to keep his eyelids from dropping. He hadn't expected a warm welcome, but Solon could at least have masked his derision.

'Then why? Why, after all these years, have you shown your face again? And at my home of all places?'

'It seems the Moirai have brought us together. No doubt it amuses them. Are you going to invite me in?'

Axil had decided to visit Solon at his home to avoid detection. He had few friends in the close circle of lawgivers. If anyone saw him, questions would be asked.

'The hour is late. What is your business, Bellerophon? State it then go.'

Axil winced. It sounded strange hearing his birth name, so long and clumsy.

'I think what I have to say will interest, and I'm not saying it out here on the street.'

Solon looked around, assessing whether anyone had seen Axil on his doorstep. He lived in a large townhouse on the outskirts of Ismarus. The town was the main trading hub of Atalantea, and it was prosperous because of its markets. To trade in Ismarus, you had to pay a local tax, and most businesses traded in Ismarus because it was the epicentre of the island. Solon had made himself rich over the years through various investments, and through his legal practice, which specialised in debt recovery. There wasn't much legal about it. He took a cut from the amount recovered, and that money funded his decadent lifestyle.

Axil had walked down a long drive lined with olive trees to reach the door to Solon's house, and the closest main road was a good walk away. They were alone.

'My family is inside,' Solon whispered.

'Please don't insult me. We both know that's a lie. No woman would ever look at your pox-ridden face or live in a place like this.'

Solon's house, whilst grand, had fallen into serious disrepair. He had left rubbish in the garden, and paint was coming off the front of the house in big chunks. He would have money to pay for the repairs, but no doubt gambling and whorehouses were higher priorities. There were plenty of both in Ismarus.

Solon looked away, confirming the lie.

'Do you think I would ride for half a day just to say hello?' Axil said, growing angry.

'Very well,' Solon replied, 'come in, say what you need to, then leave.'

Axil walked into Solon's house. The inside was no better than the outside. Dust had piled up on old furniture, and years of grime caked the windows, making it difficult for light to get in. Solon led Axil through to what he assumed were the living quarters and sat down in a chair. Piles of papers littered the floor, and a dusky odour hung in the air. Axil saw something scurry across the floor and shivered. He decided to remain standing.

'Speak,' snapped Solon, picking a paper up off the top of a pile to read.

Straight to the point, as always. His anger hadn't diluted over the years. 'I've heard you've risen through the ranks here in Ismarus and are head of the lawgivers,' Axil said. 'Not bad for someone who belongs in the gutter.'

'If you're going to insult me, you can leave right now.'

Axil couldn't resist. 'You must have dirt on a lot of people to get to where you are. You were an utterly hopeless tutor and an even worse lawgiver.'

'You're quickly running out of time.'

Axil took a deep breath. His old tutor brought out the worst in him. 'An opportunity has arisen, and it just so happens that you're the ideal candidate.'

'What opportunity?' Solon put his papers down and glanced at Axil, one eyebrow raised.

'The high lord is going to need new counsel.'

'You mean high lady? And why? What's happened to Borus?'

'The less you know, the better, but you can be sure that new counsel will be needed.'

'Why would I want to work for that girl?'

'You wouldn't be working for her...' Axil let the sentence hang.

'What's happened to Hestia?'

'It doesn't matter. All you need to know for now is that soon Attalus will be high lord...'

'What have you become involved in, Bellerophon?'

'... and Attalus would like new counsel,' Axil continued, ignoring Solon's question. 'Counsel who agrees with the old world view.'

'Speak plainly. Why me, and what's the catch?'

'I know your views. I know you hated the high lord and his meddling. I'm allowing you an opportunity to reverse his decisions.'

'And I know your views. What has changed, Bellerophon? What has made you see the light? You believed the high lord's changes were for the good. I recall you saying they were progressive. You were ignorant of the Order and the wider repercussions of ignoring His will. Now suddenly, you want me to believe that you've changed?'

'My path is not what I'm here to discuss. I'm here to ask, if an opportunity were to present itself, would you put yourself forward?'

'It would only be natural for me to put myself forward. But let me guess, if I do, there's a catch? If I put myself forward, you'll expect me to go against the governors and advise the new high lord to repeal recent changes?'

Axil nodded.

'And in doing so, I will become hated by the governors and the people. Why would I do that?'

'It's not like you have any friends now, and everyone knows your views. It would be your opportunity to correct everything you think is wrong with the world. For the good of the ten realms.'

'On whose orders?'

'What?'

'Who is pulling the strings behind all this? Come on, Bellerophon. Who is gaining from all this? Who is paying you? Who will pay me?'

'Put yourself forward and follow my instructions, and you'll be fine. Like I said, the less you know, the better.'

Solon smiled. It was a cruel and vindictive smile. It was the only smile his face knew. 'You don't know,' he said, wagging his finger at Axil, and then he laughed.

It was Axil's turn to look away.

'Your time's up.' Solon stood up and walked towards the door.

'What is your answer, then?' Axil asked, following.

Solon stood in silence with the door open. The fresh air felt good on Axil's face.

'If the high lord or high lady needs new counsel, you will have my answer.'

CHAPTER XLI

Parosean Forest, Paros

Xee and Klemides followed the Artemisiai as they set a relentless pace through the forest. Xee's injuries groaned with every step, and his throat felt dry.

'Can we stop?' he asked, unable to continue. He was about to lose sight of the party in the sticky vegetation, and his voice didn't carry. 'Can we stop!' he shouted with more than a hint of desperation. Everyone turned to look at him.

'I've twisted my ankle,' he lied and took some deep breaths to compose himself. The air felt heavy, and stopping made his joints stiff. Bugs and insects attacked him and then drowned in a sea of sweat. He had at least ten bites, and large, itchy, yellow lumps had appeared on his skin. He squatted down and then cried out as a blinding pain swarmed over his thigh.

'What's wrong with him?' asked one of the Artemisiai. It was the one who had aimed her arrow at him. They all looked similar, but she had softer features and an easy, mischievous smile that was more a smirk. Xee was sure he had heard someone call her Araes, and if he had to pick, she was his favourite. Not that any of them would look at him twice.

'Cramp,' Klemides replied but did not help. 'We need to keep going,' he said as Xee pounded his thigh with his fist and grimaced.

'We'll make camp here,' said the Artemisiai in charge. Two of her companions disappeared to find somewhere suitable, and Klemides grunted. It wasn't the first time she'd overruled him, but he knew better than to argue.

It was their second night in the forest, and Xee was more than ready for a rest. He'd been too frightened to sleep the first night, flinching at every sound and creak. He'd once heard that there was a frog in the Parosean Forest that could kill you within seconds if you touched it, and he'd spent the night paranoid that one might jump onto him during his sleep. The same person had also told him that giant ants roamed the forest and ate anything that got in their way.

He didn't know whether there was any truth in any of it, and he didn't want to ask for fear of being ridiculed. Instead, he'd rolled himself into a ball, hugged his knees, and tried to think happy thoughts.

On two or three occasions, he had drifted off, but only for a few seconds, as each time, a loud, deep howl had jolted him awake. It was likely a pack hunting down their prey under cover of night, communicating with one another. They were so loud they must have only been a few feet away from their camp. It could have been snarlers. Xee knew too well what they could do. Or maybe it was something even worse, like strixes, the huge owls which fed on human flesh and blood. It was impossible to sleep with those thoughts racing through his head. Klemides didn't seem to have a problem, though. He'd slept peacefully next to him without a care in the world, his snores adding to the cacophony of noise.

They'd set off at the break of dawn to make up ground on the tridents. Everyone was rested and fresh-faced, save for Xee, who could barely open his eyes. Each step was a hammer blow to his body, so the Artemisiai's decision to stop was music to his ears. Tonight he would sleep because he was too tired to worry.

They set up camp, and Xee hobbled over to his makeshift hammock next to Klemides. Off the floor meant away from the snakes and scorpions that slithered and clicked in the fallen leaves.

It had taken the Artemisiai a matter of minutes to set up camp for them, and already three snakes, a rabbit, and something resembling a small bear were being cooked over the fire for supper. One of the Artemisiai had bored a hole into a tree, and a sugary syrup was flowing out of it into a container. Another had found a water source and was boiling it over a separate fire.

Xee and Klemides watched in silence, knowing their attempts to help would only cause a hindrance.

The Artemisiai in charge approached them. 'We will catch them tomorrow. They are making slow progress. Last night, two of their number were taken.'

'By what?' asked Klemides.

'Could be a griffin. They are said to exist in this forest, although I've yet to see one. I've also heard tales of a chimera.' She watched Xee's confused reaction and smiled. Griffins and chimeras belonged in fairytales, but part of Xee suspected she was speaking the truth. 'Lots of things prowl in this forest, and your men are ill-equipped to deal with them. Such arrogance.'

'They are not my men,' barked Klemides, taking the bait. 'Not anymore, anyway,' he added softer, realising she was playing him. 'How do you know this?'

'I sent two scouts ahead. They've been watching them. Tomorrow you will have the high lady back, and we will have your men.' She smiled at Klemides, who didn't react this time. Then she turned and walked back to her camp and the rest of the Artemisiai.

Xee breathed a sigh of relief. He felt on edge whenever he was near one of the Artemisiai, like he had to impress them, be helpful, or say something funny. So far, he had failed miserably in his attempts.

The light faded, and Xee closed his eyes. At some point, Klemides brought him some food and water. It was too dark to see what it was, but it was chewy and meaty, and his stomach was thankful for the replenishment. The canopy blocked out any starlight, and his body felt numb from the day's exertions. Xee drifted off, listening to the sounds of the forest and his comrades.

A haunting scream cut through the night like an arrow.

Xee sat bolt upright, his heart pounding. Had he imagined it?

'What was that?' Klemides muttered somewhere to his right. He was already out of his hammock, dressing.

There was another scream, and Klemides cursed. Were they under attack? Had the tridents done something to Aliz or Hestia?

The sun was rising on the horizon, bringing an eerie light into the camp through the trees.

The entire forest held its breath, waiting. Xee felt like he'd received a sudden shock. Every inch of him tingled.

A large snap and a man's cry came from somewhere to their right. It was hard to say how far away he was. Had he fallen into one of the Artemisiai's traps?

Xee felt a rough hand shake his ankle, and he whimpered, then realised it was just Klemides trying to get him up. He twisted his body and fell out of the hammock. As he stood, something whistled past his ear. Xee instinctively touched the side of his head, but there was nothing there.

'We're under attack,' whispered Klemides, who was standing battle-ready next to Xee. Xee nodded and wondered what Klemides expected him to do.

'Get dressed,' Klemides ordered, and Xee suddenly felt rather foolish standing there in his underclothes.

Xee's hands were shaking so much he struggled to put his clothes on, but luckily no one was watching. An ominous silence hung over them, and Xee could hear his heart pounding in his chest. It was so loud he thought everyone must be able to hear it.

A man's garbled scream echoed around them, and Xee heard one of the Artemisiai shout, 'Clear!'

'Here, too!' came another cry.

Xee watched as an Artemisiai with red hair ran past him. 'He's here!' she shouted. 'Dead. Through the eye.'

Xee wondered what they were talking about, and then the red-haired Artemisiai dragged a man's body past them, an arrow protruding from his face. He had been standing only ten feet away.

'There were three of them,' the red-haired Artemisiai explained to Klemides. 'One fell into our trap. He's alive, for now. Another got into our camp, but he was quickly put down. This is the third.'

'I know this man,' Klemides muttered without emotion.

Xee also recognised him, although he had said very little during their time travelling together. 'How did they know where you were?' Klemides asked

'They must have spotted our scouts and followed them. Luckily, the traps we set warned us when they were approaching.'

'Did you suffer any injuries? I heard a woman's scream,' Klemides said.

'I heard a scream, too,' Xee said, trying to be useful.

'Not from us,' the red-haired Artemisiai replied and looked away.

That meant that it must have come from Hestia or Aliz.

'We will leave shortly, so make ready. Today we will have our revenge.'

They marched purposefully through the forest. The night raid had left one of the Artemisiai injured, and she had returned to her temple, and so they numbered seven, including Xee. Their assailers had lost three. The third had died from his injuries before they left camp, having first given up his group's plans following some persuasion. Xee didn't ask what measures they'd used. They were outnumbered almost two-to-one, but the Artemisiai seemed to know what they were doing and weren't as bothered as Xee about the numbers.

The sun was high in the sky when they stopped for the first time. They had seen no sign of the tridents, and Xee wondered whether they had lost them. Initially, he assumed they had stopped for lunch. He could feel his stomach rumbling, but it quickly became apparent that the Artemisiai had other plans.

Xee realized they were close. The Artemisiai in charge made some frantic hand gestures, and her comrades quickly dispersed in various directions.

'Here,' Klemides said to Xee under his breath, 'take this and hide. Don't get involved.' Klemides handed him a short sword, and Xee wondered whether the warning was because Klemides cared about what happened to him or because he was a liability.

He didn't dwell on it and did as he was told. He watched from behind a tree as Klemides joined the Artemisiai in charge, his sword drawn. The two carefully crept forwards, and Xee lost sight of them as they disappeared through the trees. He waited and listened, his senses alert to every noise and shadow. Disturbing thoughts came and went from his mind like waves crashing against the shore. He couldn't let them control him. It was so quiet. Why was it so quiet? The tension was unbearable. Maybe he should go look, maybe—

All Tartarus was let loose. Xee heard a scream in the distance and then the sound of someone running. A warning shout and then other voices joined in, creating a chorus of panic, interceded by the tuneful blast of a horn.

'Over here!' came a man's cry from somewhere to Xee's left, and then he heard a loud thump. He couldn't see what was going on. What if they all killed each other? How would he know?

There was a rustling sound somewhere ahead, and Xee peered around, assuming it would be Klemides or one of the Artemisiai. Instead, he saw a burly trident in a bronze mask carrying a long sword. Xee recognised him as EX23 by his barrel-like chest. He was part of the group that had been tasked with finding Hestia. EX23 spotted Xee and stopped in his tracks, confused. Xee remembered he was supposed to be dead.

'You!' EX23 said, his voice muffled through the mask. The big man hesitated, and then he ran at him.

Xee's legs moved before his brain had processed what was happening, but EX23 was too quick. He was on Xee before he accelerated away, tackling him from behind. Xee felt his body stumble forwards and knew he would have no chance if he landed on his front. Xee turned to face his attacker, and EX23 landed on top of him.

Xee squirmed and threw his fists at EX23, who made no attempt to move or stop him. Then Xee felt something warm and sticky on his hands and quickly shuffled back. EX23 was dead. Xee's sword was buried deep in his neck, and blood was flowing from the wound like a waterfall. He'd forgotten he even had the sword in his hand, and it must have taken EX23 by surprise. The trident's eyes had rolled into the back of his head, and when Xee went to retrieve his sword, he gagged as he breathed in the smell of faeces from the corpse.

It was the smell of death.

The sword was stuck at an awkward angle, and he had to yank it to get it out, which released another spurt of blood. Xee vomited on the ground. He hadn't meant to kill him. It had been self-defence, but still, a feeling of guilt cast a second shadow over him. He had to distance himself from the scene, but his brain wasn't functioning. He tried to wipe his bloodied hands on his top, but the blood was dry and sticky. When he gagged again, nothing came out.

He fought back his panic, needing to focus. There could be more of them. The sound of battle echoed disjointedly all around him. It sounded like the Artemisiai had prevented the tridents from grouping together and were picking them off one-by-one. It was strangely calm.

Xee walked forward, following the path Klemides had taken. He kept low and moved quickly, darting from one tree to the next. His senses were alive to any danger, and he slapped himself every time his mind wandered back to what had happened with EX23. He hadn't gone far when he spotted a body in a ditch with two arrows protruding from its back. It was a trident, but Xee decided not to investigate which one.

He nearly fell over another trident a few yards further on. This one had been taken down with a heavy sword stroke to the head. Xee could see a mixture of brain and blood on the ground. He wanted to look away but couldn't. A long sword remained gripped in the corpse's hand, and Xee decided to upgrade his weapon. He closed his eyes as he prised the man's thick fingers off the sword to claim it for himself, afraid the corpse might spring back to life. The blade was heavy, and Xee needed two hands to swing it, but it looked more threatening than the short sword he was carrying. He would keep hold of his old weapon, though, just in case.

He stumbled on, tripping up over his swords as he went. A distant cry came from Xee's right, but he couldn't see anything as he carefully scanned the area. He kept going, hoping to catch sight of Klemides or one of the Artemisiai.

After a few minutes of ducking and weaving forwards, Xee reached a clearing with a small fire. It must have been where the tridents had stopped for food. Initially, it looked deserted, but then Xee's heart leaped as he spotted Hestia and Aliz. They were tied to a tree, and a trident stood guard over them. She was armed with a bow and arrows and was wearing a sword at her hip.

It was the trident who had mutilated the high priestess.

Once again, Xee felt useless. He couldn't get close to them whilst they were being guarded.

Then he heard a familiar voice say, 'You have lost, release the prisoners.'

Xee looked. Araes had moved into the clearing and had an arrow pointed at the trident. The two of them were in a stand-off. Araes had not seen Xee.

'We still outnumber you,' the guard replied calmly. 'Where are all your friends?'

'Where are all yours?' Araes replied, moving steadily forwards.

This was his chance to prove himself. Whilst Araes distracted the guard, Xee silently edged his way around the clearing towards Hestia and Aliz. The guard now had her back to him, but he could see Aliz and Hestia, and they could see him.

Aliz's head was down. She was badly beaten and had cuts to her face. Her left ear looked like a mixture of blood, pus, and goo. Xee realised it must have been Aliz they heard screaming in the night. It looked like they had cut it off, and the thought made his blood boil. Hestia was ghostly white, but there was no obvious physical damage.

Xee felt a wave of confidence. Perhaps it was his anger overriding his common sense. He crept forwards as quickly as he dared. Araes and the guard were still talking, neither wanting to make the first move. Xee reached the prisoners, and close-up, he could see the extent of Aliz's injuries. Her lips were puffy, and her nose was in pieces. Her eyes were swollen, and her ear was a horrible mess. Xee looked away in disgust and focused on cutting the ropes with his new sword. It was a clumsy instrument for the task, so he switched to his short sword.

He hacked at the ropes around Aliz's hands and legs first, trying not to nick her, then did the same for Hestia. Araes spotted what he was doing and tried to keep the guard occupied. The final rope was tied around the tree and didn't want to give. Aliz grabbed the sword off Xee and hacked at the rope herself. The effort made her grunt, but the rope fell loose. The guard heard Aliz and realised what was happening.

Araes fired an arrow, and it whistled through the air, but the guard was expecting it. She dodged to the right, and the arrow missed by an inch, hitting a tree.

In the same heartbeat, the guard loosed her arrow. Xee watched helplessly as it struck Araes in the throat. She fell to her knees, and Xee cried out, putting his head in his hand. He barely knew her, but it felt like the arrow had struck his heart.

The guard grabbed another arrow from her quiver, placed it on the bow, and drew back.

Xee was lost in a mist and didn't notice, but luckily Aliz was alert to the danger. She cried out and threw Xee's sword at the guard. It was a weak throw, but it did enough to force the guard to fire her arrow harmlessly into the trees. Aliz grabbed Xee's long sword and charged. It was desperate, but it was also ferocious and filled with venom. The guard wasn't expecting the charge and hesitated, caught in two minds. She didn't know whether to fire another arrow or draw her sword. Her hesitation was her downfall. Aliz's leap swallowed the ground, and she plunged the sword into the guard's stomach.

Aliz and the guard collapsed on the ground together. Aliz rolled away, and the guard tried to sit but couldn't. Her hands gripped the sword that impaled her, a look of confusion on her face. Aliz gingerly stood up, then she grabbed hold of the hilt and slowly twisted it. The guard screamed and begged her to stop.

'Did you stop for me?' Aliz asked and pulled the sword out quickly and decisively. The guard looked horrified as her innards fell out onto the forest floor. Then her limbs fell limp, and her head flopped to the side.

'Aliz!' Xee shouted as another trident appeared in the clearing, but the man fell forward as an arrow struck him from behind.

The Artemisiai in charge appeared. 'Araes!' she cried as she saw her friend on the ground. She ran to her, and Klemides followed. His armour was splattered with blood, but he looked uninjured.

'Uncle!' Hestia cried as she saw Klemides. She ran to him and threw her arms around his shoulders. Klemides smiled awkwardly.

'Are you okay?' Xee asked Aliz as she collapsed. It was a stupid question, but it was all he had.

'I'll live,' she replied, and her mouth curled into the semblance of a smile. 'You did good,' she muttered, and despite everything, Xee couldn't wipe the smile off his face.

One-by-one, the Artemisiai entered the clearing. 'They ran,' one of them said, and then she spotted Araes on the floor and ran to her.

'I thought I told you to stay put,' Klemides said to Xee angrily, suddenly aware of him.

'I did,' Xee said, scratching his face, 'but then one of them found me and ran at me.'

'Then how are you alive?' asked Klemides.

'I… he landed on me funny, and your sword went into him,' Xee mumbled. He didn't want to be reminded of it.

'Hey, go easy,' Aliz croaked, 'if it wasn't for him, we might not be free.' She gave Xee a look of approval, and he smiled at her.

The Artemisiai in charge regained her composure and stood up. 'We are not safe here,' she said, wiping her eyes with the back of her hand. 'The leader, the one they call EX6, escaped with a few others. I suspect they will head back to the one they refer to as the Paymaster, but we can't be sure.'

'I will take Hestia to Governor Gadeirus,' Klemides declared. 'He was a supporter of the high lord, my brother, and I know he will keep her safe.'

'No,' Hestia said, standing. 'Take me to Arcadia.'

'Governor Ampheres?' Klemides queried.

'Yes,' replied Hestia, confidence returning to her voice. 'I know Gadeirus would have my best intentions at heart, but I need an army, and Amos Ampheres commands the largest force I can trust.'

Klemides furrowed his brow and scratched his head as he thought about the suggestion. 'Very well,' he said after a long pause, 'Arcadia it is. I think you can trust Ampheres, but I didn't get the chance to question my sources. I reached Erineus and then heard about tridents destroying a tavern there, so I rode back as quickly as possible. From what I've heard, Ampheres is a good man.'

'We will escort her,' said the Artemisiai in charge. Klemides made to argue, but she silenced him with a look. 'Your fight is not here, Klemides. Find men, loyal men, and head east into Milos. Our high priestess foresaw we would travel with you and told me to send you that message.'

'And what will I find in the Milos, other than a volcano and a few builders?'

'I do not know, but there is a girl, and she is key.'

'How do you expect me to find anyone, or anything, based on that?' Klemides griped and threw his hands into the air.

'Head east, and your path will become apparent. That is all I know.'

Klemides stood and looked at the Artemisiai, his jaw clenched. Ignoring an order from a high priestess was as good as ignoring an order from their god. 'I will travel east, as you say. There is a trident stronghold on the border of Tinos and Milos. There are men there. Men that I trust. We will travel through Milos as you suggest, but if there is nothing, we will head south and join back up with you in Arcadia.'

'If it pleases you,' the Artemisiai in charge replied and then turned to Hestia. 'We are the Artemisiai from the Temple of Artemis. My name is Metis, and we will accompany you to Arcadia to ensure your safe passage.'

'Can I travel with you?' Xee asked meekly to Metis. It seemed like everyone had forgotten about him and the role he had played. Metis looked at him scornfully.

'He travels with us if he wants to,' Aliz answered. She forced herself to stand and hobbled over to the group. Xee wanted to thank her but knew it wouldn't go down well, so instead, he acknowledged her with a nod and a smile.

'Very well,' said Metis, her eyes focused on her fallen friend. 'Do as you will, but we will not be stopping for you.' She turned her back on Xee and shouted at her comrades to dig a grave.

Xee took a deep breath. He finally felt like he was on the right side, and it felt good.

CHAPTER XLII
The Capital

You can check out any time you like. But you can never leave! Shep sang to an empty room. He was trapped, a prisoner. They said he wasn't, but he was. He couldn't go anywhere without eyes on him, watching his every move.

He'd made a half-hearted attempt to escape once. He'd planned it all in his head, but when he'd approached the gate and saw the icy stares of the guards, heard the chink of their blades, and felt the beads of sweat down his forehead, he'd quickly turned away and pretended that he was on one of his daily walks. A guard had laughed as he strolled off, and Shep knew he was laughing at him. They all were.

With nowhere to go, he spent his days making the most of the hospitality, the food, the drink, the women… the drugs. Oh lord, the drugs. Shep had smoked his fair share of weed at university and even tried some harder drugs in his post-university days, but this was a different level.

His first experience was with a girl they sent to his room. She was a tall blonde with cold, green eyes and silky, golden skin. She'd walked straight past him and sat down on the bed with a peculiar-looking pipe in her hand. It had a thin tubular shape and was curved like a banana with a bulbous end.

Shep had no interest in the pipe. He wanted his latest harlot to undress and had been angry when she just sat looking at him like a halfwit. Then she lit the pipe and guided it to Shep's lips. He was hers to command and obliged.

He took a deep breath and almost choked on the fumes when they hit the back of his throat like a bullet train. The girl looked to the side, masking a smile at his reaction. The fumes had an earthy taste with a hint of sweetness, like if you threw some honey into a pot of mushrooms. They left a bitty texture in his mouth, which made his teeth and gums itch. He breathed out and became disorientated as thick black smoke filled the room.

He took a second drag, embarrassed by his initial reaction, and the impact was instantaneous. He was flying, and it was amazing. The wind was in his hair, and the sun was on his back. The freedom was intoxicating. With no way to actually escape, smoking became Shep's alternative solution. He smoked every opportunity he got, which was most evenings.

At first, he had no influence over where he went. But as he got used to the feeling, he found he had greater control over it, until he could soar wherever he wanted. He could soar out of the palace, over the land, across the sea, but always he was stopped at the same place. An immovable force prevented him from escaping beyond the reach of the island. He'd looked for Alfred on one occasion and found him in a small cottage on the edge of a forest. He'd flown up to the window and shouted at him, but his friend was too busy looking into the eyes of a woman to hear him. Eventually, he had given up and carried on, soaring ever higher until it was time to return.

After each trip, he would wake up on his bed exhausted, his limbs heavy, and his mind drained. He would lie there, sometimes for hours, with barely a thought passing through his head. Then the hunger would hit him, and he would wait desperately for someone to bring him a meal, chewing his nails and grinding his teeth to appease his cravings.

As the days passed, Shep's ventures out into the palace and the gardens became increasingly sporadic and fleeting. They had lost their splendour. Now when he looked at the gardens, he could see weeds amongst the roses. The faces on the statues looked ill-proportioned. The paintings didn't look as striking. He might as well stay in his room.

Shep stood up and walked around, debating what he should do. A pipe sat invitingly by the bed. He knew he needed to resist. It was taking control of him, and he needed a clear head to think up a plan to escape.

It was staring at him…

Could he climb the wall? No, they would see him.

Trick the guards? He couldn't even speak the language.

Calling his name…

Could he overpower the guards? He laughed out loud at the thought.

Maybe he could tunnel, like Andy Dufresne in *The Shawshank Redemption*? He liked that film. He'd watched it about ten times. Yes, that could work. Maybe there were already tunnels. He decided there had to be. All palaces and ancient buildings had underground tunnels. The Viracocha would know. He knew everything. Maybe he could try to work it into the conversation. Not that he'd seen the Viracocha recently. He had seen no one. He was lonely all the time.

Except when he…

He needed to look outside the confines of the palace for a solution. That was the only way. He would find his answer outside the palace. Then tomorrow, he would start afresh.

Shep inhaled from his pipe and felt his body relax. He needed four or five puffs now for it to release him. He closed his eyes.

What would he do if he escaped the palace? Where would he go? He couldn't get off the island. The Viracocha had told him that. *I don't want to get off the island,* he thought as he took another puff.

The life he'd left behind wasn't one he wanted to go back to. He was a murderer. Alfred had told him so, and Alfred didn't even know the full story. It had been Shep, fuelled with jealousy and alcohol, that had been the aggressor.

He could picture it, clear as day. The dark alleyway. The boyfriend. The anger in his veins. The knife in his hands. The surprise at how easily it pierced the skin. The look in his victim's eyes as he desperately pressed his wound. The panic. And then the rock. It had been a split-second decision. Him or me, and it had to be him.

Shep inhaled again, remembering the onlooker pressing frantically at the keys on his phone, blocking his escape. He'd run at him, and the onlooker had swung his fist and nearly knocked him out. Adrenaline was the only thing that kept him going. Then he'd ran, and ran, and ran some more.

Shep inhaled again.

He looked at his shaking hands and saw blood on them. He tried to wipe it off on his top, but he couldn't. Guilt stained them, a permanent reminder of what he'd done. Of what he was.

He couldn't go home. If he did, it was only a matter of time before the net would close in on him. Better being a prisoner in a palace than a prisoner in a jail cell somewhere in the States, in amongst the rapists and the serial killers. Shep shouted in anguish. He needed a plan. Could he climb the wall? No! He was going in circles.

Shep inhaled again and felt his spirit lift free of his body. He stared down at his pitiful figure crumpled on the bed and felt sickened by what he had become. He looked like an old man, touched by death, with yellow teeth and eyes which stared endlessly into oblivion. His skin was grey, and his clothes fell loosely around his fragile frame. When he'd left England, he had been burly, gladiatorial even, but now he had no form. He was just a lump of meat thrown carelessly on a plate. He couldn't bear to look at himself anymore, so he flew off.

Shep woke to a knock on his door.

His head pounded, and it felt like someone had poured sand down his throat. His eyes had crusted over, and the cotton bed sheet had stuck to the side of his face.

His visitor didn't wait for a response. It was the Viracocha. 'You need to be careful,' he said as Shep gingerly lifted his head. 'Black magic has some unusual side-effects. You have been overindulging.'

Shep rubbed his head and scoured the room, desperate for a jug of water. He found one, but it was empty. He licked around the roof of his mouth and felt his teeth move. Shep couldn't remember the last time he had brushed them.

He grunted in response. 'Why are you here?' he asked, unable to muster the energy for pleasantries.

'I bring news,' said the Viracocha. 'News that you will be happy about.'

Shep sat up. The effort made him light-headed.

'We have restricted your movements. It has been,' the Viracocha leaned on his staff and tried to think of the word, 'unfortunate, but necessary. For your safety. I can see that it has not been good for you.'

The Viracocha sat down on a chair and played with his beard as he thought.

'On the eve of Saviour's Day,' continued the Viracocha, 'there will be a decision.'

'A decision about what?' asked Shep in no mood for the Viracocha's riddles.

'About you.'

'What do you mean? What is Saviour's Day? And what are you deciding?' Shep asked, his anger seeping through.

'You do not realise your importance. You are the first outsider we have had here since the Event, and some believe that you are our key to lifting the curse.'

'So you have said, but how do I do that?'

'That is what they must decide.'

'Right, and then will I be free to go?'

The Viracocha looked at him and thought about the question. 'You will have your freedom,' he said. 'One way or another.'

CHAPTER XLIII
Oropus, Attica

A xil watched the governor from a distance as he made his way through the dusty streets. He'd been watching his movements for four days, desperate to find out if his hunch was correct. Desperate to find a way out of the terrible mess he'd found himself in.

The governor was old, slow, and walked with a bent back, making him easy to pick out, despite his attempts to remain undetected. He wore a tatty grey tunic, like a beggar, and carried a crooked wooden staff which clacked on the cobbled floor with a steady beat, interrupting the otherwise silent evening.

The governor looked around, and Axil merged into the shadow of a building that had once been a bustling market. The signs had rusted. Plants and grasses had forced their way through stone and rubble to reclaim their territory.

The governor took a hard left and quickened his pace. Axil listened as the tempo of his clacks increased and then followed, pulling the hood of his black cloak further over his face. The paths were narrow and empty, with few hiding places which left him exposed, but luckily, the governor wasn't paying attention. He reached a small, white stone house on the edge of the street and tapped on the door with his staff.

The house was dilapidated, just like all the others in Oropus. A pox had washed through the town five years ago. The town counsellor had walled it off and imposed a complete prohibition on anyone entering or leaving. The actions taken contained the pox, but the town never recovered, and most of those who survived had long since abandoned it.

The governor disappeared into the house.

Axil waited a few moments, then crept up and peered into a window. The front room of the house, a small living room, was empty. Axil held his breath and gently opened the front door. It creaked, and Axil waited, but nothing happened. He opened the door further to find a short corridor. Two hushed voices sounded from the rear of the house. Axil crept along the hall as far as he dared. The men were oblivious to the fact that they were being overheard.

'You have it?' said the man who wasn't the governor. His voice was nasal and hoarse. Axil was sure he recognised it.

'I have what remains of the gorgon blood. We have no more, so take care with it. He must be alive on the eve of Saviour's Day. The people must see him,' replied the governor.

'Do not speak to me like a fool. I know perfectly well how to administer it. Was the high lord's death not perfectly disguised?'

'The girl suspected.'

'She knows nothing. She is but a girl and nothing but reckless to wisdom. There is a reason the Saviour created the Order the way He did.'

Axil felt his heart rate quicken. His mouth felt dry. How foolish he had been. For years he had worked for the Paymaster, following his every instruction like a whipped dog. The Paymaster had stripped away his soul, leaving him an empty shell of a man, too weak to question his orders. It had rendered him blind, deaf, and dumb to his master's voice.

He had never questioned or considered who was paying him. The knowledge would have been an inconvenience, but the stakes were too high now. The Botanist had known it immediately, and he had felt pathetic in front of her. It had taken her courage to shame him into questioning himself and his actions until he couldn't think of anything else. So he had followed his instincts, and they had led him to Attica. Now he knew his suspicions were correct. His Paymaster and the governor were one and the same. They had to be. It was the only thing that made sense, and the realisation was sickening. The acts he had committed on the Paymaster's orders were all the more heinous knowing they had come from the governor.

Bile rose in Axil's throat, and he swallowed deeply. The gorgon blood he'd collected from the Botanist had been used to kill the high lord. His breath caught in his throat. He'd committed treason. If his role in the high lord's death ever came to light, they would give him the traitor's death. They would fix a cage to his body and tie him to a rock. Then they would put an eagle in the cage and leave it to starve. With nothing to eat, the eagle would slowly peck him to death. People called it the Prometheus Price after the sentence Zeus laid upon Prometheus for stealing fire from the gods to give to mankind. It had been hundreds of years since the State had punished anyone in such a way, but the penalty for treason still stood.

They must have added the poison to the high lord's drink, or perhaps his food. A few drops would be enough to kill anyone instantaneously, but the effects of such a dose would have been obvious. His muscles would have tensed, his body going rigid as blood flew from every orifice as it thinned. Then his heart rate would have increased until the organ exploded, putting the victim out of their misery. The high lord didn't die in such a way. If he had, the news would have spread. The stranger in the room must have carefully administered the dose over a prolonged period, causing a heart attack. The poison would have eventually turned his blood black and thick, but that wouldn't have shown until after the initial autopsy.

That was why they needed to kill the high physician. He was a loose end and so was murdered by his men on his orders.

'We have her. The girl.' The governor coughed, and Axil snapped back to attention. 'My men found her, and they are bringing her back. We will deal with her when she arrives, but we need a contingency. She has shown herself to be quite a handful, and my men should have been back by now. I haven't heard from them, and I don't like it, something's not right. So what of the boy?'

'Attalus is out of his depth. He holds on to my every word. He will reverse the decisions of his father and restore the Order. Of that, I have no doubt. Soon everything will be put right, and the Saviour will look down on us favourably once more.'

'Good, good. But can we legitimise his rule while the girl still lives?'

'Do you not trust me? The high lord breached the Order. He had no right to put forward the measures he did, destroying our greatest protectors and permitting female rulers. The Saviour does not take kindly to us interpreting His rules as though we are His equals. You just need to make sure the girl does not attend the swearing-in ceremony. The boy has power at the moment, so long as his sister remains absent, and the State cannot appoint her high lady if she is not at the ceremony.'

'Yes, but many disagree. They say the ceremony is merely a formality.'

'Many are wrong, and we need to show them they are wrong. Once they realise, once they see the middling and the destruction his life guarantees, they will back the boy.'

'The curse?'

'It is the only way. Those who disrespect the Saviour by revolting against the Order and the prophecy only have themselves to blame when they suffer His wrath. It is what He would want. We are merely the vessel to His wishes. It is the only way to maintain order and ensure the future of this land.'

The governor grunted in acknowledgement. 'Do you need anything else from me?'

'The deed has already been done. The curse will fall soon, and the people will witness the Saviour's wrath on the eve of His day. But we will appease Him, and then they will know. Then they will see.' The man banged something on the floor, and it echoed through the empty house. 'Just deal with the girl. Make sure she stays away from the ceremony.'

'The governors will revolt. They will see it as an act of war. As ignoring democracy.'

'Then so be it,' snapped the man. 'We will be ready.'

Axil listened intently, a large lump in his throat. He crept around to catch sight of the man whose voice sounded so familiar. He could see two shadows. The governor was standing with his back against the wall at a ninety-degree angle to Axil. The other man had his back to Axil, but he could see his staff with its snakehead, and shock slammed into him. He knew who it was, but it made no sense that it was the Viracocha. Two of the high lord's most trusted advisers had plotted his downfall.

Then a thought struck Axil. Perhaps he was only seeing part of the picture. The governor didn't care about the Saviour. He wasn't a believer and never had been. He had other interests, though...

Axil was so deep in thought he didn't notice that the two men had fallen silent. The change of atmosphere crept over him like a shadow. Axil looked up to see the governor pointing his long, bony finger at something. It was a mirror, and that mirror was facing him.

The Viracocha turned around and looked straight at Axil, his dark eyes a mixture of anger and fear. Axil froze momentarily, his initial shock paralysing him. His brain recalibrated as the two men made to move, and then he ran.

CHAPTER XLIV

Kea

Alfred's left arm felt numb. Ariadne's weight had been squashing it for the last hour, but he didn't mind. With his free hand, he traced the contours of her back to the base of her spine and then back up to the nape of her neck. Her skin was silky soft and warm. He gently brushed her hair from her face, tucking it behind her ear. She stirred and muttered, 'Morning.'

Her English had improved over the last few weeks. Unfortunately, Alfred's understanding of the Atlantean language had not. It wasn't through lack of trying. He just couldn't connect the words. He did better with the reading, and he'd almost mastered their alphabet, which had thirty-two letters, many of them similar in sound to their English equivalent.

According to Ariadne, the Atlantean language was the forefather of all vernacular, making it easier for Atlanteans to learn different variations. The same way musicians who have mastered the scales can easily turn their hand to a tune, but Alfred wasn't sure. He didn't know what to believe. He still thought it was a practical joke.

'Morning,' Alfred replied and kissed her shoulder. He slid his arm out from under her and flexed his fingers to get the blood flowing again. 'You slept well.'

'You tired me out.'

Alfred closed his eyes and revisited the previous night in his head. 'I think it was the other way around,' he said and sat upright. Most of his injuries had healed, but a few lingered. His shoulder still ached when he twisted it, and he struggled to bend the fingers on his left hand.

'My poor baba,' said Ariadne, and Alfred realised he must have groaned when he sat up.

'I'm fine,' he said as Ariadne moved around and massaged his shoulder. Her fingers dug into his muscle and gently eased out a pressure point. 'Actually, that's good,' Alfred said and felt the tension melt away on his neck. 'Do you think we could get out of the house soon, maybe go somewhere? I want to see Atalantea. I want to see all those things you've told me about, the temples, the gardens, the pyramids. I still don't believe you,' he teased.

Alfred hadn't ventured further than the house and the garden. He hadn't been physically able to, but now he'd recovered, he could see no reason for remaining housebound.

'No, it's not safe, baba,' said Ariadne. 'Not yet. No, no, no.'

Alfred wasn't sure whether he liked his pet name, but he let it pass. 'Why?'

'You think you can walk around no questions? You don't know the language. You don't know the people. You don't know the area. You know nothing. At the moment, people are fighting. There have been killings. They hate the thought of strangers landing on our shores. They think it means the beginning of the end. It is what they have been taught. If they see you, they will take you or kill you. Maybe. I don't know.' Ariadne had jumped off the bed and was pacing the floor, shaking her head.

'I don't understand. Why would they want to kill me?' Alfred asked. He loved that she cared, but his house arrest was taking its toll. He was desperate to explore. It was like he was trapped inside a computer game and couldn't get past level one. At the very least, he needed to try to make contact with someone back home, although he had no idea how he would do that if there was no internet, electricity, or phones. How could such a place exist?

Ariadne turned to look at him, a pained expression on her face. 'Before you, we had no strangers. We were alone for thousands of years.' She said it slowly, as though speaking to a child.

Alfred had heard her tale before. Anyone who had attempted to leave Atalantea had suffered a similar experience to him as he had entered but hadn't been as lucky. They had turned back, or their bodies had washed up on the shores a few days later. He didn't understand how it could be possible, especially with the wizardry of modern technology, but he knew Ariadne was telling the truth.

'There was talk of a stranger. Many years ago, it was written that when a stranger arrives, our world will end. At least that's what people said. People think you are a sign. Some see hope of us returning to join the rest of the world, and the rest see doom. Here in Kea, people think you should be… erm,' Ariadne struggled to find the right word, 'offered to the Saviour.

Because that is what they are told to believe by people who have power and influence, by our governor and the priests.'

'Offered to the Saviour? What does that mean? Who's the Saviour?' It was the first time Alfred had heard anything about being offered, whatever that meant.

'The creator of Atalantea. We cannot say His name. It is forbidden.'

'Poseidon?'

'Shush!' Ariadne recoiled and looked around. 'Don't do that. If they find you, they will take you. Look at you. You stick out with your red hair and pale skin. Anyone who sees you will be suspicious.'

Alfred didn't think she meant it to sound offensive, but it came out that way. 'Take me where?'

'If you're lucky, they'd take you to the Capital. The governors would decide what to do with you. Maybe they'd spare you.'

'And if I'm unlucky?'

'They'd take you to a priest here. He'd offer you to the Saviour. You're lucky that Kaspa found you. He doesn't believe in the old ways.'

'I can't just stay here for the rest of my life, though.' Alfred sighed. 'Why don't we go to the Capital, explain what happened, and prove that I'm no threat. I could be valuable to them. I made it through the storm. Maybe I could help others through the storm?'

'No, no, no, no, no, no!' Ariadne cried, throwing her arms into the air. She punched Alfred on the shoulder, and he felt his injury jar. 'You don't know. You don't know. You say you want to help. You can't help. You try to help, and they will think the Saviour will punish us. They would kill you first. And anyway...' Ariadne trailed off.

'What?'

'It doesn't matter.'

'No, go on,' Alfred pushed.

'It's nothing. I don't want to say. Not now.'

'No, please,' Alfred pleaded. He could tell that Ariadne was keeping something from him. She looked up and hesitated. She sighed and looked away.

'It's whispers only. The news we get here is mixed and confused. I don't know if it's true, so please, I said nothing because I wanted to be sure first.' Ariadne was trying not to cry. She could barely look Alfred in the eyes. Each word seemed to be an effort.

'Hear what, Ariadne? Please. Tell me.'

Then the tears came. They created a small stream on her cheeks and dropped gently onto the floor. She wiped her nose with the back of her hand and breathed in. Alfred put his arm around her to try to calm her. He hated seeing her so upset.

'They say,' she started and then stalled before trying again. 'They say that a stranger is already here. That he is in the Capital. He arrived during the high lord's funeral, and they took him.'

Alfred didn't know why Ariadne was so upset. Surely that took the pressure off him. 'What are they going to do with him?'

'I don't know. No one knows who is in charge. They say the governors can't agree on what to do. Some say war is coming. That's why it is so dangerous right now.'

Alfred had been wondering what had been upsetting Ariadne so much, and then it hit him like a brick, and he felt guilty for not having realised it straight away.

Shep. He was alive. It had to be him. Who else could it be? He didn't know whether to be angry or elated. 'My friend,' he said. 'It's my friend. It must be.'

'Baba, no, no, no. We don't know. We don't know. That's why I didn't want to say. I knew that's what you'd think.'

Ariadne tried to grab hold of Alfred as he jumped out of bed, but he ignored her. How could she keep something like that from him? Even if it was only the remotest of chances, she had no right.

'How could you not say? How could you?' Anger consumed Alfred. He felt betrayed. 'You knew! You knew!' he shouted, pointing his finger at Ariadne. The sudden burst of energy had tired him out, and he was shaking.

'I don't know. We know nothing. You know nothing. The stranger could be a whisper. It could be a trick.'

'A trick?' Alfred sat down and laughed cynically. 'Why would they play a trick? Why on earth would it be a trick? Do you not think it's coincidental that Shep and I ride through the storm, survive, then suddenly a stranger shows up out of nowhere for the first time in thousands of years, and it's not him?'

'You speak too fast,' Ariadne pleaded. 'I don't understand. Your friend, Shep, maybe didn't survive the storm. No one survives the storm.'

'I survived!' shouted Alfred.

'I know. Please. Don't shout. Let's talk.'

'I'm done talking. You tell me lies, half-truths, or nothing at all.'

Alfred's mind had already raced forwards into thinking about how to get to Shep. If he was alive, and if what Ariadne had said was true, and that was a big if, then he needed help, and Alfred was the only person on the planet who could help him.

'How do I get to him?' Alfred snapped whilst throwing some clothes on.

'No, you can't.' Ariadne was sobbing, and Alfred suddenly felt guilty for his reaction. She was wrong for keeping it from him, but through the mist of anger, he could see that she'd done it for what she thought were the right reasons.

'Ariadne, I'm—' Alfred started, but Ariadne sprang up from the bed and ran past him. He thought at first that she was running away from him, but then he heard her retching in the other room and realised she must have come over sick. Perhaps the emotion of the conversation had overwhelmed her. Although, come to think of it, he was sure he had heard her retching the other morning. Maybe she had a sickness. Something else she'd kept from him.

Ariadne returned, wiping her mouth with a cloth. Her eyes were red, although it was impossible to say whether that was from the crying or from being sick.

'Are you okay?' Alfred asked. He tried to sound concerned, but it was difficult when he was still feeling angry, and it came out cold.

Ariadne nodded. 'I'll be okay,' she said. 'If you need to go, you go.'

The response stung Alfred. It was like she suddenly didn't care, and he meant nothing to her. 'Why?' he asked tentatively.

'You want to act on a whisper and kill yourself, you go. You leave. Leave this. Leave us. For a whisper.' Ariadne sat down on the bed and turned away from Alfred. How had he become the bad guy?

It was their first proper argument, and he'd lost. He felt terrible for shouting at her, even though it was Ariadne who had hidden things from him.

'I don't want to leave,' he said. 'I have to. It's Shep. He needs help, and I'm the only one who can help him. It has to be him. You must be able to see that,' Alfred pleaded. He needed Ariadne's approval. He couldn't go without it.

There was an unbearable silence whilst Alfred waited for a response. He could feel his heart pounding in his chest.

Ariadne turned to face him. 'I know,' she mumbled and tried to smile, but her eyes remained filled with sadness. 'I know, but I don't like it. You don't know the dangers.'

That was true. Alfred didn't understand what the dangers were, how to even travel to the Capital, or what he would do when he got there.

'Still, I have to go.'

'How do you get in?' asked Ariadne.

'Get in where?'

'The Capital. How do you get in?'

'I don't know. I'll find a way.'

'Well, let me teach you something about our history. When our Saviour fell in love with a mortal named Cleito, He enclosed the hill where she lived in alternate zones of land and water to prevent anyone from getting to her.'

Alfred nodded. He was familiar with the story.

Ariadne continued, 'Since then, and over many years, the Capital has been further fortified. If your friend is alive, he will be on the very top of a hill that our Saviour designed to be impregnable. Now, let's pretend you find the Capital, which is at least four days from here on foot, probably seven or eight for you in your condition. You will find a great stone wall surrounding it. The wall is high, so high it's impossible to climb, and there are only four ways in and out on foot. Let's say you get through undetected, and then you're into Outer Atalantea. You walk through, avoiding detection, and reach a ring of water and another wall, this one bronze. Again, there are only four ways through, but this time they guard the entrances. No one can get past without the correct stamp or document. Let's say you somehow sneak past the guards. Then you're into the Limbal Ring. You walk through and reach another ring of water and another wall, a silver wall, and guess what? More guards. Four ways in, four ways out. You get through to reach the Iris Ring, then... guess what?'

'Another ring of water and another wall?'

'A golden wall. Then you're into the Citadel, and your friend, if he's alive, and it's not just whispers, will be there. So, how will you do it?' Ariadne fixed him with a fierce stare.

'I don't know,' muttered Alfred. It sounded impossible, but he didn't want to admit it. 'I have to try, though.'

'No, you don't.'

Alfred looked at Ariadne. She had won the battle but lost the war, and she knew it.

Ariadne exhaled and put her head in her hands. 'There's only one way that you can get through the guards to the Citadel.'

'How?' Alfred asked, sitting down next to Ariadne and taking her hand in his. The earlier hailstorm had washed away, and the faint outline of a rainbow had appeared. 'Please, I need you. You could save someone.'

Ariadne tutted, dismissing him. 'Most supplies for the Citadel get unloaded in Outer Atalantea, but Kea wine is the best in Atalantea, and it's expensive. Amphorae of wine had a habit of going missing, so the high lord brought in special measures. If you're on the boat transporting Kea wine, you get a stamp to pass straight through to the Citadel.'

'Right. Perfect. That's the solution. Brilliant. You're brilliant. I lo...' Alfred was in a bubble of excitement and nearly let it overtake him, but he stopped himself just in time. 'How do I get on the boat?'

Ariadne looked at him, one eyebrow raised as though expecting him to finish his earlier thought. When Alfred remained silent, she asked, 'If I get you on, will you come back here?'

'Of course!' He squeezed her hand. 'I don't want to leave. I'm going because I have to, not because I want to. I don't want to go to the Citadel. I want to stay here with you.' It was at least half true. He wanted to stay with Ariadne, but he was also bursting with curiosity.

Ariadne was shaking, and Alfred could see that it was difficult for her. 'I can help. The wine merchant is a friend of mine. He will keep you safe. If I get you on the boat, you stay hidden in an amphora. You don't talk. You don't get off. You find out if your friend is there, then you come back in one of the empty amphorae.'

Alfred smiled. He had a feeling that Ariadne had thought up the plan a while ago, knowing he would insist on looking for Shep. 'Yes, yes. Thank you.' Alfred kissed Ariadne, catching her by surprise.

'You come back,' she said, wiping away her tears. 'You do what you need to do, and you come back here. I cannot lose you and Kaspa. Not after...' Ariadne couldn't finish the sentence. They had barely spoken about what had happened in the caves. It was still too raw. Now Kaspa had been gone a few weeks with Theseus, and they had heard no news from them.

'When does the next boat go?' Alfred asked, trying to move the conversation away from Ariadne's dead brother.

'In a few days,' she replied after a few moments. 'There is a supply going for the swearing-in ceremony. I will tell you everything I know that will help.'

'That won't take long,' Alfred teased and then realised that the comment was ill-timed. It was too soon for jokes. 'No, please,' he said, trying to make amends, 'I want to know.'

Alfred's mind was racing, his body a mixture of excitement and trepidation. He was so caught up in his thoughts that he barely noticed as Ariadne ran off to be sick again.

CHAPTER XLV
Ismarus, Tinos

Axil tried to focus. He closed his eyes and felt his body shutting down, so he shook his head and took a big gulp of water from his skin. He'd pulled his cloak tight over his face and was pretty sure the governor and the Viracocha hadn't recognised him, but he couldn't be positive. If they had, they'd already be searching for him, and so he needed to keep his wits about him.

From what he'd heard, their plan would unfold on the eve of Saviour's Day at the swearing-in ceremony. In Hestia's absence, Attalus would preside over the event as acting high lord. He would declare his father's actions ultra vires, which would make them null and void. Solon would verify the decision, assuming he accepted the role as the new high lawgiver. The high priest would appoint Attalus as the new high lord under the traditional laws of ascension.

Hestia wouldn't be able to contest the decision because she wouldn't be there. She would be dead or imprisoned, although it sounded like the governor didn't know where she was. The governors would have no say on the matter and could only watch as a decade's worth of progress vanished in one night. They planned on using the middling as some kind of pawn to justify their actions, and they had spoken of some sort of curse.

Everyone in Atalantea had been invited to the swearing-in ceremony, and it was being talked about in every tavern across the land. Most thought it was to witness the first appointment of a high lady. Instead, the governor and the Viracocha would make a statement through Attalus, which would reverberate across the ten realms.

What Axil didn't understand was why the governor would have such hatred towards the high lord? Had they not been friends? The more Axil thought about it, the more it nibbled away at him. There was only one thing that made sense.

His first stop had been to the Central Library in the Capital to consult the genealogical records. They traced the lines of the governors and the high lord back to the Saviour and his children with his beloved Cleito. Together, they had five sets of twins. Their firstborn, Atlas, was the first high lord of Atalantea. Atlas had divided the island amongst his siblings whilst keeping control over the Capital, nine siblings, nine realms. Later, a civil war resulted in the Attica realm, splitting it in two to create a tenth realm, Syros.

The genealogical records ensured each realm remained ruled by a descendant of its original governor. Strict rules were in place over who the high lord and governors could marry to ensure that their line remained true. The rules had caused controversy over the years, and so the genealogical records, and those who studied them, were of vital importance.

The Central Library housed the original copy of the records. Initially, they were closed to the public, but the last high lord had ordered the State to make them public to ensure transparency and avoid any arguments about them being manipulated.

Few people attempted to access them, though. They were almost impossible to decipher, and guards closely monitored them at all times to ensure no one tampered with them. Despite such vigilance, when Axil went to view the records, he discovered that someone had removed them. The librarian had remained tight-lipped over who had taken them until Axil had shown him some coins. It came as no surprise that Zetes Diaprepes, the governor of Attica, had taken them. The governor he had followed for four days, the governor who had plotted against the high lord.

The librarian said that Zetes had removed the records to verify and update them months ago. He had travelled with the Genealogy Master, who had confirmed the purpose. The librarian hadn't considered it unusual or suspicious, and as the Genealogy Master was the only one permitted to update the records, he had allowed its removal. The librarian assumed the records had remained with the high table because of the death of the high lord and the controversy over his replacement.

That made sense, but Axil knew Zetes' reason for removing the records had nothing to do with updating them.

The library in Ismarus held the only other copy of the records, and so Axil had travelled there along the canal networks. It was the quickest route, and it allowed him a few hours to sleep. Not that sleep was forthcoming. His mind was far too active, and the ferryman hadn't stopped talking about the swearing-in ceremony. He was expecting a busy week transporting passengers from Ismarus to the Capital. He was loudly telling anyone who would listen that they were lucky because he was about to double his prices.

Axil didn't know how the Capital would cater to so many. There were still a few days until the event. Already there was a constant stream of people making the journey on foot, and the canal networks were full. There would be nowhere for people to stay and not enough food to go around. It was a combination that could only lead to unrest.

Ismarus was bustling with people when Axil arrived. Many travelling from further afield appeared to be using it as a stopping point for their journey. Axil had no intention of staying. He wanted to check the records and then get back to the Capital via the Attica and Syros realms. He thought he could avoid the busy transport routes that way.

The library was a tall, long building in the centre of Ismarus encased in black marble. Large carvings of the nine muses guarded the entrance. Axil was so struck by their beauty as he walked in, he nearly collided with someone. Inside, books lined every wall from the floor to the ceiling, and the library looked far more cluttered than the one in the Capital. Axil felt lightheaded as he looked up at the long ladders on wheels. They reached up to a mural of Mount Olympus on the ceiling. Three old men looked in Axil's direction as his footsteps interrupted their thoughts, but they quickly buried their noses back in their books.

He walked across the first room and then through an archway that led down into a small, dimly lit, underground space. The smell of old parchment filled his nostrils and made him feel nauseous. A plump man sat at a table in the room with a scroll rolled out in front of him. Three obsidian rocks held it down to stop it from rolling back up.

'Can I help?' he squeaked without looking up.

'I'm looking for the genealogical records,' Axil said.

'Continue through into the room behind me. They are in the room on the left.'

'Thank you,' said Axil.

'There's someone there already,' said the man, his head down still.

'I'm sorry?'

'Someone is already looking at the records. He's been there all day, so you'll have to wait.'

'Who?'

The man exhaled loudly and finally looked up. 'I don't know,' he snapped, venom shooting out of his beady eyes. 'Why don't you ask him?'

Axil took the hint and left the librarian to his scroll. He followed his instructions and found a man sat pouring over the records. The room was dark, and it was hard to see his face, but Axil didn't think he recognised him. After a few seconds, the man looked up and stared at him. He had a youthful face, cleanly shaven, with large, bulbous eyes. He smiled nervously.

'Can I help?' he asked when Axil said nothing.

'I need to view the genealogical records urgently,' said Axil.

'I see. I'm afraid I might be a little while. I also have an urgent requirement. Are you a genealogist?'

'No, are you?'

'That's a shame. No.'

'Who are you?' Axil asked. There was something about the man that felt familiar.

The man paused. Axil could see the clogs ticking in his head: who's asking, and why? 'I'm Ptolemy,' he replied.

Suddenly, Axil knew who he was. 'The Viracocha's apprentice?'

The panic in Ptolemy's eyes told him that his assumption was correct.

'People have been looking for you,' continued Axil.

'Who are you?' asked Ptolemy, his voice breaking slightly.

'My name is Axil. Don't worry. I have no interest in your business. But it begs the question, what you are doing here?'

'Consulting the genealogical records, I thought that much would be obvious.' Ptolemy's tone had turned cold, and his eyes narrowed.

'Why?'

'That is of no concern to you.'

'I disagree.'

Ptolemy cleared his throat nervously. 'Who are you exactly? And what business do you have here?'

'I think we are both working to the same ends. And we might be able to help each other.'

Ptolemy looked at him, unconvinced.

Axil continued. 'I think you discovered some… unsavoury elements of your tutor's behaviour, and so you disappeared. Since then, you've been trying to piece everything together. I think you're looking for evidence.'

Axil sat back. Ptolemy gently stroked his chin. 'And why would you think that?'

'Because I've been working for Governor Diaprepes.'

Ptolemy sat up straight and gulped. Axil held out a hand to calm him down. 'I didn't know who I was working for or realise the implications of my role. Not until recently, anyway, but I need to be sure.'

'Why should I trust you?' Ptolemy asked. He'd stopped gripping the table, but he was still unconvinced.

'I don't think you have a choice. What's going on is bigger than you, and you can't do it all by yourself. We can help each other.'

Ptolemy eyed him up, his eyebrows almost meeting his hairline. 'Very well, although I'm not sure I can be of much help to you.'

The comment was sincere, but Ptolemy undermined his value. There was a reason the Viracocha had selected him as his apprentice. The earliest viracochas were the architects of Atalantea. They understood the old ways, which made many Atlanteans believe the gods spoke directly to them. Before the Event, the viracochas had taken their knowledge and skills to all corners of the world, enabling different societies to thrive. Few possessed the old skills, perhaps only one or two in a generation. If Ptolemy was one of them, he was one of the most valuable men on the island.

'Tell me about your tutor,' Axil said. He kept his voice low to prevent it from travelling down the corridors.

'He is no longer my tutor, as I'm sure you know. We parted ways.'

'I've heard rumours,' Axil confirmed. Ptolemy used to follow his tutor around like a dog, so his absence was noticeable. 'It's the why which interests me.'

Ptolemy looked uncomfortable. 'I found his views... volatile. He is more of a traditionalist, whereas I am progressive. We didn't agree on a lot of things, and so I left.'

'Who decided?'

'I decided.'

'They say that the Viracocha didn't know that you'd left until after you'd disappeared.'

'He's a clever man. I'm sure he worked it out,' said Ptolemy, and Axil smirked. It was hard to dislike Ptolemy. He had a humorous and highly unthreatening aura about him.

'In what way were his views volatile?'

'The Viracocha believes the Saviour gave him his gifts, that he is therefore connected to the Almighty and can speak for Him.'

'You don't believe that?'

'I would think the Saviour would have something a little more interesting to say.'

Axil grunted and signalled for Ptolemy to continue.

Ptolemy paused for a second, considering his next words. 'The Viracocha thought the high lord ignored and angered the Saviour by changing the Order. He predicted that the Saviour would send something as a test of our loyalty. A middling like it says in the Bard's Prophecy. He said that when the middling arrives, we will have to offer him to the Saviour to restore order. So we travelled across the realms, and I watched the Viracocha whisper words into the priests' ears. He fed them lies and forced them to rouse the people. I couldn't watch anymore, and so I left.'

Axil could tell that Ptolemy was holding back information, but he let him continue.

'Now a middling has arrived, so perhaps it is me that is wrong. Perhaps the Saviour does speak to him.'

'That doesn't explain why you are here, looking at the records?'

'No, it doesn't,' Ptolemy commented unhelpfully and sat back. 'Other strange things have been going on.' Ptolemy continued. 'I have heard rumours of people, sometimes entire villages, going missing without a trace. Someone claims to have seen a griffin. Sailors have crashed into the rocks near Harpes Island. It could all be a coincidence, but I don't like coincidences. There's something I'm not seeing.'

'Why are you here, looking at the records?' Axil tried again.

'The Bard's Prophecy,' Ptolemy said, as though that was a good enough explanation.

'What of it? It's not a genuine prophecy.' Axil wasn't interested in the words of a bard from hundreds of years ago, and it surprised him Ptolemy was entertaining such folly.

'No, but they say that he spoke to the Oracle at the Temple of our Saviour.'

Axil grunted and looked away, uninterested. He knew the story of how the bard went to see the Oracle following the death of his true love and returned with both a vision of Atalantea's future and a curse that no one would believe him.

'I can see you are sceptical,' Ptolemy said, 'but let us think about it. The prophecy mentions four things.' Ptolemy held up four fingers and looked at Axil expectantly.

'An eagle landing,' Axil said, going along with his game.

'The metal contraption that fell from the sky has the image of an eagle on it.' Ptolemy folded his little finger, leaving three fingers held up.

Axil grunted. 'The time of the cup-bearer being close,' he said.

'The night sky tells us we are moving into the age of the cup-bearer.'

'A stranger from distant shores.' Axil continued as Ptolemy folded another finger down.

'Which has now come to pass,' Ptolemy said, leaving his index finger in the air.

'And a line lost returning once more,' Axil said.

'Look here,' Ptolemy said, beating his finger down on the page in front of him. 'The line of the Attica realm was cut by the Event. When the Saviour engulfed us in this cloud, the governor of Attica was in Athens and never returned. He couldn't. The governor's sister's husband governed Attica instead. Following the Event, he took the name Diaprepes. It's all here in the explanatory notes. Since then, there have been no breaks in the chain, so if you only look at the Attica line after the Event, it looks the purest of all the realms.'

'So? How does something that happened thousands of years ago matter?'

'If the middling descends from the original governor, he would have a claim to Attica.'

Axil remained silent, lost in thought.

'That is why I'm here. I am here to look at the records. Now you tell me why you're here.'

Axil sat back and closed his eyes, thinking. 'I don't think Zetes cares about the Order or the Saviour,' Axil said after a long pause. 'He's never believed in the gods or cared about the prophecy. I don't think he's even aware of what happened before the Event.'

Axil thought of the list Zetes, the Paymaster, had given him and the names he had passed on to assassins. He chose his next words carefully. 'Of the missing people you spoke of, were any related to any of the governors?' Axil knew the answer, but he wanted to see if Ptolemy had made the connection.

Ptolemy licked his teeth and crossed his arms, processing the question. 'Yes, I believe a few may have been. What do you know?'

'I think Zetes wants land and power. I think he's weakening the lines of the other governors to strengthen his and his three sons' claims against the other realms. The Equality-For-All Motion stops this. If women can rule, his plans will come to nothing. Think about it. The current governors have few sons, but plenty of daughters.'

Ptolemy nodded. 'True. What made you suspect Zetes?'

Axil took a deep breath. He knew he should have made the connection earlier. 'The Paymaster told me he only needed five votes. The only reason he'd only need five votes would be if he was the sixth governor voting against the motion. After that, the link was obvious, or it should have been, had I not been burying my head in the ground. The governors gave Zetes money following the disbandment of the Trident Programme, but he hasn't invested it in Attica. So what's he used it for? I think he's used it to fund his campaign.'

'Yes,' agreed Ptolemy, 'I've been to Attica. There has been little invested in it over the last ten years, and Zetes' relationship with the high lord always struck me as false.'

'Historically, Attica has never aligned with the Capital,' Axil said. 'Why would it when it was the high lord who split Attica in two to create Syros following the civil war, just so the high lord's brother had something to rule over? It might have been hundreds of years ago, but it's no secret the governors of Attica have always wanted to reunite Syros with Attica to restore the original nine realms. And Zetes has been careful with whom he has assigned his sons to.'

Ptolemy thought about it, pointing in the air as he joined the dots. 'Damaris, his second son, is assigned to Cassandra Atlas of the Syros realm. Governor Atlas has no son, so without the Equality-For-All Motion, Damaris would have a claim to become governor of the realm, assuming there is no one else to stand in his way.'

Axil nodded. 'I suspect Zetes has taken care of anyone who might be a threat, but that is why I'm here.'

'Why do you suspect?' Ptolemy asked, staring intently at Axil.

Because I ordered it, Axil thought. 'I have also heard rumours,' he said, instead.

Ptolemy nodded slowly but didn't look convinced. 'There's something else,' Ptolemy said. 'I heard another rumour about the middling. Two men have been boasting about chasing him Below. They are adamant he washed up in Kea, and they are telling their tale in every tavern en route to the Capital. I sensed they weren't lying.'

'You sensed?'

'It's a skill detecting when someone is lying or withholding something.'

Axil felt the hairs prick up on the back of his neck. 'So he escaped and ended up in the Capital?' he said, hurrying the conversation on.

'Not possible. No one has escaped the Below. There's a reason it's closed off, and even if he escaped, the timing doesn't work. I think there could be two middlings. That whoever is being held in the Capital is not the person who washed up in Kea.'

Axil shrugged, unconcerned. Whoever washed up in Kea was probably dead by now. 'Will you help me then?' Axil asked.

'I thought I was,' Ptolemy said and turned the pages of the records until he found details for the Syros realm. 'Who has gone missing then?' he challenged. 'I suspect you know more than I...'

CHAPTER XLVI
Eve of Saviour's Day

Kea

Alfred waited nervously in the bowels of the ship. It was a small cargo ship carrying huge amphorae of wine. One would be enough to get an entire village drunk. They were taking a direct route to the Capital via the trade canals, which would cut the journey in half compared to travelling on the public routes.

Alfred had convinced Ariadne that he didn't have to spend the entire journey in an amphora, but there was an empty one sat waiting patiently for him in case anyone undertook a search of the cargo. Alfred eyed it up and planned how he could quickly get into it if the need arose. His heart was pounding, his mouth felt dry, and his scalp itchy. He stood up and paced the floor, taking two steps forward, two steps back, two steps forward, two steps back. Then he played with the pendant. He considered it his lucky charm, although he kept it hidden under his top to avoid drawing attention to himself as it still shone brightly.

Why hadn't they left?

Ariadne had been instrumental in securing his passage through to the Capital. The ship's captain, Soter, was a close friend of hers, and Alfred had been jealous when Ariadne had recounted stories of their childhood adventures. It was a jealousy that had silently eaten away at him until he met Soter and realised that he was at least ten years her senior and married with children, two of whom were on deck to help move the cargo when they arrived.

Soter had been reluctant with the plan at first. He believed there was trouble brewing in the Capital, and if a guard discovered Alfred, he would lose his business and possibly his life. But Ariadne's powers of persuasion were formidable. Soter had eventually agreed, subject to Alfred staying invisible and pretending to be mute if anyone saw him. When they reached the

Capital, Alfred would have to hide in the amphora for the inspection. That would be the moment of truth. If the guards properly looked at the paperwork and counted the amphorae, they would realise there was one extra and ask questions. Soter would have a hard time explaining why a mute man was hiding in one.

If they got through, Soter and his son would carry Alfred, hiding in the amphora, straight into the palace. He would have an hour at most to find Shep and extract him whilst Soter and his sons moved the empty amphorae back to the boat. They would leave two for Alfred and Shep to hide in, but if Alfred wasn't on time, Soter had been clear he wouldn't wait.

It was a good plan. It was their only plan. So it had to work. It wasn't like they could change it because Soter couldn't understand a word Alfred said.

If he made it to the palace, and that was a big if, Alfred had no plan on how he would find Shep. No one knew the layout of the palace, and that was assuming Shep was even in there. They were working with broken chains of information and broad assumptions, but he still had to try. His conscience demanded it. If Shep wasn't there, Alfred could return to Ariadne an unburdened man. He smiled at that thought and clung to it like a warm duvet on a chilly night. He had never known an attraction so instantaneous and electric, not even with Josie. There was no build-up, no hesitation, and no need for any words. It was just there, as though written on a neon sign, obvious and overwhelming.

Alfred stumbled as the ship lurched into action. One of Soter's sons, the older one, popped his head below deck, causing Alfred to panic and dive behind the amphorae. He laughed at the silly stranger and then disappeared again. They were finally going.

They chugged along at a steady pace, and Alfred tried to relax. He hated being powerless. There was so much that could go wrong, and it was impossible to plan for anything. Different scenarios played out in his head, and he could feel his veins clogging with the stress, his cortisol levels flying. He had no way of gauging the time or how long they had been travelling, and he didn't know how Soter would warn him if an inspection was about to take place. They should have thought all this through a bit better.

Occasionally, Alfred heard Soter shouting to other carriers. He sounded jovial, as if it were just another day. How could he be so calm when Alfred's heart lurched at every creak? What if Soter sold him out? Could he trust him? Would it be better for him to be hiding in plain sight, pretending to be deaf and dumb onboard? At least then, he could keep an eye on the captain.

Alfred sat down and squeezed his eyes shut, attempting some meditation. It used to help him at work, but now it just added to his anxiety. What if they inspected the boat whilst he was meditating? How would he explain that?

Alfred went back to pacing back and forth, his body demanding that he do something.

They drifted along the canal, moving further from safety. Then the boat came to a stop, and Alfred could hear voices. Soter's son appeared and pointed at the amphora. Alfred nodded, suddenly out of breath, and put his thumb up. Soter's son looked horrified and pointed frantically at the amphora. He must have misunderstood the signal, thinking Alfred intended to come up. Alfred made amends by moving over to the amphora and climbing into it. He'd rehearsed getting in and out a few times, and there was no dignified way of doing it, but luckily the container was so big it was relatively straightforward. He squatted down so that his head wasn't showing, and then the light disappeared as Soter's son put the lid on it.

Alfred waited. This was it, the moment of truth. He could hear muffled talking, which grew louder and clearer as men descended the stairs. He heard a floorboard creak and papers rustle. They were standing perhaps three or four feet away. There were three male voices, Soter and two others. Alfred breathed in and out slowly, conscious of every movement he made. The men spoke, and then someone banged the top of the amphora next to him. He could feel the small vibrations as they fanned out, their footsteps on the floor reverberating through his container. He breathed in. If they banged on his, they would know it was different by the sound. But they didn't.

Alfred listened as their voices and footsteps faded. He breathed out a sigh of relief as they started moving again a few minutes later. A feeling of discomfort replaced Alfred's anxiety as his inability to move aggravated his muscles and bones. Then the boat stopped again, and Alfred felt himself being shaken around as a pulley system lifted him off the boat. At this rate, he would be lucky if he was alive by the time they dropped him off at the palace.

He sensed he was moving forwards on the back of a horse-drawn carriage. Then, after a few more minutes of lifting and grunts, he came to a stop. Someone knocked on the amphora and lifted the lid. Alfred tried to stand, but being thrown and twisted about had left him disorientated, and it took a few moments for him to steady himself. By the time he could focus, Soter had left with his sons to collect the next load, and he was alone.

He climbed out into an empty underground storeroom filled with amphorae, bottles, and crates. There was one way in and one way out, so his first decision was easy.

He told himself that he would have a quick look and then get back as quickly as possible. If he saw anyone, or if it proved too difficult to search for Shep, he wouldn't risk it. He just had to see. That he'd made it so far was a miracle in itself, but it wasn't time to celebrate just yet.

Alfred climbed the stairs and put his ear to the door at the top. When he heard nothing, he gently opened it and peered through into an enormous kitchen with an oak table dissecting the room. Pots and pans hung from the walls, and a monstrous fire blazed in the corner, its smoke disappearing up a large chimney. Something was cooking on the fire, and the aromatic smells tingled Alfred's taste buds. A pallet of pomegranates and figs had been left temptingly on the side, but Alfred resisted the urge. Time was of the essence, and he couldn't waste it.

He moved through the kitchen into a corridor and found a spiral staircase. Alfred sensed that if Shep was in the palace, they would hold him on one of the higher levels. From a psychological perspective, it would distance him from thoughts of trying to escape, and Ariadne had told him that the workers would most likely occupy the rooms on the lower levels. Alfred waited a moment, listening carefully for any footsteps, and then tip-toed his way up the stairs. It seemed peculiar that there was no one around, but he wasn't complaining.

He moved along the corridor of the first floor. Gigantic paintings of regal-looking men hung from the walls, and a strong woody smell hung in the air. In front of him, a cabinet displayed old and weathered-looking weapons, no doubt bearing some special significance. Alfred looked through the first door he reached. It looked like a room for entertaining guests, with dozens of chairs and a makeshift stage.

Alfred froze when he heard footsteps. He ran back to the stairs and listened until the footsteps disappeared.

The first floor didn't feel right. He didn't have time to search the entire palace. It would take all day. He had to go with his gut, and his gut was telling him the first floor was a waste of time.

More footsteps, this time they were coming down the stairs. Alfred tucked himself into a shadow and watched as two maids hurried down, chatting in hushed voices as they went. They were carrying some bedsheets, and one had a wooden bowl with some leftover food in it. Someone was upstairs. It could be Shep. It could be anyone.

Alfred waited a minute to see if any other maids were coming down and then ran up to the second floor, taking the steps two at a time. Most of the doors were open on the second floor, and it allowed Alfred to look into the rooms without having to break stride. They were all bedrooms, and all of them were empty, the beds neatly made. Then he reached the room at the end of the corridor. The door was shut with a key in the lock.

If this isn't it, I'm going back, Alfred thought to himself. He pressed his ear to the door but couldn't hear anything. He took a deep breath and then winced at the noise created by the friction of the metal as he turned the key. There was no response from within, so Alfred opened the door and looked inside.

A strong earthy fragrance hit him, like the smell of grass clippings after rain. A disheveled figure was on the bed. At first, Alfred thought it was a corpse, but then one of his hands twitched, and Alfred nearly jumped out of his skin. He took a few steps into the room, and his heart sank as he realised it was Shep, but not the Shep he'd left England with. This one looked like the shell of the man he knew.

'Shep!' Alfred whispered as loud as he dared, but his friend didn't wake up.

Alfred didn't have time for pleasantries, so he grabbed Shep by his shoulders and shook him vigorously. He was all skin and bone. 'Shep,' he said again with urgency.

This time Shep did wake up, or at least he prised an eye open and then closed it again. What had happened to him? His face was yellow, save for the big black rings under his eyes, and his hair had receded, making him look like an old man.

Alfred sat Shep up and noticed that he had bitten his fingernails down, and they were red raw. One had even fallen off. How was he supposed to get him down the stairs? There was some water on the side, so Alfred picked it up and threw it into Shep's face. It had the desired effect.

'What?' Shep said to Alfred. He looked straight at him, but his eyes betrayed no hint of recognition.

'Shep, it's me. It's Alfred. What's happened to you?'

'Is it time?' asked Shep. Alfred noticed that his teeth had turned yellow, and some had dropped out.

'Time for what?'

'Time for me to go. You said yesterday that I could go today.'

'Shep, do you know who I am? It's Al. We met at university and travelled here together. You know me, Shep,' Alfred pleaded. He'd never expected to see his friend again, and even though he'd found him, he was still lost. 'You need to come with me, Shep. I can get you out of here.'

'Yes. Out of here. They said I could go. Are you here to take me?' Shep stared at a spot on the wall.

'Yes, we need to go now.'

'To the show?'

'To the what?'

'You said there was going to be a show and that everyone would be there. You said I'd be the star.'

'What show, Shep? You're not making any sense.'

'But you promised. You promised to take me away from here. You said... you said... that there would be a decision. That... um... I forget. You look different. Who are you?' Shep looked at Alfred, but there was no emotion behind his eyes, just a deep abyss.

'It's me,' Alfred tried again, 'Alfred. We're friends.'

'Alfred,' Shep repeated slowly. 'You speak my language. How do you know my language? Are you here to take me?'

'Yes, you need to come with me now. We need to go.' Alfred tried to pull Shep off the bed.

'Give me a few minutes,' Shep protested feebly and slapped Alfred's hands away before turning onto his side and closing his eyes again.

Alfred wanted to scream at him. 'What have they done to you?' he muttered to himself. He picked Shep up and put his arm over his shoulder to carry his weight. There was no way that he could carry him all the way, but if he could find something to carry him on—

Footsteps along the corridor disrupted Alfred's thoughts. Someone was striding purposefully towards them, and then they paused at the door. The key! It was still in Alfred's hand. The door opened, and Alfred darted under the bed. Shep collapsed on the floor. He was helpless without Alfred's support.

From under the bed, Alfred watched two men walk into the room. They spoke quickly, and then one of them laughed and prodded Shep in the side with his foot. Shep barely moved. The men scooped Shep off the floor and dragged him away. He didn't register what was happening, and Alfred felt his blood boil.

Alfred waited a few seconds in case they returned, then peered out of the room. Shep was being taken down the corridor towards the main staircase. There was no way he could follow without being seen. Ariadne had told him about a swearing-in ceremony in the Capital for the new high lady, whatever that was. Apparently, everyone on the island was headed there. That must be where they were taking him.

Alfred knew he needed to follow, but first, he had to get back to the boat. He wouldn't be able to do anything if he was trapped in the Citadel.

CHAPTER XLVII
The Capital

After their meeting in the library, Axil and Ptolemy travelled to the Capital together. Two heads were better than one, and Axil liked his new companion. He was a welcome tonic to his recent exploits.

Zetes and the Viracocha planned on taking Atalantea back to the dark ages, and despite Axil and Ptolemy's endless discussions, there was little they could do to stop it. Their only hope was Hestia had somehow escaped Zetes' men, Axil's men, and could stop the ceremony. But that was a forlorn hope. She could be dead already. Their only crumb of comfort was that she was missing when Axil spied on Zetes and the Viracocha, which was curious, if not conclusive.

The journey was slow. Despite taking a longer route to avoid traffic, every town and village on route to the Capital was full of people making the same journey. There was no way around or through it. They just had to join the queue and hope that they would make it on time for the ceremony. It was a goal they accomplished just as night overpowered day.

The ceremony was taking place at the Pagaros Pyramid in Outer Atalantea. Axil muscled his way through the crowds, with Ptolemy following close behind. There was tension in the air, and he didn't like it. The whole thing could turn violent in the blink of an eye. Most people had sensed this wasn't a normal swearing-in ceremony. No one had seen or heard from Hestia since the governors' annual meeting, and rumours were rife. On top of that, people were nervous about the middling. They wanted to know what was happening.

A small fight broke out on Axil's right. A man fuelled by alcohol had taken offence at something someone had said, and he was being held back by his friend. Someone was on the floor, and Axil could see blood, although it was difficult to see much through the mass of bodies.

A guard was quickly at the scene, trying to calm things down. The high guard and tridents were everywhere, although they wouldn't be able to do much about it if trouble erupted.

They reached an abandoned carriage in the middle of a path leading up to the pyramid and climbed on top of it. It was about as close as they could get, and it gave them an unobstructed view of the proceedings.

'I have a bad feeling about this,' Ptolemy commented.

'Me too,' Axil replied. 'There's nowhere to breathe. If trouble erupts, there will be chaos.'

Ptolemy nodded in agreement.

A large horn sounded, and Axil felt butterflies in his stomach. More horns joined in until a wave of noise washed over everyone. After a minute, they fell silent. Over one hundred thousand people stood, waiting. Not one person spoke.

*

Alfred reached the storeroom just as Soter was preparing to leave. He had left two empty amphorae as promised. Alfred shook his head when he saw him, and Soter shrugged his shoulders. It made no difference to him. Alfred climbed into an amphora and allowed Soter and his son to carry him back onto the boat. This time, though, after they had passed the checkpoint, he crept on deck to see what was going on.

The canal that dissected the Capital was narrow, just broad enough to allow two boats to pass each other. A path abutted the canal on one side, and a swarm of people were walking along it as though on route to a football match. The atmosphere was a mixture of excitement and tension. In front of them, a silver wall stood proudly, and Alfred knew that meant they were about to pass out of the Iris Ring and into the Limbal Ring. To his right, the sun was fading, and a crescent moon sat low in the sky as though resting on the wall. A second checkpoint was ahead, and the boat slowed, pulling up to the side. A guard shouted, and Soter responded. Alfred noted a tone of panic in his voice. Something was wrong.

The guard jumped onto the boat amidst protestation from Soter and walked around.

Alfred didn't have long to act. The guard had his back turned to Alfred as Soter remonstrated with him. Soter spotted Alfred, and a look of recognition and fear passed over him, but he recovered before the guard registered the reaction. Soter quickly led the guard down for the inspection. Alfred took advantage of the opportunity and climbed off of the boat onto the path unnoticed. He kept his head down, following the throng of people towards the ceremony.

He passed over a dusty horse racing track, followed a circular canal, and walked through a garden filled with long greenhouses. Everyone walked with urgency, and barely anyone spoke. When they did, it was in hushed tones as though they were up to mischief. Few registered him as they walked, although he got a few sideways glances and curious looks. Ariadne had dressed him in an old tunic, suitable for heavy lifting, to go along with the premise he was working on the boat. Everyone around him appeared to be well-dressed and carried a wealthy confidence. It was only then that Alfred remembered that only the upper classes of society lived in the Iris Ring, the physicians, lawgivers, members of the high table, and anyone else who held favour with the high lord. Alfred suddenly felt self-conscious, but no one stopped him. They had other things on their mind.

After a while, he reached a bronze wall, which meant that he was heading into Outer Atalantea. There was a checkpoint at the bridge leading across the wall and over the canal, but it was unguarded. Alfred breathed a sigh of relief as he walked across unchecked. He spotted Soter's boat as it progressed slowly along the canal, having completed the additional checks. He wanted to shout at him, to let him know he was okay so he could report back to Ariadne, but that would only draw attention to himself. How would he get back to her again? He would find a way, he had to, but first, he needed to find Shep and escape the Capital.

Outer Atalantea differed significantly from the inner rings, and as Alfred crossed the bridge, the atmosphere changed from apprehension to excitement. Rather than gardens, fountains, and showpiece buildings, basic white stone houses filled Outer Atalantea. Ariadne had told him most of the residents who lived in the Capital resided in the outer ring of land. A huge bazaar filled the main street, and it was abuzz with merchants selling food and clothes. The sweet smell of honeyed nuts roasting on a fire made Alfred's mouth water. He hadn't eaten in hours, and everything looked tempting. Even the stall with the pot of curried insects, which seemed to be an Atlantean delicacy, whet his appetite.

The merchants scurried around as they tried to bring people to their stalls. Most attempts failed, but today would still be a profitable day for them. Alfred stared at the floor to avoid making eye contact with anyone. People knocked into him, grabbed hold of his shoulders, and threw items in his face to get his attention, but he brushed them off and picked up the pace.

The bazaar ended, and Alfred reached what looked like a town centre with a temple in front of him. A statue of a warrior with a shield and spear sat on top of it. Alfred followed the flow of people down the side of the temple and then watched as a scuffle broke out in front of him. A group of five men had set upon a man who had been standing on top of a wall preaching. Whatever he'd said had hit a nerve. No one stopped to help as the group of men brutally threw the preacher to the floor and repeatedly kicked him in the head. They just walked casually past as though it was perfectly acceptable behaviour. Alfred also kept walking, cringing at the hypocrisy of his emotions.

Past the temple, the landscape opened up, and Alfred let out a little gasp as the destination became clear. It was a pyramid, as big as the Great Pyramid of Giza, but shining a brilliant, almost blinding white in the setting sun. It looked out of place like someone had randomly stuck it there with no regard for the surrounding buildings. Thousands of people were gathering around it as though waiting for an act at a festival. Whatever was happening, it somehow involved Shep, and that thought made him sick. Perhaps if he was close by, he could do something.

Alfred continued walking and squeezed his way past a group of men. He felt eyes on him and was sure he recognised someone, but he dismissed it. He didn't know anyone in Atalantea and was too preoccupied to think about it any further. So, he continued walking until the mass of people, pressed together in a tight nucleus, made it impossible to progress any further. A fight broke out a short distance away. Alfred saw a woman fall to the ground and disappear beneath a sea of feet. Guards were patrolling the area to keep the peace, but they were massively outnumbered.

Alfred spotted an abandoned carriage that two people were using as a makeshift vantage point. He pushed his way through and climbed onto the back of the carriage, oblivious to the fact his pendant had come loose.

Then a horn sounded.

*

Shep snapped into consciousness. He was being dragged through the palace by two guards, but he didn't have the energy to resist. Let them, he thought.

He'd had a strange dream where Alfred had appeared. It had seemed so real. He could see his pale, worried face and hear his voice even now, urging him to leave. But in his dream, he'd forgotten who Alfred was, and he'd dismissed him. It couldn't be real. Alfred was dead. Wasn't he? The strings of reality and fantasy had rolled into one confusing ball, and he could no longer untangle them.

Shep's joints felt sore like they needed a good grease, and he had bruises all over his body, but he did not understand how he had come by them. He could feel grime clogging the corners of his eyes, and his lips felt dry. He needed water, but there was nothing he could do about that now.

Was he awake, or was he high? Or was this another dream? It felt like he was awake, like what was happening was real, but nothing made sense anymore. He squeezed the skin on his hand and felt a gentle nip. His hands didn't look like they were his. They were too pale and bony, with blue veins bulging out of them. They were cold and looked like the hands of a dead man. Was he dead?

'Water,' Shep muttered, and the surprise at hearing his own voice made him jump. It was a weak, pathetic voice filled with angst. His tongue was like sandpaper, and it felt swollen in his mouth. The dehydration made his head pound.

Two guards were sitting with him, but neither moved. 'Water,' Shep said again, forcing the word out of his throat. The guards looked at each other and shrugged.

Shep breathed into his hands to create some moisture and put his palms against his mouth. It did nothing to appease his thirst, but it provided some comfort and warmed his hands.

The carriage took off, and Shep could feel every stray stone and pothole as the wheels rolled thoughtlessly across the paths. He closed his eyes to think but found himself drifting off into another stupor. He needed to stay awake, assuming he was awake, but he was so tired, so sore, so thirsty.

The Viracocha had said something about a show, but then the Viracocha had said a lot. And all of it in incoherent riddles his brain couldn't process. It tired him out just thinking about it. His desire to sleep was a powerful magnet pulling him inevitably towards the source. Maybe if he closed his eyes for a few seconds, it would help.

No! He needed to stay awake, but his eyes were so heavy.

Was that a horn?

Just a minute or two…

*

The horns stopped, and a man appeared on a platform near the top of the pyramid. 'The high lord,' he announced, and his voice carried over the swathes of people, naturally amplified by the positioning of the pyramid and the surrounding buildings.

A deathly silence swaddled the crowd as Attalus appeared, dressed in the bronze armour he had worn to his father's funeral.

The crowd didn't know how to respond. There were a few claps, but most people remained silent, confused. They had been expecting Hestia.

'He's already calling himself the high lord,' Ptolemy whispered to Axil, who grunted in response. It was his fault Attalus had grounds for calling himself the high lord.

'Welcome,' Attalus said and held up his hand as though expecting a cheer, but he had grossly misread the mood of the crowd. He quickly moved on. 'I stand before you as the acting high lord, and no doubt many of you are wondering about the whereabouts of my sister, Hestia. I am afraid, it is with the heaviest of hearts, that I must share this news with you. You must hear, and see, for yourselves the grave mistakes made by the previous high lord, my father, and the repercussions of those mistakes. But fear not, for today we will rectify those mistakes, ensuring the future of Atalantea and the future of each and every Atlantean.'

Attalus was reading from a script, and he made his comments with little emotion. A low murmuring from the crowd crescendoed until Attalus shouted, 'Silence!'

He regained his composure and carried on.

'You are all aware of the changes implemented by the previous high lord, with the endorsement of the high table. It has come to my attention that members of the high table were compromised in their positions. They guided the high lord negligently and for their own gain. More importantly, they guided the high lord to act in contravention of the Order. An act of treason against the Saviour. I have evidence, eyewitness reports, that my sister, Hestia, fraternised with members of the high table to force through laws which acted in direct contravention of the Order to ensure her future role as leader of this great nation.'

Some people booed, but most remained silent, still unsure what was happening.

'And where is she now?' Attalus continued. 'I am afraid that as soon as Hestia became aware of the allegations and the investigation, she fled. Her guilt is undeniable. She must now stand trial and face the consequences of her actions. Anyone assisting her will share her punishment.'

Axil took a deep breath and scratched his chin. 'These are the words of Zetes or the Viracocha,' he said to Ptolemy. 'There's no way Attalus would show such cunning.'

'She must have escaped,' Ptolemy said, squinting at the pyramid. 'Otherwise, she'd be here, standing trial.'

Axil felt a glimmer of hope rise in his chest.

There was a ruckus in the crowd, and Axil turned to see what was going on. A carriage was being pushed slowly through the crowds, and there was a cage on top of it with a naked man cowering within. People were trying to get out of the way, afraid of what they could see. As it approached, Axil could see that the man had black spots covering his body, some of them weeping a yellow puss. The man was in a lot of pain. He lifted his head and cried out. His face looked badly mutilated, and Axil turned away in disgust.

'The man before you now,' boomed Attalus, 'is Borus, former high lawgiver on the high table. He has suffered the wrath of the Saviour for his part in the betrayal. He advised the high lord to turn his back on the Order. The Saviour has responded by casting him with the pox and removing his eyes so that he stands before you as vulgar as his acts. This is what happens when you ignore the Saviour. This is your warning.'

'He's mad,' muttered Ptolemy. 'This is wrong. It's wrong.' He was shaking his head and looking at his feet.

Axil could only nod his head.

Attalus continued. 'But it is not too late. We can make amends, and we have taken steps, necessary steps, to ensure your future, the future of your children, and the future of Atalantea. The Equality-For-All Motion is in violation of the Order. As acting high lord, it is my role, no, my duty, and my right, to reverse the decision to follow the current legal counsel to the high table. The decision will be reversed with immediate effect. You are all witnesses to this historic event. This righting of wrongs. This victory against tyranny.'

The crowd became agitated. Many were protesting. Attalus's words had turned the temperature up, and the crowd was at boiling point.

'It is as we predicted,' Axil said.

Ptolemy nodded in agreement. 'I fear Attalus is nothing more than a puppet. He does not understand the implications of his decision, other than it paves the way for him to be high lord. The governors who sided with the motion will revolt. He has undermined them all and made them look like fools. Worse, he has called them traitors.'

Axil thought about his meeting with Solon. He had known it was a mistake, but he had been too afraid to follow his heart.

Attalus hadn't finished. 'As you know, our Saviour has also sent us a test, an opportunity for us to ask for his forgiveness. You are all aware that a middling arrived on these shores, providing undeniable evidence of a world outside of the storm. It is a world that threatens ours. A world that could destroy ours unless we take action and unless we appeal to our Saviour. When the middling arrived, I immediately brought him under control whilst others, including Hestia, stood and watched. Some of you may have been there and witnessed it yourself. I know there are some who would have us welcome the middling and have him live amongst us. I appeal to those now. The middling's influence and treachery will grow like a cancer and destroy us if left unchecked. We cannot allow it.'

'He's challenging the governors,' said Axil, but Ptolemy wasn't listening. Something behind him had distracted him.

'It's them!' Ptolemy said.

'Who?'

'The two men who claimed to have chased the middling Below.'

Axil followed Ptolemy's line of sight and saw two large men who looked like they had to stay together at all times to share a brain cell. 'It's not surprising they are here,' Axil said, not sure why Ptolemy was bothered.

'Yes, but they have an unhealthy interest in whoever it is that is sitting in the back of this carriage.'

Axil hadn't even noticed there was someone behind them. Whoever it was, they were oblivious to the fact that they were subject to so much attention. The man had ginger hair and pale skin. He was staring so intently at what was happening with the middling Axil was sure his eyeballs would pop out. He also had an unusual pendant glowing from his neck.

'What are you thinking?' Axil asked.

'I think we don't lose sight of whoever it is in the back of this carriage. I have a feeling that the two oafs have an interest in him, and I want to know why. And that pendant is unusual. It's the sort they used to use for human sacrifices so that the Saviour would recognise the offering. I would be interested to know where he obtained it from,'

Axil didn't know, so he turned back to listen to Attalus.

'… we have kept the middling under strict control during his stay. However, not strict enough, behold those who angered the Saviour by fornicating with his test.'

A group of naked women were ushered onto the platform. Like Borus, they were also covered in black, pulsing spots from head to toe. They tried to hide their dignity, but some were too weak or too far gone to realise what was happening.

'The curse,' muttered Axil to himself.

'The curse?' asked Ptolemy.

Axil had not told Ptolemy about how he'd spied on Zetes' meeting with the Viracocha. 'They want to create fear by showing that anyone who fraternises with the middling will suffer the curse.'

There were some shocked gasps from the crowd. Many looked away. Some were shouting for blood.

'He's certainly putting on a show,' Ptolemy sighed, one eye on what was happening behind him.

Someone removed the cursed women from the platform, and the high priest joined Attalus, dressed in his finery. Attalus moved to the side to let him speak.

'We are here today, not only to correct previous errors but also to witness the swearing-in of our new high lord. In light of recent amendments and following the traditional laws of ascension, that is, the laws of our Saviour, it is my honour and privilege to welcome the new High Lord, Attalus Atlas, eldest son of Critias Atlas and rightful heir to the highest seat.'

There was a muted cheer as Attalus kneeled and gave his oath whilst the high priest placed his hand on Attalus's head.

'I, Attalus Atlas, truly and sincerely swear in the presence of our Saviour that I will serve the ten realms in the interests of the State as the rightful and lawful heir to the highest seat. I will honour the Order, or shall the Saviour strike me down from where I kneel.'

Axil half expected a trident to explode from the sea and nail Attalus to the pyramid. He was disappointed when nothing happened.

The high priest allowed Attalus to stand. 'Before I ask the governors to swear their allegiance to the new high lord, as is tradition, we will now make an offering to our Saviour to bring good luck and prosperity to the high lord's reign and to repent for past mistakes.'

*

Shep woke up disoriented. Where was he? It was dark, and he could hear hushed voices. The air was dry, and he could feel sand underneath his bare feet. 'Alfred,' he said aloud, although he didn't know why. He'd been having strange dreams recently, such strange dreams.

He was leaning against a big stone block in a dark corridor, although he didn't know how he had made it there. Why was it so difficult to move? Voices whispered around him, ghosts tormenting him in a foreign language.

291

Invisible hands manoeuvred Shep around the low, tight corridors, and then he walked up some steps, each one a monumental effort. Every time he stopped, he felt a sharp jab in his back, forcing him to keep going. After what seemed like an eternity, he turned a corner and saw an opening leading to the clear night sky. Someone was talking. It sounded like a preacher, and he could hear boos, shouts, and the occasional cheer. He couldn't tell whether the preacher was liked, but he didn't care. He just wanted to go home.

Someone pushed Shep towards the opening, and then the preacher appeared. He was wearing a white robe that draped along the floor and had a large hood covering most of his face, but Shep could see that he had a thin, bitter smile. His limp wrists and fragile hands suggested that an old man hid under there. He felt a chill go through his body. He felt awake now, adrenaline suddenly kick-starting his brain. Every alarm bell in his body was ringing.

Shep turned and saw a guard who gave him a cruel smile. The preacher held out his right hand and curled his long, arthritic fingers around Shep's arm. Shep stuttered forwards, surprised by the old man's strength. Or was it his frailty? He didn't want to go, but his body didn't seem to react to his instructions. He felt like a computer swamped with viruses. As he moved forward, the noise of the crowd outside grew. He tried to protest, but nothing would come out of his mouth. His vocal cords had frozen. His body was slowly breaking down, piece by piece.

The preacher grabbed him around the waist and helped him to stay upright. Together, they walked towards the light until they were both standing on a platform midway up a giant pyramid. Shep could see the sea and the plains of Atalantea around him. It was beautiful. He breathed in the air, and for a moment, felt at peace with the world. The preacher shouted something rhythmically. It sounded demonic, but Shep wasn't paying attention. He was looking at the thousands of people who stood watching, his mouth agape.

The preacher grabbed Shep firmly, and he sensed a change in atmosphere. The crowd was suddenly silent, waiting. But what for? Was he supposed to do something?

The old man let go, and without his support, Shep fell onto his knees, his legs unable to hold his weight anymore. He looked out at the crowd, but his eyes failed him now, showing only a blur of light fading to darkness. They wanted to close and grew heavier with every second.

The preacher pulled Shep's head back, and a memory floated into Shep's head of when he used to get his hair washed at the hairdresser's in one of the uncomfortable sinks. He had secretly fancied the hairdresser, whose soft hands had caressed and gently massaged his scalp. He smiled tiredly at the memory and then grimaced as the preacher's bony fingers grabbed his hair and forced his chin up.

Was this some sort of baptism ceremony? Viracocha had said that he was going to be the star of a show. He didn't feel much like a star. He didn't feel like anything.

His senses dulled. First, his eyes closed, then his hearing faded just as a strange sounding horn erupted in the distance. It was like someone was pulling plugs out of him, slowly turning him off.

Something cold and sharp licked his neck. At first, it tickled slightly, and then he felt it dig in. It felt like someone was slowly drawing a line across his throat with a sharp pen. A sharp iron taste filled his mouth, and he coughed violently, blood splattering everywhere. He couldn't get rid of it. He tried to clear his throat, but it was impossible. There was too much. He thrashed and coughed, panic setting in. What was happening to him? He tried to cry out for his mother. Shep wanted her to tell him everything was going to be alright, but when he opened his mouth, all that came out was a sea of blood. He just wanted to go home.

And then a gentle peacefulness overcame him...

It was Shep's fifth birthday, and he was in his back garden, playing swing-ball whilst his father cooked meat on the barbecue. His mother was sunbathing away from the smoke, and his older sister sat with her feet in the paddling pool. She never wanted to go in, unlike Shep, who jumped in at every opportunity. The smell of burgers and sausages drifted over, and Shep inhaled it. He had his new toy bike to play with from his mother, but that could wait. He was enjoying hitting the ball around as fast as he could, watching it whizz up and down on the pole. Later, his friends would be around for a birthday party, but this was his favourite part. All of his family together for him, a temporary truce with no tension and no shouting. Not today, because today was his birthday.

Shep was home.

*

'We're too late,' Hestia said and then said it again when no one responded.

She was sitting on a white gelding next to Aliz and Governor Gadeirus in some woods just outside of the Capital. The horse was more temperamental than what she was used to, but he was quick and didn't startle easily, so it was ideal for the task ahead. The Adelphi army marched in a thin line behind them. Just shy of two thousand men. It wasn't enough.

Ganymede and his household troops marched alongside them. Only twenty men, but all of them loyal to their future leader. After Hestia's disappearance, Ganymede had sent men to look for his betrothed, and he had quickly ridden to her aid as soon as he received word of her whereabouts. Hestia wasn't sure how she felt about that. She didn't enjoy owing him a debt, especially after how his father had forced her hand during the governors' meeting, but she was thankful for the additional soldiers.

She would have liked the Artemisiai to have joined her, but they had left to rejoin their temple, explaining that they didn't get involved in State matters. She felt naked without them. They had transported her safely to Gadeirus along long-forgotten routes and paths to avoid detection. Without them, she would have been helpless.

'Perhaps not,' Aliz muttered. Her body had recovered quickly after her ordeal, especially after Gadeirus's physicians had looked at her and applied their ointments and herbs. Still, the mental scars would linger for much longer. Hestia had tried to convince her to stay behind and recuperate, but there had been no talking to her. She was a wild animal pulling on the chains which restrained her.

Aliz pulled at the bandage covering her ear and scratched at the cavity behind the material. There had been nothing the physicians could do to help with that, and Hestia shuddered at the thought of what the tridents had done to her. It filled her with anger.

'They have sounded the horns,' Hestia said. 'The ceremony is underway. We should have set off earlier.'

Gadeirus shifted uncomfortably on his horse. 'It is not an easy thing, high lady, amassing an army spread out over an entire realm, in secret, for a cause which cannot be communicated. However, it would appear that our approach will be unchecked, which is a victory in itself. They will not be expecting an army.'

Hestia felt guilty. She had spoken out of turn and hadn't meant to upset Gadeirus. He had availed himself to her without question and had acted with honour and integrity, qualities few of the governors seemed to possess. 'My apologies, Gadeirus. I meant no offence.'

'None taken, high lady. You are right though, we must move with haste, but we have to wait for my scouts. If there is any danger ahead, we need to know about it. If they have blocked the eastern entrance, we may need to devise another plan.'

As if in answer, three scouts galloped towards them, and Hestia breathed out in relief. Xee, the young man who had helped rescue her, was one of them. He was desperate to please and followed Aliz around like a love-struck puppy, clinging to her every word. It was Xee who had stayed by Aliz's side whilst she recovered, and part of her wished she could switch places with him.

'The way is clear,' a scout said. He addressed Gadeirus, and Hestia felt irritated at his slight, however unintended.

'And what of the gate?' Gadeirus asked.

'We saw no one. No guards,' the scout replied. Xee nodded eagerly beside him.

'No guards?' Hestia remarked, incredulous. The gates were always guarded.

'It would seem everyone is at the ceremony, high lady,' the scout replied.

'It's true,' Xee said, 'you can march right in, and no one will notice.'

'I suppose that makes things easier,' Gadeirus said, turning to Aliz.

They had planned to send a few riders ahead to capture the gate should it be guarded, but it seemed they wouldn't need to.

'It could be a trap,' Aliz said. 'As soon as we pass through, they could descend on us and trap us in Outer Atalantea. It would be a slaughter.'

'Not if we hold the gate to ensure our exit,' Gadeirus replied. 'I don't think we have another option if we are to stop the ceremony. They will know by now that you escaped, but they will think you've gone into hiding. They won't be expecting a direct attack. Nevertheless, they'll be looking for you here as well, if they have any sense.'

'And I intend to let them find me,' Hestia pledged, with fire in her stomach.

'Send Ganymede and his guard ahead to secure the gate,' Aliz said, taking a swig from her waterskin. 'If there is anyone there, they won't suspect anything if they see Ganymede. Then once they've given the signal, we can head through and march on the ceremony.'

'Give the order,' Hestia confirmed, keen to get moving.

She watched as twenty shadows rode past her up the hill towards the gate, imagining what was happening at the ceremony. What was Attalus doing and saying to drag her name through the mud? She had spent many hours thinking about the people who might have betrayed her, thinking about what she would do to them. In her head, she had made an example of them, drawing inspiration from the punishments dished out by Hera, Queen of the Gods, but she knew she wouldn't be able to live with herself if she took such ghastly methods. Perhaps she was a weak leader. Perhaps she didn't have what it took to rule.

A torch waved in the distance. It was the signal.

Hestia's senses tingled, alive to every movement, noise, and smell. She was calm. It didn't feel like the next few minutes would shape her future. She looked at Aliz and Gadeirus, wondering what they were thinking. Were they worried or concerned? They didn't look it, although it was hard to tell in the fading light. She took a deep breath and squeezed her legs gently. The gelding responded immediately to the command and cantered forward. Two thousand men followed.

*

Alfred threw up on the ground. He hadn't been able to turn his eyes away. His brain couldn't accept what was happening. It was a stunt, wasn't it? The reaction of the crowd told him otherwise. Shock. Disgust. Disbelief. Elation.

Shep's body had thrashed and sputtered before dropping like a rock onto the platform. The priest stood, his robes soaked in disgrace, shouting a rhythmic incantation. His voice became lost as the crowd grew agitated. Groups congregated, throwing rocks and other random items, inciting disorder. Guards had their weapons drawn, making no pretence of their intentions.

Alfred watched, lost amidst his reflections, unable to process what he had witnessed, refusing to accept it. Then he felt a raindrop land on his nose. It was the first time he could remember it raining whilst he had been on the island.

Thunder rumbled in the distance, a deep growl of discontent, and then the heavens opened. The change in weather sparked panic in the crowd. People had been standing around, frozen by what they had witnessed, but now they ran.

Alfred's survival instinct kicked in. He needed to get out of the Capital and back to Ariadne. He jumped down from the carriage and barely noticed that he'd knocked someone over. People were fleeing, families and groups desperate to stick together amidst the chaos, impervious to anyone else. On Alfred's right, a lone man challenged a group of topless young men who had been jumping up and down, yelling wildly, and taking delight in what they had seen. The group ran at him, and the man briefly stood his ground before being knocked to the muddy ground and swarmed by his assailants.

Pockets of fights had broken out everywhere, making it impossible to pick a safe escape. Flashes of lightning lit up the madness, and a soundtrack of snarling thunder and thumping rain accompanied it.

A horn sounded to Alfred's right, and the ground shook. A mass of soldiers appeared from nowhere, marching towards him in a tightly knitted wall of shields and spears. Behind him, guards had formed their own wall, but they were outnumbered and haphazard, unprepared for such an attack.

Alfred ran, trying to outflank the guards to reach safety. He saw a spear penetrate a soldier's thigh and a sword slash across a woman's back, but the events were a blur. It was like they were taking place in a different world. All around him, people were falling, screaming, and cursing in their strange language. A man turned to look for his family and then fell as an arrow pierced his throat. Alfred jumped over his body and kept going.

A mob of at least a hundred men attacked a group of soldiers. They ran at them with makeshift weapons, all courage and no sense. They fell onto the spears of the waiting army. Their foolhardiness created a gap for Alfred to run through, and as he reached the other side, the sounds of the massacre dissipated.

Alfred ducked around a corner, taking a few seconds for a breather. He was standing there, panting and trying to think of a plan when he felt a presence hovering over him.

He spun around to find two men looking at him. One of them smiled. Alfred recognised the grin and the big dent on his forehead. It was the men who had chased him through the forest. Alfred turned to run, but he was too late. This time, he couldn't evade them. He felt his legs disappear from under him as he slipped on ground churned up by rain and panicked feet. He tried to scramble up, but there was a knee on his back, pinning him down and forcing his head into the mud. Then something hard hit him on the back of his head, and his vision faded.

Freezing water splashed around Alfred's waist. He had a headache, and the back of his head felt sore. As he made to touch it, he realised his hands were tied behind him. He wriggled to free himself, but the ropes were tight, cutting into him. A wave of salty water splashed up against his chest and bombarded his face. Cautiously, Alfred opened his eyes.

His hands and feet had been tied to a rock in a small pool that was quickly filling with seawater and rain. The tide was coming in, and the waves had already moved up to his chest. The storm thrashed overhead, relentless and unforgiving.

Alfred rubbed the rope against the rock to create friction, but it was no use, and his wrists were quickly in tatters.

Two giant pillars stood a short distance away to his left. Alfred knew they marked the entrance to the Capital from Ariadne's instructions. He hadn't been taken far by his captors. They must have dragged him out of the Capital amidst the riots and found the first secluded spot they could to tie down his unconscious body.

He'd watched them brutally sacrifice Shep. Bile rose in his throat at the atrocity, and now he was suffering the same fate.

The wind picked up, whistling playfully around his ears, and then he saw a wave rising threateningly in front of him. It crashed before it reached the pool, but it was only a matter of time before one would engulf him.

Alfred shouted, praying that someone might hear him, but the howling of the wind drowned him out. His mind turned to Ariadne, and he felt tears in his eyes as he realised he wouldn't see her again. She had made the whole godforsaken journey worth it. The storms, the caves, the battles, the injuries, he would do it all again for her. She'd told him. She'd begged him not to go, and he'd ignored her. He'd tried to play the hero, believing himself invincible, but as the water rose to his chin, he knew he was about to be proven wrong.

He tipped his head back and shouted out again, but as he did, he swallowed a mouthful of water, nearly choking. He pulled his arms with all of his might, feeling his skin and muscles tearing, but something moved. Alfred pulled harder, tensing every muscle in his body. With a jerk, his arms moved forward, freed from their restraints. Part of him rejoiced, but he remembered his feet were still tied, holding him down.

Alfred took a deep breath and plunged his head beneath the waves to work his feet free with his hands, but the resistance of the water forced him back up. He tried again, this time pushing down as hard as he could. They had bound the ropes around his feet tight, and his fingers couldn't find a way in. He returned to the surface, but he could only just crane his neck high enough to suck at the air. Alfred pulled at the ropes binding his legs again, using the last of his energy reserves, but still, they would not budge.

A clock was ticking in his head like a metronome. Tick. Tock. Tick. Tock. Brrrrrrrrr.

He needed air, but when he straightened his body, he couldn't reach the surface. Alfred flapped his arms and kicked his legs to fashion himself an extra inch, but it was no use, and a familiar stinging feeling hit his chest.

Then he felt a movement as something swished by his feet. At the same time, a strong arm pulled his hands upwards, and he felt his shoulders sockets strain as the ropes held him down. It's no use, he thought to himself, *it's too late!* But then his feet were suddenly free, and he was being pushed over the side of the pool into a boat. Rain was still hurling down, and the boat rocked precariously as it tried to ride the waves.

Alfred took some deep breaths. He wasn't sure what had happened, and he didn't care. He just needed to breathe. A man knelt beside him and smiled as Alfred gasped desperately. He had friendly, curious eyes which seemed to burst out of his head. Alfred's instinct told him he had nothing to fear from this man, and he relaxed slightly.

'Greetings,' said the man in Atlantean. 'I'm Ptolemy.'

CHAPTER XLVIII

Saviour's Day

Kea

'There will be a war,' said Ptolemy matter-of-factly. 'Of that, we can be certain.'

Axil nodded and paced the room, his hands on his hips. The middling's sacrifice had resulted in chaos in the Capital. Brawls had erupted as far as the eye could see. Mostly it was young men drunk on the occasion with beliefs and opinions entrenched over many years of indoctrination. Men, unable to see reason or process the true consequences of their actions. Men, incapable of opening their eyes and ears wide enough to understand what was happening.

Then Hestia arrived with her army or, more correctly, Governor Gadeirus's army. They had surprised everyone. The high guard and tridents had tried to put up some resistance. Various groups had joined them, keen to make a stand, the why being irrelevant, but Gadeirus's army quickly overpowered them. The scene turned into a massacre with hundreds of innocents caught in the crossfire. It was a sickening display of wanton slaughter which shamed every Atlantean. People were describing it as the Carnage in the Capital.

Ptolemy's hunch about the person in the back of the carriage had proved correct. They watched as he ran blindly into the middle of a battlefield with two large oafs in close pursuit. They had followed, jumping and slipping over fallen bodies. A man, trying to shepherd his family to safety, was bludgeoned over the head. His children screamed as his wife tried to revive him. A girl, on the verge of womanhood, had fallen in front of them. She had a look of confusion in her eyes and a knife buried between her shoulder blades. A young boy, lost and alone, had slipped on the mud and then suffocated as the army marched over him.

They'd kept their heads low and their wits about them as they tried to keep pace with the two oafs. It was difficult with the mass of bodies crisscrossing in front of them, and they'd lost sight and ground when two groups clashed in front of them. By the time they'd found a way around, the two men had caught their prey and were dragging him off. Axil and Ptolemy followed from a distance, unable to catch them.

The two oafs had taken their prey through the Pillars of Heracles and tied him down as an offering to the Saviour, hoping to garner divine favour for themselves. With the tide turning violent, they'd quickly disappeared, afraid the Saviour might claim them as well. Axil and Ptolemy rushed to help, but they couldn't access the pool via land as the tide had come too far in. Instead, they found a rowing boat and struggled to maneuver it against the waves.

They reached the middling just in time. A few more seconds, and he would have drowned. Axil couldn't make sense of how he had broken free from the ropes around his arms and legs. There must have been a weak point in the ropes, but that explanation seemed more convenient than accurate. There had to be more to it.

The middling had told Ptolemy that his name was Alfred, and then he'd pleaded with him to take him to someone called Ariadne. Alfred was able to direct them in the right direction, and after a day following the Tibune into Kea, they reached their destination. Alfred wept when they arrived, his relief and ecstasy too much to contain. Axil could see why. Ariadne was not only a pretty girl, but she was fierce!

Axil and Ptolemy waited in the front room while Ariadne put Alfred to bed. It was Saviour's Day. A day for eating and dancing around the fire, listening to bands in the communal areas, and sharing presents. Instead, they were planning a war.

'What happened?' Ariadne asked as she entered the room, her face tense with stress. Axil relayed what had happened. When he described how the men had tied Alfred down as a sacrifice, she went white and gripped the chair, her tendons jumping out of her skin. 'I told him,' she said. 'I told him they would try to kill him. I should never have helped him. I should have tied him down.'

'Why was he there?' Ptolemy asked softly.

'To save his friend. He wanted to save his friend.' Ariadne explained her part in the story.

Axil listened intently as she told them about how Kaspa had found Alfred on the beach and how he had been chased Below. Ariadne cried when she described his escape and the loss of her brother. He couldn't believe what he was hearing, and he prayed she was mistaken about the Androphogi. She had to be.

'He told me in there,' Ariadne said, pointing to the bedroom, 'that he found his friend, but he couldn't get him out. What have they done? Why have they done this?' Ariadne's head was in her hands. The events had left her exhausted and her emotions tied in knots.

'To start a war,' Ptolemy said. 'I think Governor Diaprepes and the Viracocha have been working together. The Viracocha wants to return to the old ways to appease the Saviour, and Diaprepes wants to take control over Syros. It would make him the most powerful governor in Atalantea, especially with Attalus as his puppet and with control of the high table and the high guard.'

'But Hestia took control of the Capital, didn't she? She stopped it?' Ariadne looked up, hope in her eyes.

'Not quite,' Ptolemy said. 'By the time Hestia arrived, the damage had already been done. She may have taken control of the Capital, but she only has Gadeirus's army. By law, Attalus is the high lord, and Hestia is a usurper with no right to claim the Capital.'

'That can't be right,' Ariadne gasped.

'Maybe not,' Axil agreed, 'but it is the law, and many of the governors will stand with Diaprepes. They are old men, set in their ways. The thought of a woman ruling fills them with horror.'

'They are worse than Eris,' Ariadne spat, referring to the Goddess of Strife and Discord.

'And now they think the Saviour is on their side, having made a huge offering to Him. They made a show of a curse which was brought on by the Saviour, and now Attalus has sacrificed the middling. The curse will no doubt be lifted, proving that they were right to act as they did.'

Axil grimaced. Whilst human sacrifice was an abhorrent act and one which had been confined to the history books for thousands of years, standing against Attalus would mean sullying the sacrifice and risking the wrath of the Saviour. Most Atlanteans were fair-weather with religion, but many harboured beliefs which blossomed in the darkness or when convenient.

'Where are Governor Diaprepes and Attalus then?' Ariadne asked.

'Attica.' Ptolemy said. 'At least, that's my best guess. He'll be amassing his army and calling on the other realms to swear their allegiance to Attalus, which they would have done at the ceremony had Hestia not arrived.'

The three of them sat in silence, processing their thoughts.

'Alfred is the key to all of this,' Ptolemy said, breaking the silence.

Ariadne shook her head. She knew what was coming.

'He survived the mouth of the storm, he escaped Below, he got into the Citadel, and then he survived an attempt on his life—'

'Because you saved him,' Ariadne cut in.

'Yes, we arrived and got him, but his ropes were already loose. Either he's very lucky, or someone is looking out for him. I think the Bard's Prophecy could be true, and I think he is the only one who can help us out of this hole.' Ptolemy gave Ariadne a sympathetic smile.

Ariadne exhaled and gently cupped her stomach. It was only a brief gesture, but Axil noticed it and stayed quiet.

'How? How can he help?' Ariadne asked, raising her voice. 'Has he not suffered enough?'

'He can't stay hidden here forever.' Axil smiled, trying to calm Ariadne.

'I don't know how he can help,' Ptolemy conceded. 'I just know that he is the key, and we must try. For the future of Atalantea, we must try, and that means riding to Hestia's aid. Only Alfred can expose the lies of Attalus and Zetes.'

Ariadne didn't answer but looked like she was about to explode. She knew Ptolemy was right and that she couldn't hide Alfred away, but the realisation was a hammer blow. She'd only just got him back. 'He needs to recover here,' she demanded through gritted teeth.

Suddenly there was a movement in the room next door, and Alfred emerged from the bedroom, his hair a tangled mess and bags drooping under his eyes. He looked around at them expectantly. Axil looked him up and down. Their chief weapon in their battle for Atalantea could barely stand. But even so, they would march on the Capital and start a war they had no chance of winning.

Honour and morality demanded it.

CHAPTER XLIX
Milos

Kaspa halted and watched as Theseus knelt. He touched the ground and then surveyed the landscape. They were on a dusty path cutting through some overgrown trees with the Alakasta Volcano, watching their every move on the horizon. Kaspa followed Theseus's gaze but couldn't see anything untoward.

They had begun by following rumours, tales of entire villages going missing. Invariably, the villages were cut off from the rest of society. They were difficult to locate and even more difficult to access. Most of the rumours had proven to be true, but it was impossible to know whether that was because of the Androphogi or some other reason. In the hopes of containing the pox should it hit their realm, many governors had built villages deep in isolation as a fallback measure. They were rarely occupied unless there was a contamination, but sometimes exiles moved into the houses.

'People have been this way recently,' Theseus mumbled to himself, his eyes on the ground. He often spoke like that and rarely addressed Kaspa directly.

'How can you tell?' Kaspa asked. He couldn't see anything to show that anyone had been there for a long time.

'Look at the ground,' Theseus explained.

Kaspa looked down, confused. It was dusty and dry.

'There are footprints,' Theseus said, as though it was obvious. 'They're difficult to see because dust has settled on top of them, but when the light hits it at the right angle, you can tell. Tracks both ways, but the tracks coming back this way look heavier.'

Kaspa focused on the path in front of him. Maybe there were footsteps, but he couldn't see them. His eyes were not trained to see such things.

'I reckon maybe a few days ago?' It was more a statement than a question, and Kaspa nodded in agreement.

So far, their trip had been fruitless. Frustration and exhaustion had replaced Kaspa's thirst to avenge Erik's death. Theseus was relentless and didn't seem to have the energy levels of a normal human being. He never tired and only rested when Kaspa insisted. To get help from the State to remove the Androphogi, they needed proof that they existed in the bowels of the earth. Most people thought they existed only in nightmares.

Theseus had heard rumours of strange happenings and disappearances that he thought must involve the Androphogi. He knew they harvested humans. He had seen it, and not all of them could be cavers. He was convinced that they must be escaping somehow. Their plan, if you could call it that, was to locate any entrances to the Below where Androphogi could be escaping and then…close them? Fight the Androphogi? Get help? Kaspa wasn't sure. He didn't think Theseus was sure, either.

Theseus had wanted to return to where they'd lost Erik, but there was no way Kaspa was going back there, and it was pointless anyway. The Androphogi couldn't climb out of that cave without assistance, so they must be escaping from somewhere else. They needed to find out where.

'The village will be at the end of this path,' Theseus muttered.

How do you know? Kaspa thought to himself.

They continued along the path in silence, and Kaspa felt a pang of annoyance as a village became visible in the distance. He wanted Theseus to be wrong every once in a while. If only to show that he could be mistaken. A local farmer had told them that the village should be inhabited, but no one had been to collect food or supplies recently. There was no sign of life, and an eerie silence hung in the air.

A small house stood at the entrance to the village. It looked well maintained, but the front door had been left wide open, which was curious.

'Wait here,' Theseus said.

Kaspa was more than happy to follow orders on this occasion. He stood waiting, his senses primed for any sign of danger.

After a few minutes, Theseus reappeared. 'Nothing,' he said. 'It's the same as the village we saw a few days ago. People have been living here recently. There are embers in the fireplace, and the rooms are full of clothes and items. They left in a rush. I can't see any signs of a fight or a struggle.'

'What do you think happened?' Kaspa asked.

'I don't know, but it doesn't feel right.' Theseus clicked his tongue and then marched off towards the village. Kaspa scurried behind him.

They found the same scene in the village. No sign of life, and every house abandoned in a hurry. An enormous bonfire had long since burned away in the centre.

'There was a bonfire in the last village we visited, as well,' Theseus mused.

Kaspa had noticed that. It wasn't unusual for small fires to be lit at night. Locals used them as gathering points and communal cooking spots, but this was a large, almost ceremonial, bonfire. Saviour's Day was a few days ago, and so it wouldn't have been surprising for one to have been lit then to celebrate, but if that was the case, where was everyone? Kaspa sighed. Usually, he'd spend Saviour's Day with Erik and Ariadne, celebrating and drinking rather than scouring the land for monsters. The thought made him well up, and he struggled to push the emotions back down.

'What are you thinking?' Kaspa asked, looking away, his voice almost breaking.

'Two bonfires, two deserted villages. It can't be a coincidence, can it? There must be a connection.'

Kaspa's eyes widened as a terrible thought suddenly flashed through his mind.

Theseus read it. 'No,' he said. 'It's not big enough for that. The smell would travel, and there would be remnants in the ashes, teeth, bits of bone. The only thing that's been on this fire is wood.'

Kaspa breathed out, relieved. But what purpose had the fire served? Kaspa looked up and saw movement from a window. It was only for a split second, but he was sure that he had seen something. He tried to focus his eyes. 'Up there!' Kaspa said to Theseus and pointed at a house a short distance away.

Theseus followed Kaspa's finger. 'I can't see anything,' he said.

'No, it's gone, but I'm sure I saw a movement up there.'

'I'll go check,' Theseus said and stood up. 'It won't be Androphogi,' he added, seeing Kaspa's hesitation. 'If they're coming up, they won't be doing it in broad daylight. They are creatures of the night.'

He wandered off, leaving Kaspa alone to sit and ponder. Theseus was confident, and he knew more about the Androphogi than anyone, but he didn't know everything. If he did, they wouldn't be spending so long trying to locate them.

Kaspa heard a scream and jumped up to see where it had come from. It sounded like a girl's scream, and it pierced the silence like a lightning bolt. He looked up to see Theseus standing in the window of the house. He had hold of someone. A few seconds later, he emerged with a small girl roughly thrown over his shoulder. She was squirming, struggling to escape.

'What are you doing?' Kaspa asked, aghast.

Theseus just smiled at him. 'There was a hidden door,' he said, apparently pleased with himself.

'Put her down!' Kaspa demanded, and only then did Theseus realise that he'd traumatised the poor girl. He set her on her feet but kept hold of her by the scruff of her neck.

'It's okay,' Kaspa said, raising his voice to be heard over the girl's screams. 'You're okay. We're not going to hurt you. We're not going to hurt you,' he repeated.

The girl took a few deep breaths, although Kaspa wasn't sure if she was calming down or just catching her breath to scream again. 'I'm Kaspa. What is your name?' he asked, giving her the friendliest smile he could muster.

'Me-Me-Metis,' the girl managed and wiped her button nose with the back of her hand, drawing a string of snot. Her voice was squeaky like a mouse and full of sorrow. Kaspa felt his heart melt. She was only five or six and still learning how to pronounce her words.

'And where are your ma and pa, Metis?' Kaspa asked.

'I... I don't know,' she said and started sobbing again. Theseus let go of her and stepped back. He was out of his comfort zone, and Kaspa finally felt useful.

'Metis, listen to me.' He crouched down, so he was at her height. 'Listen to me, Metis,' Kaspa said again, and she looked up at him. 'We're going to do all we can to help find them, but we need you to tell us what happened.'

Metis's eyes lit up. They were large, green, and filled with the innocence of youth. 'You can find them?' she asked, and Kaspa saw Theseus pull a face.

'We'll do everything we can, but we need your help. Can you help us?'

Metis sniffed and nodded.

'When did everyone disappear?' Theseus asked abruptly.

Kaspa held up his hand to tell him to stand down. 'When did you last see your ma and pa?' he asked.

'I don't know,' the girl cried.

Her hair was a mass of knots. She had mud on her face and clothes, suggesting they had been gone for at least a few days. Kaspa heard Theseus sigh behind him in frustration, and he resisted the urge to punch him. His time Below appeared to have robbed him of any compassion.

'That's okay. Have you been in your room all the time?' Kaspa asked, and the girl nodded.

'She's not left her room,' Theseus confirmed. 'You could tell by the smell. She's been living off scraps of food and stale water.'

Metis looked at the ground and wiped her eyes again.

'There's nothing to worry about,' Kaspa said. 'How about we get you some new clothes? Once you get washed, and we get you some food, then you might feel a bit better.'

'We don't have time for this,' Theseus complained.

'We don't have a choice!' Kaspa said as calmly as he could. 'Why don't you scout the area, see what you can find? See if you can work out where they went. With all of these empty villages, there has to be a way they can get in and out. They can't just vanish.'

Theseus, oblivious or indifferent to the anger in Kaspa's voice, considered the suggestion and decided that it was a good one. 'I'll look,' he confirmed. 'You get what you can out of the girl.'

'Her name is Metis,' Kaspa said before turning to her. 'Don't worry about him,' he said. 'We'll get you sorted.'

Kaspa helped Metis to get herself washed and changed. As normality and a sense of security returned, so did her confidence. Based on her account, everyone disappeared four or five days ago, shortly after Saviour's Day. The poor thing had been hiding in her room the entire time. She described seeing a monster on the night that everyone disappeared. She said it had two heads, a tail, horns, and black scaly skin. Her mind had likely embellished what she had seen, but Kaspa nodded and listened intently nonetheless.

There wasn't any food around, so Kaspa shared his bread and fruit with Metis, watching as she gobbled it up. He'd always thought he would make a good father, but no woman had ever been interested in him. Not as far as he could tell, anyway. People thought of him as odd or different, and the women he knew didn't want to be tainted with the same brush. Most men his age were busy drinking ale and inhaling black magic, but that didn't interest Kaspa. It left him with no close friends. He didn't mind his own company, though. It was rare for him to feel lonely, but the thought of settling down and having children occasionally crossed his mind.

Theseus returned. Metis fell silent, hiding behind Kaspa's leg.

'I followed the trails,' Theseus said.

'And?'

'And they disappear like they always do. It makes no sense. How can everyone just disappear with no sign of a struggle?'

'Do you usually have a bonfire here?' Kaspa asked Metis.

'No,' she said, 'but we were celebrating.'

'Celebrating what? Saviour's Day?'

Metis shrugged. 'Erm... the man said that it was to celebrate an offering to our Saviour. Everyone was there.'

Metis reeled off the names of everyone she knew, counting them off on her fingers as she went.

'... and there was music and dancing, and everyone was drinking and eating, but Ma wouldn't let me drink because I'm not old enough, but the other children were drinking. It wasn't fair. And then we went home because Ma said she didn't feel well—'

Kaspa and Theseus exchanged a look, and then Metis stopped talking and cocked her head to listen.

The sound of hooves was growing louder.

'Who is it?' Kaspa wondered aloud.

'How should I know?' Theseus replied.

Around thirty horsemen appeared in a cloud of dust and stopped a few feet away. The man in front took off his helmet, revealing a trident tattoo.

'They are tridents,' Kaspa hissed.

'I can see,' Theseus responded.

The lead man jumped from his horse and approached them. His leathery, tanned skin was weather-beaten, and Kaspa placed him in his fifties. Past his prime, but still a force to be reckoned with.

'You look familiar to me,' Theseus said to the man as he approached. He was squinting with his mouth ajar.

'And you to me,' the man replied with a big grin. The rest of the riders remained seated, watching.

'What business have you here?' Theseus asked.

'Do you not know who I am?' the man asked. 'It has been a few years, but I haven't changed that much!'

Theseus studied the man intently before shaking his head. 'I suspect you have misplaced me. What is your name?'

'You will have known me as Klemides, although I go by my trident name these days.'

'Klemides,' Theseus repeated slowly and shook his head.

'I know of you,' Kaspa said. 'You are the leader of the tridents, aren't you? The high lord's brother? The old high lord, at least.'

'Yes,' replied Klemides. 'And who might you be?'

Kaspa felt Metis clinging to the back of his leg. Klemides, with his armour and tattoo, had scared her, and Kaspa could see why. 'I'm Kaspa, and this is Theseus,' he said.

Klemides laughed. 'Theseus, you say? Who came up with that name?'

'What do you mean?' Kaspa asked. How did Klemides know that wasn't his name?

'I escaped the Below thanks to Kaspa and his brother Erik,' said Theseus, cutting straight to the point. 'I had no name, and so now I go as Theseus.'

'So what are you doing here?' asked Klemides, unmoved by their tale.

Theseus exchanged a glance with Kaspa. 'Androphogi,' he said. 'There's Androphogi Below, and they're growing. Not only that, but now they're coming up.'

'Impossible!' spat Klemides.

'That's what everyone else says,' muttered Theseus. 'Which is why we need evidence to take back.'

'Look around you,' said Kaspa. 'The entire village has gone. The only person left is this little girl.'

Kaspa felt Metis bury her head against the back of his thigh. 'I know it sounds unbelievable,' he said. 'But I've seen them, fought them. Theseus has been fighting them for years. They killed... they killed my brother.' The last words didn't want to come out of his mouth, but Kaspa knew it was the only way he could convince people. 'We know no one will believe us, so we need evidence to take to the high lady to raise an army.'

Kaspa had decided that was his plan. He hadn't consulted Theseus with it.

'Even if what you say is true,' said Klemides, shaking his head, 'there will be no army.'

'You don't understand!' shouted Kaspa.

'No, you don't understand,' Klemides replied calmly. 'There will be no army because there is going to be a war. Most of the tridents have already picked a side. I have with me all that is left. Men loyal to me.'

It wasn't enough. It wasn't close to enough. News of a massacre at the swearing-in ceremony had reached the towns they'd visited in Milos, but it was impossible to discern what had happened from the various accounts they had heard. That was the first time Kaspa had heard anyone mention a war.

'So, what are you doing here?' Theseus asked as Kaspa dithered.

'I was sent to look for my nephew,' replied Klemides. 'I was told by the Artemisiai that he will need me.'

'You're joining with Attalus?' Kaspa asked, shocked.

'No, my other nephew,' said Klemides. 'Dyon.' He said the name slowly, watching Theseus closely.

'But he's dead!' stuttered Kaspa. 'Everyone in the ten realms knows he—'

'Disappeared.' Klemides finished Kaspa's thought. 'And now you've found him.' Klemides's eyes remained on Theseus. 'Perhaps just in time to stop this nonsense.'

Theseus stared at the ground, his eyes wide as he processed the thought. 'Dyon,' he said under his breath, as though trying to remember. 'Dyon,' he said again, and then he looked up and laughed, the sound loud and hysterical.

Kaspa watched as Klemides sat down with Dyon away from everyone else. They had a lot to discuss. Kaspa couldn't believe he'd been travelling with the high-lord-in-waiting. It was such a shock he didn't know how to respond, other than to stare at his feet and allow the thoughts to flow around him.

There is going to be a war, Klemides had said. A pointless war unless Dyon could stop it. But was it too late? And what about the Androphogi? What about Erik? For the first time since he was a little boy, Kaspa prayed…

And the Saviour must have smiled because the age of inertia was over. It was time for the age that would define Atalantea.

The age of heroes.

ACKNOWLEDGEMENTS

There are many books and works on Atlantis. So many you could fill a library with them. The obvious person to start with is Plato, who introduced the concept of Atlantis in his dialogues, *Timaeus* and *Critias*. They are a quick read, but provide such a detailed and vivid description of Atlantis that people have strongly believed the account to be factual for thousands of years. So powerful is the depiction given by Plato, I have tried to stay faithful to it where possible.

One individual who spent a lifetime in pursuit of Atlantis was former U.S. Congressman Ignatius Donnelly, who set out his theories and arguments in his 1882 work, *Atlantis: the Antediluvian World*. Whilst some of his theories have now been discredited, others have been repeated and considered in subsequent works by modern scholars. His belief that Atlanteans colonised the rest of the world enabling advanced civilisations to form and grow, essentially taking mankind from a barbarian state of existence to a more formalised and civilised one, is a theme throughout the book.

Many still believe Plato's description that Atlantis sits at the bottom of the ocean waiting to be discovered, although the exact location is subject to heated speculation. Charles Berlitz argued that Atlantis is located in the vicinity of the infamous Bermuda Triangle in his 1974 book *The Bermuda Triangle*, and this theory provided the backdrop for the transatlantic race and the mysterious and deadly storms that Alfred and Shep faced.

Other works that have provided inspiration for the narrative include: *When the Sky Fell*, by Rose and Rand Flem-Ath; *The Atlantis Blueprint*, by Colin Wilson; and Graham Hancock's *Fingerprints of the Gods*. All are well worth a read for anyone with an interest in Atlantis, and this book certainly would not have been possible without the insight they provided.

Writing this book has certainly been a labour of love, and it would not have been possible without the support of my wife and family, who have been my cheerleaders throughout the writing process, despite having Greek mythology forced upon them.

A special thanks to Emma White, who helped create the map of Atlantis, which brings the story to life. Many thanks also to my editor, the very talented and patient Aisling Mackay who provided amazing feedback and guidance.

ABOUT THE AUTHOR

D.M. White is an author and lawyer located in Beverley, England. Tales of Atlantis: The Dawning of a New Age is his debut novel. He has previously written for an online magazine and has had a short story published by Rewritten Realms. He can be found on Twitter @TheLostDialogue. Further information on the author can be found at:

www.thelostdialogue.com.

Printed in Great Britain
by Amazon

77180798R00181